A WARRIOR'S PENANCE

SAGA OF THE KNOWN LANDS

BOOK FOUR

By

JACOB PEPPERS

This book is a work of fiction. Names, characters, places and incidents are either the product of the author's imagination or are used fictitiously. Any resemblance to actual persons, living or dead, or to actual events or locales is entirely coincidental.

A Warrior's Penance: Saga of the Known Lands Book 4
This book is licensed for your personal enjoyment only. This book may not be re-sold or given away to other people. If you would like to share this book with another person, please purchase an additional copy for each person you share it with. If you're reading this book and did not purchase it, or it was not purchased for your use only, then you should return to the retailer and purchase your own copy. Thank you for respecting the hard work of the author.

Copyright © 2022 Jacob Nathaniel Peppers. All rights reserved, including the right to reproduce this book, or portions thereof, in any form. No part of this text may be reproduced, transmitted, downloaded, decompiled, reverse engineered, or stored in or introduced into any information storage and retrieval system, in any form or by any means, whether electronic or mechanical without the express written permission of the author. The scanning, uploading, and distribution of this book via the Internet or via any other means without the permission of the publisher is illegal and punishable by law. Please purchase only authorized electronic editions, and do not participate in or encourage electronic piracy of copyrighted materials.

The publisher does not have any control over and does not assume any responsibility for author or third-party websites or their content.

Visit the author website: http://www.jacobpeppersauthor.com

To mom

There's no way to thank you for all that you've done for me,

Not without making this dedication a second book

Still, let this stand as yet another poor attempt.

Thank you. For everything.

I could not ask for a better mom, nor my children a better mema.

Sign up for the author's mailing list and for a limited time receive a FREE copy of *The Silent Blade*, prequel to the bestselling fantasy series *The Seven Virtues*.

Go to JacobPeppersAuthor.com to get your free book now!

CHAPTER ONE

He knelt on the hard packed earth of the training circle, panting for breath. His fingers clawed into the dirt, and there was a dull but painful throb in his back where the practice sword had struck him. The ground was blurry beneath him from the tears gathering in his eyes, tears not of sadness or pain but of rage, a rage that seemed, at any minute, that it might sweep over him like some great tide, carrying him where it would.

"*Get up, boy,*" a voice said.

But he could not be back here, for he knew this place, just as he knew that it did not exist any longer. It was from a time before the Skaalden came, before the world had gone dark. *I'm not a boy,* Cutter thought. *I'm a man grown. I have been for a long time—too long, I think.* He knew this, yet he knew too, that he *was* a boy, and that boy knew little else at that moment but his anger. Anger which made him snatch up his own practice sword from where he'd dropped it when struck.

He rose to his feet, his chest rasping with breath and turned to regard Darius, his father's master-at-arms.

But that can't be, he thought, *you're dead. You died to the Skaalden.* And yet, despite this, the man stood before him, his arms crossed, the look on his face the one that he often got when Cutter—when *Bernard*—disappointed him. "It isn't fair," Cutter said, waving at his opponent only to see that it was not, as he'd expected, one of the children he'd so often trained with. Instead, it was only a shadow. It could have been anyone or no one.

"It isn't fair," he said again. "It's too much. They...they're too strong."

The next he knew, Darius was no longer standing but kneeling in front of him without having moved. "Look at me, boy. *Look* at me."

Left with no choice, Cutter did.

"Do not tell me that it is too hard, that they are too strong," the master-at-arms said. "*Life* is hard, boy, and any man who wants to live it had better learn to be hard too, do you understand?"

"I...I..."

The world blurred then, shifted, and when it resolved he was no longer standing in the circle of the training ground but instead inside in the audience room of his father's castle. People were everywhere, milling around, clearly terrified. Cutter stood at a strategy table with his father and the king's closest advisors. "You are strong, Bernard," a voice said, and he looked to see that it was Darius again, standing next to him, "even you do not fully understand that strength, but you will in time. Use it—protect them."

He opened his mouth to answer but then the audience room, too, was gone, vanishing as if it had never been. In another moment he stood in his old room in his father's castle. His father stood at the window, gazing out, his hands clasped behind his back. "Do you know what the greatest challenge is for a king, Bernard?"

"I...I don't..."

"It is not dealing with the merchants—though they present their own...*unique* challenges. Nor is it dealing with rebellions or bandits or taxation or any of the other issues my advisors so love to discuss. Instead, a king's greatest challenge is the same as that of any man or woman on the face of the world." He turned then, regarding Cutter with that questing expression he often had when he was trying to teach him something. "Do you know of what I speak?"

Father, he thought. *Oh, fire and salt, how I have missed you. Please, help me. Tell me what to do.* But he was not in control here, not any more than he had been in control at the training grounds with Darius, so instead he said, "No, and I don't care. I am *sick* of your lessons, Father, sick of always being told I'm not good enough."

"*No one* is good enough, Bernard," his father said softly. "You should never be satisfied—for a contented man does not grow, he only lingers. Now, answer my question, and I will leave you in peace. What is a king's greatest challenge?"

The young Cutter snorted. "Getting his sons to listen to him, I imagine."

His father smiled sadly at that, and Cutter felt his heart reach out to him, wishing he could take back the words. But the past lay in the past, beyond his reach, and he could not change it no matter how much he might wish to. "Son," his father said softly. "A king's greatest challenge, the greatest challenge of *all* men, is to get back up. The world will knock you down, Bernard, and the higher a man rises the greater that fall may become. It *will* knock you down, and the greatest challenge you will face, when it does, is getting back up again. Do you understand?"

"I guess."

"Listen to me, Bernard," his father said, meeting his eyes. "You must *always* get up. No matter what happens, no matter what difficulty you face, you must always *keep going*. Do you understand? *Keep going*."

"Alright," he said, "alright. I will."

"*Bernard? Bernard? Bernard!?*"

He roused as if from a dream, giving his head a shake, and saw that he no longer stood in his old quarters in his father's castle. Instead, Cutter now stood in the Black Wood, the home of the Fey and seat of their power. Feledias stood several feet ahead of him, frowning, a worried expression on his face.

"What?" Cutter croaked. "What, is it, Fel?"

"You seemed...I don't know, out of it."

"I'm fine," Cutter said, giving his head a shake to rid it of the vestiges of the daydream. He immediately regretted it as a wave of dizziness swept over him. He stumbled and would have fallen had Feledias not reached out and caught him.

"Fire and salt, Bernard, you're far from fine," Feledias hissed. "And no wonder. Why you've got so many wounds it looks like someone took it in mind to butcher you for meat."

Cutter winced. "Okay, then I'll *be* fine," he said. "I just need a little rest, that's all."

Feledias snorted. "What you *need*, brother, is a good healer—maybe a team of them—and a month to recuperate."

Cutter sighed. "Your company, Fel, is all the remedy I need."

His brother rolled his eyes. "Make jokes if you want, but I'll be more than a little pissed off if you die before the Fey get to kill you. I wouldn't care to be the sole target of their attentions."

"No doubt my corpse would be very concerned about your anger," Cutter said. "Now, if you're done, how about we look for a place to camp for the night?"

"Fine," his brother said, "but as soon as we stop, I'm going to take a look at your wounds."

"You know something of healing?"

"Some," his brother said defensively. "Anyway, I don't see anyone else volunteering for the task. Now then, where would you want to set up camp?" He gestured to their left. "How about that menacing copse of trees there? Or, if you prefer, there is the equally-menacing copse of trees on our right."

"Why don't you choose?" Cutter said.

"Joy," Feledias muttered dryly. "Well, come on. I suppose when a man is searching for his own gravesite, one spot is really as good as another." He led them to a small, secluded patch of ground in between several giant trees. Normally, such a place would have given Cutter some comfort, for the massive trunks of the trees, wider than he was at the shoulders, would serve well to hide them from any peering eyes. The problem, of course, was that, in the Black Wood, a man could not shake the feeling that the trees themselves were watching them.

Despite the assurances he'd given his brother that he was fine, it was a trial to walk the short distance, his feet shuffling through the newly fallen snow. Finally, though, they reached it, and Cutter started to remove his pack from where it was slung over his back only to wince as the movement caused a spasm of pain in several of his wounds.

Feledias glanced at him, raising an eyebrow. "I swear, nothing has changed since we were kids. Why, you'll even go so far as to nearly get yourself killed if it means avoiding work. Just...just *stand* there, if you can. I'll set up camp. When I'm done, maybe you can find another task you'd like me to do, you know, considering that by all appearances I might well be your servant."

"Well," Cutter said, doing his best to turn his grimace of pain into a frown, "my boots are looking a bit scuffed up. Might be they could do with a little polishing."

Feledias snorted. "Jokes again. Careful, brother. Just because I've decided to hold off on killing you doesn't mean I can't change my mind. They don't call me Feledias the Mercurial for nothing."

Cutter frowned. "No one calls you that."

"Give it time," his brother said, walking to Cutter and removing his pack before setting it and his own down on the snow. He began to take out their meager possessions; it did not take long. Two bedrolls, some flint and tinder, and some wrapped dried meat they had purchased from a small village on their way here. Not much, but Cutter told himself that a man didn't need much to die.

Feledias was done in a few moments, then he was turning back to Cutter. "Well? Go on and sit down, prop against that tree there. We'll see what can be done."

Too tired to argue, Cutter did as he was asked, stumbling to the tree and half-sitting, half-collapsing into the snow.

Feledias crouched down beside him. "This would be a whole lot easier if my fingers didn't feel frozen stiff," he complained. "Of course, it'd be even *easier* if someone didn't take it in mind to serve as target practice for seemingly any person who owns a knife or sword in the whole damned kingdom."

"You have my sympathy," Cutter said dryly.

"I choose to ignore the sarcasm in that," his brother said, raising an eyebrow, "considering the fact that I am about to try to help heal the man I spent the better part of the last fifteen years trying to kill."

"Life's funny like that."

"Yeah, and it can be short too—now shut up and let me work."

Exhausted as he was, Cutter was pleased to comply. He shut up as requested, leaning his head back against the tree and closing his eyes. Unwise, maybe, to allow himself to be so vulnerable in the Black Wood, but then they had left wisdom far behind them when they had come to this place. So he sat while his brother unwrapped the bandages covering his wounds and peered at the flesh underneath.

"Damn," Feledias cursed after examining one such wound on his arm, and Cutter groggily raised his head. "What?"

His brother sat back, rubbing at his nose. "Damn thing stinks. That, of course, would mean infection."

Cutter winced. That wasn't great. He'd been in battle plenty of times, and he had seen soldiers suffer often minor wounds, celebrating their luck only to succumb to infection a few days later when the rot somehow got into the wound. He didn't suppose there was any good way to die, but from what he'd seen that was likely one of the worst.

"How bad?"

"Well, it isn't great, brother mine," Feledias said. He rubbed his hands on his trousers, then cupped them to his mouth, blowing on them in an effort to work some warmth back into them. "Damn," he said again. "I've got to get some herbs." He rose from his crouch, glancing around. "I'll be right back."

His brother started away, pausing when Cutter spoke. "Fel?"

"Yes?"

Cutter met his eyes. "Don't go too far."

His brother grunted, glancing around at the giant trees, their branches seeming to reach out, eager to cover the whole world. "Wouldn't dream of it."

While his brother was gone, Cutter busied himself with removing his axe from the sheath at his back. It was a task that normally would have only taken a moment, but his weakness coupled with the pain of his wounds made the weapon seem heavier than it had ever been. By the time he was done, his face was covered in a cold sweat, and his skin felt flushed with heat.

He lay the axe down beside him in the snow, making sure that the handle was within easy reach. Likely it wouldn't matter, as given his current state, he probably wouldn't be able to defend himself against a child throwing rocks, let alone a Feyling, but then a man shouldn't let a little thing like nearly being dead make him sloppy.

Besides which, despite his efforts to clear it from his mind, the memory he'd had in his delirium while they walked still remained, so vividly that he could almost see his father's face before him.

"I'm sorry," he told that specter of the past. "For everything."

The specter, unsurprisingly, did not answer. With a sigh, Cutter leaned his head back against the tree. He was tired. His wounds, the exertion of the last few days, that was part of it but not all—not even most, in truth. He was tired in body, yes, but more than that, he was tired in his soul. Weary beyond belief. He wondered, as he sat there, if it would really be so bad, being dead. The dead, after all, had nothing to worry about, for the worst had already happened.

He remembered once, long ago, Maeve saying that it wasn't his strength that made him so dangerous, but his will. Cutter had been drunk at the time—he had often been drunk in those days—and had laughed it off. But in the days since, he had thought about that often. A creature of will. He had played at the idea, worried at it like a dog with a bone, over and over again, turning it this way and that, examining it, trying to understand it.

Perhaps she was right, but then, if that were so, what happened to a creature of will when that will began to fade? Did the man fade along with it? Cutter thought that maybe he would, that maybe he *was* fading, had been fading for a long time now. Soon, perhaps he would fade out completely, and he thought maybe that would not be such a bad thing. Not for him and certainly not for the world he'd leave behind.

A life spent at war, at bloodshed, and what good had come of it? A kingdom that was broken—or nearly so—a brother betrayed, and a son who had seen the entire life he had known set ablaze. Cutter knew that Maeve, Chall, Priest, and perhaps even Matt would grieve his death, but they would get over it, in time. Priest would have his faith, Matt his kingdom, and as for Maeve and Chall, they would, if they could only stop being so stubborn, have each other. The thought entered his mind that his death might even be the thing that finally brought them together.

He liked the idea of that. Liked to think that if he could do no good in his life then at least, perhaps, he could in death.

Keep going.

He frowned, giving his head a shake. The memory was close, it was true, so close that he could almost see his father's face, could almost hear his voice. But as close as that memory was, as close as that *voice* was, the darkness was closer. Darkness that was complete and unbroken, darkness that promised, if not peace, then oblivion, and he thought that in the end he could be satisfied with that. After all, it would be closer to peace than he had ever gotten anyway.

He sat there with his eyes closed, the frigid snowflakes falling around him, and Cutter, the Crimson Prince, as he so often had in his life, thought of death and little else. Only, this time it was not the death of his enemies which he considered but his own. And he did not *just* consider that death—he welcomed it.

The greatest thing that could be said about such a story as his, perhaps the only really *good* thing was that sooner or later, it ended. Sooner or later it *must* end. And perhaps it was fitting that he would find that end here, in this place shadows and monsters.

There had been a time—a long time, in truth—when he had thought himself invincible, and certainly attaining victory in battle after battle had seemed to support that idea. The bards had sung of those victories, that invincibility, and he had drunk and reveled in those songs. Now, though, he knew the truth—the world killed everyone, in the end.

And now that death was not far off, on some distant, ill-considered day. No, it was close. Pressing all around him. He would not have to draw the knife he had kept for so long for the purpose to do it either. It seemed then, in that moment, that all he had to do was *let go.* To let loose the life to which he had so desperately clung for the last fifteen years, telling himself that he could be better, that he *would* be better. But then that had been a lie—evidence of that lay among the scattered ashes of the farmer Alder's barn, the man dead for no other reason than he had met the messenger of death, Cutter. And death, as everyone knew, only ever sent one message.

Yes, he could do it. He could let go. He *wanted* to let go.

Keep going, the ghost of his father told him.

You are stronger than you know, the ghost of Darius, his father's master-at-arms said.

But Darius was wrong—he was not strong. He never had been, not really. Or, if he was, that was only because there were many forms of strength and his the least of them all. And keep going? Why? What was the point? He'd marched into the Black Wood, into certain death. What did it matter if that death found him tonight or tomorrow or the day after? It *would* find him in the end. And even if he were not in the Black Wood, still he would want it, would court it, for his was a death that had been coming a long time now, one well-deserved, well *earned.*

Get. Back. Up.

His father's voice again, and Cutter, his eyes still closed, shook his head slowly, drunkenly, against it. "No," he muttered. "No, I do not want to."

Want has nothing to do with it, Maeve said, her voice the ghost of a half-remembered memory.

We are what we are. Priest's voice, this time.

The best thing about living, Prince, is living. Chall's voice, pragmatic and a bit cynical as always but possessed of a wisdom greater than he knew.

"Leave me alone, ghosts," Cutter growled, "*leave me be. I have done what I can, and it has all come to naught. I am fire, don't you see? I am fire, and all I touch turns to ash.*"

Bernard?

He froze then. It was her voice, Layna's. He had not heard it in more than fifteen years, yet he knew it, *remembered* it as if he had heard it only yesterday.

"Layna?" he croaked. "Are you another ghost, then? Will you try to convince me that life is better and never mind that I have an entire life to prove otherwise?"

Bernard, do you not see? Deeds done in the darkness bear fruit in the day.

He frowned at that, wondering at what it was supposed to mean. But he decided, then, that he did not care. He was done caring, for what matter whether the axe cared or not as it reaped its bloody harvest? It was an axe, after all, and care or not, it could only do the one thing—cut. No. It was better to die. Better to let it go, all of it.

Father?

He felt as if someone had punched him in the stomach, and his breath caught in his throat. *No,* he thought desperately, *not you. Please, gods, anyone but you. Is it not enough? Have I not suffered enough?*

You cannot die, Father, Matt said, only his voice was not that of the Matt grown, but that of Matt as a child, when he had often come to visit Cutter on his lonely hilltop home. Matt before he had understood the true meaning of loss. Matt before he had learned, before Cutter had *taught* him, that everything a person had, all the foundations upon which they had built their life, could be taken, could be *stolen* in a moment, in a single night of fire and death.

We need you, the voice, his *son's* voice said, *I need you.*

"Please," Cutter said, "please…"

Will you not help us? Will you not save us?

"Fire does not save, lad," he said softly, and he could feel an icy tear running down his wind-blown cheek. "It only burns. It knows nothing else."

The youth said no more. That feeling of a presence suddenly vanished, and Cutter was alone. More alone, in that moment, than he thought he had ever been in his entire life. Alone to listen to the slow beating of his heart in his chest, and the whistling of the wind through the treetops. Left alone to make the decision, to rise or fall to the challenge that his father had said every man, king or commoner, faced. To give up…or to get up. To let go…or to keep going.

"Fine, lad," he said, "fine. I'll stay."

"Of course you'll stay. Where in the name of the gods would you go?"

Cutter opened his eyes and saw standing before him not Matt, as he had thought for a brief moment, but Feledias. His brother was holding a bundle of what appeared to be several different herbs.

"Fel," he said. "It's you."

"Who else would it be?" Feledias moved toward him, eyeing him closely. "Everything alright, Bernard?"

"Yes," Cutter lied.

Feledias watched him for a moment, as if he understood some small bit of the thoughts that had been going through Cutter's mind seconds ago. "Fine. Well, I've got some herbs to grind. You just sit there and don't die, alright?"

"Don't worry, Fel," Cutter said tiredly. "I'm not going anywhere."

For that, too, is my curse: to linger.

Always to linger.

CHAPTER TWO

"I still don't like it," Matt said, a troubled expression on the youth's face.

They sat in a small study near the king's quarters. Not *in* the king's quarters, as the castle servants were still busily cleaning up the mess Maeve had left on the floor when slaying the assassin Felara the night before.

Maeve glanced around the room at Priest and Chall. They both looked as exhausted as she felt, as Matt looked as well, and why not? It had been a trying night—a trying few months, come to it—and none of them had slept, had instead spent the hours since they had rescued Matt from the Feyling Emma's control trying to decide what to do. Grueling, exhausting, worrying hours and with very little to show for it.

Both of the men looked to her, waiting for her response, and she sighed. "What's to like, Majesty?" she asked. "But we can't go storming off to the Black Wood, you in particular. After all, it wouldn't serve for the people of the Known Lands to get their king back only to have him traipse off to a place that likely means certain death." She winced as soon as the last words were out of her mouth, wishing she could pull them back. It was too late, though, and she cursed her exhaustion, for she surely never would have slipped up in such a way were she not so damned *tired*.

"Certain death?" Matt said. "See, but that's exactly what I *mean*, Maeve! My father and uncle are going to the Black Wood—for all *we* know, they are there already. And if we don't stop them, if we don't *help* them..." He trailed off, unable—or unwilling—to finish.

"Oh, but it isn't so bad as that, lad," Chall said, giving a smile that wasn't convincing in the slightest. "After all, your father is the most dangerous man, the most dangerous *thing* I've ever met, and your uncle is no slouch with those swords he carries. It'd take more than a few Feylings to take them down. Why, it'd take a whole...well..."

"A whole forest full of them?" Matt finished.

Chall glanced at Maeve and winced, as if to say *sorry, I tried*.

"What I believe Chall is trying to say, Highness," Priest said, taking his shot, "is that while we all care deeply for your father, for you to travel to the Black Wood now would be...reckless. After all, we do not even know how much damage the Feyling caused while she possessed you, nor do we yet have a clear understanding of how many conspirators colluded with her."

Matt winced at that, clearly trying to think of some argument he might make, and Maeve felt her heart go out to him, a young man wanting only to save his father. "But we have to do *something*," he said finally. "My father and uncle are out there!" He rose and jabbed a finger in the direction of the Black Wood, "and it's my fault. *I* sent them there."

"But you know that's not true, lad," Maeve said softly. "You're not anymore responsible for sending Cutter and Feledias to the Black Wood than we are—you didn't have control over your body."

"Maybe," Matt said, "but that's easier for you to say—after all, it wasn't *your* body that ordered them to the Black Wood. It was mine."

Maeve rose, moving toward him then, meaning to comfort him, but Matt held up a hand, forestalling her. "I'm alright," he said. "And I'm sorry—I didn't mean that." He paced for a moment. "What about this—what if we send a contingent of the army? Enough to rescue my father and uncle? That way, I can remain here, but we can still help them."

Maeve and her two companions shared doubtful looks at that, and Matt frowned. "What? What is it?"

"A contingent that might be made up partially or wholly of traitors, Majesty," Chall said apologetically. "The simple fact is that there's no way for us to know who is loyal and who isn't. For all we know, we'd be doing more harm than good by sending anyone after your father."

"What of this guardsman you told me of?" Matt said desperately. "This Nigel? Didn't you say that you believed he might be able to help us with that?"

"Yes," Maeve said patiently, "and if you'll recall, Majesty, we sent for him over an hour ago. He should be here soon. But even if Nigel *is* able to help us, it will still take time to examine each guard, to ferret out who is loyal and who is not. By the time that's finished..." She trailed off, and Matt frowned.

"By the time that's finished my father and uncle might already be dead."

There didn't seem to be much to say to that, so Maeve didn't bother trying. Instead, she chose to change the subject. "First, we need to figure out everyone in the castle who might have been part of the conspiracy. We can't very well worry about the rest of the city when, for all we know, any serving maid could be an assassin waiting for our backs to be turned."

Matt nodded slowly, a grim expression coming to his face, one that somehow reminded her of Cutter. "I have some idea of where to start."

"Oh?" Maeve asked.

The youth gave a nod. "Follow," he said, that and nothing more before he rose and walked out the door.

The other three were left staring at each other.

"That one's becoming more and more like his father each day," Chall said.

"Let's not hope *too* much," Maeve said.

"Did you see the look on his face?" Priest asked thoughtfully. "I've seen that look before."

Chall met Maeve's eyes. "Shit," the mage said, "we'd better hurry."

Then the three of them were rising, rushing out of the door but despite their haste, by the time they made it out into the castle hallway they were only able to catch a glimpse of Matt turning a corner. They hurried after him.

The young man wasn't running, not quite, but then he wasn't far from it. "Where are we going, Highness?" Maeve said as she and the others caught up.

"To see my bodyguard," Matt responded without bothering to so much as turn and look at her. Staring at him as they walked, Maeve decided that Priest was right—she had also seen that look before. Never on Matt's face, maybe, but she had seen it on his father's often enough to know it. It was a determined look, an angry look, and if her past experiences with his father were anything to go by, it meant that someone—or perhaps, several someones—was getting ready to have a really bad day.

"Bodyguard, Majesty?" Chall said. "Do you mean—"

"Rolph," Matt said.

"What um...what are we going to see him about, Majesty?" Maeve asked, glancing worriedly at Chall.

Matt didn't speak, only continued marching through the empty hallway, his mouth set into a grim line. Matt walked on purposefully, as if, should a wall appear in front of him, he wouldn't bother to so much as turn but instead choose to walk right through. And, just then, Maeve was possessed of the thought that maybe he could have.

She and the others followed in his wake until he reached a door. Maeve thought the youth meant to barrel into it but he stopped at the last moment, giving the door a knock.

"Screw off," a man's voice called from inside, sounding strangely muffled. "I'm busy."

Matt's hands knotted into fists at his sides and before Maeve could say anything the youth brought his foot back and gave the door a kick where the latch must have been. Maeve thought, as she watched, that it was useless. After all, this was not some cheap inn in the poor district, but the king's castle in the capital of the Known Lands where the doors were made thick and made well.

She watched with complete shock as the door cracked beneath the blow, swinging open. Matt didn't so much as hesitate, marching inside.

Maeve turned and stared at her two companions, Priest studying the door as if it was a puzzle he didn't understand.

Chall, meanwhile, stared at her aghast. "It seems…" He paused, swallowing. "It seems that his looks aren't the only thing the king got from his father. Got some of his strength too."

"More than some I'd say," Maeve said, "now come on."

They stepped inside in time to see a man rising out of the bed from beneath the forms of two half-naked women, which, Maeve supposed, went a long way toward explaining the muffled sound of his voice when he'd called out.

"Just who the fu—" The man, Rolph, who they had first seen in Two Rivers, cut off as he took in the four of them, his wide-eyed gaze moving to Matt. "Majesty?" he asked. "What are you—"

"You are my bodyguard, are you not?" Matt said, his voice cold and hard.

"O-of course, Majesty," the man said, shoving one of the women aside and pulling a sheet over him to cover his nakedness, "but what does—"

"And yet," Matt growled, "an assassin, one by the name of Felara, was allowed not only into the castle but into my *quarters* unchecked."

The man licked his lips nervously, trying for a laugh. "Majesty, I thought…that is, the woman assassin, she was a friend of yours, wasn't she? Meant to protect you from—"

"From whom?" Matt demanded. "From these, my companions?" he said, gesturing at Maeve and the others.

"I…well, yes."

"I see," Matt said. "And so, if what you're saying is true, then why were you not there to protect me from my *friends* when they broke into my room?"

The bodyguard winced. "Yeah, well, sorry about that. Thing is, I'd had a bit too much to drink—it's amazing how much wine this place has, all kinds, and—"

"Gather your things," Matt said.

"My…my things, Highness?" the man asked uncertainly.

"You heard me," Matt said. "Oh, do not worry. We will still find you some other accommodations." He paused, giving the man a humorless grin. "After all, it is the least we can do to reward your…service."

"Other accommodations?" the man asked, frowning now as he got over the worst of his shock.

"Indeed," Matt said. "I think the dungeons should suffice. You see, Rolph, I have some questions for you. Some questions that I mean to have answered."

"Bullshit," the man spat, giving up all pretense of civility now as he rose. He was quite a bit bigger than Matt, a head taller, Maeve thought, probably five years older, too, and by the way he stood it was obvious he knew it. "You ain't takin' me anywhere, you fuckin' child. I ain't listenin' to the orders of some innocent little babe lost in the woods and all of a sudden decides to grow a pai—"

The man never got a chance to finish. Matt's hand flashed out, his fist taking him in the face. Maeve winced as she heard the unmistakable sound of Rolph's nose breaking, and the man stumbled away with a squawk, bringing his hand to his bloody nose.

"Y-you broke my fucking noshe," the man said.

"Yes," Matt said calmly, letting his hand fall back to his side, the knuckles bloody from where they'd scraped against the man's face. "And I will break more than that if I have to. Get your things. Now."

"*You son of a bitch,*" the man growled, lunging under the bed and pulling something from it before he charged at Matt.

It took Maeve a moment to realize what it was. "*Matt, he's armed, watch out!*" she called, starting forward and knowing even as she did that she would be too late.

She needn't have bothered, though. The man swung in an awkward, unpracticed strike. The training sessions Matt had gone through with Cutter must have made a difference, for the young king stepped easily into the man's guard, wrapping his arm up underneath his own. Matt let out a growl of effort then gave a savage twist, and Rolph screamed as his arm snapped, bending at an unnatural angle, the sword it had held dropping to the floor, forgotten.

Rolph stumbled away, but Matt wasn't finished. He grabbed the older man by the front of his jerkin with both hands and slammed his forehead forward, into the man's already ruined nose.

Rolph let out a guttural, watery scream, was still screaming when Matt brought his foot down, hard, on the inside of his knee and there was a loud *crack*.

The Two Rivers man cried out, falling to his knees. Before he could do anything else, Matt brought his fist around and into the man's face. Rolph grunted, falling onto his back on the ground and staring dazedly up at the sky.

"Matt—" Maeve began, her words barely more than a whisper at her shock.

"Not now, Maeve," the youth said as he stepped forward, kneeling before Rolph. "Look at me."

The man was blubbering, gasping and crying all at once. "*Look at me,*" Matt growled.

Rolph did, turning wide, terrified eyes at him, and Matt gave a single, satisfied nod. "You're right," he said. "I'm young. But don't ever make the mistake of thinking me innocent."

Maeve and her two companions were left staring in surprise as Matt rose, turning to them. "Summon the guard," he said. "I want my ex-bodyguard taken to the dungeons. We will question him there."

"Y-yes, Matt," Chall said, licking his lips, "that is…I mean, Majesty."

"Are…are you okay, Majesty?" Maeve asked.

Matt raised his bloody fist, looking at it thoughtfully as he flexed his fingers. "I'm fine," he said after a moment. "Scraped knuckles is all."

"That isn't what I meant," Maeve said, "and I think you know it."

Matt turned on her so abruptly that Maeve found herself taking an involuntary step back. It did not seem as though she was looking at the youth she had first met in the Black Wood, not any longer. He seemed more akin to some wild beast, one that, having tasted blood, decided it liked it. "I did not fight hard enough," Matt said, "with Emma. Because of that, my uncle and father have been sent to their deaths, and that is only the beginning of the suffering that she…that *I* caused. I did not fight hard enough, Maeve. It will not happen again."

"Matt—" she began, reaching out, but he turned away.

"I'm fine," he repeated. "Now come. There are others to whom I would speak. My advisors, after all, were, like my bodyguard, chosen not by myself but by Emma. We have a long day ahead of us."

He didn't wait for a reply. Instead he glanced once more at the broken man lying on the floor in a pool of his blood, then at the two women, prostitutes, Maeve guessed, still in the bed. "Get out," he said.

The two women, their eyes wide and wild, didn't need to be told twice. They gathered their clothes and rushed toward the exit.

"Not everyone is an enemy, lad," Chall said. "Those girls—"

"Are not my concern," Matt said. "Now come."

And with that, he turned and walked out the door.

"Did...did you *see* that?" Chall said in shock.

"I saw," Maeve said, finding that, suddenly, her mouth was unaccountably dry.

"Fire and salt, I wonder what the prince would have thought if he'd been here to see it," the mage said.

"Best that he isn't."

They both turned to stare at Priest, and the older man shook his head, staring at the door through which Matt had walked. "All men have faith in something, Challadius," Priest explained. "For some, it is the gods; for others it is themselves. For Prince Bernard, I believe it is in goodness. Not his own, for he believes that he has abandoned that long ago. Or, perhaps, that it has abandoned him. Instead, he takes faith in the goodness of the king, his son. Had he witnessed this, today, then that faith would have been shaken. And like most men, it is his faith that serves as the foundation upon which the prince has built himself. Should that faith come crumbling down...all that they are crumbles with it."

Maeve found herself staring at the man, her old friend. She had always taken it for granted that Priest was okay. No matter what terrible odds they faced, what terrible things they saw, she could always count on him to be steady, to not waver. Now, though, the man did not seem steady, not at all. "Valden," she said, "what's wrong?"

The man gave her a small, humorless smile. "Come," he said. "I do not think the king will wait."

"Fine," Maeve said, "but we will talk. Later."

The man paused on his way past her, turning to her and giving a single nod of his head. "We will talk."

He turned and walked out of the door then, after the king.

"Come on, Chall," Maeve said after a moment, "best we keep up."

"Maeve," Chall said, "there's something I want...well, maybe I need to talk to you about."

She frowned, turning to glance at the mage. "What is it? Did you have a dream?" She moved forward, grabbing his shoulder. "Is it about Cutter? Has something happened to the prince?"

"No, no," Chall said, wincing, "it's nothing like that. Or...well, I suppose maybe it is a dream, I don't..." He let out an angry huff, shaking his head. "I'm not doing this right. Look, it isn't about Bernard. It...it's about Matt."

Maeve breathed a heavy sigh of relief. "Relax, Chall. I know that Matt is acting strangely now, but he's angry, that's all, and if you ask me, he has a right to be. I can't imagine what it was like, being imprisoned in his own mind, watching everything happen but unable to do anything about it." She shook her head. "Considering that, I think he's got the right to be a little angry."

"Of course he has a right to be angry," Chall said, "it isn't...what I mean, Matt's eyes—"

"I know, I know, Chall," Maeve said, "they looked like Cutter's. I get it. But Matt *isn't* Bernard, alright? He's just a young boy who has had a terrible couple of weeks, that's all. He'll be okay, you'll see. Now, we need to—"

"*Maeve, just be quiet!*" Chall snapped, and Maeve, who had never heard the mage raise his voice in such a way and *certainly* never at her, stared, wide-eyed.

Chall winced. "Sorry, Mae, really, I don't...it's just that I'm a little scared is all. Do you remember how I went into Matt's mind, to see if I could find him, help him, somehow?"

Maeve nodded slowly. "I remember."

"Well...I *did* find him," Chall said. "First on the day he was crowned king, then at the mayor's house back in Two Rivers, and lastly, I found him at a cabin in some snow-swept wilderness, what I can only assume, from what the boy told me, was the prince's home during his exile."

"I see," Maeve said. "But...what does any of this matter, Chall? After all, we got him back. Matt's back."

"Yeah," Chall said slowly. "Maybe it's nothing but...Maeve, when I found Matt, it wasn't long before the Feyling, Emma, found us. I tried to stand against her, but her will was too strong. In the end, it was Matt who saved me. He stood against Emma and, within his mind, he was far more powerful than she could ever hope to be."

"Okay?" Maeve said impatiently. "What difference does that make, Chall? She's beaten, the Feyling. We don't need to worry about her."

"It's not *her* I'm worried about," Chall said. "Look, Maeve, when Matt was beating her, when he was…when he *destroyed* her, or whatever was left of her anyway, he was grinning as he did it." He held up a hand, silencing her before she could say anything to that. "I know, I know. He'd been through a lot, and the gods know I've seen his father smile while he fought. Stones and starlight, I've listened to him laugh while he cut his enemies down. But that's not what bothers me. What bothers me, Mae, is that when Matt defeated the creature—when he destroyed her—his eyes glowed green. And not just any green—a Fey green."

Maeve frowned, waiting. When the mage said nothing more, she raised an eyebrow. "Is that it?"

"Well…" Chall said, clearly taken aback, "yes, but…but Maeve, the only creatures whose eyes I've ever seen glow like that are Feylings."

Maeve sighed, shaking her head. "Fire and salt, Chall, you had me terrified. Okay, so Matt's eyes glowed green, so what? You were in a *dream*, remember. Think of it—the Feyling, Emma, we killed her back in Two Rivers, right?"

"Yes…"

"And so she only existed like a parasite in Matt's mind. A mind which you were stomping around in. You said you saw him in three different places, said, too, that Matt was only a child when you found him at Bernard's cabin. Well, is he a child now?"

"No, but—"

"Of course he isn't," Maeve said. "You were in his mind, that's all. He was distraught and angry and scared from the creature Emma's torture—there's no telling what you might have seen in a mind as troubled as that. If you ask me, seeing his eyes glow green is just about as lucky as you can hope for."

Chall frowned thoughtfully. "I guess…well, I guess maybe you could be right. It just…it was strange, that's all."

"You were inside another person's mind, battling a Fey creature who had invaded it and taken it over, Chall," Maeve said dryly. "I'd say the whole thing qualifies for strange and then some, wouldn't you?"

Chall nodded slowly. "So then…you don't think it was anything?"

Maeve gave him a small smile, stepping forward and cupping his cheeks in her hands. "He's back, Chall. Matt's back, okay? And we've got plenty enough enemies to deal with without inventing more phantoms to fight. Alright?"

Slowly, a smile spread across the mage's face. "Alright," he said. "You're right, I'm sure. Thanks, Mae."

She leaned in and kissed him. "Thank you for talking to me. Now come on. Matt may not have green eyes like a Feyling, but there's no telling what he might do if we leave him alone for too long."

CHAPTER THREE

"Well, look at you. And after all that talk of being careful, watchful. Seems a bit hypocritical to me."

The words sounded as if they were coming from far away, and Cutter opened eyelids that felt as heavy as if they'd had weights tied to them. "Fel?" he asked, staring up at his brother. "What...what happened?"

"What happened is that while I was over here toiling away at saving your life, you fell asleep," Feledias said. Then frowned, shrugging. "Or maybe you passed out. It's really hard to say."

"I...see," Cutter said, wincing and looking down at his body to see that fresh strips of cloth had been tied around the wounds on his arms and chest.

"Damned fingers started to cramp, I had to do so much tying," Feledias observed. "I'll warn you, brother, you'd best not get wounded anymore—not unless you want me using your shirt or trousers for bandages, that is, for we're just about out of everything else we might use."

Cutter grunted. "I'll do my best."

Feledias nodded. "See that you do." He walked over and crouched by a small fire he must have made at some point while Cutter had lain unconscious. Only when he saw his brother turn a small stick spit holding the skinned body of what appeared to be a squirrel did Cutter become aware of the smell of cooking meat. No sooner did he smell it than his stomach roiled hungrily.

"I'm...not sure that's wise, brother," Cutter said.

Feledias glanced up. "The fire or the squirrel?"

"Both, maybe," Cutter said. "This is a dark place, a cold place. Such light, such warmth, it might well draw attention we do not want."

"You said yourself you think they know we're here, brother," Feledias said, "so it seems like it's too late to worry about that. And the squirrel? What's wrong with it?"

Cutter considered that then finally nodded. "I guess you're right. As for the squirrel...I don't know. It seems to me that the Black Wood twists things. Might be that it's poisonous."

"We're going to be on a short mission indeed if we can't eat, Bernard," Feledias said. "We're out of the supplies we brought with us, if you'll recall. Besides, if there really are creatures coming to kill us, and if we really are going to die, then I'd just as soon die on a full stomach."

Cutter grunted. "Pass some of that damn squirrel, why don't you?"

Feledias grinned. "Sure."

A moment later, Feledias handed him a large piece of cooked meat. Cutter resisted the urge to swallow it all down at once, knowing that if he did, with his wounds, exhaustion, and time since he'd last ate, he'd probably get sick. Instead, he ate slowly, sucking on the small morsel one piece at a time, enjoying the warmth of it in this cold place.

No sooner had he finished than Feledias handed him another big piece of meat on a stick, and Cutter frowned as he noted that, all told, he would be eating nearly three quarters of the squirrel. "What about you, Fel?" he said, glancing up at his brother.

Feledias shrugged casually. "Just not all that hungry. I guess maybe marching to my imminent doom has stolen my appetite."

Cutter frowned, watching his brother. "You're lying. You never were good at it, not since we were kids."

Feledias raised an eyebrow. "And you were never good at avoiding being target practice for anyone holding something sharp. What a pair we make."

Feledias was still holding out the cooked meat to him, and Cutter shook his head. "Eat it, Fel."

"You should have it," his brother said. "It is no easy thing for me to admit, Bernard, but despite all my training I know that I am not the fighter you are. Should something come, we will need your strength."

"Should something come," Cutter said, "then I will find what strength I need. And do not look so glum, Fel. Perhaps I am a killer, but then I was born to it. There are many other things in the world than being good at killing. Far better things."

Fel nodded slowly, turning away.

"What is it?" Cutter asked.

"Those people," Feledias said, "in that village you stayed at, Brighton. How many do you think there were?"

Cutter winced. "Fel, it doesn't—"

"*How many?*" Feledias grated, his voice raw with emotion.

"A little over two hundred, I think."

"Two hundred," Feledias repeated, his voice dry, hollow. "Two hundred dead. You are wrong, brother. You are not the only killer. We were both born to it."

Cutter could hear the pain in his brother's voice and how not? After all, he knew that pain, that shame. Few knew it better. He wished that he could say something to comfort his brother, to take the worst of it away, but if such words existed, he did not know them. Otherwise, he would have told them to himself long ago.

"We can't...we can't change what we've done, Fel," he said. "The only thing we can do is to keep going, to try to be better."

His brother nodded, saying nothing, yet Cutter could see a slight tremble to his shoulders that said he was weeping, and he thought that was a good thing. Monsters, after all, did not cry. Cutter himself could not remember the last time he had shed a tear, if he ever had. Some men might have considered such a thing a mark of strength, but then, some men were fools.

They sat in silence for a time, Cutter allowing his brother his grief, his shame. Eventually, Feledias spoke.

"I wish I could take it back...what I did," he said, his voice little more than a whisper.

"I know," Cutter said.

"I...I don't know why I did it," Feledias croaked. "It...I was just so angry. It was just at you, at first, but over the years...it got to where I was angry at everything, everyone. I blamed you, yes, but I blamed everyone else, too. I began to hate...everything. Those things which were once sweet turned sour in my mouth, and those things which were once fine became foul to my sight until I grew convinced that there was nothing good left in this world."

"I know," Cutter said, "and I understand, Fel. Maybe no one else would, but I do."

His brother raised his head then, and Cutter saw tears coursing their way down his cheeks. "I know that men can turn into monsters—" He paused, giving a ragged, sobbing laugh. "How could I not? But tell me, Bernard, do you believe that a man, once he has become that monster, once he has forsaken all decency, all kindness and compassion, do you think that he might find them again? Do you think that monster, that wretched beast, might once again become a man?"

His brother's face was pale, and he trembled with his grief, his shame. Cutter found himself rising, climbing his way to his feet, clawing at the tree to gain his balance.

"You should not move," Feledias said, his voice weak, thready. "You risk opening the wounds. You might begin to bleed again."

"Then I will bleed," Cutter said. He shuffled to his brother, holding in a grunt of pain as he knelt on one knee, placing his other hand on his brother's shoulder. He took a minute, finding that he was out of breath from the exertion. "Listen to me, Fel," he said. "I...I wish that I could tell you yes, that I knew that a monster could turn into a man again, but I don't."

Feledias nodded, his eyes going to the ground. Bernard tightened his grip on his brother's shoulder, and Feledias looked up again. "But he, Fel, *we* can try. We can do the right thing, the *good* thing. And perhaps, in time, with enough such things, we might find our way back again."

"The good thing," Feledias said thoughtfully, running an arm across his eyes. "You mean like venturing into the Black Wood, counting on mercy from creatures who have none to seek peace when all they seem to want is war?"

Cutter gave his brother a small smile. "It might be we overcorrected."

Feledias let out a breathy laugh but this one, at least, was genuine. "I miss you, Bernard," he said softly, and in that moment he was not a man grown, but the small child, so innocent and clever, that Cutter had known so long ago. "Even when I hated you for what you had done, I still missed you."

"I miss you too, Fel," he said.

"I wish..." Feledias began, then cut off, clearing his throat. "I..."

"I know, Fel," Cutter said. "Me too. More than anything."

"But a man can't change his past," Feledias said, "no matter how much he might want to."

"No. He can't."

Feledias met his eyes again. "He can only move forward. Can only try to be better."

Cutter gave a single nod of his head.

Feledias grunted. "It's a bitch though, isn't it?"

"I think, brother, that becoming something new always is. Now, will you rest? I can take first watch."

Feledias snorted. "Is that so? And what will you do if something comes for us? What *can* you do? Besides scream, maybe?"

Cutter smiled wider. "I'll scream loudly."

Feledias shook his head. "There are your jokes again, far better at putting a man to sleep than any lullaby."

"Prove it."

Feledias sighed, rolling his eyes, then made his way to his bedroll and lay down. "You really are starting to get far too clever for your own good."

"No, Fel," Cutter said, staring at his brother's back as he turned on his side, feeling as if something shifted inside him, some great mountain that might crush him beneath it, "you're the clever one—you always were." *Just as you were always the good one, the kind one. At least until I betrayed you, ripping that kindness from you the way I might have stolen your toy as a child.*

"Goodnight, Bernard," his brother said, his voice already sounding thick and muzzy with exhaustion.

"Goodnight, Fel. Goodnight, brother."

It took a monumental effort to make his way to his feet again, more so as he was determined not to disturb his brother or to make him worry. Feledias had more than enough to concern him without Cutter adding to it. By the time he was standing again, he was covered in sweat. His hands trembled, and his legs felt as if they might give way beneath him at any moment. He made his way back to the tree, *his* tree, and eased himself down so that he sat once more with his back against it.

Once he had gotten his breath back, he found himself thinking once more of his brother's question. *Can a monster become a man?*

"Only time will tell," he said quietly, into the darkness. But then, he was not sure that they had much time left to them. The Fey would come, sooner or later, that he did not doubt. In truth, he was more curious as to why they had not come already. Certainly, they hated him as much as Feledias had, and had he marched into Feledias's place of power even a year ago, he was confident that he would have been dead or, at least, been in the process of being tortured within minutes.

But then, the Fey were not men. They hated like men, but they did not think like them. That much, he had gleaned from his conversations with Yeladrian, the Fey King, before he killed him. "What are you waiting for?" he said into the darkness. But the darkness, as ever, hid its secrets jealously.

Cutter found himself growing anxious as he sat there. It was not the darkness that unnerved him, nor was it the thought of his impending death—he had made his peace with death long ago. As for darkness, that without was nothing compared to that darkness which lurked inside him. No, instead, it was the quiet.

When battle was joined and men charged forward, shouting their fury, he did not falter. Neither did he flinch at the ringing sounds of metal on metal as men bled and died. For in that cacophony, in that chaos, he could forget, at least for a time, who he was, *what* he was. Monsters, after all, never felt more alive than when they were surrounded by death.

But in the quiet, in the stillness, with no cries of rage or pain to distract him, with no stroke or counterstroke to demand his attention, with nothing upon which to vent the anger which he always felt, he could hear them, could see them.

Voices, crying out from the grave, faces floating in the dark. Dead voices. Dead faces. Guttural and recriminating hisses, cold, dead eyes, empty—yet somehow accusing for all that. So many faces. Hundreds and hundreds of them, men he had cut down in battle or simply for sport. So many voices, telling him what he was, what he had always been. A monster.

And not all of those faces, those voices, were human. There were others scattered among them, their visages sometimes kind and sometimes cruel. The faces of the Fey. And they, at least, did not call him monster, did not call him a fiend or a murderer. They had one word for him—one word and one word only.

Destroyer.

The faces were all around him, floating in the darkness, huddled there, so close that when they voiced their recriminations he could feel their breath upon his face. He had told Priest of the voices once, long ago. At the time, he had thought them little more than an annoyance, some imbalance of humors that might be remedied by the right tincture or potion. But they had not gone away, and so he had spoken to Priest again, telling him that he was haunted, that the ghosts never left him, trailing him, always.

Priest had told him that there was no such thing as haunting, that what haunting a man felt, he did to himself. Perhaps that was true and perhaps it was not. Cutter did not know. What he wondered, though, in the still, quiet moments, moments like now with the darkness pressing close, the faces, twisted in pain and fury and death hovering all about him, was whether or not it mattered. Whether the ghosts came from him or somewhere else, they came nevertheless. That much, at least, was not in doubt.

"*Go away,*" he rasped to the faces. "*Go away.*"

But they did not. They never did. Not even sleep was an escape from them. They followed him into that darkness, for darkness was their domain, and in the stillness, in the quiet of sleep, their power did not diminish but only grew.

He found his hand creeping to the axe handle where it was propped against the tree. Foolish, he knew, for the dead were dead already and could not be killed again. He knew this, for he had tried. Countless times he had roared his anger and his fear out into the darkness, his axe flashing this way and that but passing through those ghosts as if they were nothing.

Still, the axe felt good in his hands. Right. As it always had. He wondered, sometimes, at that. Did a smith's hammer feel right in his hands? Feel so natural? And if it did, did it feel that way because of years spent bent at his labors or simply because he had been born to be a smith and that hammer only completed him, like a puzzle that had long been missing a single piece only to finally find it?

No, the ghosts could not be slain, nor could they be banished for the wanting of it. So Cutter did what he always did in such times—he waited. He waited for the sun to return, for the sounds of the day, of the living, to come back and drown out those dead voices. He waited, the sweat turning as cold as ice against his skin, the air itself cool and somehow foul as it entered and left his lungs.

He waited for as long as he could, waited until his courage was eaten away bit by bit by the darkness, until it was left in ragged tatters. Then he rose and made his way to Feledias. Or, perhaps, it would be more correct to say that he fled to him. It was not the ghosts, really, that scared him. At least not their faces. It was the evil things they said, the cruel, hateful, *true* things.

He woke his brother, and Feledias rubbed the sleep out of his eyes, taking up position to watch. With that task done, Cutter made his way back to his bedroll and lay down. And then, Prince Bernard, known as the Crimson Prince, the most feared and powerful warrior in the world, pulled the blankets over his head in a childish and vain attempt to keep out the darkness.

He lay there, in the dark.

He lay…but he did not sleep.

CHAPTER FOUR

Feledias woke him in the morning, though it was not so easy to tell. Here, beneath the great boughs of the Black Wood's trees, there was little difference between night and day, between light and darkness. For very little of the sun's illumination managed to make it through the reaching canopies of those ancient sentinels to the ground beneath.

And what little did was no great comfort, for the light which fell was a pale, sickly thing, and the warmth of it against Cutter's skin was not comforting as it might have been. Instead, it felt like the warmth of some disease coursing through his veins.

Feledias hunted for game with which to break their fast but he had no luck and so they ate berries from some nearby bushes. They looked like blueberries, smelled like them too.

"They could be poisonous," Feledias said as they gazed at the bushes.

"Aye," Cutter said, grabbing a handful. "They could be."

Feledias shrugged, then followed suit. The berries might have looked like blueberries, but they were sour to taste, and even though they knew they needed to eat as much as they could for strength, they could stomach no more than half a handful each.

They ate in silence, each of them focused on keeping the foul fare down and doing their best not to contemplate the road that lay ahead. And both of them—on that last part, at least—failing miserably.

Finally, when Cutter decided he had stomached all he could, he rose and repacked his bedroll as Feledias did the same. "Ready?" Cutter asked.

"Oh, why not?" Feledias asked. "It isn't as if I've anything else going on."

They traveled on through the wood, talking little, each of them nursing his own thoughts. Cutter's body ached with each step, but he found that his wounds hurt less than they had. Whatever Feledias had done, it had clearly made a difference. And what pains remained, he did not let concern him. After all, he had felt pain before—little else, in fact. They were his constant companions, the pain without and the pain within, and he knew them both well, never mind that he did not like them.

The axe strapped at his back felt heavy, heavier than he could remember it feeling, but this, too, he ignored. Instead, he kept a tight rein on his thoughts, allowing himself only to be concerned with the path ahead of him, the mission that his son had given him.

Peace, Father. Matt's voice inside his head. *We must find peace.*

Perhaps not Matt's words, not exactly—the truth was, Cutter couldn't remember—but near enough, he thought, as to make no difference. Peace. He wondered at that. Ever since he could remember, it seemed that he had been fighting someone or another, fighting for some *thing* or another. His life was made up of little else but that constant fight, that never-ending struggle.

Peace.

It was like an alien word, an alien concept for a man who had lived the life he had. He was not even sure that he knew what it meant. And should he and Feledias somehow succeed—a thought that seemed all but impossible—should they gain the peace that his son wished...what then? Cutter felt like a clerk grasping for a hammer, or a warrior a pen. They might grab it, in time, but once they did, how could they have any idea what to do with it, that thing with which they were so unfamiliar?

But he told himself it didn't matter. He did what he did not for himself but for Matt. For the first time in his life, he did not seek his own ends but someone else's and who better than his son? His son who had been kind and compassionate from a young age, never joining in when the children of the village mocked one another but always defending, stopping in a race he would have easily won to help up his opponent who had fallen.

No, it was far better to do what such a boy, such a man, wanted than to follow his own heart, his heart which had only ever led him to blood and more of it. So he walked deeper into the Black Wood, ever deeper, and the man who was known throughout the land as a ruthless killer, as the Crimson Prince, thought of one thing and one thing only—he thought of peace.

Feledias had motioned him to the front as they began, he said, because if anything came upon them with the intention of giving them a good chew, he would prefer they started with Cutter. In truth, though, Cutter thought it was because his brother wanted to be able to keep an eye on him, so that he might notice should Cutter's flagging strength fail him.

Cutter loved him for that as he loved him for so many other things, and he wondered, as they walked, at how he might tell him. For he saw the pain in his brother's eyes from the night before, pain and shame at what he had done, regret that even the magic of sleep could not dispel. Guilt. That, Cutter understood and far better than peace, for he had known it for more than fifteen years, known it since he had taken the small babe and walked into his exile. He wished that he could take some of the pain away from Feledias, but he could not, for despite the fact that he had known that guilt for so many years, he had found no answer to it.

None, at least, save moving forward, ever forward.

And so he did.

They continued into the forest as dawn came and went, the day dragging on, and Cutter found that he was tired. His wounds were part of it, sure, but he did not think that they were all. It was this place, the Black Wood, a cursed place, as inimical to mortals as the light of a torch was to shadow. He felt worn down, used up, as if some vital part of him were being slowly leeched away by his surroundings.

Peace, he told himself. *You go because Matt asked it of you.*

It became like a mantra in his mind, a spell repeated over and over in the hopes that it might stave off the worst of that leeching, might slow the spread of that creeping despair he felt growing in him.

He walked on, lost in his own thoughts, until he noticed an odd thing. Where, moments ago, trees and bushes had crowded either side of the dirt trail on which they walked, now, suddenly, the ground on either side was clear. The grass this revealed looked almost black, yet even stranger was that, among that grass, he saw holes in the ground with what appeared to be fresh dirt scattered about them. Some small, no bigger than his finger, others much larger, as if all the bushes and the trees in the area had suddenly decided to uproot themselves.

He noted this, but he did not stop to regard it. This, he knew, would not be the only manner of strangeness the Black Wood offered, and he had to focus on his mission, on the mission his son had given him.

He continued on until suddenly, he was forced to a stop. For the path ahead was gone. Or, if it remained, then at least he could not see it. It had been covered by a wild growth of trees and bushes, all so tightly packed together it seemed impossible. He stood, frowning at this unusual barricade, the hairs on the back of his neck stiffening.

He was still standing that way, staring at the impossible growth, when Feledias came to stand beside him. "Huh," his brother said. "Well, I guess that's that. Suppose we better turn around, head back to the capital. We can tell my nephew that we tried, honestly we did, but there were just too many bushes."

Cutter shot Feledias a sidelong glance. The man shrugged, trying to appear casual, but Cutter could see in the way his eyes were slightly narrowed, his jaw set, that his brother was as unnerved as he.

"Something's wrong here," Cutter said.

"Just now noticing that, older brother?" Feledias asked. "Why, I've been trying to keep from pissing myself for the last day and a half. With decidedly questionable results, in case you were wondering."

"I wasn't," Cutter said, frowning around at the trees, the impossible snarling tangle of undergrowth blocking their way.

"Well," Feledias said. "I suppose you could put that axe of yours to work."

Cutter considered that then shook his head. "It's too much. It seems to go on forever. We'd lose days at it."

"Maybe," Feledias agreed, "but we're liable to lose a lot more than that if we step off the path. Wasn't it you who told me not to wander too far in the Black Wood?"

Cutter nodded slowly. "So it was." He hesitated, trying to decide what to do. He did not like the idea of leaving the trail. The trail might not be safe, but in the deepness of the Black Wood they would be robbed of even what dubious security it provided.

Yet the alternative was to spend days hacking away at the brush with no way of knowing when it ended or even *if* it ended. No, they would have to go around. Despite the obvious dangers that entailed, Cutter didn't see any choice. Leaving the trail was not wise, but spending several days in the Black Wood, days in which anything might come upon them, was an even greater folly.

"We turn around," he said, "backtrack. Maybe we can find a place where the trail splits."

"And if not?" his brother asked grimly.

"If not," Cutter said, "then we will journey into the Black Wood in truth. Come on," he said, turning, "let's—" But he cut off as soon as he turned around, his muscles tensing. He had meant to backtrack along the trail, as he had told Feledias, but the trail, it seemed, had had different ideas. For now, the path upon which they had walked only moments ago was gone. In its place was undergrowth and trees as thick as what lay behind them.

"What?" Feledias said. "What is it, Bernard?" He turned, following Cutter's gaze, then took an involuntary step back. "Shit," he breathed. "Where'd the path go?"

"I don't know," Cutter said, eyeing those trees and bushes now blocking the trail behind. "Your swords," Feledias," he said quietly. "Draw them."

Feledias frowned. "And do what, exactly? I'm not going to do battle with shrubs and thorns, Cutter, however much those bastards deserve a good thrashing."

"*Just do it,*" Cutter growled, suiting action to word and drawing his axe from his back.

"Fine," Feledias said, drawing his own blades, "but your axe is far more suited to the task of plant-murder than my swords."

"Quiet," Cutter said, as a feeling came upon him, a distinct foreboding. He'd had such a feeling before, usually when danger approached.

"What?" Feledias said, licking his lips. "Scared the plants will overhea—"

"*Quiet,*" Cutter growled again. "Something comes."

They stood there in the silence, and for a moment, nothing happened. Then, slowly, Cutter became aware of a slight breeze across his fevered flesh, one that had not been there before. It picked up in a moment, scattering the fallen leaves which had dotted the ground around them into the air. Only, those leaves did not blow away as they should have. Instead, they began to swirl around the brush and Cutter and Feledias, swirl in a wind that was growing more and more powerful by the moment. In seconds, it felt as if they stood in the midst of some great, swirling maelstrom.

Cutter held up a hand in front of his face, trying to peer through them but he could see nothing.

"*What do we do now?*" Feledias shouted, forced to yell to be heard over the driving wind.

"We fight," Cutter said quietly. The pressure of the wind against him grew stronger and stronger until he thought that he might be knocked from his feet by its power.

Then, suddenly, the wind vanished as abruptly as it had come, the leaves which had swirled around them, obscuring their vision, falling to the ground. But being able to see what was now around them was little comfort.

The bushes and trees which had blocked their path were no longer there. Or, at least, they had *changed.* Now, those thorny bushes, those thick trees and reaching vines had transformed, melded themselves together to form three vaguely mortal-like shapes. Though those shapes, Cutter noted, his mouth turning into a grim frown, towered over him and Feledias, seven and eight feet tall. And within each of their mock faces formed by leaves and vines and thorns, two sullen emerald spots glowed like green coals.

"*The Destroyer has come,*" a voice said, one that sounded like the rasp of leaves or the whisper of grass in a breeze. "*You should not have braved the Wood, Destroyer, for now you will find your doom. We will show you to it, just as you showed the King Yeladrian to his own.*"

"Bullshit you will," Feledias growled. "Damn if I'll get killed by a plant." He gave a cry then, rushing forward.

"*Fel, wait!*" Cutter yelled.

But his brother was beyond listening. He charged toward the nearest figure of branch and thorn, lashing out with his sword, lightning fast. The creature only took the blow, and Fel was rewarded for his efforts with the tiniest of knicks in one of the branches that comprised the creature's form. He struck again, then again, his blades darting in and out, but each strike had no more effect than the first.

Feledias was continuing his assault when the creature swung its arm at him. The arm seemed to grow by the instant, the vines which comprised it twisting and turning as if alive, growing larger, thicker, and Feledias let out a cry of pain and surprise when it struck him, sending him flying backward.

Feledias hit the ground in a roll, coming to stop near Cutter's feet, his swords lying on the ground roughly equal distance between them and the monstrosities.

"*Bastard,*" Feledias wheezed in a pained voice.

Cutter offered his brother his hand. Feledias took it, and he pulled him to his feet. "You okay, Fel?"

Feledias grunted, rubbing at his chest where the creature had struck him. "I've been better," he croaked.

"Stay behind me," Cutter said. "This is not a job for swords. As you said," he went on, glancing at his brother, "this is work for an axe."

"Stay behind you and do *what* exactly?" Feledias wheezed. "Cheer you on?"

Cutter glanced at the three creatures arrayed in front of him, taking their time, in no hurry and why would they be? They were confident of how the thing would end. "Start a fire," he said quietly.

Feledias frowned. "A fire? Forgive me, brother, but I don't think the cold is the worst of our pro—" He cut off, his eyes widening. "Ah. Of course. And I think I might just have some idea on what to use for kindling. Still…" He paused, glancing at the three creatures before looking back at Cutter, "you think you can keep them busy for long enough?"

"One way to find out," Cutter said, his eyes watching the three forms. He started forward then paused, glancing back at his brother. "And Fel?" he said. "Make it a big one, will you?"

"You…got it," Feledias said, still trying to catch his breath.

Cutter nodded, leaving him to it as he turned back to the three creatures.

"Now then, Destroyer, are you prepared? Your death is coming."

"It's been coming for a long time now," Cutter said.

Then he charged.

The creature, perhaps aware of the lethality of the axe he wielded, did not allow him a free strike as it had his brother. Instead, it lashed out with its arm, which had grown as massive as a tree trunk by the time it reached him, and Cutter narrowly escaped it by falling to his knees, hissing in pain as his wounds made themselves known at the sudden movement.

He slid across the leaf-strewn ground, and once he came within range of the creature he rose, pivoting, and with a roar, swung his axe at the roots and vines making up the creature's legs. Normal swords might have had little effect, but the Fey weapon cleaved deep into the creature, and it cried out in a voice that sounded like the building of some great storm as the black blade sliced through first one leg, then the other.

It fell to the ground on what would have been its back, had it been a man, and lashed out at Cutter for another strike. Cutter batted the blow aside with his axe then stepped forward and smashed his foot down on what made up the creature's face with a roar.

It stopped moving then, dead, and in its death the magic that had held together that great conglomeration of vines and thorns and leaves dissipated, and it all collapsed to the ground. Cutter turned to the other two. "It's what my people do with trees that are in our way," he growled. "We cut them down."

The creatures lumbered forward, not content to come at him one at a time now that they'd seen their companion cut down so easily. Cutter circled, trying to keep them from getting around behind him, for he knew that while the first might have fallen easily enough, that was only because it, like most of the Fey, was arrogant.

These two, though, seemed intent on not making the same mistake, and they came on as a pair, following his movements. Cutter was exhausted, weak, and it was all he could do to keep his feet as he backed warily away. At least, that was, until he fetched up against something. He spun to see that a wall of vines and thorns had grown behind him, hemming him in and keeping him from maneuvering.

"Fine," he growled. "I won't make you wait any longer."

Left with no other choice, he rushed forward, his axe leading. The nearest swiped out with a blow that would have likely taken his head from his shoulders had it connected. Cutter ducked beneath it, continuing forward only to be met with the creature's other arm, thrusting toward him. He lunged to the side, out of the way of the attack and with a roar buried his axe in the creature's arm.

Or at least he meant to. His axe was only moments from cleaving into it when something struck him in the side, hard, and he was sent stumbling backward into the wall of undergrowth. The wall, though, seemed to come alive at his touch, and vines and roots reached out, trying to grab him.

Cutter growled, ripping himself free only to have pieces of twigs and thorns still clinging to him, crawling across him like worms. He hissed in disgust, sweeping them off him with his free hand as he turned back to see the two creatures bearing down on him.

His side ached where the creature had struck him and, worse than that, he found that the brief exchange had sapped much of what little strength had remained to him. Still, there was nothing to be done but stand and so he did, watching his death come, and it was all he could do to hold his axe up in front of him.

"Come on then," he growled as the creatures lumbered forward, wiping an arm across his mouth where a line of blood had begun to leak out.

The creatures seemed all too happy to oblige, quickening their pace as they moved toward him. Cutter bared his bloody teeth in anticipation—but suddenly, there was a shout from behind the creatures and they froze.

A moment later, Cutter became aware of the smell of something burning.

"*Burn, you bastards, burn!*" Feledias roared.

And, as if by way of reply, the creatures did. They let out strange, rasping wails as fire blossomed within the vines and leaves which formed them. The flames spread across them hungrily, eager to devour the meal which had been placed before them. Soon the two giant creatures were two giant blazing torches, stumbling forward, reaching their burning hands toward Cutter.

In their agony, though, whatever magic had held together the wall of vines vanished, and he was able to retreat backward until the creatures collapsed in front of him, little more than piles of smoldering ruins.

Feledias shuffled around them, one arm across his chest, a still-burning torch held in his other hand. "Bastards," he hissed, spitting on them as they burned.

He came to stand beside Cutter. "You okay?" Feledias asked.

Cutter bared his teeth in a bloody grin. "I've been better," he said, echoing his brother's words from earlier. "What took you so long?"

"You wouldn't believe the difficulty I had getting a fire going," Feledias said. "It's not easy here. It's as if this place doesn't like the flames."

Cutter grunted, glancing back at the burning creatures. "I can see why."

Feledias nodded. "Well. What do we do now?"

"I don't know about you," Cutter breathed, wincing at the pain in his side, "but I was considering passing out."

"Don't you bloody *dare*," Feledias said. "Hauling your ass behind me like some damned mule once was enough—don't you start making a habit of it. You pass out again, there's good odds I'll take it in mind to leave you, understand?"

Cutter winced, nodding. "I understand."

Feledias shook his head, glancing around. "Well, at least the path has returned."

Cutter followed his gaze to see that, indeed, his brother was right. The path ahead was clear once more. "Come o—" He cut off as the wind began to pick up again.

"Shit," Feledias said, "what now? More of those things?"

"No," Cutter said as he watched all of the shrubs and underbrush on one side of the road come together, forming a creature that was at least fifteen feet high. "This one's bigger."

The creature formed a dozen feet away from them, towering over them, and Cutter glanced at Feledias to see him looking at his torch doubtfully.

"Stay behind me," Cutter said. "Wait until I distract it." He started forward then, but paused when the creature spoke.

"Be at peace, Destroyer," the creature said, *"for I mean you no harm."*

Cutter frowned. "These others did," he said, indicating the smoldering corpses of those creatures which had attacked him with a tilt of his head.

The creature turned its massive head to regard the piles of ash and vines, then slowly it began to change. Leaves and twigs all swirled and moved around it until, in time, what stood before Cutter was not a giant any longer but a creature near his own height. *"They were young,"* the creature said, moving forward, and Cutter thought he detected a note of sadness in its alien voice, *"and in their youth they were arrogant."*

"But...aren't you mad?" Feledias ventured. "I mean...that we...well..." He trailed off, glancing at the charred forms.

Cutter winced, turning back to the creature. *"I am not angry,"* the creature said. *"Instead, I am sad. These here have set themselves against the Destroyer and so, in turn, were destroyed. As I said, they were younglings and did not know better. They were consumed with their pride and their hatred, for they follow the teachings of the Green Man, and the Green Man knows only hate."*

Cutter frowned. "The...Green Man?"

The figure inclined its head. *"You know of him, for you have met. The name by which you know him is Shadelaresh."*

"So...is he the new king? Of your people?" Feledias asked.

"My people have no king," the creature said, *"not any longer. Yeladrian is dead, and so we are kingless until the next Coming. No, the Green Man is not our king. He is more like what your kind might call a shaman or a priest."*

"A priest," Feledias repeated.

"Yes, but a powerful one. He was not always as he is now, but his hatred for you, Destroyer, has twisted him, has made what was once fine a cruel, evil thing that cares only for vengeance."

Cutter winced, sharing a glance with Feledias. "Because of Yeladrian?"

"Yes. The Green Man and King Yeladrian were very close, were life friends since birth. Once, the Green Man taught peace, and he spent many hours wandering the woods, listening to the sounds of

the trees blowing in the wind, feeling their shade. It was he, in fact, who bade the king seek peace with your people. Now, he revels in his hatred, his thoughts only of revenge, of how he might best make you—and all mortals—suffer. Now, tell me, Destroyer, Slayer of the Fey King Yeladrian, why have you come to the Black Wood? Will you kill Shadelaresh, the Green Man?"

"No," Cutter said.

"*Why?*" the creature asked, not sounding just curious but more than a little disappointed.

Cutter frowned, turning to Feledias to see that his own surprise was mirrored in his brother's face. "I...I have come seeking peace."

"*Peace,*" the creature repeated, as if it had never heard the word before. "*It has been so long since I have known it, I wonder if I might even recognize it, should I have it again.*"

Those were surprisingly close to Cutter's own thoughts from earlier, so he nodded. "Yet, I have come seeking it. If the Green Man is the closest you have to a king now, then it seems that it is him to whom I must speak."

"*Then you spend your life without purpose, Destroyer, and there are few worse things than that. The Green Man will not accept any peace, for he has no peace within himself. He has abandoned even the pursuit of it, so that the only peace he might know is the peace of the grave. Now, tell me, again, Destroyer, why have you come?*"

"I told you," Cutter said, "I've come for peace."

"*A destroyer come for peace. Even were it here to be found, and it is not, you would not be the one to find it. Do not frown, please, for I mean no offense. It is not wrong, nor cruel to tell the rabbit that he is such, or to tell the lion what he is. It is only cruel to tell the rabbit that the lion is something else, something kind, so that he knows naught of his peril until he feels the bite of that great cat's teeth. Do you understand?*"

"I...don't think so," Cutter said.

"*What I speak, Destroyer, is that if you are to win peace for your people and for mine, you will not do it with a kind word, not with all the good intentions of the world. You will only gain it the same way you have gained everything in your life.*" Its gaze traveled then to Cutter's back where he had sheathed his axe, and he was suddenly very aware of the weapon's weight strapped against him. "*If you are to win peace, you will win it not by word but by deed, not by speech but by blood. It is the only way the Green Man understands any longer, for the other knowledge has been lost to him. So, too, is it the only way you understand."*

"You would have me kill him," Cutter said. "You would have me kill your priest."

"He is not my priest, Destroyer, nor is he my master, no more than the rain might be said to serve the wind."

Cutter frowned, thinking that through. "Do you mean to say that you are as powerful as he is? But...if that's true, why do you not just defeat him yourself?"

"There are many forms of power, Destroyer, and my path is a different one. I know this, for I have seen it. I saw it even before your first visit to the Wood, many seasons ago, when you came with your men and your steel and your fire. And even should I raise my hand against the Green Man, it would serve no purpose but to subject my people to even worse tragedies, to embroil them in a war where kin was set against kin, where those who had once played together as younglings ripped the life from each other." The creature gave a powerful shake of its head. *"No. This I will not, cannot do. If the Green Man is to be destroyed, then it must be you who does it. You...and the Breaker of Pacts."*

Cutter considered that. A lifetime of blood, a lifetime of corpses at his feet. What was one more among that pile? But that answer, at least, he knew. It was everything. "I am no assassin," he said, "and I will not kill him."

"Then you will die, for he will surely kill you. He thinks of little else but how to get it done. Only how to make you suffer as much as he might before your end."

"So...let's say we did want to kill him," Feledias said, pausing as Cutter abruptly turned on him. Feledias raised his hands. "Just *saying* that we did. How would we do that? Just the old axe to the throat trick?"

"No," the creature said. *"The Green Man has spent these many seasons since Yeladrian's death in preparation, weaving about himself glamours and protections, ones so powerful that even the Breaker of Pacts would not find purchase on his flesh. No, the Green Man cannot be slain, not in that way. But there is another. One that lies far to the north, past what your people call the Barrier*

Mountains. Among the snow and the ice of that forsaken wilderness might you find it."

"Find *what?*" Feledias asked.

"It doesn't matter," Cutter growled. "We haven't come to fight—we're here for peace."

"And should you continue your search for it," the creature said, *"then you will find it, but only that peace which might be found in the grave. You are what you are, Destroyer. And like a fish seeking to be a man, you will only suffer should you try to be anything other than what you are."*

"Listen…" Cutter paused. "Sorry, I didn't get your name."

"My true name is one beyond your ken, for it is not spoken as much as it is felt, felt in the quiver of the leaves before the coming storm, in the quiet rustle of branches in a crisp autumn wind. It is felt in the coolness of the spring air on early morning, and in the warmth of a summer sun on flesh."

"How about 'Bob'?" Feledias offered.

The creature cocked its head, and the vines and twigs which made up its countenance seemed to split into what might have been a smile. *"Feledias Stormborn. It is what they call you, is it not?"*

Feledias frowned, glancing at Cutter who only gave him a shrug before turning back to the creature. "Or asshole," he said. "I've heard both."

"Yes," the creature said. *"Yours is a tale of pain, is it not? For I can see it writ upon your face. But do not fret, Stormborn, for all pain fades, in the end. It can do naught else."*

"Uh…was that like the most obscure threat ever, or…?"

"My name," the creature went on, *"or at least what might serve for your purposes…well. You may call me the Gray Man."*

"The Gray Man," Feledias repeated.

The creature inclined his head.

"Very well, Gray Man," Cutter said. "Anyway, we thank you for your offer of help, but as I've said, we must be going."

"Yes, you must," the Gray Man answered, *"though I would not worry overly much, Destroyer. After all, a man's death is the one thing that will wait for him, always."*

Cutter turned to Feledias. "Come," he said. "It's time we left."

He started away, shuffling, the many aches and pains of his body making themselves known now that the fighting was over.

"*Your wounds pain you,*" the creature said.

"Yes," Cutter agreed, turning back, "but I'm used to pain."

"*As all the living become, should they survive long enough,*" the creature said. "*Still, if you will allow me, Destroyer, I would see you and your kin healed. If you insist on moving forward and seeking the Green Man, and if you wish to have any chance of surviving to make it to him, then you must be made whole once more. Or, at least, as whole as you might be made.*"

"Do you...do you mean you can heal us?" Feledias asked.

"*It is within my power to heal some of those hurts which plague you,*" the creature said. "*Some, but not all for some hurts are beyond help. Do you understand?*" the creature asked, regarding Cutter.

Cutter had lived his entire life in one form of pain or another, and while the healers and their arts might go a long way toward mending those physical hurts which he'd accrued over his life, none of their tinctures, their potions and medicines, ever touched the emotional ones. For there was no cure for shame and regret, for the hatred a man felt for himself. "I understand," he said.

"*Come then, Destroyer, come to me, and I will do what I may.*"

Cutter started forward, but paused as Feledias grabbed his arm. "Bernard...are you sure about this?"

"No," Cutter said, "but we cannot continue like this, Fel. I'm hurt, and you're little better. The shape we're in, I doubt if we'll survive the night."

With that, he turned and walked toward the creature, stopping in front of it.

"*Such rapid healing as I will perform...there is a cost,*" the creature said. "*There will be pain. Great pain.*"

"Nothing I haven't felt before."

"*Perhaps,*" the creature agreed, nodding its head as if in assent.

Then it reached out toward him, twin vines crawling around each other in a spiral, moving closer and closer to him until, finally, they alighted on his forehead.

A soft, gentle touch, as soft as if a snowflake had landed on his fevered skin. And then...

Pain.

Hot, incredible pain, lancing through him, roaring through him like some raging fire. Washing over him, pouring over him in a flood. Pain of red and white, blasting through his head, his mind, and then…only blackness.

The next thing Cutter knew, he was on his knees, gasping, his breath pluming in white clouds in front of him.

"Bernard!?" Feledias's voice, sounding as if it came from some great distance. "What have you done to him, you bastard?"

There was the familiar metallic sound of a weapon leaving its scabbard, and then Cutter's brother stepped in front of him, interposing himself between Cutter and the Gray Man. "I'll kill you, if you've hu—"

"I'm fine, Fel."

Feledias glanced over his shoulder, raising an eyebrow. "Oh, sure, that must have been what all the yelling was about."

"Yelling?" Cutter asked, frowning.

"Yes, *yelling,*" Feledias snapped, "gods, you must have yelled for ten minutes straight."

Cutter's frown deepened. "I…I don't understand. I thought…that is, he only touched me a moment ago."

Feledias snorted. "I thought you said you'd fix him, not drive him insane," he said to the creature. "Or…well…insaner."

"How do you feel, Destroyer?"

"I feel…good," Cutter said. And he was surprised to find that it was true. Whatever magic the Gray Man had called upon, it seemed to have mended the ache and pain of wounds he had all but forgotten about over the years. For the first time that Cutter could remember, he did not hurt. At least not physically. True to the Feyling's words, those other pains—emotional, mental—he found were still there.

He rose, feeling stronger than he had in some time, and inclined his head to the creature. "Thank you."

"Do not thank me, Destroyer," the Gray Man said, *"for you go to Shadelaresh, to your doom, and what I have done is no more than face paint upon a corpse."*

"But what a handsome corpse he'll make," Feledias said. "Now then, brother, are we ready to go now? You know, we've got dying to be about and all that."

"Go ahead, Fel," Cutter said. "Let him help."

Feledias grunted. "I'm fine."

"You're not fine," Cutter said. "You think I can't see the way you're favoring one side? How many ribs are cracked? One? Two?"

"Oh, let's not make a game of guessing," Feledias said, rolling his eyes. "Still, I must admit I'm not particularly inclined to go through whatever that was."

"More inclined to die because you were too stubborn to take help when it was offered you?"

Feledias sighed. "Fine, but if he kills me, brother, know that I will haunt you until the end of your life."

Cutter gave him a small smile. "Couple of days, then? I think I can deal with that."

"Don't be so confident, brother," Feledias said, raising an eyebrow, "it might well be sooner."

"Done stalling yet?" Cutter asked.

His brother heaved a heavy sigh. "Come on then, Feyling," he said. "Do your worst—show me what you've got."

The Gray Man stepped forward, reaching out, and then it showed his brother what it had. Which, based on Feledias's shout, was quite a lot.

It went on for several minutes until Feledias collapsed to a sitting position on the forest floor, his shoulders slumped, blinking dazedly.

"Fel?" Cutter asked. "You alright?"

"That uh..." Feledias took a slow breath, swallowing hard. "That really packs a punch, doesn't it?"

Cutter laughed, offering him his hand. "Yes, yes it does. Now come. We'd best be getting on."

"Sure," Feledias said. "It'd be wrong to be late for our own executions."

"Outright rude," Cutter agreed.

CHAPTER FIVE

She lay in her soft bed in the castle, glorying in the warmth of the sun where it shined through the window and fell upon her naked skin. She could not remember the last time she had been proud of her body, *comfortable* in it. Not for many years, anyway, not since age had begun to take its hold on her, since those things which had once been smooth and supple began to sag and skin that had been flawless began to wrinkle.

And she didn't *just* feel comfortable now—she felt beautiful. Silly, maybe, as she was far more Maeve the Mummified than Maeve the Marvelous. Yet...she did. And that feeling came not from the shallowness of her outward appearance as it had in the past, but instead from the inside. She felt beautiful because *he* thought she was.

Challadius yawned in his sleep, scratching at his ample stomach. Maybe not the sort of man that women fawned over, not anymore, at least. Certainly not the type of man the young version of herself would have fawned over, but then the young version of herself had, by and large, been a complete fool.

And while the years had taken some things from her like a thief in the night, unlike that thief, they had also left some things in their place. Her once famous, celebrated looks had been stolen from her, but she had been given a certain degree of wisdom instead—not just wisdom, either, but humility. It was for this reason that she understood, finally, that it was not the outside appearance that counted, but what was inside.

And Challadius, no matter how much he tried to hide it, had a kind, loving, compassionate soul. She reached out, running a finger through his curly hair. He snorted, waving a hand at it in his sleep as if he were swatting away an annoying fly, and Maeve smiled. It seemed strange to her that so many people spent their lives searching for something, some sort of meaning, some sort of happiness, only to realize when they finally found it, that it had been right in front of them all along.

She ran her fingers down his cheek and his eyes eased opened. A slow smile spread across his face as he saw her there, and Maeve thought she had never seen anything so wonderful as that smile. "Morning," he said.

"Good morning," she said back.

"Feels like I'm dreaming."

"If you are, then don't you dare wake up," she responded.

He kissed her then. It was a good kiss—with him, they all were—and it went on longer than she meant for it to before she finally, reluctantly, pulled away. "It's time."

He grinned. "Again already? Alright, just give me a minute, let me get woke up. I don't...well, you know, wake up as easy as I used to, and—"

"No, no, Challadius," she said, laughing, "I mean it's time for us to get up and go find Matt."

The mage heaved a heavy sigh. "By find him you mean trail after him like puppies as he storms about the dungeons, interrogating one advisor after another over and over and over again like he's done for the last three days? Asking the same questions, threatening the same threats?"

She smiled. "Something like that."

"Well, if you say so," Chall said. "Just...give me a minute."

He eased himself out of the bed, yawning and stretching as he shuffled toward the chair upon which he'd hung his clothes the night before.

Maeve shook her head, unable to keep the smile from her face as she watched him in all his overweight glory. Then she heard a strange sound, one that made her smile freeze on her face. It was a familiar sound, a sort of *click*, but she couldn't place it. Yet place it or not, the sound set alarm bells ringing in her mind. Challadius, though, didn't seem bothered in the slightest, beginning the process of tugging on his pants.

"What do you say we go out in the city tonight?" he asked over his shoulder. "Just the two of us?"

"That would be nice," she said distracted, trying to place the sound.

"You alright, Maeve?" he asked.

He began to turn and, as he did, the sunlight coming through the window abruptly shifted, light flashing across the room, and in the same moment, Maeve realized where she'd heard that sort of click before. *"Chall, get down!"* she screamed, leaping from the bed as she yelled and rushing toward him.

Chall didn't have time to get down—barely had time for his mouth to open in a surprised 'o'—before she was tackling him. They hit the ground with him on his back, her on top, and he grunted in pain.

"Damn, Maeve, no need to be so forceful, you could have just—"

He cut off at the sound of shattering glass followed a moment later by splintering wood. They looked up to see that a crossbow bolt had buried itself in the wall, no more than a foot above their heads, and was still quivering from the impact.

"What the fu—"

"Stay down," Maeve hissed, then she rolled off the mage, back in the direction of the bed. Making sure to stay low so that the thick mattress blocked her from view, she crawled back to the bed then grabbed it in both hands. With a grunt of effort, she lifted the mattress up out of the frame, forced to rise with it. Another crossbow bolt flew through the mattress, appearing out of the stuffing as if by magic, missing her by less than half a foot and sending feathers into the air.

Growling with the effort, Maeve finished lifting the mattress, shoving it forward so that it landed propped against the wall, blocking the window.

"Shit," she heard from the other side of the mattress. A male's voice.

She knew she only had moments before whoever it was shoved the mattress aside, exposing her and Challadius, so she darted past the mage, gesturing for him to stay down as she hurried toward the door. As she did, she snatched up a small butter knife from where it lay on a silver platter along with the remnants—crumbs mostly—of their dinner from the night before.

She reached the door and threw it open.

"Maeve, what are—"

"*Quiet,*" she said, low but not so low that she thought the assassin outside wouldn't be able to hear, "*come on, we have to get out of here.*" Yet even as she spoke, she motioned for the mage—a very confused, terrified looking mage just then—to stay down.

Then she moved back toward the window as quickly and as quietly as she was able. She heard another curse from outside the window as she was hurrying back and no sooner had she reached one end of the bed before it was thrown forward.

As she had hoped, the assassin, fearing that his quarry was escaping, had traded caution for haste. He threw the mattress aside with a grunt and climbed through the window. Or, at least, he tried to.

He was no more than halfway through, one hand grasping the top of the window frame, one foot on its bottom, when Maeve lunged forward and plunged the butter knife into his throat. Blood fountained out, proving beyond doubt that she had struck the artery for which she'd been aiming, and the man let out a soft wheeze before all the strength seemed to go out of his body and he fell backward, disappearing through the window. Maeve darted her head out, looking first one way then the other to make sure that there weren't any more assassins, then looked down to the street to see their attacker's body—or at least what was left of it—smashed on the cobbles far below.

Dead, that much was sure. If the knife hadn't done it then the fall certainly would have. Satisfied that the immediate threat of danger had passed, Maeve turned back to Chall. "You okay?"

The mage's face was white as parchment, and he was staring, blinking, at the blood-stained window frame. "I...you just...who was..."

"Snap out of it, Chall," Maeve said.

He cleared his throat, giving his head a shake as if to clear it. "Right, no, you're right. I'm...I'm okay." He paused, glancing down at himself. "At least, I think so. Though I don't mind telling you that

I could do with taking a piss just now. Who was that bastard anyway?"

"I didn't really have a chance to ask him," Maeve said dryly, "you know, I was too busy saving us and all."

"Did I not seem thankful?" Chall asked. "Trust me, Mae, this is me thankful."

"Good," she said then moved forward, her heart still racing, her eyes beginning to tear up, a reaction to the abrupt violence. She ran a hand along his face. "Are you sure? That you're okay?"

"I'm fine, Mae," he said. "Really."

"Good," she said again, then ran an arm across her eyes. "Now, come on—we need to go find Matt, make sure he's okay. Then check on the body, figure out who this bastard was."

"Sure, but Mae—"

"I know, Chall," she said, turning back from where she'd been heading to the door. "I know." Then she let out a heavy sigh. "And...I'm glad you're okay, too. But really, we need to go. If an assassin was sent after us, one might well have been sent after Matt or Priest as well. Now, let's—"

"But Mae—"

"Chall, please," she said, "we really have to go."

"And I'm *willing* to go, Mae," he said. "I just thought maybe you'd want to get dressed first."

Maeve frowned, glancing down at herself and realizing that she was still completely naked. She felt her cheeks flush. Maeve the Marvelous indeed.

"Don't get me wrong," Chall said, "I don't believe you've ever looked better, not in all the years I've known you." He grinned but it quickly faded. "Except for the blood that is."

She glanced at her arms, coated in the man's blood from where she'd driven the blade into his throat, then winced. "You're right. Maybe a quick clean up, then I'll get dressed and we'll go."

He sighed. "If you must."

She grinned at that, giving him a wink, but she knew that it was just an act for both of them, each trying to deal with the shock of what had just happened and the terror at what nearly had. She hurriedly set about the task of using some of the water that remained in the pitcher a servant had brought them last night—

along with two goblets, both of which were empty of wine, Chall had seen to that much—to wipe the worst of the blood away.

When she was satisfied that she was clean, or at least as clean as she was going to get, she began to dress. Chall was already finished by the time she dressed, and she looked at him where he'd been sitting watching her. "You know, people get arrested for that sort of staring."

He gave her a grin that clearly didn't come cheap. "Very well, then I put yourself at my mercy."

She laughed, shaking her head. "Later."

He sighed, nodding, and then they started through the hallway at a brisk walk. As they moved through the castle toward Matt's quarters, Maeve's eyes roamed every intersection and every doorway they passed, ready to draw one of the many blades secreted about her person and defend herself or Chall, and forced from time to time, to wipe at her eyes in an effort to keep away the tears that threatened to come.

She noted Chall watching her out of the corner of his eye as they walked, just as she couldn't help but notice that he asked if she was okay three times. She assured him that she was just as he assured *her* that the man had been a bad man and that she shouldn't feel bad for killing him.

She didn't bother correcting him but the truth was that she didn't feel bad about that much in the slightest. After all, she had killed before, many times, and the cold reality was that the feeling of guilt and shame that came after was something that a person got over with time.

No, it wasn't the dead assassin that was affecting her. In fact, if she could bring the bastard back to life and kill him again she thought that probably she would. What brought the tears, what terrified her, was the thought of how close she had come to losing everything she cared about, how close the *bastard* had come to succeeding. They were alive more because of luck more than anything she had done, that was the simple truth. If the assassin had fired a moment sooner, if she hadn't happened to notice the change in the light, Chall would be dead, for it had been obvious that the man intended to kill him first.

And if he had managed it, Maeve thought that she might have only stood and let him finish her off as well. She had been alone before, for the last fifteen years she had been alone and never mind that her "husband" had shared a bed with her. She could not go back to being alone, not anymore, not after remembering, after being *reminded* of what it felt like to have someone. Better to be dead than that.

Still, she scolded herself for allowing her emotions to show. After all, they would do her no good, not now. She tried to seek some consolation in the fact that both she and Chall were still alive, but that did little to better her mood.

She was still trying to work her way past it, had only just managed to gain control of the tears that kept threatening to come, when they turned down the hallway that led to Matt's quarters. Normally, when the king was present in his quarters, two guards stood outside his door with another two stationed at the end of the hallway. Now, though, she saw that the hallway was empty.

She frowned, glancing at Chall before looking back down the hallway. Had the guards simply left because Matt had risen early this morning? Or were they missing for some other, more nefarious reason?

"Come on," she said, grabbing Chall's hand and almost-but-not-quite jogging down the hallway to the door.

They reached it, and Maeve's breath caught in her throat as she saw that the door was slightly askew in its frame. She met Chall's eyes, bringing a finger to her mouth to beg for silence, then reached into her tunic, withdrawing a knife.

She eased the door open with her free hand, her body tensed, ready to explode into action. She continued to push it open slowly, carefully, until the door let out a creak. The moment that it did, Maeve shoved it open the rest of the day, leaping into the room, her gaze sweeping across it. She caught sight of a figure, and she darted forward, putting her knife at the figure's throat.

But the figure was not an assassin as she had expected. Instead, judging by her simple linen shift—and the soapy rag in her hand—she was a servant come to clean the room. A particularly terrified servant, her face pale, her body trembling.

"Oh gods, I'm sorry," Maeve said, pulling the blade away and sliding it back inside her tunic. "I thought someone was attacking the king."

"K-king's n-not here," the woman, who appeared to be in her early twenties, managed as she held her hands up in front of her, clearly terrified. Maeve noticed that the woman wore a ring with what might have been stylized wolf on it, but then her mind shoved the random, useless observation away as the woman continued to speak. "I-I was only, only cleaning, is all."

"Right," Maeve said, wincing, "sorry about that. I—"

"You'll have to forgive my companion," Chall said as he walked into the room. "She really does enjoy showing off her knives at every chance she gets Miss...forgive me, but I didn't get your name?"

The woman smiled shyly, glancing at her feet. "It's Margaret, my lord, if it please you. And beggin' your pardon, but you...well, you're Sir Challadius, aren't you? Challadius the Charmer?"

The snort came out of Maeve's mouth before she could stop it, and Chall grunted. "That's just right, Margaret," Chall said, scowling at Maeve as he did. "Anyway, I wouldn't worry about Maeve here—she's safe enough."

"Maeve?" the woman said, her eyes going wide. "You mean, that is, as in Maeve the Marvelous?"

The woman might have seemed shy, even flirtatious when she'd discovered Chall's identity, but her reaction to Maeve's was considerably different—namely, terror. "I'm afraid so," Maeve said. "Anyway, that was a long time ago. I'm...well, I'm considerably less marvelous now."

"O-of course, ma'am," she said, licking her lips nervously. "Well, if you would like to look over the king's room, I can leave—"

"That won't be necessary, Margaret," Maeve said quickly, "we'll be leaving in just a moment. Only, the king: do you know where he's gone off to?"

"My mistress—the mistress of the servants? She said that he'd gone to the dungeon, told me to get in here and clean 'is Majesty's quarters proper-quick on account of there was no knowin' when he might be back to use them. That's all I was doing, cleaning, I wasn't up to anything, I swear, and—"

"I know you weren't, Margaret," Maeve said, reaching out a hand, but the woman took an abrupt step back, looking more terrified still.

"Easy, Maggie, easy," Chall said, stepping forward, giving Maeve an apologetic look as he did. "Just take it easy—can I call you Maggie? Does anyone else?"

"N-not anymore," the woman said, allowing Chall to place a hand gently on one of her shoulders. "N-not since my mom passed."

"I see," Chall said, nodding. "Well, then maybe it'll just be our special thing, how'd that be?"

She smiled prettily, if not completely over her terror then pretty damned close by Maeve's estimation, just as she thought that the feeling most prominent in the woman just then wasn't terror but something else altogether. "I...I think I'd like that."

"Sure, and it would be my privilege. Anyway, Maggie, we really appreciate all your help, truly. So much, in fact, that well, you see, we're sort of friends of the king, and I'll make sure to mention to him just how lucky he is to have a fine lass like yourself looking after his quarters for him."

"You mean...really?" the woman asked, shocked. "You'd do that?"

"Of course," Chall said, smiling, and in that smile, even so many years later, was the reason he had been known as the Charmer. "I'd be happy to. Now, we've got to go. I'm afraid we're in a bit of a hurry but thank you, so much, for your time."

The serving girl flashed him another smile, batting her eyelashes and blushing, and Maeve found herself gritting her teeth.

"Of course," the girl said.

"Come on, Chall," Maeve said. "We wouldn't want to keep the king waiting."

She grabbed him by the arm, and he let out a squeal of surprise as she started toward the door, dragging him after her. "And just what was all *that* about?" Maeve demanded when they were in the hallway.

"Nothing, Mae, nothing," Chall said, "I was just trying to keep the poor girl from fainting is all."

"And if she had," Maeve said, angry at herself for her jealousy but unable to stop, "I suppose you would have taken care of her out of the kindness of your heart."

"Someone is in a bad mood," Chall said.

"Of course I am," she snapped. Then took a slow breath. "Sorry, Chall. It's just, well, having an assassin try to kill me always does play havoc with my temper, and the fact is I'm worried about Matt. There's no reason to believe that the assassin that came for us is the only one roaming the castle."

"I'm with you, Mae."

She smiled at that, she couldn't help it, and then she started down the hall, toward the dungeons where the serving girl had told her she would find Matt. They reached the dungeons a short while later, waiting while the guard stationed at the entrance which led to the prisoners' cells unlocked the door.

No sooner had he done so than Maeve heard a voice she recognized as Matt's, raised not in fear or pain, but anger. She glanced at Chall, who winced. "Seems he's still not satisfied with what the questioners have found out so far."

Maeve nodded grimly, starting into the dungeon. Maeve expected to find the king shouting at one of the prisoners, issuing threat after threat as he had been, but when she reached him, she saw that she had been wrong. It was not one of his advisors or his previous "bodyguard" at which the king was yelling. Instead, two men stood before him, both of whom Maeve recognized. It would be hard not to have, of course, since, at Matt's bidding, she and the others had spoken with them constantly over the last several days.

The first was Sergeant Bilster, a broad-shouldered, tall man who also happened to be the man in charge of the dungeon guards. Maeve had asked around about Bilster—deciding it was vital to check everyone, given the conspiracy they faced—and the man, while loyal, was also known for his dangerous temper. A temper that, just then, he was clearly choking back with a will as he stood stiffly, studying the ground, his face growing an increasingly alarming shade of red as he weathered Matt's angry shouts.

Next to the sergeant was Chief Interrogator for the Crown, Falstid Aberath, a man who appeared to be the sergeant's opposite in nearly every way. He was a thin man, short, and where the sergeant's back was straight, this man hunched, giving off an impression of age when, in fact, Maeve knew that he was at least ten years her junior. And while Bilster might have looked far more physically imposing, there was something in the smaller man's eyes that made Maeve think now—as she had over the last several days in their company—that he was the far more dangerous of the two.

If Matt's anger bothered the interrogator, he hid it well, only standing and accepting the king's wrath without complaint, his expression emotionless.

She walked closer, stopping where Priest stood with his hands clasped behind his back, watching silently. She glanced around and saw several of the nearby prisoners watching the king berate two of what were no doubt the most feared men in their lives.

"How long has this been going on?" Maeve asked Priest.

The man frowned, giving his head a small shake. "This time? Thirty minutes, at least."

Maeve winced, looking at the king as he continued his steady tirade. "He looks tired. Did he not get much sleep?"

Priest glanced at her. "The king did not get any sleep, Maeve. He has been up all night, looking into the matter of the conspiracy. He only just allowed Guardsman Nigel to seek some rest a little more than an hour gone, then he came here."

"I see," Maeve said, wincing, though she thought surely Priest must have been exaggerating. After all, the serving girl who had been cleaning the prince's room had had her work cut out for her, with everything thrown about as it had been. The man had clearly spent time in his quarters.

"He can't keep going like this," Chall said, the unmistakable worry in his tone pulling Maeve from her thoughts. "He's young, so it'll take it a bit longer, but it'll all catch up to him just the same. It always does."

Maeve nodded, glancing over to see the two men watching her. She grunted sourly. "And I don't suppose either one of you bastards volunteers to be the one to talk to him about it?"

"I would, Mae, really," Chall said, "but unfortunately, I'm too busy...you know, *not* getting yelled at."

Maeve sighed, glancing at Priest.

"I have tried to speak to him," the man said, "but to no avail. The king does not seem interested in listening to me, I'm afraid. Still..." He paused, smiling. "I once knew a woman famous for convincing people to do what she wanted. It was, despite the commonly held opinion, what I believe to be her greatest talent."

Maeve grunted again. "That was a long time ago. These days, that woman can't even convince her back not to ache when she gets out of bed." The man said nothing, only giving her a small, tight smile, and Maeve sighed. "Fine," she said, "but I don't hold out hope—maybe you'd best say a prayer to that goddess of yours."

Maeve turned then, and so she did not see how her words caused the smile on her old friend's face to wither and die. She started forward. "Majesty."

Matt cut off his steady stream of rebukes, turning to see her. "Ah, Maeve. You're awake. Good, I was just saying to Sergeant Bilster and Chief Interrogator Aberath that—"

"Yelling."

Matt paused, blinking. "I'm sorry?"

"Forgive me, Your Grace," Maeve said, "but you were not saying—you were yelling."

"Fine," Matt said, "then I was yelling. Anyway, I was just telling them that the speed at which we are uncovering the conspiracy within the city is unacceptable."

"I see," Maeve said, glancing at the two men. "And have you said what you intended, Majesty?"

Matt frowned. "What?"

"I only ask," Maeve pressed, "because, if you have, it may be best to consider allowing them to leave. After all, it will be particularly difficult for them to attend their duties if they are forced to remain here for you to...say things to them."

Matt's frown deepened, and he glanced back at the two men. "Do you both understand the importance of us finding out how far this conspiracy goes, then?"

"Yes, Majesty."

"Of course, Majesty."

Matt studied them for a moment then gave a single nod. "Very well. You are both dismissed."

Maeve favored the two men with an apologetic look, saying nothing as they made their way past her. Meanwhile, Matt had already begun pacing back in forth in the dungeon hallway, his hands on his hips, his head down, a look of obvious frustration on his face.

"That was poorly done, Majesty," Maeve said.

Matt paused in his pacing to look at her. "I'm sorry?"

"Berating them that way," Maeve said. "It was ill done."

"Ill done?" Matt said. "I'll tell you what's *ill done,* Maeve. This entire *investigation!* My father and uncle are parading around the Black Wood, meanwhile my dungeon guards and my interrogators are doing nothing to find out just how far this conspiracy goes, a conspiracy that is keeping me from offering my father and uncle any aid."

"And tell me, sire," Maeve pressed, "do you believe that berating them will do any good?"

"Nothing else seems to!" Matt snapped. "Maybe they're in on the conspiracy after all. It would explain why they have barely managed to uncover anything regarding it since I set them the task."

"You know that they are not, Majesty," Maeve said. "I have looked into the matter personally—both men appear as innocent...well, perhaps not innocent," she went on, thinking of the chief interrogator and the dangerous gleam that always seemed to be in the corner of his eye, "but at least as *loyal* as anyone can be. Unless, that is, you do not believe that I did a thorough job of checking into it. I wonder, will you yell at me now?"

Matt turned on her sharply, opening his mouth, and for a moment, she thought that he was preparing to do exactly that. Then, after a moment, he took a slow, deep breath. "I was wrong, do you think?"

"To call them traitors?" Maeve asked. "Yes. I don't pretend to know much about politics, Your Grace, but I know a little something about relationships, and this much I can tell you. If a woman calls her husband a cheater enough, he'll likely become one. And should a king insinuate—or, as you did, outright claim—that his loyal subject is a traitor..."

"Then he might make a traitor out of an honest man."

Maeve gave him a small smile. "Or a man, anyway."

Matt nodded, rubbing at his eyes. "You're right, of course. It was wrong, to talk to them that way. They are only trying to help. I shouldn't...I shouldn't have lost my temper."

Maeve stared at him, feeling a little astonished. In many ways, Matt was his father's son, but there were differences, also. Certainly, the Bernard Maeve had known had never been so ready to admit to being wrong. He'd kill first—she knew, for she'd seen him do exactly that. Matt, though, seemed all too ready to accept that he was wrong and to hold himself responsible for it. "Well," Maeve said, "it's understandable that you're in a bad mood, you know, considering that you haven't slept."

Matt glanced up at Priest. "Told you that, did he?"

"I would like to think, Majesty, that there are few things Priest would not tell me. We have, after all, been friends for a long time."

Matt sighed. "Please, Maeve, enough with the 'Majesty' talk. Just call me Matt. I get more than enough bowing and scraping from everyone else; from you, Chall and Priest, I'd really just love some candor."

Maeve glanced at the others then back to the young man, looking old and tired beyond her years. "As you say, Matt. And in the spirit of candor, might I say—you look like shit."

Matt laughed. "Thanks, Maeve. You really know how to make a person feel good. I can see why they called Chall the Charmer and not you."

"Matt, you can't go on like this," Maeve pressed, refusing to allow herself to be distracted. "You're running yourself ragged, and you can't keep going this way. You're exhausted—don't deny it, for I can see it in your face. You need to take it easy."

"Take it easy?" Matt said, turning to her. "Take it *easy?* Listen to me, Maeve. You told me that I could not leave to go and help my father. You told me that it was a king's place to remain with his kingdom, and I agreed. Then you told me that I could not send soldiers to help my father either, for there was no way to know whether the men I sent were good or evil and to that, also, I agreed. But my father and my uncle are out there, risking their lives, and the only way for me to help them is to deal with this conspiracy as quickly as possible. And I will do that. So do not tell me to take it easy. I will do whatever is necessary to right the wrong that I did, to help my father. If that means losing a little sleep, then so be it."

"It's not just sleep, Matt," Maeve said. "Look at how you were acting to those two men. Those two men who are some of the most loyal, the closest, the most *important* people you have. Those things which need to be done will be, Matt, but you cannot do everything yourself. You must trust others. Your job as a king is to look after your kingdom. Allow us, your friends, to look after everything else. Or at the very least, to *help* you."

"And how do you mean to help me, Maeve?" he asked honestly. "Will you somehow make those bastards, my advisors, talk? Or what of my bodyguard? Will you make him tell you everyone he knows that was in on the conspiracy?"

"No, Matt," she said. "I cannot do those things. What I can do, though, is to tell you that you are pushing yourself too hard. Now please, will you not rest?"

The young man looked clearly frustrated, but he took a slow, deep breath. "Fine. Always your way, Maeve. Tell me, is that why you came? To lecture me?"

"No, Matt," Maeve said, hurt by his words. "Chall and I came because an assassin came to our room this morning and tried to kill us. We wanted to check and make sure that you were okay."

Matt's eyes went wide at that and the angry, sullen expression left his face in an instant. "Are you serious?" he asked, then before she could answer he rushed forward, pulling her into a tight embrace. "Fire and salt, Maeve, I had no idea. I'm so sorry."

Maeve glanced at Chall and saw the mage favor her with a small smile, one that reflected the relief she as well felt. Perhaps Matt had gotten harder, tougher, but then the world had made him that way. It was good, refreshing, to know that beneath that hard exterior was still the sweet boy they had first met in the Black Wood.

"I'm fine, Matt," she said softly. "Truly."

"Something to be thankful for, at least," Matt said, pulling back and turning to Chall. "And you, Chall? Are you okay?"

"Oh, I'm fine, Matt, thanks for asking. Besides, nothing gets as man going in the morning quite like a good assassination attempt."

Matt shook his head, running a hand through his hair. "Stones and starlight, here I've been complaining, and someone tried to kill you. But what of the assassin? Perhaps we can question him, find out who sent him and—"

"I'm afraid that isn't going to be possible, Matt," Maeve said wincing.

The youth cut off. "Oh?"

"Not unless you have a way of talking to the dead, that is," Chall said. "That fella decided to take a nosedive from our window to the cobbles far below. Well...maybe *decided* isn't exactly the right word." The mage glanced at Maeve. "He might have been helped along a bit."

"I see," Matt said.

"Yes," Maeve said, "we were actually going to go check on the body, we only stopped because we wanted to make sure that you were okay."

"Oh, well I'll go with you," Matt said.

Maeve shared a look with Chall and Priest. "Are...that is, are you sure, Matt? There's really no need to—"

"Of course I'm sure," Matt said. "If someone tried to attack you and Chall, I want to know about it just as much as you do." He let out a deep breath. 'I know I'm bad at showing it sometimes and that I can be a jerk, but you are all my friends. The only friends I have. Besides," he continued, giving that self-deprecating smile that was his and his alone, "I think I'm just about all yelled out for the time being."

Maeve, seeing that she wasn't going to talk him out of it, nodded. "Very well, as you say, Majesty."

***

"Fire and salt," Chall breathed, turning away from the assassin's body—or what was left of it—and bringing a hand to his mouth as he focused on the nearly overwhelming urge to vomit. He'd seen a lot of corpses in his life—far more than any man ought to, truth be told. He'd seen plenty of other terrible things besides—as it turned out, war rarely made for pretty sights. But he could count on one hand the number of things he'd seen as bad as the assassin's body after the great fall he'd taken. Didn't even seem human at all. More of human *paste* maybe. Chall's stomach rumbled threateningly at the thought. The acidic, sour taste of bile filled his throat, but he swallowed it down with a will.

"Stay back, lad," Chall said, one hand on his knee as he bent over, the other held out to where Matt still stood some distance away, flanked by several guardsmen that had accompanied him through the castle. Thankfully, Matt obeyed without argument, which was just as well, as with how Chall was feeling then, any argument was likely to end with him spewing last night's dinner out onto the grass, an occurrence that was pretty damned likely anyway.

For his part, Priest stared at the ruined body of the assassin with an expression not of disgust but of sadness. Maeve, on the other hand, examined the body with an almost detached clinical sort of look that Chall had no idea how she managed to pull off.

Probably the same way she managed to keep a straight face the first time she saw you naked, fat man, he thought. And that was alright. Anything, he thought, to keep him from thinking about the body, all smashed, like a jam-filled biscuit someone crushed in their fist. And there was the bile again and the fight against his stomach's gorge resumed in earnest.

"And you're sure that no one's touched the body?' Maeve asked.

"No one, lady," the guard captain who, along with two of his guardsmen, had been standing around the body when they arrived. "Guardsman Adelin here was on patrol when he came upon the..." The man hesitated, clearing his throat, no doubt fighting the same struggle against puking that Chall himself was. "That is, before he came upon the body, ma'am."

"I see," Maeve said. "And you did not touch it or mess with anything?" she asked.

"Gods be good, ma'am," the man said, "who would want to touch it?"

"Anyone wanting to hide their tracks, that's who," Maeve responded. She moved forward then, and Chall tracked her as best he could while pointedly avoiding looking at the pile—or puddle, it was hard to decide which—of the man's body.

She moved closer to it, and Chall grunted. "Fire and salt, Maeve, tell me you're not going to..." He trailed off, unable to finish which didn't seem to matter much as Maeve didn't appear to be listening anyway.

She knelt over what remained of the assassin's body, examining it with a critical eye. She then removed a dagger from the inside of her tunic and began poking around in the man's remains.

"Damn, Mae," Chall croaked, "is that really necessary?"

"No way to know without doing it," Maeve responded, continuing to prod at the body without bothering to so much as look away.

Slowly, Chall turned, wincing as he did, to regard the body. "So...what are you looking for exactly?"

"Anything to help me figure out who this man was or who sent him here."

"Don't suppose you can just look at his face, get a description?" Chall asked.

"Look at his face?" Maeve said then grunted, gesturing with the knife. "Which part?"

That just about managed it, and Chall's stomach tried to do a flip. "Anything I can do to help?" he managed.

"You can help by staying back," Maeve said, and it was all Chall could do to keep from breathing a heavy sigh of relief. "There's not much to go on, but—" she cut off, giving a sharp intake of breath as she used the knife to remove one of the man's shoes and stare at the bottom of his foot.

"What is it, Mae?" Chall asked, noticing the way her face had paled. "What's wrong?"

Maeve slowly rose, catching a cloth tossed to her by Guardsman Benedict, one of the guards normally stationed in the dungeon, and wiping the tip of her blade on it before sliding it back into place. "I don't know who wanted him to come here," she said, turning to look at Chall and Priest, "but I know who sent him."

Chall frowned. "Listen, Maeve, I enjoy a riddle as much as the next person—which means not at all, people hate riddles—but I'm thinking maybe now's not the time."

"It's not a riddle," Maeve said, turning to the guard captain. "Thank you for your help, Captain. That will be all."

"Ma'am?" the captain asked, clearly surprised by being dismissed. "You don't...that is, you will not require our help any further?"

"We will not," Maeve said. "Except to send someone to clean this mess up."

The man bowed. "Very well, lady." Then he turned on his heel and left, followed by the other two guards. Chall, though, barely paid them any attention. He was too worried over the way Maeve was acting and also feeling a stab of pity for whoever the poor bastard was that would be tasked with cleaning up the mess.

"So what is it, Maeve?" he asked when the guards had left. "What's got you looking so scared?"

Maeve shook her head slowly, pointing at the corpse. "You see that?"

"I've been trying my best not to," Chall said.

"Not the *body*, Chall," she said in an exasperated tone. "I mean the bottom of his foot. Do you see it?"

Chall frowned, looking over at it, but it was Priest who spoke. "A scar."

"Yes," Maeve said, "and not just any scar. A brand."

"And...it is a brand with which you are familiar?" Priest asked.

"It would be hard not to be," Maeve said. "After all, the same scar marks the bottom of my own foot.

Chall frowned. "And I don't guess this is just some strange coincidence, like you both stepped on the same nail?"

"Not likely," Maeve said. "I can't speak for this man, but I can tell you with certainty that my scar, at least, wasn't caused by a nail, nor did I receive it by happenstance. No, it was given me when I first began training as an assassin at the Guild. It is a way for the guild masters to mark you as one of their own, to show you that, from then on, you belong to the Guild, from the top of your head—"

"To the bottom of your feet," Chall finished, wincing.

"That's right," Maeve said, nodding.

"Don't suppose they could have just taught you a secret handshake."

Maeve gave him a tight smile, one that he could see the fragility in. "I don't guess so. Come—I need to talk to the king."

Maeve walked past them toward where Matt waited, far enough away that Chall wished he could have been as lucky to have not seen what had happened. Chall shared a troubled look with Priest then followed after her.

"Did...did you find anything out?" Matt asked.

"I did, Majesty," Maeve said, then turned and glanced back at Chall, an apologetic expression on her face he didn't like, before turning back to Matt. "I'm afraid I have to go, Majesty."

Matt blinked at that, clearly as taken aback as Chall felt. "Go? Go where?"

Maeve winced. "There is a scar on the man's foot, a very unique scar that marks him as a member of the Assassin's Guild. I must go and speak to them. Perhaps...I may be able to figure out who is behind the contract on my and Chall's lives and get to the bottom of it."

"Well, I'll admit it's been a close contest," Chall said, "but I've got to say, Maeve, I'm impressed. That is actually the *stupidest* idea I've heard in my entire life."

Maeve frowned. "Listen, Chall, there isn't any cho—"

"No, *you* listen, Mae," Chall interrupted, doing his best to fight down his panic. "I know that you're a tough woman—the gods know I've never met anyone tougher, save perhaps for the prince, and he's not a woman. Shit, I'm not even sure if he's a man. But tough or not, what you're talking about is *suicide*."

"I don't mean to commit suicide, Chall," Maeve said softly.

"Maybe not," Chall agreed. "And maybe the man who jumps in the water to swim with the sharks doesn't mean to commit suicide, but when one of those sharks turns out to be hungry, his intention isn't going to stop it from taking its meal. And even *that* man isn't doing something so foolish as this. After all, you are talking about walking into an organization a member of which just tried to *kill* us. Or are you trying to tell me, Mae, that this man's attempt on our life had nothing to do with the Guild? Do you suppose maybe he's just doing some freelancing, is that it?"

Maeve shook her head. "No. The Guild doesn't allow such things. They are very jealous with their...operatives."

"I see," Chall said. "So then your great *plan*—if anything so foolhardy can even be said to *be* a plan—is to go traipsing into the midst of dozens, perhaps hundreds of killers, maybe skipping while tossing flowers to and fro, and hope that no one murders you before you open your mouth, let alone figure out what's actually going on. Is that right?"

"I told you, Chall," Maeve said, "I don't mean to be killed."

"Very few people wake up on the morning of their death looking for it, Maeve. It finds them just the same, and it tends to find them a whole lot faster when they travel into an *Assassin's Guild*. Or are you trying to say no one is going to try to kill you?"

"I didn't say that, Chall," Maeve said. "I only meant that there's a big difference between trying and succeeding."

"No, Maeve," Chall said. "There isn't a big difference—it's no wider than a dagger's blade or an arrow's tip. Not big at all."

"And what would you suggest then?" she demanded. "That we just sit around and wait for the next assassin to come? That we count on getting lucky again like we did this morning? Don't you *get it?*" she said, tears gathering in her eyes. "That man could have killed us. He could have killed *you.*" She broke down then, the tears pouring down her face, and Chall found himself rushing forward, pulling her into a tight embrace.

"It's okay, Mae," he whispered softly as she shuddered and shook against him, burying her head in his shoulder and dampening it with her tears. "It's okay." "No, Chall," she whispered. "It's not. We can't sit back and count on being lucky again. We have to *do* something. Please, don't try to tell me not to—I don't want you to hate me, but better that then you die."

"I don't hate you, Mae," he said. "I love you." He cleared his throat, finding himself getting choked up. "But I don't want to lose you either."

"You won't," she said, sniffling.

"Promise?"

She gave him a small, fragile smile. "I promise."

He nodded. "Well. If you believe you have to go, then let me go with you." He held up a hand, forestalling the argument he saw her preparing to make. "I can help, Mae. I know I'm no assassin, but I've got my own skills, my own talents."

"You can't come, Chall," Maeve said. "Wait, please, listen to me. It isn't that I wouldn't want you to—you just can't. I'm taking a chance that they will even speak with me—a risk, but a calculated one, for they know me. I was once...and perhaps, in many ways, I still am, one of them. I don't believe they'll kill me without listening to what I have to say. But if you come, too...that chance goes out the window. Do you understand?"

Chall gritted his teeth, looking at Priest. "And what of you?" he demanded. "Don't you have anything to say about this? Or are you going to just sit there and watch her throw her life away and refuse any help?"

The other man winced, his eyes brimming with compassion. "I believe that Maeve is right, Chall," he said. "The Assassin's Guild is, by its very nature, secretive. Even if they meant to talk, they would not do so with you there, would not risk giving up any of their secrets. Maeve already knows those secrets and so she is a minimum risk."

"Majesty," Chall said, turning on Matt, desperate now, "please. Tell her not to go. It's suicide, surely you must see that. I can't...she can't..."

"I'm sorry, Chall," Matt said softly, turning and looking at Maeve. "But if Maeve believes that this is the right thing to do, then I trust her. The same way that I would trust you, if you said as much."

"You can't be serious," Challadius said. "You have been so worried about your father and uncle and now you're willing to watch her throw her life away? The Assassins Guild might not be the Black Wood, *Majesty,*" he spat, his fear for Maeve making him angry, "but it isn't all that far from it either. Or do you love the prince so much that you can spare no love for the rest of us?"

No sooner were the words out of Challadius's mouth than he regretted them, wished he could take them back, a wish that was even more powerful when he saw the wince of almost physical pain that came over the boy's face. "Listen, Matt," he said softly, "I didn't—"

"No, Chall," Matt said, giving him a small, tender smile. "You need not apologize. I understand that it is your love for Maeve that makes you afraid, and you are right to question me. To answer your question, I love you all. You are, each of you, like family to me. A family that I have not had since my mother..." He cut off, clearing his throat. "That I have not had in a very long time. But just as it is your love for Maeve that makes you fear for her, it is my love that makes me trust her. Do you understand?"

Chall let out a heavy, shuddering breath, then glanced at Maeve, watching him. "I begin to," he said softly. "I'm sorry, Majesty. I was wrong to say that—I want you to know that as much as you think of us as family, we think of you as the same, all of us."

Matt gave him a bigger, more genuine smile at that, nodding his head in appreciation. "Thank you, Chall."

Challadius turned to Maeve. "When will you go?"

"Immediately," she answered, an apologetic look still on her face. "I dare not wait, Chall. The Guild has clearly taken on a contract for our deaths, and one assassin dying will not stop them from the fulfillment of that contract, will not keep them from sending another."

"And will anything else?" Chall asked. "Stop them, I mean?"

She met his eyes, frowning. "Only the one thing."

Chall felt his mouth go dry at that, and he nodded. "Fine. But do…do you know when you'll be back?"

She stepped forward them, cupping his face in her hands, giving him a small smile. "As soon as I can."

He tried to return the smile, but it fell apart almost immediately. "Don't leave me alone, Mae," he said, knowing that his voice was breaking, knowing too, that in his fear, he was speaking loud enough that Matt and Priest could hear and not caring in the slightest. "Please, don't leave me. It would break me."

She smiled then, her eyes shimmering with unshed tears. And then she kissed him. A great kiss, perhaps the best they had ever shared. He could only pray that it would not also be the last.

She pulled away in another moment, far too soon. "I'll come back, Chall." she said. Then she turned to Priest, nodding her head at the man who returned the gesture. She looked at Matt, giving him a bow. "Majesty."

"Maeve," Matt said, returning the bow. "Good luck."

"Thank you."

She gave him one final look, then turned and walked away, toward the city. As he watched her go, Chall heard her final words to him, repeated over and over in his head.

I'll come back, Chall.

He wondered how many widows, how many widowers, had heard much the same from their husbands and their wives as they had gone off to war. He wondered also how many had, in the end, found that those words, however comforting, had been no more than a lie. "Priest," he said softly, his voice barely loud enough for him to hear, "do you think…would you say a prayer for her? To your goddess, I mean?"

"I will try, Challadius," Priest said softly. "But I do not know that my goddess listens to me, anymore. I am not even sure that I might presume to call her 'mine.'"

Chall turned on him then, his body tensing. "Then you *make* her listen, damn you," Chall said. "If I've had to listen to your lectures all these years, all your holier-than-thou criticisms and complaints, then by the gods, Priest, you had better *make* her listen. And you make sure that she comes back to me. Do you understand? Do you?" The last was asked in a broken, hitching voice, and then Chall felt the tears coming, felt them but did not bother trying to stop them. After all, he knew that that, at least, would be a battle that he could only lose. She was gone, that was all, and there was no knowing whether or not she would ever come back.

"I will do everything I can, Chall," Priest said. "You have my word."

Chall nodded, turning back in time to catch the barest glimpse of Maeve as she stepped around the corner, heading toward the castle gates that would lead her into the city. *Please, gods,* he thought, *do not let that be the last time I see her.*

He did not know how long he stood there, watching that emptiness where she had been. Minutes, hours. In his worry, in his fear for her, time had lost much of its meaning. All he knew was that, eventually, he felt a hand on his shoulder and turned to see Priest standing there.

The man said nothing, only gave him a small, sad smile, and Chall sighed. "Now would be a good time for one of those platitudes you're always so fond of throwing around, Priest."

The man winced. He opened his mouth, as if he meant to say something then closed it again.

In the end, it was not Priest who spoke but Matt. "My father," the young man said, walking up, "not Cutter, understand, but my...well, the one who took me in when I was a child. He used to say that things are never as bad as they seem."

No, Chall thought, *no, he was right about that much—normally they're far worse.* But he knew that Matt was only trying to help, the same way that Priest was trying to help, so he forced on the best smile he could manage—not a good effort, he was sure—and nodded. "Thanks, Matt."

The young man gave him a small smile. "Of course. So what do we do n—"

"*Your Majesty!*"

They all spun to see Commander Malex rushing toward them across the castle grounds. The commander was nearing his sixties and had spent the last few weeks in a dungeon until recently but save for some hard lines on his face and a slightly-thin look, Chall didn't think a person could have told it. Even now, the commander, when he came to stop in front of them, had a...well, a *commanding* presence, with broad shoulders and a face that Chall used to joke appeared to have been manufactured using a template for army commanders. A soldier's soldier if there ever was one. Or, at least, so Chall had always thought.

"Commander Malex," Matt said surprised, "is everything alright?"

"Forgive me, Majesty," the man said, "but I meant to ask you the same thing."

Matt glanced at Chall, his confusion writ plain across his face. "Um...oh, of course, you mean the assassin. Yes, well, as it turns out the assassin did not come for me, Commander. Instead, he came for Chall and Lady Maeve."

"Yes, I have been apprised of the situation, Majesty, and I assure you I have the best of the castle guards—those already proved loyal—looking into it. But that is not the reason I came here, searching you out."

"Oh?" Matt asked. "Then what is, Commander?"

Malex opened his mouth then hesitated. "Perhaps, Highness, it would be best to show you, if you would follow me?"

"Of course," Matt said. "But, just a moment please, Commander." He turned to regard Chall and Priest. "You have both had a rough morning and with very little sleep—you in particular," he went on, glancing at Priest. "I kept you up, and I'm sorry. But now that things have calmed down, why don't you both go and get some rest? I intend to do the same just as soon as I'm finished with whatever Commander Malex needs to show me."

"Forgive me, Matt," Priest said, "but that will not do. We will accompany you until you are back in your quarters with those guards there to protect you."

Matt winced, glancing at Chall who gave him a nod. "He's right," Chall said. "Besides, Matt, with Maeve leaving the way she did...I've got pretty much no chance of getting to sleep, and even if I did manage it somehow—which I seriously doubt—well, I'm not exactly excited at the sort of nightmares I expect will be there to greet me."

Matt frowned. "I still think you should both get some rest. I've been terribly unfair, keeping you both up late, robbing you of sleep. I've been a fool."

Chall waited for Priest to say something, to offer the young man comfort as he so often did, but Priest said nothing and after a moment Chall cleared his throat. "You aren't a fool, Majesty," he said, "just a son who is worried for his father, a nephew his uncle. You have nothing to be ashamed of."

Matt's expression grew dark and he nodded slowly. "Thanks, Chall. But I'm afraid you're wrong—I have much to be ashamed of. Still, I will not argue with either of you—if you wish to come with me then I will, of course, be glad for the company."

He turned back to Commander Malex then and gave the older man a nod. "At your pleasure, Commander."

The older man inclined his head in a bow. "Majesty," he said, "this way."

***

As it turned out, Commander Malex's "pleasure" was to practically sprint across the castle ground and through its hallways so that, by the time they arrived at their destination, Chall was panting for breath, his body soaked with sweat. But even fighting for air as he was like a fish thrown onto the riverbank, Chall couldn't help but be surprised to find that their destination just so happened to be the hallway which he knew led to the prince's quarters.

Malex finally slowed his pace—a thing for which Chall was grateful—as he followed the commander toward the guards stationed at the hallway entrance, guards who had been proven loyal by their investigations.

"Any problems?" Malex asked.

"No sir, Commander," one of the guards said, bowing his head. "It's the same as you left it."

"Commander?" Matt asked. "What is it? What's happened?"

The commander turned back to them, a grim expression on his face. "As I said, Majesty, I think it would be better if I showed you."

"O-okay," Matt said.

The older man nodded, then turned and started down the hallway.

More guards waited nearer the doors to the king's quarters, four in total. Three stood with serious expressions, their blades drawn, while the fourth consoled a gray-haired, matronly woman who was sobbing quietly.

Commander Malex nodded to the guards but did not stop as he moved toward the door to the king's quarters, then opened it and stepped inside.

Matt, showing far less certainty and conviction than he had in the past days while hunting down his traitorous advisors, followed in a nervous shuffle. Chall glanced at Priest, the two of them sharing a troubled look, before they went after them.

Inside the room, Matt's quarters were much as they had been hours ago when Chall and Maeve had come searching for the king. Clothes lay everywhere, as if the king had been in a rage the night before and had taken it in mind to throw every article of clothing out of his closets across his room. The drawers of the wardrobe in the center had been opened, the stable and nightstands tossed on their sides, and Chall edited his further thought. The room didn't look as messy as it had when he and Maeve had seen it earlier that morning—it looked worse.

At least, he thought it did. He couldn't be sure as he hadn't paid as much attention to the room as he might have since they'd been busy trying to find Matt and make sure he was still as un assassinated as he had been the day before. And, of course, there had been the serving girl. "Whoever she was," he muttered, "she did a piss poor job."

"What's that, Chall?" Matt asked, turning and glancing back at the mage.

"Maeve and I came here first, looking for you," Chall said. "After the assassination attempt, that is. Only, you weren't here. A serving woman was, though, set about the task of cleaning. I was just saying she did a terrible job."

"But what happened here?" Matt asked. "To make this mess, I mean?"

Chall blinked in confusion at that. "I had thought...well, Maeve and I had thought...that is..."

"That I'd done it myself," Matt said, wincing. "You thought that I was so angry, so upset that I wrecked my own rooms?"

Chall cleared his throat. "Well...I mean, I was a teenage boy once myself, Majesty, begging your pardon. And I guess I broke more than a few of my things in anger over the years, trashed quite a bit of them too. Doesn't make sense, of course, as then in addition to whatever had angered you in the first place, now you're just left with some of your own shit you broke. But then, in my experience, teenage boys—even kings—" he added softly, "rarely do things that make sense."

"I suppose I'm not in a position to disagree with you," Matt said with a sigh. "At least, not most of the time."

"Are you saying you didn't do this, Majesty?" Priest asked. "To your rooms, I mean?"

Matt shook his head, a guilty expression on his face. "I did not. In truth, I have spent very little time in my rooms of late."

"This serving woman," Malex said, "the one you saw. What did she look like?"

Chall frowned. "I thought you would know that, wouldn't you? I mean, as the man in charge of all the castle's guards, I thought you'd be aware of all the servants too. Or is there a schedule or something someone else is in charge of?"

"The mistress of servants, Madam Olaphasia—the woman who we passed in the hall—is in charge of assigning the servants daily tasks," Malex said. "That said, I make it a point to keep myself apprised of those schedules."

"But if you already know who was here, then why ask?" Chall asked.

"Humor me, Sir Challadius," Malex said.

Chall had known the commander years before, during the Fey War, and he had never known the man to do anything frivolously or without cause, so he nodded, forcing down his impatience.

"Shit," he said, thinking, "what was her name? I know she told us but..."

"But you can't remember?" Priest said unhelpfully.

"Well, I was a bit distracted," Chall snapped, "you know, having only just escaped death at the hands of an *assassin*. Anyway," he went on, rubbing at his temples, "it was something...started with an 'M' I think. Maria, maybe or...Martha or...no, that's not it. Wait, I've got it—Margaret!"

Malex's eyebrows drew down, and he studied Chall carefully. "Are you sure?"

"Sure I'm sure!" Chall said. "It's Margaret—no question about it."

"You are certain?" Commander Malex pressed.

"Yes, of course I'm certain," Chall said, feeling his patience finally give way. "Fire and salt, man, do you think I'd lie about such a thing?"

"No," the commander said, a grim expression on his face. "No, I did not think that you would lie, Sir Challadius. I only look to be sure, you see, because I know the names of all the servants and there is no Margaret to be counted among them."

Chall frowned. "But...but that can't be right. Of course there's a Margaret. I *met* her. That was her name, I'm quite sure of it."

"Perhaps...if you described her..." Priest said.

Chall let out his breath in a huff, angry and annoyed and confused. "Fine, but I don't know what good it will do." He rubbed at his temples, trying to think past his frustration and annoyance. "Let's see, she had black hair—no, no brown hair, yes, it was brown. Her eyes..." He sighed. "They were brown too. A pretty girl, I suppose, if it a bit waifish. And..." He laughed. "I suppose that isn't helping any. Oh, wait. There was one more thing. She was wearing a ring."

Commander Malex raised an eyebrow at that. "A ring?"

"That's right," Chall said. "I only noticed it because it seemed a bit strange, a servant wearing jewelry. Not the sort of thing you see every day. Also, the ring itself was a bit...odd."

"Odd in what way?" Malex said, studying him.

"Well," Challadius said, "it was a signet ring, a black back drop with some sort of animal silhouette in crimson. A coyote, perhaps, or a dog...maybe—"

"A wolf," Priest said, and there was something about the way he said it, the way he sounded, that made Chall turn and frown at him.

"Yes," he said slowly, "yes that might well have been it." He shrugged, turning back to Malex. "Some sort of ring, anyway. It seemed like a pretty expensive trinket for a serving woman working in the castle."

"Expensive indeed but that is not the true cost."

Chall frowned, turning to Priest who had said the words in little more than a whisper. "What was that?"

"Nothing, nothing," Priest said, shaking his head. "Only thinking out loud."

Chall watched the man carefully, trying to decide if he'd heard him right and, if he had, what he had meant. He was still watching him when Matt spoke, pulling him from his thoughts.

"But...why would someone pretend to be a servant only to sneak into my rooms?"

"I can think of a few reasons, Majesty," Commander Malex said grimly, "but that is not the worst of it. There is one more thing I would like to show you, if you would allow it."

"O-of course, Commander," Matt said.

Malex gave a single nod then turned and moved farther into the room to a doorway which Chall knew led to the large walk-in closet that held the king's wardrobe.

Chall noticed, as they followed, a crimson puddle leaking out of the doorway.

"Is...is that blood?" Matt asked, his voice sounding slightly breathless.

It is, Chall thought, feeling his mood grow darker still. After all, a man didn't lead the life he'd led without coming to know intimately—far *too* intimately, in fact—the look of blood when it was spilled. Walking at the closet from the side as they were, whatever lay beyond, whatever—or *who*ever—had caused the bloody spill was beyond his sight and, for a moment, Chall was overcome with a powerful conviction. Whether that conviction was born of his fears or his gift he did not know, but it was strong. Strong enough that he felt the hairs on the back of his neck stand up, and he shivered as a sudden chill washed over him. A conviction, but more than that, a presentiment. *Of doom?* he wondered, and he thought surely it must be. After all, people never talked about presentiments of happiness, did they? And prophecies, at least in his experience, were most always dark. He'd yet to read the one that claimed that a man would wake up and find that someone had left a bag of gold coins outside his door.

That blood was significant. It meant something. It was not just the blood nor the cause of it—there was something else. Something...momentous. It was as if he stood at the foot of a great mountain and he, and the kingdom along with him, had taken their first step up its summit. And what waited for him at the top, what waited for *all* the people of the Known Lands, was anyone's guess.

"*Chall?*" a voice said, and he grunted, giving his head a shake as he was pulled from what felt like a trance to see Matt standing before him, a concerned expression on his face.

"You don't have to yell," Chall said muzzily, rubbing at his ears. "Stones and starlight, you're liable to pop my ear drum."

"Sorry," Matt said, flushing, "only you would not answer."

"Well," Chall said, "I don't mean to try to tell you how to live your life, Majesty, but if you want someone to answer, you might want to consider trying to call their name at a normal volume first."

"He did try, Chall," Priest said, and he turned to see the other man watching him carefully. "We all did. For five minutes we've been trying."

Chall blinked. "Five minutes? That's...that's impossible. I've only been standing here..." He paused then, realizing that, in truth, he had no idea how long he'd stood there. It might have been only a moment or it might have been far more than that. The truth was he had been too lost in the trance to be able to say with any certainty.

"Is everything alright, Challadius?" Priest asked. "Was...was it something to do with your gift?"

Now, like always when such episodes overcame him, Chall found himself feeling embarrassed, almost ashamed. This reaction made no more sense now than it ever did, he knew, for his "feelings" and his "dreams" had saved his own backside more than once. But knowing that feeling a certain way made no sense and being able to keep yourself from feeling that way were, Chall had discovered over the course of his life, two very different things.

"I...I don't know," he said honestly. "Maybe. But maybe I'm just a bit...out of sorts."

"Understandably, if that's the case," Priest said.

Chall nodded, glancing back at Commander Malex. "Forgive me, Commander, please, proceed to show us what you meant to." *Even though I do not think I want to see it,* he thought, *not at all.*

Malex gave him a nod in return, then turned about and continued the short walk to the closet.

"Gods be good," Matt breathed as they all took in the grizzly sight.

Not likely, Chall thought, swallowing and feeling as if his throat was suddenly unaccountably dry. "This is..."

"The real serving woman," Malex finished, "tasked by madam Olaphasia to clean his Majesty's quarters. It would appear that the serving woman—by the name of Lucia—must have come in and interrupted the impostor while she was about her work and the impostor, whoever she was, killed her to keep her silent while she made good her escape."

Chall winced, thinking he now understood why the mistress of the servants had seemed so inconsolable outside in the hallway. She, after all, was the one who had sent the serving woman to the king's quarters which, as it turned out, had been sending her to her death. No doubt she blamed herself, thinking that it was her actions that had doomed the poor girl. It wasn't true—no one was responsible for a murder except the one who did the deed—but he knew that, even should he tell the woman as much, she would not hear him. Not yet. In time, she would, but for now anything people tried to tell her would be drowned out by her own voice of recrimination.

"But *what* work?" Matt asked.

Chall was pulled from his thoughts, turning to regard the young man. "What's that?"

"I said, *what* work?" Matt repeated. "Why was she *here?*"

Chall winced. "I don't mean to worry you, Majesty, but it seems to me that she would probably be looking to do what most people would, assuming they were ballsy enough to sneak around in a king's chamber by themselves, not to mention willing to kill someone that interrupted them to keep whatever their mission was safe."

"The crimson wolf hunts alone," Priest said in a quiet whisper, one barely loud enough to hear.

Chall frowned, glancing at the man, realizing that he hadn't said a word since Commander Malex had shown them the body. "What?"

"Nothing," Priest said, shaking his head like a man coming out of a trance. "It's nothing."

"Don't bullshit me, Valden," Chall said. "If you know something about this, you'd best tell us."

The other man winced. "It...I thought that I might, Challadius, only, what I thought cannot be true. It is...it is impossible."

"Impossible," Chall said. "Seems to me I remember hearing someone say that making it to the capital and seeing Matt recognized by a prince and then, furthermore, becoming the king of the city was also impossible."

"You were the one that said that," Priest said, raising his eyebrow.

"Which only goes to show that I'm that much more sure it was said," Chall countered. "Now, maybe whatever it is that's got you all twisted up is crazy and maybe it isn't, but in a world where village boys become kings, army commanders become prisoners only to become commanders once more, and fat mages with sharp tongues manage to live to see their first gray hair, I'm willing to accept that just because something's crazy doesn't mean it isn't true."

Priest sighed, nodding. "Have any of you ever heard of the group called the Crimson Wolves?"

Chall frowned, scratching at his chin. "Doesn't sound familiar." He glanced over at Commander Malex and Matt to see both of them shaking their head.

"I suppose that is not so surprising," Priest said. "After all, they have not existed, at least so far as anyone knew, for a very long time."

"Crimson wolf," Matt said thoughtfully. "You mean like the one Chall saw on the woman's ring?"

"Exactly that," Priest agreed. "Each of the Crimson Wolves used to wear just such a ring, or so witness accounts claim, though those were always inconsistent and usually coming from the mouths of one terrified individual."

"So these Crimson Wolves," Chall said slowly, "they were what? Some sort of criminal organization? Like a gang?"

Priest considered that for a moment. "There were certainly some who thought so—Prince Feledias among them. You see, the Crimson Wolves arose during the Fey War. Or, at least, that is so far as anyone knows. They were a very secretive group, one whose apparent mission was not criminal activity. Or, at least, not the sort of criminal activity that most people think of. Instead, they were a group of vigilantes. Men and women who apparently had become disabused of the world, who had had their fill of the evil in the world and had decided to band together and deal with it themselves."

"And these vigilantes," Chall said, "I'm guessing their idea of dealing with evil wasn't to write a strongly-worded letter?"

"No," Priest said, meeting his gaze. "No, their methods were far more...*final* than that."

Chall found his eyes going to the serving woman then back to Priest. "I see. So...what happened to them? Did the city guard wipe them out or something? Or maybe one of the other crime bosses?"

"No," Priest said, shaking his head. "No, though any and all of them would have loved to do exactly that. The problem, though, was that the Crimson Wolves were extremely good at remaining hidden. In fact, they were *so* good at it that many at the time thought them no more than a rumor, a made-up tale created by drunks to garner attention for themselves or, perhaps, by one criminal organization or another, a bogey man to scare their competitors, that sort of thing."

"And what do *you* believe?" Matt asked.

The man appeared to consider that for several seconds, scratching his chin. "I believe that they were real," Priest said. "Though, having said that, I do not believe—I *cannot* believe—that the Crimson Wolves are behind this."

"But why not?" Chall said. "You said yourself that the only people who had those rings were members of their, their club or whatever. And the woman did have the ring, that much is sure. Or do you think I made it up? Is that it?"

"Of course not, Challadius," Priest said. "Only, I still do not believe that they could be behind this."

"Well what other options are there, Priest?" Chall asked. "Fine, I guess maybe the woman, whoever she was, might have found one of the rings. Shit, maybe she killed someone and took it. I mean come on, isn't it obvious? The woman, whoever she was, was a member of this Crimson Wolves you've been talking about."

"That...isn't possible," Priest said. "For one, the Crimson Wolves haven't been seen or heard from for more than fifteen years. And even if it *was* them, they would have never slain an innocent. Anyway, they would not have stood idly by and let criminals take over the world as Belle and her ilk have done in the prince's absence. No," he finished, shaking his head firmly, "it could not be them."

"Huh," Chall said, frowning thoughtfully. "Well, it seems to me that there's only one way to know for sure."

"What way is that, Chall?" Matt asked.

"Simple, Your Majesty," Chall said. "If you are wondering whether a cat is nearby, who better to ask than the rats? They, after all, are always the first to know." He turned and glanced at Priest, and the man watched him for a moment before shaking his head.

"No, Challadius," he said. "There is no point. They would know nothing of the Crimson Wolves' return because the Crimson Wolves *have not* returned."

"So what do you suggest then, Priest?" Chall asked. "Should we just wait around until the next time an assassin comes for the king? And what if, this time, she isn't scared off by some poor serving girl? What if this time, she succeeds?"

He saw the hurt on the man's face and immediately regretted the words, wishing he could take them back. But he could not. "Listen, Priest, I didn't mean—"

"I suggest, Chall," the man said, clearly struggling to contain his emotions, "that we let the guards, Commander Malex and his men, do their jobs. They will investigate and, I do not doubt, find the truth of matters. Anyway, if it helps, Majesty," he went on, turning to look at Matt, "I do not believe that this woman was here to kill you."

"You...don't?" Matt asked, sounding relieved which, Chall supposed, was no surprise. After all, nobody was very thrilled by the idea of having assassins—or at least something close enough as to make little difference—out to kill them.

"I do not," Priest said.

"Forgive me, sir, but why is that?" Commander Malex asked.

"For a few reasons, Commander," Priest said. "For one, she had already hidden the serving woman's body in the king's closet. She could have, after concealing her crime, lain in wait for the king to return to his quarters, if assassination had been her goal."

Chall glanced over at Matt, saw him looking around the room nervously as if expecting some assassin wielding a bloody dagger to present herself, charging at him as if to oblige Priest's theory. "Well, I'd say that the king might have been somewhat suspicious," Chall said, glancing at Priest, "when he came back to see that his entire room had been turned upside down, all of his belongings thrown everywhere."

"And so, Chall," Priest said, "you have touched upon the other reason why I am confident that the woman's presence was not an assassination attempt. It is clear by the state of His Highness's quarters that she was searching for something. The question we must ask ourselves is, what might that something have been?"

"Or, perhaps," Chall said, "did she find it?"

Priest considered that then slowly shook his head. "I do not believe so. I believe that it was the appearance of the serving woman—and her subsequent murder—which led the intruder, whoever she was, to flee. After all, it would only be a matter of time before the guards stationed outside in the hall or, alternatively, the mistress of servants, wondered at how long she was taking. No, I think it likely that whatever the woman came for, she did not find it, though of course there is no way to know for sure. However, as to the matter of *what* she was looking for..." They all slowly turned to regard Matt who blinked, looking like nothing so much as a hare who has just realized he's gained the attention of three particularly hungry-looking lions.

"I'm sorry, what?" Matt asked.

"Whatever it was that the woman was searching for, Majesty," Chall explained, "she expected to find it *here,* in your quarters."

"But...but what could it be?"

"I do not know, Highness," Priest said. "In truth, I was hoping that you might tell us."

"But...but I have no idea," Matt said. "I don't have anything that an assassin might want. O-or these Crimson Wolves. Honestly, nothing that I can think of."

Priest glanced over at Chall, a troubled expression on his face, and Chall fought back the urge to sigh. It seemed that it would be up to him, then. "We believe you, Majesty," he said. "Of course we do. Only, while you may not have had anything that might have interested the woman, perhaps the...*other* might have."

"The...other?" Matt asked, confused. Chall said nothing, only watching him, and so he saw clearly the look of hurt, of shame, that came over the young man's face as realization struck. "You mean...you mean her," he said. "Emma."

"Yes, Majesty," Chall said softly. "Is there anything you can remember from...that time? Anything she might have brought here? Whatever it was, it had to be important, for the woman was obviously willing to risk breaking into a castle with dozens of guardsmen and coming to the most defended part of that castle to search for it."

Matt shook his head. "I...I don't know," he said, a strained expression on his face as he thought back. "I...I can't think of anything."

"Try, Majesty," Priest said. "Anything you can remember might help us. Focus, think back."

"I...it's difficult," Matt said. "It...it is as if there's a fog over it, like it was someone else's life...and they only told me about it." His eyes were squeezed shut now, tears leaking from the corners as if he seemed to be struggling against some great weight.

"*Try, Majesty,*" Priest hissed. "*Try.*"

Matt did, his entire body tensed, trembling. "I...I can't," he moaned "I...I can't—"

"*Yes you can, you* must," Priest said, leaning closer, and Matt let out a sob, his body shaking.

"*Enough,*" Chall snapped, glaring at Priest as he moved to Matt, putting a hand on the young man's shoulder. "It's alright, Matt," he said, "let it go."

Matt did, his shoulders slumping, appearing exhausted as if he had just run for miles.

"Easy, Matt," Chall said. "Easy, it's alright. We'll figure out what happened here—don't you worry about that none, lad."

A Warrior's Penance

The young man nodded, swallowing hard, looking unsettled, used up.

"Commander," Chall said, "the king is very tired and has had a long, trying few days. I wonder if you might find him somewhere safe to rest?"

"O-of course," Commander Malex said.

"No, Chall," Matt said, a sort of desperation to his voice, "I...I should stay and help. I want to help. The serving woman, Lucia, she...she died because she was sent to clean *my* rooms. I..."

"It's not your fault, Majesty," Chall said. "You did not cause this."

Matt nodded slowly, but the look on his face showed that he did not believe it. "Very well, Chall. I will rest...only, there is something I need to do first. I am going to speak with the mistress of servants, ask after this woman's family. She died cleaning my quarters; it is the least I can do to break the news to them, to...to help them, if I can."

He turned, with that, and started toward the door.

Chall glanced at Commander Malex who was staring after the young man, a look of evident shock on his face. "Everything alright, Commander?"

"O-of course," Malex said. "Only...the king, he seemed genuinely concerned. For the poor girl's family that is."

"He is a good king, Commander," Chall said. "A good man. The best I have ever known, in truth."

"A good...king," Malex said slowly. "I wonder...what does that even look like?"

"You just saw it, Commander," Chall said.

Malex stiffened, then turned to him. He met Chall's eyes, nodding his head in a bow, then turned, hurrying after Matt.

Chall waited until they were both gone then rounded on Priest. "Fire and salt, Priest, just what was all that about?" he snapped.

"I...I don't know what you mean," the man said.

"I'll be damned if you don't!" Chall snapped. "You ask me, *Priest,* just then you looked less like a holy man and more like a torturer at his trade—shit, I was just waiting for you to bring out the hot irons. You had the boy in tears, and for what?"

"I only did what I did to protect him," Priest said. "If Matt remembers something, *anything*, then we might use it to discover the identity of the woman who came here, or at the least to understand *why* she came in the first place."

Chall watched the man for several seconds then finally shook his head. "No. No, there's more to it than that. You've got a personal stake in this somehow. So what is it, Priest? Did you used to have a Crimson Wolf as a buddy, is that it?"

The man winced. "Chall, it isn't—"

"Or a woman?" Chall asked. "Was that it? Did you fall in love with a wolf, Priest? A dangerous game, surely, but—"

"*Shut your mouth,*" the other man growled, and Chall, shocked to see the normally calm man appear on the verge of attacking him, did exactly that.

Priest colored, looking miserable. "Forgive me, Chall. I did not mean that. Only...the Crimson Wolves, you see, they used to stand for something. They were brutal, perhaps, vigilantes who lived by their own code certainly, but they were men and women who were only tired of all the killing, all the world's evil, and sought to make the world a better place. I cannot believe that such men and women as that would resort to...to killing innocent serving girls."

"Well, Priest," Chall said, "sometimes things aren't always what we want them to be, and it's a hard fact of life that those things which we put our faith in are not always deserving of it."

The man turned to regard him then and Chall saw something in the man's eyes that gave him pause. "Priest...is everything okay?"

The man continued to look at him, and Chall amended his previous thought. It wasn't what he saw in the man's gaze that had so bothered him—it was what he didn't. Hope, maybe. A belief that things would work out in the end. No one would have seen such a thing in his own gaze, wouldn't have seen his own hope for the future unless they were able to travel back in time to when the young, twelve-year-old Challadius—not the Charmer then, far from it—first asked Miss Layla Edinbaugh to dance. To which she replied no and that in no uncertain terms. She hadn't used words so much as laughter, but that had been more than enough to get her point across.

A Warrior's Penance

Priest, though, he had somehow managed to keep hold of that hope through the years, to retain the belief that no matter how dark the night got, morning would still come. Chall had no idea how the man had managed not to fumble that hope through all the bumps and bruises and batterings that life gave a man, but he had. And it had been that hope, compared to the absence of his own, that had made Chall hate the man from time to time. It was also the thing that had made him love him. And staring at the man, at that great voided absence where that hope had been, Chall realized that even though it had driven him crazy—and quite nearly to murder—he had come to rely on it. To rely on it in the same way that a man walking into the darkness counts on the ground to remain beneath his feet even though he cannot see it there.

"I'm fine, Chall," Priest said.

"You're fine," Chall repeated.

"That's right," the man said. "I...I think I'm just tired, that's all. Matt's right—I need some rest. I think we all do."

"Uh-huh," Chall said. "So you just mean to go back to your room and go to sleep?"

"Of course," Priest said. "What else would I do?"

Chall watched him for a moment then sighed. "Very well, though I doubt I'll get any sleep, not with Maeve gone."

Priest put his hand on his shoulder. "She'll be okay, Chall. If there's anyone better at taking care of themselves than her, I've yet to meet them."

"Doesn't mean it'll be enough," Chall said, feeling a lump gather in his throat. Ridiculous, maybe, to be worried about her. They'd traveled together for years, had taken on all manner of Fey creature and mortal soldier, and she had made it through it all fine. But that didn't give him as much comfort as it might have. After all, they had finally found their happiness, and if you're going to pull the rug out from underneath someone's feet, you've got to wait for them to step onto it first. And the world, while it had a cruel streak, was also one patient bitch. "Thanks," he said.

"Of course," Priest said. "I'm always here for you, Chall. You know that, don't you?"

Chall found himself touched, giving the man a small smile. "Thanks."

"Now then," Priest said, returning the smile, "I'm to bed. You?"

"Sure, why not?" Chall said with a sigh. "It isn't as if my floors are going to pace themselves, is it?"

CHAPTER SIX

Cutter gave an exhausted swipe of his axe and the last of the brambles fell away. He stepped through the undergrowth, his eyes trained ahead of him, then stopped, panting, letting his axe hang at his side.

He waited a moment, listening to the sounds of Feledias shambling up before finally coming to a panting stop beside him. "*Is…is it real?*" he asked in a dry croak.

Cutter shook his head slowly as he stared at the lake in front of them. "I don't know," he said, his own voice rasping from his dry, parched throat. The water they'd brought with them had run out two days ago. Left with no choice they had traveled on, growing increasingly thirsty with each step as they went deeper and deeper into the Black Wood. Cutter was no expert in woodcraft, but he had done what he could, guiding them into low ground where water would most likely be discovered. Yet for two days they'd had no luck.

But that had not been enough of a cruelty for the Black Wood. Since the first morning they had woken to find they had no water, he and his brother had heard a sound, coming it always seemed from only a short distance ahead. A sound they both knew—that of rushing water. But no matter how far they walked, that sound seemed to always be up ahead somewhere, never getting any closer.

Even now, he could hear it, off in the distance, but he paid it no mind. The Black Wood was full of tricks and its tricks, he'd long since discovered, were always cruel ones.

"Well, there's one damn way to find out," Feledias wheezed. He started forward, and Cutter put a hand up, stopping him.

"Wait," he said.

"For what?" his brother asked. "For us both to shrivel up like a couple of prunes?"

"It could be dangerous," Cutter said, glancing around at the trees looming around the lake. There was still another hour of daylight left, perhaps two, but the shadows seemed to gather around the lake, crouched and waiting for them.

Feledias gave a snort. "Of *course* it's dangerous," he said. "Fire and salt, brother, have you forgotten where we are? Trees that attack you and try to kill you, berries that run through you like they're in a race, and snow as cold as…as…"

"Ice?" Cutter offered.

"My point," Feledias went on, sounding annoyed, "is that everything here is dangerous. But if I'm to die, I intend to die with cool water in my throat instead of what feels like sand."

"Just do me a favor and stay here for a moment, alright?" Cutter asked. "I'll check it out."

"Don't you go drinking all the damned water," Feledias grumbled.

Cutter glanced at the large lake in front of them then back at his brother, raising an eyebrow. "I'll try not to."

Cutter moved forward, keeping his axe in his hand instead of returning it to the sling across his back. In normal circumstances, he wouldn't have been so cautious, but then, the Black Wood was far from normal. A hostile place where everyone—and everything—wanted to kill you and where none of them had any compunction about giving it a try.

The walk to the lake, at least, was easy enough. The ground was flat and soft and clear of any obstacle, a pleasant change from the thick, choking brambles and undergrowth through which he and his brother had been forced to travel practically since entering the woods. Still, Cutter did not allow himself to relax. After all, if a man relaxed enough, he died and that was truer nowhere than in the Black Wood.

As he moved toward the lake he noted what appeared to be a deer standing at the far side. Despite his thirst, Cutter found himself pausing to gaze at it. They had been in the Black Wood for days now, and it was the very first sign of any normal creature he had seen. It seemed incongruous in that place of perpetual shadow, and its very presence stole some of the woods' menace, some of the dark magic that seemed to fill it.

The deer was licking at the pool, quenching its own thirst, and it seemed to sense his presence, freezing for a moment before slowly raising its head to regard him. Cutter half expected it to turn into some giant, rampaging monster and attack him. After all, if he had learned anything in the Black Wood it was that those things which appeared the most innocent were also often the most dangerous. At the least, he thought that the creature must be somehow deformed, somehow twisted, and a part of him recoiled in anxiety as it slowly raised its head, expecting, *knowing* that he would be treated to a terrible, perverse sight.

But the creature did not transform into some humongous beast of fang and claw. Neither did its movement reveal the twisted, hideous features of some monstrosity. Instead, it continued to be a deer—a fawn, in fact, less than a year old, if Cutter was any judge—and he had grown to know some bit about wildlife in his time spent in Brighton where he had fed himself mostly through hunting and gathering so as to minimize the chances of anyone discovering his identity.

"Well?" Feledias called from behind him. "*Are you just going to stand there all day, Bernard?*"

Cutter glanced back to see his brother impatiently staring after him. Then there was a *splash,* and he turned back to the lake, his fingers tightening around his axe. But no threat presented itself. He did note, however, with a frown, that the fawn had vanished. As he stared at the place where it had been, noting a slight rippling of the water's surface, a powerful feeling of disquiet overcame him.

Relax, part of him thought, *it only turned and scampered back into the woods while you were turned. Likely your very act of turning was what scared it away. And that ripple in the water? Surely only caused by the deer disturbing it to drink.*

But as comforting as the thought might have been, he did not believe it. Perhaps it would have been a reasonable explanation in some normal wood, some normal lake, but there was nothing reasonable about the Black Wood. Cutter took his time moving to the lake's edge, letting his gaze travel around its perimeter, across the trees surrounding it, into those shadows which seemed to huddle against their trunks.

His was a practiced, experienced gaze, but if there was any danger to be found, then it knew well how to hide itself. He was so intent on his search that he was unaware how close he had grown to the lakeshore until he felt cool water against his toes. He looked down to see that he stood at the very edge of the lake.

He glanced to his left where he saw a small strip of ground stretching out a few extra feet into the deeper waters of the lake. He walked toward it, stepping out onto the small promontory and moving to its edge, focusing on all his senses, for any half-imagined sight, or momentary sound that might alert him to danger.

He paused at the water's edge for a moment. When nothing happened, he slowly knelt. In the pale light of the failing sun, he saw his reflection staring back at him. A reflection whose haggard, drawn appearance stood testament to the difficulties he and Feledias had endured since leaving the capital. He looked thinner, and nowhere in that grim countenance staring back at him with dark eyes did Cutter see proof of the unending strength for which he was known.

But then, he knew that there was little of that strength left. Enough, he hoped, to make it deeper into the woods, to find the Green Man and broker with him some peace, a peace that would be Cutter's gift to the people of the Known Lands, and likely his parting gift. He did not know if what strength remained to him would be enough to make it so far into the Black Wood as he must go. But he knew, with a certainty, that it would not be enough to make it back.

A one-way trip then, but he thought that some part of him had always known it would be. He thought that some, quiet part had *hoped* it would.

"*You didn't fall asleep, did you, Bernard?*"

Feledias's voice, and Cutter glanced back once more. "*A moment more,*" he called.

Cutter leaned down with a hand, meaning to scoop out some water to taste, to see if he detected any foulness to it.

But as he drew closer to the lake's surface, a strange thing happened.

The reflection of himself began to change, the thin, cracked lips of his mouth stretching wider and wider. At first, he took it as no more than some trick of the water and the fading light, but in another moment, Cutter paused, his hand hovering only inches above the water's surface, the reflection of himself grinning widely, baring its teeth, madness dancing in the dark caverns which were its eyes.

"Shit," Cutter said.

And his reflection seemed to grin wider, only for an instant. Then something massive exploded out of the water's surface. Cutter gave a shout as he was flung high into the air by the force of the blow. He wondered, as he hurtled upward, what it might have been that had struck him, but he did not have to wonder for long, for that thing was suddenly shooting toward him, a massive, gray tentacle, three-feet thick at least, wrapping around him.

Cutter cried out in pain at the shocking strength of it as the tentacle grasped him, high above the water's surface, and sought to squeeze the life from him. Cutter had managed to hold onto his axe, and with a breathless growl he brought it down into the undulating tentacle.

The Fey weapon dug deep into the gray, writhing flesh, and there was a terrible, ear-splitting screech from somewhere below the lake's surface as black ichor fountained out of the wound. Then Cutter wasn't being squeezed to death anymore. Instead, he was plummeting toward it, falling toward the lake that seemed to lie miles beneath him.

But despite how far away it seemed, the water rushed toward him shockingly fast. Cutter had time enough to take a sharp, quick breath but no more than that. He was still trying to orient himself so that he would plunge in feet first and was only halfway there when he struck the lake's surface.

Falling from such a height, it felt as if he landed on stone. The momentum of his fall drove him deep into the lake, the dark water closing around him like the giant maw of some hungry beast. Cutter was dazed from the fall, and for a moment, as the lake drew him farther and farther down, he thought it would be so easy. So easy to let go, to not fight. To not fight for once in his life. It would be over quickly. The need for air, small at first, then desperate, then all-consuming, and then nothing. Assuming, of course, whatever that giant tentacle belonged to did not finish him first.

But no sooner did he have the thought then he remembered the voices. Those voices which, for the last several nights, had filled his dreams. His father's, Matt's, his old sword master's. Their words were different, but they all meant the same thing. *Keep going. Stand up and keep going. It is what a man does. It is what a warrior does.* And so, now, as he had for the last several days, Cutter noted that desire for self-destruction within himself. And now, like those other times, he discarded it, casting it away—but not so far, he knew, that it would not return again.

It was dark within the lake's water and so difficult to know which way was up and which down. Cutter gave the best guess he could, orienting himself so that his feet were pointed at the bottom, his head at what he *hoped* was the lake's surface.

He kicked his legs, then again, the weight of the Breaker of Pacts seeming to pull him down toward the lake's bottom, but he dared not let it go. Threats to his life came and went, but the axe remained, for it was his burden to bear.

His chest was beginning to ache with the need to draw breath, to ache so badly that it seemed as if it might explode, when finally his head broke the water's surface and he gasped in a deep, desperate breath. He did not get a chance to take another, however, before something wrapped around his waist from beneath the water and with one powerful *jerk*, he was pulled under once more.

Cutter tried to break free, to bring his axe to bear, but the tentacle had wrapped up his arms, and he could barely move them. He called on every ounce of his strength, but it was all he could do to keep the constricting tentacle from crushing him—he had no chance of breaking free of its grasp.

Pulled by the tentacle, he surged through the lake water, moving faster and faster, as he strained against it until he was pulled into the center of the lake where the tentacle's efforts suddenly began to slow.

Cutter wondered at that, thought perhaps that it was due to Feledias making an effort on his behalf, but realized in another moment that the creature's pull had slowed for a very different reason. Namely, because it had gotten him where it intended.

A massive form slowly rose out of the lake bottom, at first no more than some enormous shadow, the features of which became clearer the closer it got. Finally, Cutter was left staring at a giant, alien face.

If, that was, the term "face" could be used for something which contained nothing more than one single eye, the diameter of which was as long as Cutter was tall, and a giant maw filled with sharp teeth, each of which was longer than his axe, handle and all. And within that maw, within those teeth, Cutter saw several pieces of debris. Seaweed in clumps, bones, and some grisly remains that were, he suspected, those of the fawn he had seen earlier.

Cutter's chest was burning, and he continued to fight against the creature's grip as it studied him with its one massive eye. There was a pressure in his lungs, his chest, one that was growing by the moment, and he knew that it would not be long now before he was unable to fight his body's urge to draw a breath. Not that he suspected he would have time to drown, not with the way the creature was slowly reeling him toward its waiting maw, its teeth gnashing in a sort of eager anticipation.

As he was brought closer and closer to his doom, Cutter continued to struggle against the grip holding him. Even though he knew that it was useless, he fought on. Fought because he had always fought, because his life had been little more than one fight after the other and he knew nothing else.

He was only feet away from the creature's mouth, its great eye as large as the moon in front of him, when suddenly it gave a jerk. The tentacle spasmed, its grip abruptly loosening. Not all the way, not so much that he was let loose, but enough that, coupled with his own efforts, Cutter was able to break one arm free of the tentacle's hold. Which was all he needed. His chest feeling as if it might explode at any moment, Cutter lifted the Breaker of Pacts and buried it into the creature's giant eye.

There was another terrible screeching, so loud that Cutter felt his ears pop. The creature jerked away, its entire body seeming to convulse within the dark water of the lake. It began to thrash, and the space all around Cutter was suddenly filled with giant, writhing tentacles, slapping at the water, curling and furling through it. He'd just managed to pull his axe free of the creature's ruined eye before one of those thrashing tentacles struck him with the force of a runaway carriage.

The blow sent him surging through the water, breaking his concentration. The next thing he knew, he was gulping in water, great mouthfuls of the stuff, choking and gagging and gulping all at once as he was hurtled through the water. And then not through the water at all but up and out of it, sailing into the air, turning end over end, still choking, still gagging, still *drowning* on the water he'd swallowed when he struck the ground with bone-jarring force. Then he was rolling, tumbling end over end, grunting and hissing and wheezing until, finally, he came to stop on his back, his entire body aching from the force of his landing.

"Bernard!"

He tried to turn at the sound of Feledias's voice but he found that, just then, he could not. He was still gagging, spitting out lake water, feeling weaker than he could ever remember feeling, his side aching where the creature had struck him.

He finally managed to regurgitate the lake water he'd swallowed and then was lying there, gasping and wheezing for breath, when a familiar figure appeared standing over him.

"Are you okay?" Feledias asked, and Cutter heard the panic in his brother's voice, was touched by it even past the pain.

"I'm...alright," he croaked, and he thought that, surprisingly, he was. He ached, but nothing was broken so far as he could tell, and he was only partially drowned which, on the whole, was far better than he had expected. "What...happened to you?"

Feledias looked down at his sword, coated in black ichor, then at his shirt and trousers, covered in the stuff. He ran an arm across his face, an effort which only smeared more of it on his forehead and cheeks. He winced. "Saw that damned thing grab you, like some monster out of a nightmare. Anyway, I went in after you, ran into a bunch of its tentacles. Guess it was distracted tryin' to eat you, so..." He glanced at his sword once more then shrugged. "Well. Say our friend the lake monster is going to have to borrow someone else's tentacles to feed himself from now on." He offered Cutter his hand and Cutter took it, allowing himself to be pulled to a sitting position where he draped his arms over his knees, staring out at the lake's currently placid surface.

"What of you?" Feledias asked. "Did you have a pleasant swim?"

"I've had better," Cutter said honestly.

"Well, if you're done taking your leisure," his brother said, "then maybe we'd best get on—I'd rather not hang around for that sea monster to decide he wants a second go at things."

"I don't think we're going to have to worry about that," Cutter said.

"Oh?" his brother asked as Cutter rose gingerly to his feet.

"Yeah, an axe in the only eye you've got would, I imagine, make you rethink some things. At least until you died, that is."

Feledias shook his head, and they both glanced back at the water. "Still," he said. "That thing was damned horrifying. When it came out of the water and grabbed you, well, I thought you were doomed."

"You and me both," Cutter said.

"Another nightmare to add to the list anyway," Feledias said.

Cutter grunted. "It'll have some stiff competition."

Feledias sighed. "True enough, I suppose," he said, a grim expression coming on his face, a far cast to his eyes that told Cutter he was thinking of his past. Of the demons—him chief among them—which lurked there. "Nightmares I deserve anyway," his brother said softly. "After all, I do not doubt that I feature in the nightmares of some few others."

Cutter knew that he was thinking of Brighton and of the other wrongs he'd committed, the people he'd hurt in his quest to find Cutter and make him pay for his sins. He knew this just as he knew that any words he said could not go so deep as to touch that hurt, a hurt, a scar that went to the very center of his brother, like a crack in a great stone. A crack that might be missed, in a glancing look, but one that, in time, might well prove enough to destroy the giant boulder altogether.

"Come, brother," Cutter said, kneeling and retrieving his axe from where he'd dropped it. "Let us go and fill our waterskins. And then..."

"Time to keep going?" Feledias asked quietly.

"Yes," Cutter said, offering him a small smile. "A little farther, yet."

CHAPTER SEVEN

He waited in the darkness as the figure approached. He noted its furtive movements, the way its cowled head turned this way and that, shooting questing glances in all directions. Moving like a thief come in the night, only one not seeking entrance but escape.

He waited until the figure was upon him, then he let the illusion drop. *"Hey."*

The figure moved in a shockingly fast blur, and the next thing Chall knew, there was a knife at his throat. Less than an inch, and he'd be having a really bad day. Anymore than that, and his day, he figured, would be well and truly over. *"Challadius,"* the figure said surprised, then reached up with its free hand, pulling back its cowl to reveal Priest's features. "What are you doing out here?"

"Hoping not to get skewered just now," Chall said, not daring to move as he stared at the knife poised so close to his throat.

Priest frowned and pulled the blade away, and Chall hoped he only imagined the brief hesitation before the man did so. "What do you want, Chall?"

"I'm thinking maybe a medal," he said, doing his best to keep the relief from his voice. There had been a moment—a wild, insane moment—when he'd thought the knife was going to move in the other direction. Crazy, of course. He and Priest were friends, and the man had saved his life countless times. Only, the man standing before him did not seem like the same one Chall had known for so long. He seemed *less* than that man.

"And why would you get a medal?" Priest asked sounding impatient, also a first as far as Chall knew.

"Well," he said, "I figure it isn't every man can say they've had a priest lie to them. Has to be some sort of record, hasn't it?"

His friend's frown deepened at that. "Lie?"

"Sure," Chall said. "It's what it is, isn't it? You telling me you were going to let it go, that you were going to allow Malex's men to investigate?"

"I...I do not know what you mean," Priest said. "It is only that I could not sleep and so have stepped out for a walk, hoping to clear my mind."

"A walk," Chall said.

"That's right."

He sighed. "You really are shit at lying, Priest, though I guess that's no real surprise considering you haven't had the practice at it I have. Still, let me give you a little tip—in case it ever comes up in the future. If you want anyone to actually *believe* the lies you tell, then you had best try to make them *believable.* For example—" He paused, reaching out before the other man could react and patting his tunic where he felt the hard edges of several sheathed blades. "I have a difficult time believing that a man going for a walk would insist on bringing quite so many knives along with him."

"One might argue," Priest said, "considering that a murder and an assassination attempt have both taken place within the castle—the latter of which seemed to have you as one of its targets—that a man could not be too well-prepared."

Chall grunted. "Huh. Well, maybe you're not so bad at this lying thing after all. Can't help but wonder what that goddess of yours would say to that."

"I do not know."

Chall frowned. "Anyway, fine, maybe you weren't up to anything untoward, though if you don't want to be mistaken for a man up to sneaky shit, I might recommend not moving so damn sneakily. Maybe you really are just going for a walk. In which case, I'd be happy to accompany you."

"That won't be necessary, Chall," Priest said, a little too quickly for his liking. "I would prefer some solitude. Besides, you no doubt have some business of your own to attend."

A statement which from most people would have elicited a polite and predictable response. The problem, though, was that Chall was not most people, and he was in no danger at all of being called polite. "Not really, no," he said, giving the man his best, toothy grin. "See, the thing about being worried to death for the woman you love is that you're not much good for anything else. And as for preferring solitude, well, I'd prefer Maeve not be risking her life going to the Assassin's Guild or for the prince not to be wandering around the Black Wood. It's a sad fact of life, Priest, that what we prefer really has very little to do with it."

Priest watched him for several seconds, and Chall, having found himself in such a situation often when he'd tried to sneak out of the room of one farmer's daughter or another, could almost see what he was thinking. First, that perhaps if he pushed a little more, he might yet convince Chall—or, in Chall's case, the farmer in question—that he wasn't up to anything. Then, shortly after that thought, the understanding that a person would have to be shockingly stupid to believe such a thing and, finally, the feeling that Chall had seen mirrored on so many women's' faces when waking up next to him, particularly since he'd put on so much weight. Namely, reluctant acceptance. "I cannot talk you out of following me?" Priest asked.

"You'd have to do a lot more than just talk to manage that," Chall said, glancing once more at the knife and barely resisting the urge to lick his lips nervously.

Priest glanced at the knife as if he'd forgotten he was holding it then winced, sheathing it inside his tunic. "Forgive me, Chall. I did not mean..."

"Never mind that," Chall said, mostly because he didn't want the man thinking too hard about having almost stabbed him—after all, if someone were looking for a reason—or reasons—to stab Challadius the Charmer, well, they never had to look very far. "How about you just tell me where we're going. Or would you prefer it remain a surprise?"

Priest sighed heavily. "I will tell you but let us speak while we walk. Already we have wasted too much time."

They started through the castle hallways then. Chall gave the man several minutes to speak. When he did not, Chall finally did. "Well?" he asked. "You planning on keeping me in suspense after all?"

The man winced. "It is not that, Challadius. It is only that I am trying to figure out the best way to express my thoughts. You remember the Crimson Wolves, the ones I told you about?"

"It'd be pretty hard to forget," Chall said. "Sounded like pretty damned terrifying bastards, if you ask me."

Priest nodded. "Well, I imagine there isn't a criminal in the whole of New Daltenia, at least any over twenty-five, who would not agree with you. As I said, the Wolves pursued what they believed to be justice, seeking to destroy anything or any*one* they determined to be evil, and they were not shy or subtle in their methods. Not any more than the gardener who, discovering that weeds have begun choking out her flowers, seeks to rip them out one handful at a time."

"So are you telling me that you think that they're back after all? These Crimson Wolves, I mean? Because I seem to recall you telling me that they haven't been around for nearly twenty years or more and that they never killed innocents."

"And there, at least, I was not lying, Challadius," Priest said. "The Crimson Wolves have not been seen or heard from in a very long time, and those I once heard of never would have hurt an innocent, certainly not killed one. For in so doing they would have only become that which they sought to destroy."

"So what, then? After all, *someone* killed that serving girl, and I think it's probably too much to imagine that yet another person intruded after the woman with the ring left."

Priest hesitated as they reached the entrance of the castle and did not speak again until they were past the two guards stationed there. "As I said, the Crimson Wolves have not returned to New Daltenia *as far as I know.* You must understand my problem, Chall. You see, I *know* that the Crimson Wolves would never have harmed an innocent, just as I know that they have been gone for twenty years. Yet, I also know that this is exactly what happened. So I decided that I would do some asking around of my own."

"I see," Chall said, a sinking feeling entering the pit of his stomach. "And I don't guess there's much point in me asking who it is you're thinking to talk to about it."

They reached the castle gate, and Priest nodded to the guards there, he and Chall pausing as the men set about opening it. "Well, you said it yourself, Chall," he said, turning to him as they waited. "Who better to ask, when wishing to know whether or not the cat has returned, than the mice who might be its next meal?"

"You mean to find some criminals? Interrogate them?"

"I don't have to find them, Chall," Priest said. "I know exactly where they are—I always have. After all, I'm one of them."

And with that he turned and stalked toward the open gate, leaving Chall staring after him for a moment. He didn't know what was happening to Priest, but he thought that whatever it was, it wasn't good. He wished Maeve was here to talk to. She would know, would have some idea of what to do, what to say. And if not her, then Cutter. The prince was, from time to time, surprisingly adroit at understanding others' emotions, of saying the exact words—usually in a low, threatening growl—that they needed to hear. Assuming, of course, that he wasn't busy hacking those emotions out of them with that great axe of his.

But Maeve was nowhere to be seen—*but she will be, soon* he thought desperately—and as for the prince...well. There was no way of knowing if the man still lived, though Chall somehow thought he did. Not a prophecy that, or at least if it was, not one born of his gift but one of his knowledge of the man. In truth, hardly a man at all. The prince was more like a force of nature, a great storm, at the coming of which any person of sense would hide before it. A storm, yes, and one could not slay a storm, surely. A man could not, nor could a haunted forest of Feyling creatures out of nightmare...or so Chall hoped.

But whatever problems the prince and his brother faced, they would have to face them alone, for Chall's own task list was quite full at the moment. After all, Maeve or the prince might have been better suited to dealing with the problem of Priest—certainly better suited to following him into a den of murderers and thieves, at least so far as Chall was concerned. But then, Chall thought that a man would be hard pressed to find someone *not* better suited than him to discover what had caused that absence he had seen in Priest's eyes and set about finding some means by which to mend it. But the task, it seemed, was left for him. He, a philandering rake, a man of little substance, excepting perhaps that that substance was ale. A man who avoided serious discussions, serious thoughts, with great effort—the ale helped, of course.

But there was no one else. Him and him alone. And so Chall did the only thing he could do, the only thing, it seemed, that he had been doing since he could remember.

He followed his friend into the darkness.

He followed, and now as all those other times, he did so reluctantly.

CHAPTER EIGHT

Maeve sat on a stool in a dark corner of a dark common room and waited, doing her best to hide her impatience.

The barkeep did not seem to have noticed her yet, too busy wiping at the wooden bar counter with a rag, fighting a battle with the grime and grit and bloodstains marring it that anyone could see had been lost long ago.

Still, Maeve waited. The waiting, she told herself, was only a part of it. A part of the dance, a part of moving from one world to the next, from a world of castles and kings, of ballrooms and ballgowns to a world of whispers in the darkness, of deals offered and deals struck. Of blood on the edge of blades and those who breathed one moment and did not the next. The *real* world, the one which hid beneath the façade civilization provided. Though, it had to be said that the façade had begun to crack of late, and those who had once lived in abject denial, if not abject ignorance, had been forced, more and more in the last years, to gaze upon the world's true face.

The true world, the world of assassins and contracts and blood traded for gold time and time again, was one that Maeve knew well. Or at least she had. Once. Despite her confident words to Chall, Maeve, though she had known this world once, had not traveled its winding corridors and shadowed alcoves for many years. And she knew that those corridors, and those shadows within them, changed quickly so that even a week away might well find the unfortunate returning soul lost among them, swallowed up.

She gave a soft laugh at that. Chall would have had words to say about those meandering thoughts, she was sure. Would have told her that the world was complicated enough, surely, and that there was no need to go complicating it further by dissimilation and obfuscation. He would tell her what he had so often told Priest during one of his meandering stories, stories that, in their time, inevitably revealed themselves to be lectures. That the best stories, the best tales, were simple tales told simply. Or, better yet, not at all.

The simple tale, then, was that Maeve was scared. Terrified, really. Yes, she had traveled this world before, had been thought of as, if not its master, as close as any might come, but having walked a path many years ago did not mean that a woman might still remember her steps. Steps which, should she get them incorrectly, would reveal pits beneath her, chasms into which many before her had fallen but from which few, if any, had ever returned.

She was scared, and she was alone. When Chall had offered to come with her, it had been all that she could do to refuse him, to not leap at the prospect of it. In the end, she had done so because loving him, she could not bring him on this journey with her, was not confident she could lead him through the shadows safely when she herself had long ago forgotten the way.

"Ma'am?"

Maeve was startled from her thoughts, looking up to see the barkeep standing before her, an expression that was a mixture of concern and annoyance on his face which made it clear it was not the first time he had hailed her. "Is there anything I can do for you?"

Maeve cursed herself for a fool. It did not do, at the best of times, for a person to allow themselves to become distracted and even less when her goal was to find entrance into the Assassin's Guild. "Forgive me," Maeve said. "an...an ale, please."

The man watched her suspiciously but gave her a gruff nod before moving off. Maeve found that her heart was hammering in her chest, and she cursed herself inwardly for a coward. *You have nothing to be scared of, old girl, not yet,* she told herself. Only, she didn't think that was right. She had entered that world again, was entering it even now, and while those who remained within civilization's falsities, like rabbits hesitating at the edge of a glade, not seeing the lions lurking in the tall grass, were not safe, they were certainly safer than the rabbit who ventured inside.

Still, she would not stop, *could not* stop. Someone had tried to kill her, had tried to kill *Chall,* and not just *any* someone, but one sent from the Guild. Which meant that someone else had taken out a contract on one or both of them, and she had to find out who that person was or else she might not be so lucky next time. *Chall* might not be so lucky.

And while she might not be aware of everything going on in this world any longer, she told herself that there were still things she *did* know. Things such as the fact that there were certain doors upon which one might knock, certain shitty stools in shitty taverns upon which they might sit, certain words which they might say, that served as markers. Or, if not markers, then passes, passes of admittance those possessing the knowledge of which might use to gain entry. Sometimes, after all, a shitty tavern was a shitty tavern and sometimes it was far more than that.

If, she thought sourly, *that possessor of knowledge is not too cowardly to use it.* She waited for the barkeep to return and set her ale on the counter before her.

"Ah," Maeve said, staring at it then tossing a coin back onto the counter, meeting the barkeep's eye. "Sorry, but I've changed my mind. I seek a different doom than this," she went on, initiating the challenge.

She waited, tense, for the man to respond with the answer, to complete the phrase. The barkeep raised an eyebrow at her then grunted, shrugging. "Don't make no mind to me, just so long as you pay for it," he said, then he scooped up the coin and turned, walking away.

Maeve watched him go, frowning. That most certainly was not the answer to the challenge. Sometimes shitty taverns were something more...but sometimes, she thought, sighing, they were just shitty taverns.

That was the problem with being out of the life for so long, she decided. The secret world of assassins was like a house, one seen to by a mad carpenter who was never satisfied with it and so was constantly rearranging things, changing the locations of the doors that might gain entrance, the windows that might give a person a look inside. The only way to truly be aware of what the carpenter changed was to be inside the house when he did it.

Just a tavern then, and just a barkeep. Worse yet, this was not the first false start she'd had but the fourth. There had been the abandoned church—a site that saw few visitors save those who sought the Assassin's Guild. A church that had, at least, been made to *look* abandoned, though Maeve had been there, and she could say with some certainty that it was abandoned now, in truth. The second she'd tried had been a small trinket shop, one which had once sold ribbons. Ribbons that a person might tie about their wrist or use to adorn their hair and which might, in time, bring someone to speak with them. Only, the trinket shop was a trinket shop no longer. It had been purchased and it, with several surrounding buildings, had been turned into a tannery, one which Maeve had braved the smell of to verify with her own eyes.

The third she had tried had been a particular homeless man who tended to linger on a particular corner. Only, the homeless man was not there, perhaps, she supposed, having found a home at last. Though, she thought it far more likely, considering those forces with which the man had been acquainted, that he had found a fate far more permanent and considerably less spacious—coffins, after all, were far from roomy—than a home.

This, then, this tavern smelling of blood and sweat and ale gone sour, had been her next chance. Worse, it had been her last one. She was out of ideas, all of the old avenues of ingress blocked to her, and as she sat there, thinking, despairing, Maeve found her eyes going to the ale sitting on the counter before her. "Oh, why not?" she muttered. She lifted the glass and took a long drink before setting the cup down.

She felt desperate, thinking again of how close Chall had come to dying, of how close they had both come. So desperate that she was tempted to simply ask the barkeep, who she noted eyeing her sidelong out of the corner of her gaze, if he knew any assassins.

The thought caused her to freeze, her hand still on the mug. It was unlikely that the barkeep did know any—or at least, if he did, didn't *know* he knew any, for assassins were nothing if not particularly guarded about their work. But whether or not the man knew any was irrelevant. *Maeve* herself knew one.

Knew her in the form of Emille, Ned the carriage driver's wife.

"But I cannot," she said softly. "I cannot call upon her, not for this."

"What's that?"

Maeve glanced up at the barkeep, waving her hand dismissively. "Nothing."

Only, it wasn't nothing. It was something. A dangerous idea, to involve the woman. The woman who, along with her husband, had risked her life, her happiness, more than once to help Maeve and the others. It was a cruel way to repay her kindness, *their* kindness, to involve her in this. After all, while the woman, Emille, might work for the Guild, that did not mean that the Guild, and those who ran it would be appreciative should one of their own aid another seeking uninvited entrance among their ranks.

It would present a problem for the Guild, would in turn mean that *Emille* herself was a problem, and it was perhaps not surprising to anyone at all that the Assassin's Guild had one way above all others in which it favored dealing with problems that presented themselves. A particularly final, particularly *cutting* method, as it happened.

"*But what choice do I have?*" Maeve muttered.

What choice but to risk the assassination attempts continuing? And that was no real risk at all, she knew, for they *would* continue, there could be no doubt of that. The Guild, at least so far as contracts were concerned—and more particularly the coin with which those contracts were paid—was nothing if not determined. They did not fail, that was all. They could not *afford* to fail. For an Assassin's Guild that became known for being unable to fulfill those obligations for which it was contracted was not an Assassin's Guild at all but simply a street gang. And street gangs, it had to be said, while certainly brutal, did not enjoy the same reputation for efficiency that the Guild did and, therefore, were unable to charge the same prices for their services.

And *that,* Maeve knew, the reputation as much as their exorbitant prices, was something the Guild would be eager to protect, to protect at any cost. A cost that, as it turned out, included the lives of any—and if necessary, she did not doubt *all*—of the assassins who served within their employ.

But the assassin's life, the life of her husband, was not all that was at stake. At stake, too, was Chall's life. And her own. But even that was not all of it. For should whoever was behind the assassination attempts be successful and get what they want, what would stop them from going further still? These conspirers who were more than willing to send assassins into the castle itself, the very seat of power for the kingdom of the Known Lands? Would they then decide, once she and Challadius were out of the way, that they would go after Priest next? And would they stop there? Would they not go further yet, and mark Matt, Cutter's *son,* as their next victim?

No, that Maeve could not countenance and so, she rose, tossing another coin onto the counter for the barkeep. Then she turned and, hating herself more than a little, left the tavern.

It took her longer than it might have to reach Emille and Ned's home as she took a circuitous route, one which led back on itself more than once so that she might ensure that she was not being followed. She also stopped from time to time, pretending to admire the wares of this shop or that, so that she might glance around to see if she saw any faces that seemed a touch too familiar or, failing that, a touch too interested in her.

None did, but then that gave her little comfort. Assassins, after all, did not advertise themselves. Yet while each wasted minute left her feeling frustrated and impatient, she forced back the urge to hurry. After all, it had been some time since she had walked among the shadows and, like someone performing a dance nearly lost to memory, it would not do to move in haste. She was confident that, if she took her time, if she allowed those memories of the dance, of the woman she'd once been an opportunity to resurface, they would do so, and she would remember. And, if she found herself unable to become Maeve the Marvelous once again, the most feared assassin in all the land, then at least she might be some pale ghost of that proud, deadly woman.

So she took her time, slowly remaking herself into that woman or at least trying to, sewing together the frayed and torn pieces that had once comprised her, casting it about herself like a cloak or a gown and, in time, she stood, safe and unfollowed, at the door of Ned and Emille's home.

Maeve hesitated staring at the door, but she did not hesitate for long. She had come, after all, she was here, and what decision was to be made had been made already. She stepped forward and knocked.

She stood there for several seconds and, after a moment, began to believe that perhaps they would not answer. After another, she began to hope that they would not. She was just starting to turn away, relieved and disappointed all at once, when the door eased open, revealing the exact woman whom she had come to see.

Maeve was not sure in what manner she had anticipated Emille or Ned receiving her, if they chose to do so, but she had certainly not counted among those that she might find Emille in the midst of what could only have been a good cry.

The assassin-healer saw Maeve standing on her stoop and looked both surprised and embarrassed at once, running an arm quickly across her eyes and sniffling. "Maeve, is that you?"

"It is, Emille," Maeve said. "I thought..." She glanced around and saw no one, but then only a fool took chances when there was no need. "Well, I thought I might...visit you. And Ned, of course."

Emille snorted at that, a decidedly unhappy sound. "Good luck. Ned isn't here just now." And then, in a considerably quieter tone that Maeve believed had been meant for Emille and her alone. *"He rarely is."*

Maeve frowned at that. She had seen Emille take on two assassins without showing even an ounce of fear or emotion. It was some shock, then, to see her red eyes, an obvious sign she had spent a fair amount of time crying, and to hear in her something that Maeve had never heard before, not even when she and the prince and the others had risked her and her husband's life by coming to them for help—bitterness.

"Emille..." Maeve said, "is...is everything alright?"

"I'm...I'm fine, Maeve," the woman said in a voice that made it clear she was anything but fine. "Now, if there isn't anything else, I've got some tasks I need to get back to and—"

"Why have you been crying, Emille?"

"What?" the woman asked defensively. "This?" She gestured to her red, teary eyes. "No, no, I was just, cutting some onions, that's all." She gave a soft, incredibly unconvincing laugh. "I never have been able to cut one without tearing up. Ned, he says I wouldn't shed a tear if he got runover by his own carriage but get me near an onion and..." She cut off, sniffing again, running her arm across her eyes. "Anyway, I'm sorry, Maeve, but I'd really better be going. I'm...I'm afraid I'm poor company just now."

She stepped back into the door, beginning to close it. "I will call upon you at the castle soon, I promise, just as soon as I'm feeling better. I'm sure you've better things to do, so—"

"Nonsense," Maeve said in her best I'll-brook-no-argument tone as she pushed her way past the woman and into her house. "Besides, I've got nothing going on, and if it's onions need cutting, well, after all you and your husband have done, it's the least I can do, isn't it?"

She made a show of glancing around the room, aware of Emille letting out a heavy sigh as the woman stepped into the house behind her, closing the door.

"So," Maeve said, turning back to the woman, "what are we fixing?" She allowed her eyes to drift to the cooking pot hung above the fireplace—which currently had no fire going—before turning back to Emille and raising her eyebrow.

The woman winced. "Well. I...I suppose I should offer you an apology, Lady Maeve. There isn't...that is, I wasn't actually slicing onions."

"You don't say?" Maeve asked, not bothering to hide her sarcasm. Then, she moved toward the woman, putting a hand on her shoulder and when she spoke again her voice was softer. "What is bothering you, Emille? Whatever it is, you must understand that I'll help, if I can."

The woman gave a fragile smile. "I appreciate the offer, Lady Maeve, but I'm sure this isn't why you came. Now, if you'll just tell me what I can do—"

"What you can do is have a seat and tell me what's bothering you," Maeve said. "And if you appreciate the first offer, then you'll love this next one—I'm not leaving until you tell me what's going on. So if you want to get me out of your hair so you can get back to...you know, cutting onions, you'd best get out with it."

Emille sighed again. "I'm really not going to get rid of you, am I?"

Maeve said nothing, choosing instead to favor her with a smile, and the woman nodded. "Very well. Only, let me fix us some tea, at least," she said, clearly scrambling for a way to, if not completely avoid the conversation, at least delay it.

"Why don't you just have a seat?" Maeve said. "I'll fix the tea."

The woman shook her head, an expression on her face that was a mixture of annoyance and admiration. "Fine," she said, "if you insist."

"I really do," Maeve said. "Now then," she went on as she set about the task, "why don't you tell me what's bothering you? And have you told Ned about it?"

Emille gave another snort. "No, no I don't think that would do, not at all. You see…Ned, well, he's the problem."

Maeve frowned, glancing back at the woman from where she'd been hanging the pot over the fire. The last several times she'd visited the couple, they had seemed as close as—if not closer than—any other married couple she'd ever met. "What is it?" Maeve asked. "Do you mean that you and Ned are having problems?"

Emille grunted. "Hard to have problems when he's hardly ever around."

"Been working a lot, has he?" Maeve asked.

"Or so he'd have me believe," Emille said, not looking just sad or hurt now but angry.

"I…don't understand," Maeve said.

"According to Ned, he's been forced to work extra a lot lately."

"And…you don't believe him?"

"Oh, I did," Emille said. "Of course, I did. After all, he's my husband. If you can't trust your husband, who can you trust?" she asked, a sharpness to her tone. "He's been working so much, in fact, that he's missed more dinners than he's attended lately. I felt bad for him, of course, so I thought that I would just go by and deliver some food to his work—you know, that way at least he'd have a good meal. Only…he wasn't there."

Maeve frowned. "Not there? Well, he's a carriage driver, Emille. I'm sure that's not so unusual, right? Likely he was out on a job."

"So I thought as well," Emille said. "At least until I talked to Delilah."

"Delilah?"

Emille nodded grimly. "Delilah's the woman in charge of all the comings and goings of the carriage drivers. Scheduling their pickups, making sure they're paid, that sort of thing."

"I see," Maeve said. "And what did she have to say about all the extra work Ned has been doing?"

"Not much," Emille said. "Except that he hasn't been doing any extra work at all."

Maeve blinked, shocked, and Emille nodded. "I guess that's about how I looked, too, when she told me. Certainly it's how I felt. My husband has been lying to me, Maeve, and try as I might, I can think of only one reason why he might do that."

Maeve left the tea pot to boil then moved to the table, sitting beside Emille and taking her hand.

"I think..." Emille paused, swallowing. "I think that my husband is cheating on me, Lady Maeve."

"That's ridiculous," Maeve blurted, the words out of her mouth before she could stop them.

Emille gave her a fragile, humorless smile. "I thought so too," she said. "But you tell me, Maeve. Why else would he be coming and going at all hours of the night? And why would he lie to me about it?"

"I...don't know," Maeve said.

"Neither do I," Emille said.

Maeve sat there, wanting to say something, anything, to give the woman some comfort, but try as she might she could think of no other reason for the man's absence than the one Emille herself had thought of already.

"So," Emille said after a moment, "now you understand why I am sitting alone in my house in the early afternoon crying."

"And Ned?" Maeve asked. "He's...at work?"

Emille shrugged. "So he says, but how am I to know?"

Maeve shook her head sadly, thinking, feeling for the woman in a way that she would not have been able to even a month ago. For a month ago, and for the last twenty years or so before that, she had believed herself incapable of sharing a love like Emille and Ned's. Or, if not incapable, then at least undeserving. After all, she'd had such a love once, before the Skaalden had come and ripped it away from her, taking with it everything she had ever cared about.

But then she had found Chall, had *finally* found him. Had unearthed feelings which had been there all along, like some precious jewel hidden just beneath the surface. And now, having felt that, still feeling it, she could not imagine what it might be like to have to call into question that he felt the same. She wondered what she might do if she discovered that Chall was cheating on her, but she did not have to wonder long. After all, she'd gotten quite good at stabbing people over the years—it was the sort of thing that came with practice.

"I'm so sorry, Emille."

The woman shook her head. "It isn't your fault, Lady." She sniffed. "Anyway, what is it that brings you here? Is there something I can help you with?"

Maeve winced. She hadn't liked the idea of asking for Emille's help in the first place, and she liked it even less now. Still, she'd had her reasons for coming here and those reasons had not changed simply because Ned seemed to be like nearly every other man in the world. She glanced around. Ridiculous, maybe, for they were inside the woman's home, not out on the street—it wasn't as if someone could be waiting in the shadows, listening to their words. Still, she thought that where the Assassin's Guild was concerned, a bit of extra caution was understandable.

Finally satisfied that no hidden listener was lurking underneath the table, or perhaps in her teacup, Maeve met Emille's eyes. "The thing is, Emille...I need to speak with the Guild."

"The Guild?" Emille asked.

Maeve sighed. "You know very well what I mean. Anyway, I need to speak with them. I have tried to reach out myself, but the avenues I once used are no longer...operational. And, I am afraid, I do not know the new ones."

Emille nodded slowly. "I believe that the Guild would say that, if you cannot gain entrance, that is because you are not meant to, Lady Maeve," she said, her voice soft in an effort to take the worst of the insult away.

"Maybe not," Maeve said, "but I intend to get it anyway. And I thought well, since you're a part of the Guild, that maybe you could...I don't know, help me."

The woman said nothing, only watched her, and Maeve sighed. "I need to speak with them, Emille. It's urgent."

"Most people, Lady," Emille said, "have an urgent need to *avoid* assassins, not to seek them out."

"I suspect that's true," Maeve admitted, "but it changes nothing."

Emille seemed to consider then, after a few seconds, shook her head. "I'm sorry, Maeve, truly, but I cannot help you. The Guild would not take kindly to me showing you where they are, and I do not doubt they would take their displeasure out on you and, of course, on me for showing you to them."

"That's a chance I'm willing to take," Maeve said.

"Maybe," Emille said, a sharpness to her tone now, "but I'm not. I have a husband, Lady Maeve, one that I love even if, as I begin to suspect, he does not love me. And should I go against the Guild, should I show you to them, they might well decide to take offense. Enough offense, perhaps, that not only my life but that of my husband might be in danger. I like you, Maeve, I do, but I do not like you enough to risk my Ned."

"The husband who you believe to be having an affair?" Maeve countered.

The woman said nothing to that, only watched her with a resolute expression. Maeve watched her in return, her jaw working, until in a moment, she realized that she would not be able to argue the woman into doing what she wanted. Neither could she coerce her into it. No, instead she was going to have to take on another altogether less preferable strategy...she was going to have to tell the truth.

"An assassin came for us this morning," she said. "In the castle. Chall and I were still sleeping. It's luck more than anything else that we are still alive."

Emille hissed in a sharp intake of breath. "In the castle? Are you sure it was a Guildmember? Not some disgruntled serving person or something?"

"I'm sure, Emille," Maeve said. "I might have been out of the life for a while, but I know a trained assassin when I see one. Anyway, he had the brand."

Emille winced. "I see. Well, how about this, Lady. How about I look into the matter myself. Give me a few days, and I may be able to figure out who put the contract on the two of you and why without the Guild being any the wiser."

"And in the meantime, another assassin will be sent," Maeve said. "And this time, I might not be so lucky. *Chall* might not be so lucky." She shook her head. "No. Thank you for the offer, but I'm afraid that's not good enough. I want to speak to the Guild myself, to ensure that the contract is canceled."

Emille nodded slowly. "I understand your worry, Maeve, I do, but has the thought occurred to you that by walking into the Guild, you'll only be doing the assassin's job for him?"

"It has," Maeve said grimly. "But this isn't just about me, Emille. It's about Chall, too. Coming for me is one thing but coming for him...well. I'll do what's necessary to protect him. And if the Guild has a problem with that then they'll learn that violence is not strictly the purview of those within their employ."

Emille considered that for several seconds. "I still don't think it's a good idea, Maeve. It's dangerous. I do not believe your mage would thank me for bringing you to them."

"That's irrelevant," Maeve said. "I love Chall, Emille. That's the truth. But loving him doesn't mean I give a shit what he thinks, at least not about this. And understand something—I *am* going to find the Guild, one way or the other. I'm not going to stop looking for them. So either you show me where they are, or I'll visit every tavern, brothel, and dark alley in the city until I find the Assassin's Guild or they find me."

Emille studied her for a moment, likely trying to decide if she was bluffing—which she was not. Finally, the woman seemed to come to that same conclusion, and she heaved a heavy sigh. "Very well, Lady Maeve," she said. "I'll take you to the Guild, but just know that if they take exception to it, I don't want to hear any complaining from you."

"If they take exception," Maeve said, rising, "then it's unlikely I'll be in a position to complain about anything ever again."

Emille arched an eyebrow. "If you're trying to make me feel better you're doing a poor job."

Maeve shrugged. "Never was my strong suit, I'm afraid." She paused then, meeting the woman's eyes. "Thank you, Emille. I am aware of all that you've done for me, for us, the prince and all the rest, and...thank you."

The woman gave her a small smile, rising from her chair. "Don't mention it. Anyway, I suppose that even risking the Guild's anger is preferable to sitting around here crying. And if Ned comes back and doesn't find me here, well, that serves him right. Let him be the one to worry for a change."

And with that, the woman started toward the door and Maeve followed, hoping that she had not just doomed the woman and her husband.

CHAPTER NINE

Chall reluctantly followed as Priest led them deeper and deeper into New Daltenia's poor quarter. Chall had spent plenty of time in such places over the last fifteen years of his exile. Partly that was due to him being too poor to afford anything better, a fact which might have been remedied by work, if he wasn't always—or at least so much as he was able—too drunk to do any.

Yet for all the time he'd spent in such places, he still did not care for them. Mostly, he thought that was probably due to the fact that the denizens of the capital's poor district gave him the distinct impression that they would just as soon kill him as look at him—likely a lot sooner.

Still, he had made a point of catching Priest in a lie, of meaning to go with him, and that point would have been undermined somewhat by him turning and sprinting toward the relative safety of the rest of the city, screaming for the city guard as he did. So he resisted the urge…if only barely.

Instead, he distracted himself by trying to appear dangerous, threatening, like a predator. Priest had the thing down, seeming to radiate menace, walking down the street as if he owned it, not even so much as glancing at the men and women watching them from where they sat on stoops or looked out of the windows of the buildings they passed.

Meanwhile, Chall did enough glancing for the both of them, and they'd barely been in the poor district for five minutes before he had a crick in his neck from trying to look everywhere at once. He tried to emulate Priest, the man's walk, the way he didn't seem to be afraid of anyone accosting them but, instead, somehow seemed to *hope* for it. But try as he might, Chall didn't feel much like a predator. In truth, he didn't even feel like the predator's prey, nimble and quick and standing a fair chance of making it away. Mostly, he felt like a steak with feet strutting past dozens of hungry lions and hoping against any common sense that they didn't decide to take a bite out of him.

He seriously considered casting an illusion upon himself, one that would turn his vastly overweight and vastly *not* terrifying but quite terri*fied* image into something that would give pause to anyone considering attacking him. In the end, though, he discarded the idea, mostly because he *was* terrified and meant to save his strength in case he needed it which, if the entire rest of his life was anything to go by, wasn't so much a question as it was a guarantee.

"How much farther is it?" Chall asked, not liking the way his voice seemed to fall flat and empty in the quiet air.

Priest turned to regard him, frowning. "You should go back, Chall. This is no place for someone...like you."

"Like me?" Chall asked, then frowned. "Fat, do you mean? I'll have you know—"

"Not fat," Priest said, eyeing him up and down, a hardness to his gaze that Chall was not accustomed to seeing in his friend's eyes. "Soft. Last chance," the man continued, meeting his gaze. "I cannot guarantee your safety, should you choose to come any farther."

"Maeve likes my softness," Chall grumbled, then seeing that the man didn't appreciate the joke sighed. "I might be...*soft* as you say, Priest, though I feel, considering the things I've faced, the things *we've* faced together, that saying so is unfair. But I don't expect you to guarantee my safety—after all, a castle full of guardsmen didn't stop an assassin from nearly killing me and Maeve both." He paused at that, a mixture of fear and anger roiling through him at the thought of something happening to Maeve. Maeve who, even now, was off to the Assassin's Guild. "My point is, Priest," he said, his voice trembling not with fright but anger now as he met the man's eyes, "that I love Maeve, I love the prince, and Matt too, even you, though don't ask me why. You are my friends, my only real friends in this world, and while I might seem soft, I can promise you that I will be just as hard, just as *sharp* as I need to be to make sure that my friends are safe."

Priest watched him for a few seconds, perhaps to see if the façade of confidence would break. It did not, though, would not, for that façade had been painted on by Chall's fear for Maeve and the prince, his anger that anyone would dare try to hurt them, and his determination to figure out who was behind it.

After a moment, Priest gave a single nod. "Very well," he said. "Then come, Challadius. Follow me into the darkness."

With that, the man turned and walked farther on, and Chall did not hesitate this time before following, for he had been telling the man nothing but the truth. And the sooner they figured out what was going on with the Crimson Wolves—if anything *was* going on—the better.

They moved on, eyes continuing to mark them from alleyways and windows. Chall met those eyes in challenge, almost hoping that someone would choose to accost them, if for no other reason than it might distract him from his growing fear for Maeve. Fear that was like a rat gnawing at his insides. No one approached them though, and they were allowed to walk on unmolested.

At least, for a while. Just because the lion didn't pounce at once, after all, didn't mean the rabbit was safe, only that the predatory cat was waiting for its moment.

This lion—or *lions,* Chall amended as more figures stepped into the street in front of them—had apparently decided that that moment was now. Six figures in all, but Chall's attention was drawn to the one standing at their front, a giant of a man whose size was on par with the prince. A big lion, then, but that didn't matter to Chall, at least not right then. Big or not, the man was placing himself in the way of them getting answers, answers that would help them to protect their friends, and so this lion, should he choose to pounce, would find that some rabbits had sharper teeth than one might think. Or so Chall told himself while some part of him acknowledged that two on six wasn't the sort of odds anyone would sign up for and that the man standing before them—looming really, the big bastard—looked like he could crush stones with his forehead, if he took it in mind to do so. And, based on his smashed nose and one ear that was little more than a lump, he seemed to have done just that on at least one occasion.

"*You*," the big man growled, and Chall was just fine with the fact that the giant was addressing Priest and not him.

"Me," Priest said calmly, and if he felt any anxiety at the giant man and those five others with him then he hid it well.

"Thought we made it clear you weren't welcome here the last time you came," the big man said.

Priest shrugged. "I need to speak with her."

The big man snorted, glancing at some of those behind him with a grin. "And I need a mansion on Noble Street," he said, to which several of the others dutifully laughed. "Don't mean I'm goin' to get it, does it?"

"I don't have time for this," Priest said.

"Well then you'd better make time," the big man growled. "Or better yet, why don't you and your fat friend turn around, go back to where you came from."

"We will," Priest said while Chall frowned down at his stomach, "just as soon as we get what we came for."

"You're not hearin' me," the big man said, folding his massive arms across his chest. "You ain't gettin' no farther than this. Now, this is your last chance—leave. Now. Or I'll make you."

"Fine," Priest said, "let's get this over with."

The big man started to smile, at least until Priest stepped forward, and he realized that the man hadn't meant to leave at all but instead had chosen the second option. "Alright then," the big man growled. "Let's get this done."

Several of those behind him started forward, pausing as he held a hand up. "I've got this." He moved into the street, to an open spot, and then motioned for Priest. "Come on, then."

"You can't be seriously plan on fighting that giant bastard," Chall said to Priest. "He looks like he eats boulders for his breakfast."

"Stay here, Chall," Priest said over his shoulder. "I'll be back in a minute. If any of the others jump in—"

"Run?" Chall asked quietly. "You got it."

Priest did glance back at him then, favoring him with a small grin before starting forward to stand a few feet in front of the big man.

"Valden the Vicious," the man said, grinning. "My but I've heard some stories about you. Most of 'em fake, no doubt."

"No doubt," Priest agreed.

"Still," the man went on, "can't say as I haven't wanted to put some of those stories to the test."

"Now's your chance," Priest said.

The big man chose to respond to the considerably smaller man in the same way that most street toughs responded to things they didn't like—he hit him. Or at least he tried to. The big man rushed forward and his fist lashed out in a hook that, powered as it was by an arm the size of a tree trunk, would have likely taken Priest's head from his shoulders. If, that was, it had connected, which it did not. Instead, Priest stepped to the side of the blow then brought his foot down on the outside of the big man's knee. There was a *crack,* and the big man cried out as his leg went out from underneath him, and he fell to his hurt knee.

Priest didn't hesitate, pivoting and bringing an uppercut into the man's face—more specifically, his nose. A nose which broke from the blow, spattering blood. The big man cried out again, swinging, but Priest was already moving, stepping behind him and drawing one of his blades in one smooth motion, bringing it to the man's neck with one hand while his other jerked back on the big man's hair, exposing his throat.

It all happened so fast that Chall and the street tough's allies were left to stare in shock at what had occurred. The big man also looked surprised—at least from what of his expression Chall could see past the blood on his face—but more than that, he looked afraid. "*Y...you bwoke my noshe,*" he moaned.

"I did," Priest agreed, "and I'll do worse than that, if you decide to stay in my way. Now, are you done?"

"I'm...done," the big man growled.

"Good," Priest said. He gave the man's head a shove so that he fell to his hands and knees, then he turned and started toward a building on the other side of the street. The five who had accompanied the big man parted before him, opening a path.

"You won't...you won't find her there," the big man said.

Priest turned, eyeing the man. "Where then?"

The big man hesitated, then let out a growl that was a mixture of anger and fear but mostly fear. "She'll kill me," he said.

"Maybe," Priest agreed, "but she's not here—I am."

The street tough hesitated then apparently decided that dying later was preferable to dying now. "There's a brothel, name of Florence's. It's over on—"

"I know it," Priest said. He moved back to Chall who was still watching him in shock. If the other man seemed bothered in the least by the fight he'd just been in or how close he had come to killing the big man, he did not show it. "Ready?" Priest asked as he came to stand beside him.

"S-sure," Chall said.

Priest looked sharply at him for a moment, then gave a nod. "Come on."

***

They did not speak as they continued through the streets. Chall stared at his companion's back as they walked, thinking about how brutally Priest had broken the big man down, how prepared he had been to kill him. Thinking, too, of how many times Chall had mocked Priest for one thing or another, intentionally antagonizing him.

He was still considering that—and considering how, while the world often punished people for their foolishness, every once in a while some slipped through the cracks—when they turned a corner in the street and Priest stopped.

"Florence's," he said, eyeing a building across the street.

And this, at least, he hadn't needed to say, for Chall had visited quite a few brothels over the years and knew well what they looked like. A two-story building, the top floor of which had near a dozen windows facing the street. Some of those windows were blocked with thick, velvet curtains while some few others had no such covering, revealing the warm light of lanterns from within or, half-naked women hanging out of them, beckoning when they saw Priest and Chall standing in the street.

Priest ignored them, starting toward the brothel and Chall followed. Then they were stepping inside, the common room filled with the soft, warm light of several candles, a perfumed scent in the air. Cushioned divans were spread about the room and several men and women sat ensconced in them, the women all only partially clothed and some completely naked, draping themselves across the men like garments. The men themselves appeared to be of all walks of life: some dressed like sailors, other day-laborers, some merchants, and Chall even saw one man that, judging by his dress, appeared to be a nobleman. Though there was nothing noble about him at the moment as his face—at least what Chall could see of it—was flushed from drink, most of it was currently buried in the large bosom of a scantily-clad woman.

"This way," Priest said, moving toward the bar at the far end of the room, one which, Chall couldn't help but notice, was flanked on either side by two muscular men with their arms folded, looking like a bad day just looking for someone to happen to.

Priest didn't seem bothered in the least, though, and went to the counter. All the seats were empty, save one, this one taken up by a man who appeared to be unconscious, his arms on the counter, his head buried in his arms.

Priest moved directly to him. "We've come to speak to Nadia," he told the unconscious man.

The unconscious man said nothing, just went on being unconscious. There was a man's scream from somewhere up the stairs, and Chall tensed. Priest turned and glanced in that direction. It hadn't been the sort of scream a person expected to hear in a brothel, had been one not of pleasure but of pain. Chall hoped the poor bastard had decided on a safe word before they'd begun.

"She's up there, I suppose," Priest said to the unconscious man. "I need to talk to her—I don't mean any harm, but I *do* mean to talk to her."

Chall glanced at the two men on either side of the counter and noted that they were watching him and Priest with deep frowns. They weren't moving toward them, at least not yet, but he got the impression that it wouldn't be long before they did. "Priest," he said.

"Not now, Chall," Priest said, watching the unconscious man. "I assure you," he went on, "I don't have any intention of causing her problems—I just need to ask her some questions. That's all."

"Priest," Chall said again, "maybe worry less about the drunken fool and more about the two big bastards who look like they'd love nothing more than beat the shit out of us."

"The greatest dangers we face, Challadius," Priest said, "are rarely the obvious ones. Isn't that right?" he asked the unconscious man.

The man heaved a sigh and rose, and Chall felt his eyebrows raising as well when he saw that the man had not been sleeping after all—or at least, if he had, he was a bigger fool even than Challadius himself. For what the man's arms and head had hidden from view was a small hand crossbow.

A crossbow which the man now pointed at Priest as he turned in his stool to fully face them. "She isn't in the habit of entertaining uninvited guests," the man said. "Besides, she's busy right now."

"She'll want to hear what I have to say," Priest said.

"Is that right?" the man asked. "Well, if that's the case, why don't you tell me. If your news really is so amazing, maybe I'll let you see her after all instead of pulling the trigger on this crossbow here."

"I wouldn't do that," Chall said. "You aren't going to kill him, not with that tiny little crossbow bolt, and Priest here isn't in a particularly kind mood today."

"Priest?" the man asked, blinking. "As in the man once known as Valden the Vicious?"

"That was a long time ago," Priest said.

"Maybe," the man agreed. "Anyway, I don't care how big of a name you got, it ain't gonna protect you, if I let this bolt here fly."

Chall gave a snort. "Look, I'm no expert, but—"

"Poisoned?" Priest asked, interrupting.

The man gave him a smile. "Liberally."

"The fact remains that I mean her no harm," Priest said. "And as for what I've come to talk to her about...it's the Crimson Wolves."

The man grunted at that, and he suddenly looked as if he was about to be sick. "Those bastards," he said, swallowing. "What about them?"

"They're back," Priest said simply.

Priest might as well have just issued a death threat to the man based on how he reacted, his face going pale. "That's impossible," he said. "They haven't been seen or heard from in two decades."

"Why don't you let me speak to her?" Priest said. "Let her decide for herself."

The man watched him with a frown, seeming to consider. Finally he nodded. "Wait here," he said. He glanced at the two big men who had been standing on either side of the counter and who had taken advantage of their distraction, Chall saw, to move closer. "If they try to leave or do anything, feel free to kill them," he said.

The big men nodded, looking all too eager to do exactly that, and Chall did his best not to quail in fear as the man with the hand crossbow rose and started up the stairs. Priest only watched calmly, an almost bored expression on his face of the kind one would expect to see on someone waiting his turn at a shop. Chall determined that later—assuming they survived the next few minutes, that was—he would have to ask the man how he managed to keep such a straight face.

For now, though, he was too concerned with watching the two big men who watched him and Priest in turn, looking like they were just hoping for a reason for violence and, with such men as this, Chall knew that they never needed much of an excuse.

So he waited anxiously, hoping that his face would go on being unpunched for a little while longer until, after what might have been a few minutes or a few centuries, the man with the crossbow returned. "She'll see you," he said.

"Thanks," Chall blurted, unable to hide his relief at the thought of escaping the angry stares of the two men.

The other man raised an eyebrow. "I wouldn't thank me yet, if I were you. The boss was busy, and she doesn't much care for being interrupted."

And before Chall could say anything to that, the man turned and headed toward the stairs. Priest glanced at Chall, then with a nod, he turned and followed. Part of Chall didn't want to go after the two men—in point of fact, pretty much *all* of him didn't want to. But then, neither did he want to stay here with these two big men eyeing him like he was a piece of meat and they two particularly hungry wolves. Besides which, they had come here for answers, and if the only way he was going to get those answers, if the only way he was going to make Maeve safe was to speak with a crime boss then he'd do it, would do far worse if that's what it took to protect the woman he loved.

Chall followed.

Their escort led them up the stairs and down a hallway to a door at the end, flanked by two men. He stopped, giving them a nod.

The two men regarded Priest and Chall with expressionless faces before one turned and opened the door.

"Good luck," the crossbowman said to them, and Chall grunted as the man turned and headed back toward the stairs.

"Good luck with your nap," Chall said in return. Then, far quieter, "*bastard.*"

Priest stepped through the door, and Chall followed. No sooner were they through the door than it closed behind them with a resounding *thud* of finality that he did not care for. What he cared for even less, though, was the smell that assaulted his nostrils the moment he and Priest stepped across the threshold. It was the smell of blood, but not just that—the smell of piss, too. But while what he smelled was bad, what Chall saw, as he took in the room, was far worse.

There was no furniture in the room save for a single chair placed at its center. And in that chair sat a man. Or, at least, what was left of him. His hands were bound to the chair, behind his back, his ankles tied as well. He hung limply, the bonds seemingly the only thing keeping him upright. He was not unconscious, but Chall suspected from his appearance and the quiet, shaky sobs coming from him that he wished he was. For his face—his entire body, in fact—was covered in blood, his features a battered, swollen mess.

Before him stood a big, shirtless man covered in sweat, flexing his hand as if it ached. Which no doubt it did as, if his bloodied and scratched knuckles were anything to go by, it had been put to some hard use recently.

Nearby stood a woman who might have been someone's favorite grandmother if not for the emotionless, shark-like eyes with which she stared at the moaning bloody man. "Oh, stop your blubbering, Nate," the woman said, clearly unmoved with the man's muttered, incoherent pleas. "You've acted out, that's all, and like any child who goes against their mother's wishes, you must be punished."

The woman glanced at the big man with the bloody knuckles. "Well?" she said. "Punish him."

The big man nodded emotionlessly and then, also emotionlessly, began to beat the shit out of the bound man. *Just another day at work,* Chall thought, his stomach lurching as he pulled his gaze away. But avoiding looking did nothing to keep him from hearing the sickening, *meaty* sounds of the man's fist and the half-scream, half-sobbed cries of the poor soul the woman had called Nate.

Chall wasn't sure how long it went on—mostly because he was trying, and largely failing, to distract himself by thinking of something—anything—else. All he knew was that the puncher was still punching, the punchee still being punched, when there was a knock on the door they came through. The person on the other side didn't bother waiting for a reply before stepping inside.

The man, who appeared to be in his late forties, perhaps early fifties, started into the room then paused when he noted Chall and Priest standing there. "Valden?" the man asked. "That you?"

"It's me, Catham," Priest said. "How are you?"

The man shrugged. "Oh, you know how it is, Vicious. I owe the dirt a debt, and I imagine I'll pay it soon enough."

"But not today," Priest said, or more recited, Chall thought, as if the words were part of some shared saying which, based on the newcomer's nod, they appeared to be.

"Not today," the man who Priest had called Catham agreed. "Heard we had visi—" He cut off at the sound of a particularly desperate, particularly agonized scream and sighed, shaking his head. "Damn if I ever did learn to have a taste for this sort of thing."

"It isn't something you can learn," Priest said. "It's something you're either born with or you're not."

Catham grunted. "Well, s'pose you'd know."

"So what did he do?" Priest asked.

"Him?" Catham asked, glancing over at the scene with a sigh of regret, the sort of sound Chall thought belonged on a man who went to get a piece of cake and found that someone had already eaten the last one. Certainly it didn't sound like the sort of a man someone should make when they were watching someone else getting beaten to death only feet away. "Well, that poor bastard had the honor of being in charge of coordinating a delivery of..." He paused, glancing at Chall before turning back to Priest. "Well, let's just say *merchandise.* One worth a sizeable sum."

"So what happened?" Priest asked.

"It came up missin', that's what," Catham said, "and it ain't the first such shipment that's done so over the last few weeks. Why, I guess the boss is gettin' ready to pull her hair out...or, well, maybe someone else's. See, she's got a theory about the whole thing—" He paused at another loud scream before going on as if nothing had happened. "A theory that is about how whoever keeps hittin' us is able to know exactly where our shipments are goin' to be and exactly when."

"She thinks whoever it is has someone working on the inside," Priest said.

"Exactly," Catham said.

"And...she thinks it's him?" Chall asked, wincing again at the sound of fist striking flesh.

"Seems so," Catham said. "You see, apparently she didn't tell anyone about this latest shipment—not even myself, if you can believe it." He gave a sour face that made it clear what he thought of that. "Not anyone, that is, exceptin' Nate here. So when this shipment got hit like the others..." He shrugged.

"She decided it was him," Priest finished.

"That's right."

"But...that's it?" Chall asked. "Based on that she decided to—" He glanced over at the man then cut off, jerking his gaze away, "I mean, has he ever done anything like this before? Or anything to cause her to be suspicious of him?"

"What's that?" Catham asked.

"I'm just saying," the mage said, "it seems a small reason, especially if he hasn't ever done something like this to make her doubt him before."

Priest and Catham shared a look. "In this line of business, fella," Catham said, "people rarely get second chances. Anyway, I'd best go talk to her. Got a message for her, and it probably wouldn't be wise to make her wait." He gave them both a humorless grin.

"Else, it might be me in that chair. I'll make sure to remind her you're here, Vicious."

"I'd appreciate that," Priest said, and the man gave them both a nod before turning and walking away.

Chall frowned at the man's back as he walked away. There was something about him he didn't like. Oh, he'd seemed friendly enough, but then during the course of his life Chall had gone to bed with some women that seemed friendly enough to only to wake to find that the pleasant woman he'd gone to bed with had turned, at some time during the night, into a vicious creature of regret and scorn. Besides, he hadn't missed the way the man had accepted a person literally being beaten to death without so much as batting an eye.

But even that, he realized, wasn't all of it. The truth was he hadn't cared for the easy rapport the man and Priest shared. The damning part of it all was that he thought that, had Maeve been there, she would have told him he was jealous. And even *more* damning than that, she would have been right. "Friend of yours, I take it?" Chall asked.

Priest glanced at him and seemed to consider that. "I wouldn't say that the type of person I used to be was really capable of friends, Challadius, but I suppose that Catham was as close to such a thing as I got."

"A good man?"

"No," Priest said, "no, I wouldn't say that. After all, men rarely wind up as criminals by accident. Still, in the world I used to be a part of, a world of dirty men, I suppose he was one of the cleaner ones. Plus he never tried to kill me, so there's that."

"If that's not a sign of friendship, I don't know what is," Chall said sarcastically.

Priest raised an eyebrow. "Everything alright, Chall?"

"Sure, why wouldn't it be?" Chall asked, though the truth was he could think of about a dozen reasons. The prince exiled to the Black Wood, Maeve seeking out the Assassin's Guild—which felt to him far too much like a cow walking willingly to its own butchering. Then there was the fact that he and Priest were currently sharing a room with one of the most powerful crime bosses in the city while a man got the shit beat out of him.

Priest opened his mouth, apparently about to respond, then hesitated, turning to look back toward the room. Chall followed his gaze and saw the big man—who, moments ago, had been busy beating the poor bastard in the chair to a pulp—was now walking toward them, wiping his bloody hands on a rag.

The man paused in front of them, and it was all Chall could do not to cower before him, having seen just what sort of damage he could do with those fists of his.

Priest, though, only stared at the man, an eyebrow raised, not seeming fazed in the slightest. Which Chall supposed, when he considered how the man had broken down the big guy in the street, made sense.

The man's gaze turned away from Chall, focusing instead on Priest and likely dismissing the mage as no threat. Which, if it came to a fight, Chall had to admit was nothing short of the truth. The big man studied Priest for a moment, a look on his face that, if it wasn't one of outright hostility, wasn't far from it. "Boss says she'll see you," he growled.

"Thanks," Priest said.

The big man frowned, an expression on his face that said he would have preferred the woman had given him a different order regarding them, but he stepped aside, motioning them forward.

Priest glanced back at Chall then started toward where the man, Catham, stood beside the gray-haired woman, their backs to them as they shared a quiet conversation. Chall followed after him, and they stopped a few feet away from the two.

"...like he vanished."

"*Vanished*," the woman snapped. "What is that, the third one this week?"

"Yes, ma'am. Safe to say someone's poaching our men. Either that or they're trying to—" He paused, glancing back to where Chall and Priest waited. "Well. I can tell you the rest later, ma'am."

The woman turned, regarding Chall and dismissing him in a moment, nearly as quickly as the big man had. Then she turned to regard Priest. "Valden. You'd better be careful. We keep seeing each other this much, folks'll start to talk."

Priest inclined his head. "Nadia, I came to—"

"We'll get to why you're here in a bit," the woman interrupted. "What's got me curious, Vicious, is *how* you're here."

Priest hesitated, and Chall spoke. He didn't want to, didn't *intend* to, but the thing about practicing being a smart ass for your entire life was that it got increasingly difficult to turn it off. "We walked," he said. "Thought about hiring a carriage, but figured we'd have to pay extra."

The woman slowly turned to regard him, and it was all Chall could do to keep from cowering into a trembling ball as those shark eyes fell on him. All in all, Chall decided, there might be better ways to deal with being anxious than lashing out with sarcasm, particularly when one is lashing out against a crime boss who had dozens—perhaps hundreds—of people in her employ who would be more than willing to kill him if she asked. Not that it seemed to him that the woman would have needed them.

She was an old, thin woman, likely no more than a hundred and fifteen pounds soaking wet, but that didn't keep her from exuding menace as strongly as Chall himself was no doubt exuding quiet terror. She was shorter than Chall by at least a head, yet she somehow did a better job of looming over him than the big man had.

"Challadius the Charmer," the woman said, and he felt a shock of cold fear run through him as she said his name. She must have seen some of the anxiety her words caused, for she smiled. Not a genuine sign of mirth or pleasure but instead the sort of expression that might come on a crocodile's mouth as it slowly glided through the water, preparing to pounce on its unsuspecting prey. "Oh, yes," she said, "I know who you are. How could I not? Why, you and your companions—such as Maeve the Marvelous— are all, after all, quite famous. Why, I do not doubt that there are those in the city who mark your every move, knowing—" her smile widened—"exactly, at any given time, where you are. Where, for example, you all might lay your heads."

Challadius felt another shiver of fear run through him at that, and a thought suddenly occurred to him. Maeve had seemed sure that the man who had attacked them in their room had been sent from the Assassin's Guild, but then she might have been wrong. Maybe the man had worked for the Guild at one time and maybe he worked there no longer. Who was to say that a man might not leave the Guild and then work for one of the city's crime bosses instead? And if that were true, then the woman standing before him was all but admitting that she'd been responsible for the attempt on his and Maeve's life. Suddenly, Chall wasn't afraid. Instead, he was angry, furious. "You listen to me, you *reptile*," he growled, taking a step forward, "if I find that you had anything to do with the attempt on Maeve's life—" He cut off, staring down at his throat where the man, Catham, had stepped forward, putting a knife to his neck.

Chall raised his gaze, meeting the man's eyes. "And just what do you think you're going to do with that?" he growled, looking back down. The man followed his gaze, grunting in surprise and recoiling as he realized that it was not a knife he held any longer but a fish. A fish that made a particularly metallic clank as the startled criminal dropped it and it struck the ground.

Chall wasn't done though. He was angry, furious, in fact, and his fury was mirrored by the flames that suddenly erupted all around the room, and the big man, who had been so menacing moments ago, screamed in shocked terror. Chall could feel the heat of the flames on his skin, could smell the burning timbers of the brothel, and the woman, Nadia, shrank away as he stalked toward her, her shark eyes wide with fear.

"*I had nothing to do with any attempt on your life or that of Lady Maeve!*" the woman said, shouting to be heard over the roar of the flames, a roar that wasn't strictly real.

Chall stopped then, and the flames died down, vanishing as if they had never been. The fish lying on the floor was a fish no longer but now appeared like a knife once more. Which, of course, it was. "Very well," he said. "I believe you."

"*Fire and salt,*" Catham hissed.

"Yes," the woman said, overcoming her shock quickly, her shark eyes roaming over him as if she had just found a particularly useful tool and was already considering the ways in which she might use it. "I had heard, of course, of your...abilities, but I never realized just how powerful they were. I am...very impressed."

"And you haven't even heard my singing voice yet," Chall said.

The woman watched him for a moment, then finally turned to Priest. "And I was under the impression that Prince Bernard was the one with the temper."

"As was I," Priest said, still staring at Chall strangely.

"Anyway," the woman went on, "I suppose we had best get to the matter of your unexpected visit, Vicious. I would not care to see another outburst from your friend here. Now, as I was saying, I am quite curious as to how you got here—specifically, how you knew to come *here* at all."

Priest nodded slowly. "Well. I went by the usual spot, but you weren't there."

"No, I was not," she said, "though I seem to recall leaving some people in charge until I returned. People who were not given leave to share my whereabouts."

"I asked them," Priest said.

"You asked them," she repeated.

"Yes," he said.

"I am supposed to believe, then, that you were given my whereabouts simply by the asking?"

"I asked hard."

She sighed. "Very well, Vicious, you have gone through all the trouble of coming here. It seems rude not to offer you a moment of my time. But understand that you shall have no more than that. And should I determine that you have *squandered* my time, Vicious," she said, glancing at Chall, "that the *two of you* have squandered my time, then know that I will not be pleased, not at all. And my displeasure, at least, will be more than just an illusion."

Chall found himself swallowing hard at that. He tried to come up with some sort of response other than begging for his life, but thankfully Priest beat him to it. "We've come to talk to you about the Crimson Wolves," Priest said.

Nadia started at that, and from what Chall had heard about them, with good reason. But she got control of herself a moment later and raised an eyebrow. "You have come to talk to me about a twenty-year-extinct street gang?"

"They were more than a street gang, we both know that," he said. "What you might not know, though, is that they're back."

She frowned. "That's impossible. The Crimson Wolves are gone—they haven't been seen for twenty years."

"Until today," Priest countered.

The older woman watched him carefully. "Explain."

And Priest did, telling her about everything that had transpired in the castle regarding the woman who had pretended to be a servant. At first, as he talked, Chall thought that the man was telling her far too much, but then he decided that it didn't matter. The woman was the head of the most powerful criminal organization in the city. Meanwhile, they did not even know which of the guards in the castle could actually be trusted. No doubt, one—likely several—of those guards worked for her. If she hadn't already heard about what had happened in the castle then Chall thought it likely that she soon would.

"A ring?" the old woman asked when Priest was finished. "That's all the proof you have? That's it?"

"It's enough," Priest said. "You know as well as I do, Nadia, that those rings were only worn by members of the Wolves."

"Yes, once upon a time that was true," the old woman said. "But what is to stop someone, Vicious, from having such a ring made?"

"It was tried before," Priest said. "By another of the syndicates...what was their name..."

"The Bloody Talons," the woman said, her voice little more than a whisper.

"Yeah, that was it," Priest said. "Anyway, you remember what happened to them."

"I remember," Nadia said in a quiet voice, and Chall didn't think he imagined the way the woman's face had paled slightly. Whatever had happened to the Bloody Talons, he didn't think it had been a good thing. "Still," she said after a moment, "that was twenty years ago. The Crimson Wolves are gone, Vicious, and so someone, meaning to impersonate them, need not concern themselves with reprisal. They could copy them without fear."

"Would you?" Priest countered.

The woman licked her lips, and Chall was forced to consider, again, that whatever else these Crimson Wolves had been, they had been feared most of all. Enough, at any rate, to give a crime boss pause, and Chall was fairly confident that, as far as Nadia was concerned, there were few things that might make that list. "I am an old woman, Vicious," she said. "Many believe that being closer to one's death might make one more comfortable with it, but I have found the opposite to be true. After all, when the hourglass is full in abundance, it might easily be ignored, but when those specks of sand which remain are so few that they might be counted, might be noticeably diminished as yet another grain slips through, then they are all the more precious. No, to answer your question, I would not risk impersonating a member of the Wolves for to do so would be accepting a risk—however small—and that to no purpose. But then, people do many things, Vicious, and my approval has never swayed their decisions in the slightest."

Chall didn't think that was altogether true, thought that as far as criminals were concerned, at least, the gray-haired woman's approval meant a great deal. At least, that was, if they didn't want to end up like the man who now sat unconscious in the chair, only kept upright by his bonds.

"No," the woman said again, sounding as if she were trying to convince herself as much as anyone, "no, it cannot be the Wolves. If they truly had returned, Vicious, we would know. There would be signs. After all, the Crimson Wolves were many things but subtle was not one of them."

"Signs," Priest repeated. "Signs like shipments going missing without explanation," he said. "Or your hirelings suddenly vanishing without so much as a goodbye despite the fact that such men and women know well what the consequences of leaving might be."

The woman's neck snapped around, and she glared at Catham who swallowed, holding his hands up to say he meant no harm. "Remind me, later, Catham," she said in a low, dangerous voice, "to speak with you about the proper etiquette regarding what to and what not to share with others outside of our...organization."

"Of course, ma'am," the man said, bowing his head. "I live to serve," he added in a voice that somehow managed to sound completely genuine without the slightest bit of artifice that normally accompanied such a proclamation. *Catham the Cautious indeed,* Chall thought.

Nadia, though, was not so easily impressed. She snorted. "Serve, yes, but whom?"

The man seemed to stiffen at that where he still had his head bowed to her, but he said nothing. The old woman watched him for another moment before turning back to Priest. "It is true that we have had some small...difficulties, but an operation like ours is always fraught with such. Problems caused by an opposing gang, by the city guard, or by one of our members deciding that he deserves a bigger part in the organization or, alternatively, that he has found his pay not to his liking and has taken it upon himself to rectify that problem by skimming from the coffers. They are the cost of doing business in such a profession as ours, nothing more."

"Is that so?" Priest asked. "And tell me, how have costs been lately, Nadia?"

The woman's eyes narrowed. "That is none of your concern, Vicious. Such things have not been your concern, in fact, for a long time and that by your doing. Now, I think it's time you and your temperamental friend left. I have some issues that must be seen to."

"Crimson Wolf issues?" Priest pressed.

"Normal issues," she snapped, "and I can assure you, Vicious, that what issues that have presented themselves will be dealt with—the same way that we deal with all such problems. Perhaps you could spend less time worrying about what we are doing and more time ensuring that you do not become one of those issues. Now," she went on, nodding her head to Catham, "I think it's past time you left before I lose my patience."

"Damnit, Nadia," Priest said, raising his voice in his frustration, "forget the damn secrets! The Crimson Wolves—or someone posing as them—have returned. I would let them do what they do—and we both know what *that* is—only, they came into the castle and killed an innocent serving woman. I'm sure that you want them dealt with at least as much as I do, so why don't you stop wasting our time and tell me what—"

"Enough," the old woman roared, and Chall found himself taking a step back, shocked by just how impressive a roar it was considering it came from such a small woman. "I have heard *more* than enough from you, Valden. Valden the *saint*, the killer with a heart of gold." She gave a derisive snort. "You are what you are, what you have always been. You are Vicious, you're just too scared to believe it. Well, that's all well and good—that's your decision to make, not mine. But I won't be lectured, not by you of all people, and I won't be talked to in such a way. Remember this, Valden, before you think to come back—we do not owe you *anything*. You are not one of us, not anymore, and we do not owe you a damned bloody thing. You are no better than we are, *Priest*, for at least we know what we are. We do not pretend at being different. You can put all the face paint on a whore you want—she's still just a whore underneath. Now, leave my place, *whore,* before I really lose my patience."

Priest said nothing, and Chall, noting the look of dismay on his face, one the woman's words had put there, felt angry for the man as well as feeling angry at him. "Funny," he said to the old woman, "I thought this place belonged to Florence. You know, it's right there, in the name."

The old woman gave him a humorless smile, sharp enough to cut, then motioned and the man, Catham, started forward again.

"Come on, Chall," Priest said, his voice sounding pained as if the woman's words had physically hurt him. "We need to be going."

"Going?" Chall asked, shocked. "But we don't have any answers. Listen, Priest, what she said was bullshit. Don't let her—"

"*No, it wasn't,*" Priest snapped, rounding on Chall so quickly that he found himself recoiling as if he expected to be slapped. "She's right, Chall," the man grated, his voice barely louder than a whisper. "She's right, and it's past time we left."

Catham walked up, a regretful look on his face, Chall saw, but more important, a knife in his hand. Regretful, maybe, but not so regretful to keep him from killing them, it seemed, should the woman decide to give such an order. "Come on then, you lot," the man said, "best we get gone. No hope for it when the boss gets in a mood like this but to get away fast as you can and stay away as long as you can." He gave them a small, humorless smile. "Forever, in your case."

Chall looked to Priest, thinking surely that the man would put up a fight, that he would say something more, knowing well what was on the line. He didn't, though, only hung his head and meekly turned, starting toward the door. Chall followed him out of the room, and Catham continued to walk beside them as they moved toward the stairs. "I think we can find our way from here," Chall said angrily.

"Sure you can," the man agreed, "but I think it probably best if I make sure you get there. Best all around."

Chall frowned at that, but said nothing more, simply walked beside Priest as the man moved silently toward the stairs and then down them, heading in the direction of the door.

"Everything okay, boss?"

Catham paused at that, turning to regard the man sitting at the bar, the one who had been all too ready to poke Chall and Priest full of crossbow bolts a little while ago. "Everything's fine, Shem. Why don't you go on, get yourself a drink."

The man grinned. "Don't mind if I do."

Catham grunted. "Didn't figure you would," he said, then he turned back to Chall and Priest, nodding before starting toward the door.

He led them out into the street. "See ya around, Vicious. Mage."

Chall glanced at Priest, expecting him to respond, but still the man said nothing, seemingly lost in his own little world and, judging by his haunted expression it didn't strike Chall as a happy world. He sighed, turning back to the other man. "Until next time," Chall said, hoping to the gods there wouldn't be one.

The man started to go back through the door, which he still held open, then he seemed to hesitate until he finally stepped back outside and let the door close behind him. He took a moment, glancing around the street, but if it was people he was looking for Chall thought he was likely to be disappointed. As the day faded into night, shadows crept along the street, and it seemed that the denizens of the poor quarter had decided that they had better places to be right now. Not that Chall could blame them. In fact, now that it was obvious they weren't going to find any answers to their many questions regarding the Crimson Wolves, he was eager to follow their example and disappear.

Catham, though, didn't seem perturbed by the absence of anyone else. In fact, he seemed almost relieved by it, glancing around once more, peering through the window of the brothel and then, finally, rushing toward them. *"Just a sec,"* he called.

The man jogged to where they stood in the street, then paused and glanced around once more. "This woman, the one you all saw in the castle," he said in a low voice. "You really think she's one of the Wolves?"

Chall glanced at Priest, but the man still didn't seem interested in talking. Something about the woman's words had wounded him badly, that much was easy enough to see. "We think so," Chall said. "We weren't lying—about the ring, I mean."

"Right," Catham said, and the man seemed to consider, glancing around again, his neck turning this way and that so much that Chall figured he'd feel it in the morning. "Probably I shouldn't be doing this," he said quietly, talking in a rush. "Likely the boss has her reasons, but I can't see 'em. Seems to me that, with all that's been goin' on, well, we can't have too many friends, not when the ones we do have seem to be disappearin' damned near every day, and those we end up findin' are...well. Say that they're a bit worse for the wear."

"What do you mean?" Chall asked.

Another few seconds passed as the man glanced around again. "Well, the boss was right when she said that we've been havin' troubles, but she was misrepresentin' it a bit when she said that they were the normal kind. You see, I seen my share of dead men. You don't live the life I have without that. But these last few we found? The ones been croppin' up lately? Well, they're different. Sure, sometimes we lose a hireling or two to a rival gang or another lookin' to get an edge—despite common belief, we don't just kill for the joy of it." He paused, glancing at Priest then back to Chall's dubious expression. "Well. Most of us. Anyhow, whoever's been stackin' up these bodies lately, they got more motivatin' 'em than simply business concerns."

"What do you mean?" Chall asked.

"What I mean is that, whoever's doin' this, it ain't enough for them to kill—seems to me they want to make the poor bastards they get their hands on suffer first, like maybe they want to make an example out of them. Couldn't figure why they'd do that, go through all the trouble. That is, until you all showed up, talkin' about the Wolves. Ain't seen those bastards around in a long time, but them showin' up sure does explain a thing or two."

"So what are you saying?" Chall asked.

"What I'm sayin' is," the man went on, "you all want to find these Crimson Wolves? Well, so do I. There's already enough danger in this life without damned insane vigilantes lookin' to show a man what his insides look like."

"Maybe you give it up then," Chall said. "I've heard farming's peaceful."

The other man snorted. "Me, a farmer. Catham the Calloused, maybe? No, I'm old, mage, too old to be learnin' a new trade. But that don't mean I'm keen on bein' tortured to death."

"You got something you want to tell us?" Chall asked.

The man considered that, glancing around. "Best I show you, instead."

Chall grunted. "Yeah, right."

"There a problem?" the man asked.

"Yeah, it's just that I'm not too excited about the idea of following a self-confessed criminal through dark alleys toward an unknown destination."

Catham gave him a humorless smile. "You say it like that, why, it almost sounds like you don't trust me." He shrugged. "Anyway, it's up to the two of you, of course—but understand that I'm riskin' myself just by talking to you about this without the boss's go ahead. Only, I was under the impression you all came here lookin' for answers. My mistake, I guess." He turned at that, starting away.

"Wait."

The man turned back and Chall followed his gaze to Priest who had finally seemed to rouse himself from whatever trance-like state he'd been in. "We're coming," the man said.

"Bullshit we are," Chall said. "Are you out of your mind, Priest?" he said, moving closer to the man. "Look, I know something's bothering you but whatever it is, it isn't worth killing yourself over." *Or me, come to that.*

Priest glanced at him, giving him a small smile as if he heard the words despite the fact that Chall hadn't actually said them. "Catham's right, Chall," he said. "We came here for answers—this is how we're going to get them."

"I want answers, sure," Chall said, "but they aren't going to do us much good if we have to die to get them."

"What choice do we have?" Priest asked, meeting his eyes. "He has answers that we need. Or would you rather go back to the castle and pray that we find out what's happening? Pray that we do so before you or Maeve or Matt gets hurt?"

"There was a time, one not so long ago, when you would have done exactly that."

"Maybe," Priest admitted. "But what's the point of prayers, if they aren't answered?"

Chall considered that. "It seems to me that I asked you much the same question, once, long ago. Do you remember what you told me?"

Priest sighed. "Look, Chall, it doesn't—"

"You said that a man doesn't pray to be answered—he prays to be heard. But okay, Priest, alright," he said, raising his hands, "if you think the thing to do is to follow this bastard into some dark alley...well, then I trust you. Just know that I draw the line at sticking my own head in the noose."

The normal Priest might have smiled humoringly at that, but the new Priest didn't seem to have many smiles in him. Instead, he only nodded, raising his gaze to regard Catham. "Lead the way."

The man inclined his head and then, without a word, turned and started down the street. Priest started after and, a moment later, feeling very much like a man walking willingly to his own execution, for which there was a word—namely, a fool—Chall followed.

***

Chall wasn't sure where he expected the man to lead them—an alleyway full of sharp knives and sharper smiles, maybe, or perhaps some abandoned building full of shadows that might conceal an ambush.

Instead, he led them into a common room of an inn, one which was completely packed with witnesses—*people*, Chall amended—and was so bright from the dozens of lanterns placed and hung throughout that Chall didn't think there was a single shadow in the place.

"Huh," he said, unable to completely contain his surprise.

The criminal turned back, a small grin on his face. "What did you expect? That I'd be kicking you down a pit full of snakes, that sort of thing?"

"Yes," Chall said honestly.

"Sorry to disappoint, fella."

Chall frowned, letting his gaze roam the common room for anyone that looked suspicious or particularly homicidal. But the common room was full of all sorts, whores and sailors, merchants and day laborers and none of them seemed to be paying him and

Priest any undue attention. In fact, they didn't seem to be paying them any attention at all, too focused on their own conversations.

"So what were you wanting to show us?" Chall asked, still not willing to let his suspicion go.

"It's this way," the man said. "Follow me."

"Well," Chall told Priest, "in for a penny." The room was packed, and Chall and Priest were forced to work their way through the crowd. At first, Chall cringed each time he accidentally bumped someone, sure that the people in the crowd would attack the moment they passed, the way some snakes might look innocuous at first, so that their prey would ignorantly come closer. Then, when that prey was within striking distance, they would pounce, and the prey would not even have time enough to regret its mistake.

It was a feeling that held until they passed the first man, dressed like a merchant with his back to them, then the second, a sailor, laughing at some bawdy joke with several of his mates. It even held past the third, a prostitute in a low-cut dress who was currently hanging from the neck of a round-faced, red-cheeked merchant like a necklace.

But by the time they'd made their way halfway across the common room, even Chall's pessimistic belief that things most certainly would *not* work out had begun to wane. Which, of course, was when it happened.

"It," of course, being the rug being pulled out from under him. The man who pulled it, none other than Catham himself. The rug, on the other hand, was the idea—proven particularly false in that moment—that the men crowding the room did not want to kill him. Catham, who'd they'd been following suddenly paused, waving his hand in the air as he turned back to them. "Now," he said.

Suddenly the entire room, which had up to that point been surprisingly still and calm, erupted into motion as almost every person turned toward them, producing weapons of varying shapes, sizes, and types but all of which shared one similarity—they could kill. A quick, panicked glance around the room, though, showed Chall that he'd been wrong about one thing. It wasn't *almost* every person in the common room that had risen and withdrawn a weapon with the obvious intent of killing him and Priest. Instead, it was every. Single. One.

"Shit," Chall hissed.

"What are you doing, Catham?" Priest asked, his voice having some emotion in it for the first time since they'd left the brothel.

The man sighed. "Sorry, Vicious," he said. "I really am. But you know how it is, only doing what I have to." He shook his head as if in regret. "It's a shame, but it seems to me that's about all I do."

"And all this time…I thought we were…"

"Friends?" Catham asked. "Oh, we were, Vicious. I s'pose that if I'd got news that you'd died and there was to be a funeral, well, I'd be there, with eyes wet as anybody's. Only, I didn't make it this far in life by getting hung up on things like friendship." He glanced around at the dozens of people in the room then back to Priest. "The Boss wants you dead, Priest, you and your friend here, and if it's a decision between pleasing the Boss or pleasing you, well, that's not really a decision at all."

Chall didn't bother telling Priest, "I told you so." Mostly because doing so would not stop all the knives—the many, many knives—about the room from ruining his day and making a mess of his shirt. Instead, he looked at Catham who was watching the two of them with a look of regret on his face—not that Chall thought that regret was going to do anything to save them. "Funny," Chall said, "but I didn't hear her tell you to kill us. In fact, I got the distinct feeling we were only meant to leave. You know, based on the fact that she told us to leave."

An expression of what might have been panic flashed across the man's face but was gone in another moment as he smiled dryly. "Yeah, the boss can be fickle sometimes." He gave a soft laugh. "Sometimes, I almost think she just pulls her orders out of a hat."

"Yeah," Chall said, an idea creeping into his mind, "or someone else does."

The man said nothing to that, only backed away from them through the crowd. "Well, best get it done quick," he told the room at large. "The boss insisted on it."

The boss, of course, hadn't done any such thing, but then somehow Chall didn't think he and Priest were in a position to convince the rest of the people in the common room of as much, not after they'd all gotten so excited about the prospect of getting to murder someone, that was.

"Alright," he muttered as he backed up a step to where Priest stood, his eyes not leaving the crowd of would-be and likely already-were murderers in the room as they edged closer. "What's the plan?" he asked.

The man, though, said nothing, and he turned to see Priest studying the people around them with a resigned expression on his face. "Well?" Chall pressed.

The man slowly turned to him. "I'm sorry, Challadius," he said softly in a voice almost too low to hear.

"What?" Chall asked, deciding that in all the time they'd traveled together, with all the myriad of threats they'd faced, he had never heard the man sound so resigned, so...hopeless.

"It's over, Chall," the man said, holding his gaze. "It's over, and I find that part of me, perhaps the largest part, is glad. After all, the dead do not hurt any longer, do not feel the pain of their world, those things which they had believed in their entire life cracking apart like some poor façade. It is over. Finally, it is over, and I am glad."

"Glad?" Chall asked, breathless, his voice almost too low even for him to hear. "*Glad?*" Louder this time, louder as his disbelief and his fear at seeing the normally solid man so shaken was overcome by something else entirely. Anger. "*Glad?*" he said a third time, only he did not say it, not really. Instead, the word erupted out of him in a furious yell. "You listen to me, *Priest,*" he said, "I did not come all this way, live the life I have and finally find the woman I love just to die because you want to *pout.*" Priest opened his mouth as if he meant to speak, but Chall shot up his hand, silencing him. "I know you're going through something right now and later, maybe I'll even give a shit. But now, Priest, I need you to be the man who I became friends with, the man who used to lecture me about how everything was going to work out. And if you can't be that man, then you damned well better pretend, do you understand?"

Priest watched him with wide eyes for a moment then finally nodded. "I...do. And I'm sorry, Chall. Everything...that is, everything will surely work out."

"That's better," Chall said. "Now," he went on, glancing around at the people creeping closer, in no hurry and why would they be? After all, there were dozens of them against two men, and as angry as he was, Chall knew that anger never saved a man. Unless, of course, that man was Prince Bernard, the Crimson Prince, but then Bernard was miles and miles away, too far to be of any help to them and no doubt with more than enough problems of his own to deal with. He looked back to Priest, preparing to ask the man *how* exactly he thought things might work out, but didn't bother, for he could see on the man's face that he had no more of an idea than Chall himself.

So Chall did the only thing he could do—he gritted his teeth, his hands knotting into fists, and waited for his end to come, the one consolation was that he would not have to wait long.

They both turned, trying to keep their eyes on all the people moving toward them, and then they were back-to-back.

"What of your illusions?" Priest asked quietly.

"Not a chance," Chall said. "Illusions count on people not paying attention, and they're all looking right at us. Besides...the truth is I wasted a lot of my strength back there at the brothel, putting on that show."

"A very impressive show," Priest said without looking at him.

"Thanks."

"Very well," Priest said, lifting his hands to his sides, each of which, Chall saw when he glanced back, held a knife. "Good luck, Challadius."

"Yeah," Chall said, unable to manage anything more past his dry throat.

He looked around, trying to find the man, Catham, telling himself that if the opportunity presented itself before he was murdered terribly, he would make the bastard pay. He caught sight of him working his way toward the door, his back turned, and Chall abandoned that small hope of revenge. The man might only have been fifteen or twenty feet away, but considering that dozens of homicidal—and, more importantly, *armed*—men and women separated the two of them it might as well have been a mile.

"I'm sorry, Mae," Chall whispered as he watched the mob covering the last feet that separated them. "I'm sorry."

But then, just when he thought it was going to begin in earnest, someone spoke.

"*Stop,*" a voice said.

Only a single word. Not yelled but spoken in an almost conversational tone. Yet, it somehow seemed to strike the room, to strike Chall himself, like lightning, as if a god had come into the room and issued an order which could only be obeyed. Chall felt as if some invisible wave of force swept over him, swept *through* him, and based on the way those surrounding him and Priest seemed to stagger, blinking and looking around confused, it wasn't just him that had felt it.

A single word, but it had not just seemed like a word, nor a request. Instead, it had seemed, had *felt* like a command, one that was impossible to ignore, and so powerful was the command that Chall realized, when he was forced to gasp for breath, that he had even stopped breathing in response to it.

"*Let me through,*" the voice said, calm, not raised, but with what almost sounded like an undercurrent of strain beneath it.

Then, in response to the command, the mob began to separate, opening up an avenue in their midst, one through which a single man walked.

Chall didn't know what he'd been expecting—some giant behemoth whose mere voice was enough to scare the other would-be murderers into compliance, perhaps. Maybe a golden shining god with eyes like fire that radiated power and menace.

But whoever he had expected, he couldn't have been further from the truth. For the man who was currently walking toward them, shuffling, really, his shoulders slightly bent as if he toiled beneath some great, invisible weight, was not a massive street tough nor a deity. In fact, he looked like nothing so much as a carriage driver. Which, of course, was exactly what he was.

"*Ned?*" Chall asked, the word exploding out of his mouth in a mixture of disbelief and confusion.

As he drew closer, the carriage driver who Chall had last seen at his relatively modest home with his wife—who, if Maeve hadn't been pulling Chall's leg, was actually an assassin—gave him a strained smile. "Howdy, fellas," the man said. "Makin' some new friends, are we?"

"What...what are you doing here?" Chall asked, glancing at Priest to see that the man was staring at the carriage driver with wide eyes, clearly as confused as he was.

Ned winced. "Right, well, I can explain that, but I think maybe it's better if we hold on it. You know, at least 'til we're not in danger of being beaten to death by a mob of criminals. They won't remain compelled for long."

Chall frowned. Something about that word "compelled" sounded vaguely familiar, as if he'd heard it used in a similar context many years ago. Still, he didn't spend much time thinking on it—instead, he glanced around the room and saw that the men and women surrounding them looked almost as if they'd fallen asleep. But even as he had the thought, he noticed several had begun to rouse, blinking and yawning and staring around themselves with confused expressions as if they had no idea where they were or how they'd come to be there. Whatever else Ned was then, he didn't seem to be lying about the fact that whatever he'd done to the crowd was beginning to wear off. "Lead the way," Chall said.

The carriage driver nodded and, without another word, turned and headed for the door. It took less than a minute for them to reach it, but it might well have taken an eternity as far as Chall was concerned. An eternity where they walked past dozens of sleepers, like a rabbit crossing a field in which lions lurked. Most of them deep in slumber for now, but should they wake, there would be no escaping them. An eternity of tensing at each sound, bathed in a cold sweat, too scared hardly even to breathe for the certainty that doing so would break whatever spell had fallen upon them.

But then, part of him—the very small part that wasn't cowering in terror in the corner of his mind—thought, *it didn't fall upon them, did it? Instead, it had been woven.* And the man walking in front of him, a man who he had taken for nothing more than a carriage driver, had been the one who weaved it.

Despite Chall's growing certainty to the contrary, they did reach the door. Ned turned back to them, an even more strained expression on his face, and Chall saw that he was covered in sweat. Only, he did not think the man's perspiration was caused by fear. Instead, he looked tired, exhausted, really, as if he had just run a mile at a sprint. His chest tremored with rapid breaths, and there was a decidedly more pronounced hunch to his shoulders. "Best hurry now," the man said through gritted teeth, and Chall frowned, thinking he recognized that sort of exhaustion, thinking maybe he'd felt it himself on more than one occasion.

"How are you doing this?" The question didn't come from Chall, though he'd been thinking it. Instead, it came from Priest, and they both turned to see the man watching the carriage driver with eyes narrowed with suspicion. The man's tone was full of menace, and Chall found his eyes drawn to Priest's hands and, more particularly, to the knives he still held from when he'd drawn them to fight the mob.

"There's no time to explain, honestly," Ned rasped, sounding as if whatever invisible weight he was holding up was crushing him.

"Make time," Priest growled.

"Listen, Priest," Chall said, "I think we ought to just trust him for now."

Priest blinked, turning to him. "Wasn't it you who told me that you can't be betrayed if you never trust anyone in the first place?"

"Yeah, maybe it was," Chall said, "but if Mae was here I'd know what she'd say. She'd say you got to trust somebody sometime."

Priest watched him for a moment then gave him a slow, small smile. "Lady Maeve is wise."

"Yeah, she is."

Priest nodded, turning back to the carriage driver. "Lead the way."

Ned, who looked in danger of collapsing any moment, gave an exhausted nod. "Go on through the door first, the two of you...I'll...follow."

Chall felt his own suspicion rouse at that. What was to say that there weren't several crossbowmen waiting right outside the door, ready to finish what the mob had started? But then, that didn't make sense, did it? After all, the mob had been plenty prepared to finish what it had started without any help, at least until Ned had shown up and...well, done whatever it was that he had done. "Come on," he told Priest, and then he was moving through the door.

It might not have been logical for there to be several crossbowmen waiting outside the tavern to fill them full of holes, but that didn't keep Chall from tensing in expectation of exactly that when he stepped out into the street. Neither did it keep him from *remaining* tensed for the few seconds it took him to look around and see that the street was empty. Night had fallen in truth while they had been busy at the task of preparing to be murdered, but enough light spilled out of the windows and doorway of the tavern common room to show him that much, at least.

Priest followed him and, a moment later, Ned stumbled out, nearly falling and only just managing to catch himself on the open doorway. The man's face was pale, lined with exhaustion, and he closed the door behind them.

"That's...all," he panted, staggering toward them. Chall stepped forward to help the man—who looked like he might give falling down another shot any moment—but Priest beat him to it, draping one of the man's arms over his shoulders. Chall watched this, a small smile coming to his face. Once, and not very long ago, he would have taken that sort of instinctive kindness for granted, at least when it came from Priest, but over the last few hours, few days, he had come to question some of that. It was good, then, to see that whatever change had occurred in Priest, or, perhaps *was* occurring, the man he had been, Chall's friend, was still there. Buried beneath a giant pile of doubts and fears and uncertainties, perhaps, but there nonetheless.

"That's...all I've got," the carriage driver said, sounding barely conscious.

No sooner had the man said the words than Chall begin to hear confused voices from inside the tavern, and it did not take him much effort to imagine the nearly fifty people all seeming to come out of a trance at once. Confused, unnerved, but in moments they would begin to wonder where the two men they'd meant to murder had gotten off to, and it wouldn't take them long after that before they decided they'd best go have a look.

"What's the plan now?" he asked Ned.

The carriage driver raised his head from where it had been hanging, his arm around Priest's shoulders seeming to be the only thing keeping him upright. "A bit...out of practice, I'm afraid," he said. "Now...now we run."

There was an angry shout from inside the tavern as one of the men there no doubt realized that their quarry had escaped—at least temporarily. Chall swallowed hard. "You heard him," he told Priest. "I think we may have overstayed our welcome."

Then they were running.

Or, at least, trying to.

Priest might have still been the man Chall had always known, and while that man was dangerous and wise, deadly and kind all at once, he was not possessed of Prince Bernard's strength. So he could not simply lift the nearly unconscious carriage driver as if it were nothing and barrel down the road with him.

Instead, they were forced to move with one of Ned's arms draped over each of their shoulders as they proceeded down the road in a sort of shuffling, shambling half-jog, far slower than Chall would have liked. But then, they could have been on the back of a horse-drawn carriage, careening down the streets at break-neck pace and, considering what waited within the tavern, at least for the moment, Chall still thought he would have considered it too slow.

Either way, they had not traveled far enough away from the tavern that he wasn't able to hear the sound of its door being thrown open and a mob of angry would-be murderers rushing into the street.

He and the others hadn't gotten off the road yet, for they had not come across an alley entrance, and Chall looked back to see dozens of people standing in the circle of light spilling out of the tavern, scanning the street around them.

Still, he thought they were okay, thought that the darkness would serve to hide them well enough as they made good their escape. But then he saw one man turn, peering into the darkness directly at them. Either the bastard had the best eyesight of anyone Chall had ever met, or perhaps he got lucky at some brief shift of moonlight, some reflection off of the gods alone knew what. In the end, it didn't really matter.

What *did* matter was the man stabbed his finger directly at where they were standing. "*There!*" he shouted.

Those others in the street stopped their frustrated looking and spun, following the man's gesture with their eyes. Then, a moment later, they weren't just following it with their eyes at all but were rushing down the street, all too eager to resume what they'd begun in the tavern.

Chall and Priest shared a meaningful—*I don't want to get stabbed, what about you?*—glance, and then they were running again, or at least as close to it as they could manage. The sounds of angry shouting grew louder as more and more of the mob closed the distance separating them, catching sight of their quarry and practically howling like wolves on the hunt as they chased down their prey.

Chall panted and gasped and strained as they ran, for it was hard enough to lug his own weight around, let alone the carriage driver's added—if considerably less in comparison—weight. They came upon an alleyway entrance on Chall's right, and they didn't need to talk about it considering that their other option was to remain in line of sight of the onrushing mob.

They took the alley fast, turning the corner, and Chall stopped. "They'll be here any moment," he panted, "get against the wall, both of you."

"There's no use," Ned panted. "They'll see—couldn't help but to see. Look," he went on, "you two get out of here. While you can. With any luck, you'll manage to get enough distance while they...well. While I keep 'em distracted."

Chall stared at the man then shook his head, giving a snort. "Fire and salt but you mean that, don't you?"

"Ain't no time for talkin'," Ned said, "time for runnin'. Someone has to stay, that's all, and me bein' tired as I am, I ain't got no runnin' left in me. Stayin', though, well, I figure I can do that well enough. Now, you two get on while you still can."

Chall sighed, thinking that it really wasn't an easy thing to be a selfish bastard surrounded by would-be heroes. Not easy at all. "Just shut up and do as I say," he said. "You're not the only one who knows a trick or two."

The carriage driver met his gaze for a moment then finally gave a nod, allowing himself to be led to the alley wall. Not that he would have had much to say about it either way—the man didn't look like he could have stood up to a kitten just then.

Chall glanced out of the alley, saw that the mob was closer now—terrifyingly close. He judged that in another minute, maybe less, they'd be at the alley mouth, and then the festivities would start in earnest. Unless, that was, Chall had something to say about it.

He hurried back to the two men, pressing his back up against the wall beside them.

"Can you do it?" Priest asked.

"We'll know pretty quickly if I can't," Chall snapped. "This one's going to be close. Both of you, keep your mouths shut, don't even so much as breathe. And whatever you do, don't you *dare* move."

He closed his eyes then, calling upon his gift as he had so many times before, wishing, as he had on those many other occasions, that the gods had seen fit to gift him with some other magic. Fire, maybe. Being able to shoot jets of flame from his hands would have certainly changed things. But then, he supposed the benefit about illusions was that, when compared to charred, smoking corpses, there was far less clean up.

Focus, he told himself. *Focus or you and your friends die.* Which, as it turned out, wasn't a great way to focus at all. Still, he did his best, calling on his gift, struggling to calm his heart—which felt like it had taken a personal dislike to the inside of his chest and meant to beat its way out—and to stop doing a particularly convincing impersonation of a man hyperventilating.

An empty alley, he told himself, *that and nothing more. There is no one here, certainly not three men pressed against the wall as if they mean to burrow their way into it. An empty alley. It's all there is. All there could be.* He was still trying to convince himself of that, with the help of his gift, when the first of the mob turned the corner, shouting in expectation of seeing his prey. At least, Chall hoped it was only expectation. In the grips of the illusion as he was, his eyes were tightly squeezed shut as he focused on holding together the many fine strands which made up the spell.

He could not spare even the slight bit of focus it would take to open his eyes to check and see if the man had seen them. Anyway, he figured that if he had, Chall would know soon enough without any need to open his eyes at all. So he did the only thing he could do, he stood there, his eyes closed, focusing on his gift, hoping that it would not choose this time to fail him, hoping that he would make it out of this alleyway, that they all would, but hoping, most of all, that he would see Maeve again.

He listened to the sounds of thudding footsteps, dozens of them, moving past him, and he was just beginning to think they were in the clear when something struck his foot, and he heard a man's voice crying out in surprise. His concentration broke then, and he opened his eyes in time to catch sight of the man who had tripped over his foot as he sailed through the air, striking the cobbles of the alley a moment later with a grunt of pain.

Chall shot a quick glance down the alley, saw that the mob was only slightly over halfway down it. All it would take was for the man to notice them and give a shout and he and his companions would regret it—though not for long.

Chall scrambled to gather up his concentration, feeling like a man trying to catch leaves blown about in a high wind. Then, the man began to turn back to see what had tripped him, and Chall was out of time. He used what concentration he'd managed to get, focusing on rebuilding the illusion, cobbling it together. It wasn't his best work, that much was obvious by the way the man, on his hands and knees now, was frowning at the wall, and Chall redoubled his efforts, gritting his teeth so hard he thought they might break.

Slowly, the man blinked, as if he'd just woken from a dream then rose, picking up the wicked-looking knife he'd dropped when he fell then hurrying after his companions. Chall held onto the illusion, straining against it as it wriggled and squirmed in his grasp like dozens of snakes trying to break free of his grip. He continued to hold onto it until the mob, including their delayed companion, reached the end of the alley and then split, some heading in one direction, some in the other.

Then he heaved out the breath he'd been holding, and the illusion broke apart.

"Well done, Challadius," Priest said, putting a hand on his shoulder. "Are you alright?"

"Well, I'm still unstabbed, so I don't suppose I can complain too much," Chall panted, but the truth was that the man's simple compliment felt good. Once again, he considered that people often didn't know how much they came to rely on certain things, certain people, until they were forced to confront their absence. "Anyway...what do we do now? Head back to the castle?"

Priest shook his head. "No. That would not do. They will be out searching for a while, I think, and the poor district of New Daltenia has plenty of eyes to see, plenty of ears to hear, ones who are paid well to do it. No, should we try to make it out now, we will be marked, and those after our blood will be notified of our whereabouts. We would never make it back to the castle. I doubt very seriously if we would ever even make it out of the poor district."

"So...so what do we do, then?"

Priest frowned. "We need a place to stay, to wait until they've given up the search." The man glanced at Chall who grunted.

"Don't look at me, Priest. I have no idea of any place we could go. I don't spend a lot of time in the poor district around criminals. In fact, I make it a habit to do my absolute best to avoid it. What of you? You're the one who used to call this place home."

"Things change," Priest said. "And in the poor district, they change quickest of all. Still, I suppose there are one or two places we could try, but—"

"Might be I know a place."

They both turned to regard the carriage driver, Ned, who had a reluctant frown on his face. "Might be?" Chall asked.

"Fine," the man said, wincing. "I know a place, though I don't know that I'd like to use it..."

"No?" Chall asked. "And what about being butchered by a mob of criminals? Think you'd like that?"

Ned sighed. "Alright. Follow me—it's not far."

Fire and salt I hope not, Chall thought. He was exhausted—calling on his gift so abruptly and with so much force, not to mention twice in less than an hour, had a way of doing that. Besides which he didn't think he had it in him to wander around the poor district for long, not with those mobs of people out there looking to kill them. "Lead on," Chall said, "anywhere's better than here."

A statement he came to regret very quickly.

The carriage driver led them deeper into the poor district, stopping on a deserted street, one that looked as if it had been abandoned for years. Priest and Chall shared a frown. "So, where's this place?" Chall asked.

"Just there," Ned said, gesturing to the few standing remnants of a building that looked to have burned down long ago. Only, it wasn't the burnt building that bothered Chall so much as some half-forgotten memory tickling at his mind. One that he couldn't place. At least, that was, until Priest spoke.

"The Plague Church," his companion said in a voice little more than a whisper. "You can't be serious."

"Shit," Chall said, finding himself backing away from the distant building, watching it like it was some animal that might pounce. He remembered this place now. Remembered it from when New Daltenia had still been a young city, remembered it because of the plague. They had brought it with them from the ships, a plague brought on by rats and malnutrition. They had thought it was gone only to discover, several years later, that there was another outbreak in the poor district of the city. Those unfortunate souls who caught it were brought to what came to be known as the Plague Church, where they were seen to by two priests, both of whom contracted the plague while helping their charges to die with as much dignity and as little pain as possible. It was the best they could do for there had been no cure found for the plague.

None, that was, save for fire. So after the patients and the priests succumbed, the princes had ordered the building burned to clean out any vestiges of the plague lest it take root in the populace of New Daltenia. Yet despite this precaution, no one had felt safe in rebuilding on that spot in the years since, and few were those who even dared to so much as visit this part of the poor district. Evidence of that could be seen in the dust covering the street cobbles and surrounding buildings, all of which were abandoned, for those who had lived in them had long since moved to some other part of the city.

"You can't mean that this hideout of yours is here," Chall said, his voice little more than a whisper. "Look, I don't want to be murdered by a mob of angry criminals, it's true, but neither am I all that excited by the prospect of contracting the plague. I heard the stories, and I think, taken together, I'd rather the mob than that."

"Funny," Ned said, looking at him, "you being an illusionist, I figured you'd recognize it better than anybody."

"Recognize what?" Priest asked.

The carriage driver glanced at him. "Why that things aren't always as they seem, of course. Come on—you'll be safe enough, though if we hang around in the open much longer I can't promise you that."

The man turned and walked toward the burned building, and Chall frowned. "He's right," he told Priest, "things aren't always as they seem. But then…neither are people."

He didn't much like the idea of walking into a place that everyone had been avoiding like…well, like the plague for the last twenty years or so. Particularly when the last people who had spent any significant amount of time there—at least so far as anyone knew—were all corpses. Didn't give a man much comfort to discover that those who had walked a path similar to his own before him were all dead and rotting in the ground. But then, nothing since he'd woken up to an assassin shooting a crossbow at him had felt particularly comforting so why change now?

"Seems pretty stupid to follow him," he remarked.

"Yes," Priest said. "Yes it does."

Chall nodded, content at least to know that they were both in agreement on that much of it. "Well," he said after a moment. "After you."

They were walking then, moving farther and farther toward the burned-out wreckage, their boots leaving indentations in the dust covering the lane so that anyone, should they take it in mind to follow them, would have no difficulty in retracing their steps. Not that anyone was likely to follow them. It just didn't stand to reason that there would be more than three fools of such magnitude in the city at the same time, not even with the tens of thousands occupying it.

As they drew closer to the burned-out husk of the church Chall was able to see even more clearly the degree of devastation that the flames had wrought, and he began to think that surely the carriage driver must have gotten his hideouts confused. There was nothing left among the rubble in which a child might have hidden, let alone three grown men and one of those, he was ashamed to say, far fatter than he once had been. It would be the crown on a mostly unfortunate, unlucky life, he thought, to accidentally walk willingly—in so much as he could be said to have done anything willingly since waking—into a plague-infested ruin and there find, surprisingly only to him, his doom.

He thought about saying as much, asking the man if he were sure this was the place, but he told himself that no one living in New Daltenia hadn't heard of the Plague Church before. The man knew where they were, *had* to know, and so he would have known had he been mistaken. At least, Chall hoped. Anyway, he wasn't sure he could have gotten the words out even if he'd wanted to. It was all he could do to put one foot in front of the other and only slightly hyperventilate as his breath came in shallow, ragged pulls.

He told himself he was being ridiculous. The only thing that kept the citizens of New Daltenia from building here was superstition, that was all. It wasn't as if the plague was some beast, lurking in the darkness of those crumbled doorways or by the half-broken altar, cracked by the heat of the flames. A beast that was only biding its time, waiting for some fool—some fat, illusionist fool—to stumble into its path. No, the plague was not that, not alive and so not possessed of that special brand of cruelty that only the living could really understand.

The plague was gone, had been gone for years. It could not hurt them. He was safe, or at least as safe as a man being hunted by a mob of killers could be. And the scratch he felt in his throat, the sniffle he suddenly had, was no more than nerves. Just his imagination. And the uncomfortable heat spreading through him, the cold sweat suddenly covering him, just reactions to his fears. His *unfounded* fears.

"Uh...it's a nice place you got here, Ned," Chall said as he followed the other two men through one of the crumbling doorways. "Only...I'm not sure if it's going to serve our purposes, you know, seein's as there's nowhere to hide. On account of it all being burned down. You know, on account of it being infested with the plague."

Ned paused, standing above the half-broken altar, and glanced back at Chall. "You really are a glass half empty sort of guy, aren't you, Challadius?"

Chall opened his mouth, preparing to utter a scathing remark—just waiting on his brain to think of it—when Priest spoke. "It was a fine altar," he said, sounding impressed.

Chall frowned, glancing at the altar. All he saw was stone, particularly burned, particularly scorched stone that was cracked.

Still, looking closer, he thought that Priest was right. The stone seemed to have been stylized, with whirls carved into it.

"Thanks," Ned said, "it was a long time in the doing."

Chall frowned, sharing a confused look with Priest at that. "Wait a minute, do you mean to say you were the one that made it?"

The carriage driver knelt at the altar then glanced back at him, raising an eyebrow. "Well. A man has to have his hobbies, doesn't he?"

Chall was still trying to figure out a response to that when the man reached a hand underneath the collar of his tunic, retrieving a gold band. Chall paid little attention to the necklace itself, though, for he was too busy staring agape at what depended from it. Namely, a ring. But not just any ring. Instead, this was a ring that he had last seen on the hand of a woman who had turned out to be a murderer. A ring that marked someone as a member of the Crimson Wolves.

Before he could do more than stare—and Priest breathe in a sharp hiss of breath—Ned took hold of the ring and placed it into a small, almost imperceptible indention in the cracked altar. At first, nothing happened, and Chall was just about to ask what the man was doing when, suddenly, there was a quiet, *grating* sound beneath their feet. Suddenly, the altar, cracked rubble and all slid away to reveal an open trap door and a ladder leading down into the darkness.

"Huh," Ned said, sounding pleasantly surprised.

"What?" Chall asked. "You didn't know it was going to do that?"

"Well, it used to," Ned said, "but then, it's been twenty years. My knees damned sure don't work as well as they once did; I figured it was too much to hope that this would."

"Why do you have that?" Priest demanded, jabbing a finger at the ring hanging from Ned's throat, his tone sharp, cutting. "Did you join the Crimson Wolves?"

"Join them?" Ned asked. "I created them."

Chall blinked at that, turning to look at Priest who was watching the man, his expression unreadable. "You created them," Priest said flatly.

"Well. Sort of. We need to talk," Ned said. "But we'd best do it down there." He paused, gesturing to the open trapdoor and the ladder leading into the darkness. "We're not safe here."

"Oh, I don't feel safe," Chall said. "Though can't say as I feel much better about the idea of following the man who claims to have created the Crimson Wolves down a ladder into darkness."

Ned gave a small shrug, flashing a smile. "S'pose you can stay up here, take your chances with the mob. You'll have to forgive me if I don't join you. I'm sort of partial to havin' all my pieces in their proper places."

Then before Chall or Priest could say anything more, the man climbed into the trap door and proceeded down the ladder, into the darkness. Chall glanced over at his companion but this time Priest did not turn to regard him, nor did he hesitate before moving toward the ladder, an angry set to his shoulders as he followed the carriage driver—if he even *was* a carriage driver.

Chall, in that brief moment in which he watched his companion set off after the carriage driver who was also apparently the creator of the Crimson Wolves—a violent group of vigilantes from everything he'd learned—took a second to consider the course of his life. It sometimes seemed to him that he spent his life like a man tossing a dagger into the air, hoping and praying that it would land on him handle first and, finding that he was lucky enough that it had, only tossing it into the air again. Sure, he'd been lucky so far, luckier than any man had a right to expect. But sooner or later, that dagger, his *life* was going to come down sharp end first, and he would not even be in a position to say that its landing was unfair. Going down the ladder, that felt a lot like tossing the dagger again. The problem, though, was that so did staying in the church or trying to escape the poor district. So then, if a man's choice led him to blood no matter what, Chall supposed the only real option was to choose the one that at least gave him company.

After all, misery loved little else as much. And so, with that thought in mind, he followed the two men down the ladder, into the unknown, and listened to the dagger whirl in the air overhead.

CHAPTER TEN

"You've got to be kidding me," Maeve said.

"No, Lady Maeve," Emille said quietly, "I am not. From here on, everything will be in deadly earnest. Are you sure you want to do this?"

Maeve glanced at the woman, then back to the large building in front of them. It made sense, in a way. After all, the building was certainly large enough to fit all the members of the Guild, even, she suspected, should they all choose to forego their own lodgings and stay there, something few did. It was no surprise, perhaps, that people didn't generally find nights spent among assassins all that restful. Still, it would be a building plenty large enough to house any novices and assassins in training that were taken on while they went through the Guild's lessons.

Maeve did not envy them that, for she had gone through the lessons herself and still had the scars to prove it. Those who spent their lives practicing and teaching the assassins' art were not known for their trust, but neither were they known for their mercy or compassion. A hard place, a sharp one, and one which, should those who came to stay within it survive it, would make them hard and sharp as well, would make of them weapons. Weapons that the Guild might wield in whatever way it saw fit. That loss of identity, that expectation of unflinching, unquestioning loyalty, was the reason why Maeve had left the

Guild in the first place, so many years ago. She had left, but she had felt no ill will toward the Guild, at least not at the time. Now, though, she found that she had ill will in abundance. For somewhere within that building in front of her, was a man or a woman who had listened to a certain contract, and someone else who had assigned that contract to the assassin who had tried to kill her and Chall.

Not that anyone passing by would have thought as much. Assassins, after all, were known for their subtlety, and what subtlety they possessed they owed in no small part to the Guild. The Guild which, at least for the last several years if Emille were to be believed, had foregone dark alleyways and abandoned buildings, choosing instead to hide in plain sight. And not just to hide but to do so in the guise of, according to the sign hanging from the front entrance, *Sir Chavoy's Academy of the Healing Arts.*

Maeve shook her head, staring at it. "Cheeky bastards," she muttered.

"What's that, Lady?" Emille asked.

Maeve turned to the woman. "I said, lead on, Emille. When you're ready."

The woman watched her for a moment then nodded. "Very well—this way. Only know, Maeve, that once we go farther, you will not be able to change your mind."

"I do not intend to."

Emille gave another nod then turned and started toward the gate where the sign marking the expansive, multi-storied building as a school for healers swung in the wind. They stepped through the wrought-iron gate and Emille began leading her down a cobbled walkway. On either side of the walkway were ornate, lavish gardens featuring bushes and flowers of every shape and size and color. And among those bushes and flowerbeds were hunched men and women of various ages, busy at tending to the growths, keeping the weeds out and making sure that the gardens remained beautiful. And that, at least, they did well, for the gardens were some of the finest Maeve had ever seen—yet she did not let their beauty distract her from her purpose. After all, she had once been introduced to a kind of berry, by this same Guild, no less, that was a beautiful, arresting shade of pink and that was also possessed of an incredibly potent poison, one that might kill a man or woman who was unfortunate or foolish enough to ingest it within hours.

Often, the most beautiful things of the world, she knew, were also the deadliest. So she had been taught many years ago, and nothing that she had seen or heard over the years had dissuaded her of that simple fact.

"Apprentices and novice initiates," Emille said in explanation of the question Maeve had not asked. "They are brought here, taught to care for the plants, for it is believed that much of what they learn in the doing of it will serve them in...other areas of their lives."

"Oh?" Maeve asked, but the truth was she was only half-listening. Instead, she was focused on the faces of those men and women hunched at their labors—some little more than children, in truth. But though she looked at them, she did not see them. Instead, she saw the face of another, a woman who came to the Known Lands with nothing, no husband, no child, no hope. And that woman, pitiful and wretched as she had been, had eventually found herself much like these, kneeling among the thorns and the briars, searching, questing in the dirt with her hands, not looking for anything so much as purpose. As hope. Hope that if things would not be okay then they would at least be better, in time. Bearable.

They continued down the cobbled path, Maeve noting older, authoritative figures of men and women standing over the novices and apprentices, watching their movements with careful eyes, perpetual scowls seeming to adorn each of their faces as if they were not impressed by what they saw, as if they were *never* particularly impressed.

Finally they reached the door, and Maeve was surprised, at least for a moment, to see that no guards had been posted. But then, after she considered it, she supposed it made sense. After all, the Guild was impersonating a healer's school and what school employed guardsmen at its gates? No, their presence would have caused far more problems than they solved. Besides, it was not as if those inside needed protecting from the world—far more likely, the world needed protecting from them.

Inside, the entrance to the building was large and open with several busts standing against either side of the room—busts supposedly honoring some of history's best healers and creators of medicine. There were paintings as well, ones celebrating healers and the healer's art as a noble one. That in itself was not what made Maeve's stomach feel sour—after all, healing *was* a noble art. Instead, it was the idea that all of it, the decorations, the paintings and tapestries, was no more than a disguise the Guild wore, the same way that a woman might wear face paint to cover up the worst of her flaws or a short man platformed boots to appear taller.

It was a lie. But she realized as she stared around her that even *that* wasn't what really bothered her. What bothered her wasn't that it was just a lie—it was that it was a very, very good one. Here, then, was the most dangerous thing about the Guild and its members. It was not that they were trained from a young age to kill—although they were. Neither was it even the fact that, from that young age, the men and women who trained here were indoctrinated by those at the top. Instead, what bothered Maeve the most was how damned *good* they were at hiding themselves. Much had been said about Prince Bernard, the Crimson Prince, before, during, and after the Fey War, and much of it deservedly. But say this much for the man: he did not try to hide what he was and anyone, stepping toward him with violence on their mind understood the danger, knew that they were engaging in combat with a lion.

The Guild, though, was not so honest. Instead, they disguised themselves as rabbits, as meek little creatures until one drew close enough to pet them—and then they pounced.

"This way," Emille said, drawing Maeve's attention, and she followed the woman across the room toward a large oaken desk behind which a middle-aged woman sat, her hair pulled back into a tight, severe bun, brown hair shot through with gray. She sat with a rigid back, her hands clasped over each other on the desk, looking like nothing so much as the tutor who was never satisfied with her charge's work. Maeve wondered, as they approached the desk, how the woman managed an expression that somehow conveyed boredom, annoyance, and disappointment with the world in general all at the same time. Likely, she practiced it at home while dreaming about the pupils she could make squirm and fidget beneath the weight of her gaze. Say what you would about the Guild, but people didn't tend to end up there because they were known for being overly friendly.

"Ah," the woman said in a tone that lacked any emotion whatsoever, "Instructor Emille. It has been some time since you have graced our presence. Do you have a class to teach today?"

"No, no class," Emille said. "I've come to speak with the Headmistress."

Maeve wouldn't have thought it possible, but the woman sitting behind the desk seemed to grow even colder at that, her disapproval reaching new, no doubt dreamt of heights as she let her gaze travel up and down Emille as if this were the first time she had seen her. "Do you have an appointment?" she asked with the frosty air of someone issuing a challenge to the death.

Emille winced. "No, I don't, but it will only take a mi—"

The woman sniffed. "The Headmistress, Lady Emille, is a very, very busy woman as you well know. It is, after all, thanks to her and her efforts that this academy runs as efficiently and as effectively as it does. She does not have time in her schedule to attend the whims of instructors who should know better than to expect an immediate audience with a woman of her stature. Indeed, such an instructor should feel grateful that her Headmistress accepts audiences at all and should not think, in her arrogance, to demand an immediate meeting with so important a personage."

"I wasn't demanding, of course," Emille said, "only, it is important that I speak to her...about, well, regarding a particular...class."

Maeve was beginning to think that "class" did not mean a class at all but instead meant contract. The woman sitting behind the desk frowned, turning to regard Maeve, her eyes moving up and down her, an expression on her face that showed she was not impressed. Not that Maeve could blame her—she was, after all, many years removed from the woman who had once been celebrated as the greatest beauty in the world.

"'We,' I should think you mean, Instructor Emille," the woman said.

Emille glanced at Maeve, clearly confused, before turning back to the woman. "I'm...sorry?"

"You said '*I*' would like to talk to the Headmistress. I can only assume, considering the fact that you are accompanied by another, that what you *meant* to say was '*we.*'"

Emille made a visible effort to maintain her patience, taking a slow breath and giving a small shake of her head. "Fine, sorry. *We* then. Not that it matters."

"Oh, but it matters a great deal, Instructor Emille," the woman said, giving her a sharp smile with no humor in it, no surprise that as Maeve didn't think the woman had any humor in her entire body. Likely if she found herself smiling, she'd rush to the nearest healer to discover the nature of the spasm twisting her face, no doubt prepared to pay amply for any medicine that promised to cure it. "After all, an instructor at such a prestigious institution as this should be aware of the importance of accuracy, should she not?" the woman asked.

Emille said nothing, visibly trying—and visibly failing—to keep hold of her patience. She opened her mouth, preparing to say something that while it would no doubt be satisfying, would also no doubt get them no closer to their goal, namely meeting with whoever Emille intended to meet and getting the contract on Maeve and Chall retracted.

So, knowing this, Maeve spoke ahead of her. "If the Headmistress, Her Eminence, is busy," she interjected before Emille could speak, "then what about Sir Chavoy? Perhaps we would be able to speak with him? Would that be alright?"

She was aware of Emille's wince and knew, the moment that she saw it, that she had said something wrong. That thought was confirmed a moment later as the face of the woman behind the desk twisted, closing off further as if she'd just taken a bite out of something sour. "*You* wish to speak with *Sir Chavoy?*" she asked.

"Sure, that's right," Maeve said, figuring that she was in it now, one way or the other. She had stepped her foot into some sort of trap. She had not seen it, but she had no choice now but to do the same thing as any animal caught in a snare might do—to attempt to break free and hope that the layer of that trap had left a weakness in it, one that might allow her to get out.

The woman slowly turned, regarding Emille. "I think it best, Instructor Emille," she said, "that the two of you left. Perhaps you might come back another day, without...company."

Staring at the woman, at her self-satisfied air, at the obvious pleasure she took in blocking their way if for no other reason than she enjoyed it, Maeve found herself getting angry. Angry at this officious, pompous woman. She had the urge, a very strong, almost inarguable one, to reach out and snatch the woman up by the tightly-laced collar of her dark gray dress, to see if out of all those expressions she no doubt practiced, how much practice she had at one of terror. In the end, though, it was Chall's voice in her head that made her resist the urge. Chall who had often told her that if someone wanted to catch bees, they didn't take swipes at them with a blade. Instead, they only set out the honey and let the bee come to them. She didn't like the idea of it, though, seemed to her that when the bee was as big of an asshole as this woman it didn't deserve any honey. But then, she consoled herself with the fact that, should the honey fail...well. There was always the dagger.

"Listen, Miss—forgive me," Maeve said, offering the woman a small smile, "I'm afraid I didn't catch your name."

"That would no doubt be because I did not give it," the woman said.

Dagger. Dagger dagger, Maeve thought as she flashed her best self-deprecating smile. "Of course, you're right," she said to buy herself time. She thought of the way Chall had so easily charmed the castle servant in the king's quarters, how the man always seemed to be able to charm anyone, her included. She'd asked him about it before, and he had told her that the easiest way to charm a person, to get them to do what you wanted, was to get to know them. To know what they didn't like and, more importantly, to know what they *did*.

Maeve took a moment to study the woman before her, not with the distaste that she had to that point but with a gaze devoid of any emotion. Tight bun, not bordering on severe but well and truly crossed into it. Dark hair streaked with gray, gray that might have been covered by dye as many women did but which instead had been left there. That might have meant that the woman was careless regarding her hair, but Maeve did not think so. No, she did not think this woman was careless about anything, thought that there wasn't a thing in her life upon which she did not have an opinion, and that a strong one. So why would she leave her hair that way, then? Not for the stylishness of it, no, for this woman with her drab, dark gray dress and fingernails cut so close to the quick Maeve expected they bled when she was finished clearly did not concern herself with stylishness.

Which meant she'd kept the hair for another reason, and that reason, Maeve expected was that gray hair denoted age and age was often believed to represent, particularly in people of the woman's emotional bent, wisdom. And not *just* wisdom. Many, and Maeve suspected that the woman might be counted among them, saw age as a mark of superiority, an excuse to lecture and frown and disapprove of the actions of anyone younger than—and by that, inferior to—themselves.

And *that* told Maeve a lot about the woman, about what she prided herself on, about what her soft spot was. "What I meant, ma'am," she said, noting the way the woman's eyes sparkled at the word "ma'am," "is that me and my companion here, Instructor Emille, are aware of the unusual nature, the *presumption,* of our request. Expecting to gain a meeting with the Headmistress without appointment is foolhardy, is arrogance of the worst kind. I only ask that you understand that we do not expect—we only hope. For we are desperate, pitiful creatures in need of the Headmistress's wisdom, knowing even as we seek it that we do not *deserve* it. And you, of course, displayed your own wisdom in not granting us immediate audience, and so we must only put ourselves at your mercy, at *her* mercy. Though might I say, whatever you decide, that I think the Headmistress could be naught but pleased at how diligently and effectively you carry out your duties."

That was laying it on pretty thick, too thick for most, like toast that was no bread and all butter, but Maeve had it in her mind that the woman before her might lap it up, loving it all the more for its hyperbolic nature. And, based on the approving nod the woman gave, likely against her own volition, she decided she'd been right. "I see," the woman said. "Yes, well I can only hope that I, in my small way, aid her in her just and righteous cause."

No, Maeve decided as she struggled to keep a straight face, she had not been laying it on too thick. In fact, she was beginning to think she'd spared more butter than she might have. "As we all might hope," she returned, finding it no easy task to keep from sputtering at the nonsensical nature of the conversation.

The woman, though, took her words as genuine, inclining her head with her eyes closed for a moment as if she was some priest in rapturous communication with her god—or in this case, goddess. "As we all might hope," she intoned with the breathy, meaning-injected voice of a parishioner reciting a benediction.

She smiled then, an expression that looked uncomfortable on her face. "Perhaps, I might review the Headmistress's schedule and see if something might be arranged. After all, who am I to get in the way of the wisdom she might impart?"

Maeve said nothing, didn't think she could have managed it without her incredulity betraying her true feelings. Instead, she only gave the woman a small smile, inclining her head in much the same way that she had moments before.

The woman reached below her desk and retrieved a ledger which she gently lifted and placed in front of her with the accentuated care most would show handling some priceless holy relic.

She carefully opened it, turning from one page to the next then finally looking up at Emille and Maeve with a benevolent smile on her face. "I think that something might be done. Give me but a moment—I will return."

Maeve inclined her head in a bow as the woman rose and walked through a door behind her desk. That done, she turned to check on Emille and saw the woman staring at her as if she had only just seen her for the first time. "What?" she asked.

Emille shook her head slowly. "I'd heard of you, of course. Everyone in our profession has. But...the stories, I now understand, did not do you justice."

Stupid, maybe, but Maeve felt herself blushing. "Thanks. But tell me, before she returns, why was I wrong to suggest us speaking to Sir Chavoy?"

Emille winced. "Right, that. Well, you see, you were wrong because Sir Chavoy doesn't exist."

"He...doesn't exist."

"That's right," Emille said. "He never has. The Headmistress made him up, claiming that if the school was to have any legitimacy in our current world, it would be better if it would be seen to be led by a man. Also—" she shrugged—"it would help to detract attention from her, should anyone inquire too closely into the school and its...function."

"I see," Maeve said, clearing her throat and feeling a fool. "But what of you being an instructor? Cover, I don't doubt, likely used with the other assassins too, yes? But then why did she insist on it despite the fact that there was no one here to overhear?"

"Well, that would be for two reasons," Emille said. "Firstly, it would not do for *her* to assume that there was no one listening just because she doesn't see them, but mostly because she thinks I *am* an instructor."

Maeve blinked. "I...I don't understand. You mean she thinks that this is a real school for healers?"

"No, Lady Maeve," Emille said, meeting her eyes, "I mean that this *is* a real school for healers. Men and women, boys and girls are brought here. And many of those, *most* of those, spend years training in the healing arts, going over lesson after lesson, until they are finally sent out into the world, all without ever knowing the truth of what this place is. But some few of them are selected, are chosen, and those are allowed to know the school's true nature."

"Damn," Maeve breathed, impressed despite herself. It was one thing to put on a disguise, to hang a sign at the door claiming the place a school. It was quite another for it to be a school in truth, one that the Headmistress somehow managed to continue to operate without those students and teachers who attended it ever knowing the truth, that the school was, in actuality, no more than a clever, elaborate disguise. A disguise so finely crafted, so expertly fit, that there was no way to tell that it was not real. Mostly because it was. "Damn," she said again.

She had known the Guild was secretive, of course, but she began to think, as she stood there, that it might not have been such a grand idea to have come here, that Challadius might have been right. After all, the Guild was prepared to start a legitimate academy of healing, to go through all the organizational difficulties that entailed to maintain their secret. She did not doubt that an organization that was willing to do so much to protect its identity would have many qualms about destroying one old woman whose best years were behind her, even if that old woman had once belonged to their ranks. That had been a long time ago, after all, a

A Warrior's Penance

time when the name of Maeve the Marvelous was known and feared throughout the Known Lands, if not as much as that of the Crimson Prince. Now she was just a dried-up old woman, one who'd nearly died at the hands of the assassin Felara only weeks ago, an assassin that Maeve the Marvelous could have handled in her sleep.

She thought, in some ways, that those legendary heroes out of the bards' songs, of which she must count herself a part, were better off to die young, doing some grand, heroic gesture. Better that than for them to grow old and be forced to regard the slow decay of that legend, to see the great statue of themselves slowly chipped away at by time and life's erosions until it was unrecognizable, even to themselves. Perhaps *especially* to themselves.

She found herself thinking of Chall again, of what he might say to such self-pitying drivel, and she realized she was smiling. He would find some way of pointing out her own selfish foolishness that wounded her as little as possible. He was careful, in that way, as in so many others. Now, though, she thought that he might have even been more direct, might have gone so far as to have called her a fool. And worse, she thought he would have been right to do so. After all, she did not want to die. There was a man she loved, a man she had come here to protect. She had someone who loved her and whom she loved, and those dead legends could not say that.

"So this woman," she said, pulling herself back to the present, "the secretary, she doesn't know...the truth?"

Emille shook her head. "No."

Maeve let out a low whistle and was just about to say something more when movement caught her eye and she looked up to see the woman stepping out of the door she'd disappeared through minutes ago.

She was smiling as she walked toward them. "The Headmistress has, in her kindness, decided that she will see you. Come—I will show you to where you will wait for her."

Maeve said nothing, only inclining her head. The woman turned and started through the door again, and they followed her down a hallway to a door. The woman stopped and opened it, beckoning them inside. Maeve glanced at Emille, saw her own concerns mirrored in the woman's face, but she did not hesitate for long. She knew she was going in, after all. It was why she had come. Yes, there were risks, but that had not changed. She stepped into the room.

Emille followed her a moment later, and Maeve was glancing around at the room, at the desks scattered about it, when the door closed behind her with a loud *thump*. She started, turning in time to hear it lock.

She glanced at Emille, and the two of them shared a troubled look. "Guess she didn't want us wandering around," Maeve observed, "scared we might get lost."

Emille gave her a tight smile, betraying her fear, the same fear that Maeve was feeling. "Guess so."

CHAPTER ELEVEN

Chall climbed the ladder downward. It seemed to go on forever, and he paused from time to time, glancing beneath him. Not that it did any good, for he was unable to make out his companions, or anything, through the darkness. Had it not been for the sound of their feet on the ladder as they worked their way down and the soft exhalations of their breath, he could have almost imagined that he, alone, was traveling into the depths of the world. It was not a pleasant feeling.

Yet on and on the ladder went, Chall growing increasingly convinced that he would never get off it, that he would travel on forever, one rung after the other. When he'd first gazed down into the trap door, he had felt that there was plenty of room, but now he felt as if the earthen walls of the hole through which they descended were shrinking, beginning to close in on him. It seemed to him only a matter of time before they were crushed, far beneath the surface of the world, their bodies never found, for when they had all gone into the tunnel Ned had hit a switch which had closed it back again. Which meant only that their funerals would have to be done without bodies, though he supposed that those in attendance of his own, at least, could only be thankful for that. After all, he was honest enough with himself to admit that he was no prize while alive, and he doubted that death and decay would do anything to remedy that.

So all consuming was his growing disquiet that Chall grunted in surprise when his questing foot did not find another rung beneath him but instead struck the hard-packed earth that served as the floor.

He looked around him, trying to get some sense of his surroundings but he might as well not have bothered for he stood in complete darkness. Darkness as complete as that through which he and Maeve had traveled when she had shown him the prince's secret tunnels through the castle. "Priest?" he said, not liking the desperate, breathless sound of his voice in the darkness.

"I'm here," his companion said, and Chall didn't think he imagined the way the man's voice sounded tight, tense. "I'm not sure what you wanted to show us, Ned, but I can see nothing."

"Just a minute," the man said, "know it was around here somewhere." Chall waited, doing his best to control his breathing, as he listened to the sounds of the man moving around in the darkness. He heard a thump then a sharp intake of breath. "*Damnit all,*" Ned hissed. "Know it was arou—" He cut off then, making a satisfied grunt. "There it is."

Chall was just about to ask what "it" was when he heard the sound of flint being struck and suddenly an orange, ruddy glow bloomed in the darkness.

He winced, raising a hand to cover his eyes then blinked as they slowly began adjust to the light. He looked around and saw that the light came from a lantern the carriage driver held, a lantern which revealed a surprisingly large room. Hard packed earth made up the walls which were held up by beams, the same as the ceiling overhead. Yet despite the beams, Chall couldn't help feeling a bit of anxiety at the thought of all those tons of dirt and debris suddenly collapsing down on his head.

He told himself that was ridiculous. After all, the cavern had remained for twenty years according to Ned. But as was so often the case when fear was involved, logic made very little difference. He glanced around, more to distract himself than anything else, and saw that while this main area was large, there were a few other "doorways", which were little more than openings carved in the earth that led off into separate chambers.

But while the purpose of those others might have been a mystery, the purpose of the room in which they stood, at least, was clear enough. Weapon racks had been built against the walls, holding armaments ranging from short swords to pikes, from daggers to maces and crossbows, yet it was clear by the veneer of dust covering them all that they had not been put to any use in quite some time.

"An armory," Priest observed, and his voice was so serious that Chall found himself turning away from those dusty relics of weapons to regard his companion. "The real question," Priest went on, turning slowly to regard the carriage driver with narrowed eyes, "is *whose.*"

It wasn't really question—from the menacing sound of Priest's tone, Chall thought that any questions he asked in the next few minutes would be what he'd once heard a torturer refer to as "red" ones. And the truth was that Chall couldn't blame him. Maybe it was misplaced anger, but he found himself mad at the carriage driver as well, even though the man had just saved their lives and that with little doubt.

Ned must have heard the anger in Priest's tone, for he turned to him, holding up a hand. "Easy, fella," he said, and though the words were spoken softly, they seemed to echo with shocking power in Chall's mind. He found that he'd stumbled, as if suddenly struck by a powerful gust of wind, only there had been no wind. Instead, whatever force he'd felt push against him had seemed to come from the other man's hand, one that had not struck him from the outside but had instead somehow struck *inside* him.

Chall realized, as he considered it, that he had felt the same feeling before and recently, particularly when they'd been surrounded by the tavern's patrons who'd been getting set to kill them. A feeling so unusual, somehow invasive and comforting at the same time, that he had recognized it despite the fact that he had been somewhat distracted by what had appeared to be his approaching imminent death.

Now, though, he was not distracted—not having a room full of men and women wielding weapons had a way of allowing a man to focus. And he was able to think it over. Think it over enough, to examine that feeling enough, that one word suddenly popped into his mind, a word he had not thought of for over half his life, not since his years attending the academy for magicians in Daltenia before the Skaalden came. "*Empath,*" he whispered, giving the word, the thought voice, and as he did he heard within it the ring of truth, knew even as he said the word that it was the right one.

Ned glanced at his hand with a frown, putting it back down at his side. "Sorry about that. Been a long time since...well. Say it's like a pet you ain't let out in a while and, once you do, it's a trial tryin' to put it back in its cage."

"What's an empath?" Priest asked, glancing at Chall.

"A man with the gift," Chall said, watching the unassuming carriage driver, having difficulty believing it even as he stared at him. Empaths were rare, so rare that many thought they didn't exist at all, that they were no more than a fiction created by some teacher or student at the academy, though what purpose such a fabrication might have served Chall couldn't have guessed. He himself had doubted their existence often when studying about the different users of the gift, the different forms it might take. He had doubted empaths were real—he had certainly never expected to meet one.

"You mean...like you?" Priest asked.

"No," Chall said, "no, not like me. Empaths were...well, they *are* rare. So rare, in fact," he went on, turning to eye the carriage driver with a frown, "that many of us thought they were just...bogeymen the instructors created for their own purposes."

Ned gave him a humorless smile. "Boo."

"But...if they really are as rare as you say," Priest said, "then...wouldn't the other mages look for them? Wouldn't they know what he was?"

"A good question," Chall agreed.

Ned sighed. "They do know. Or, well, at least they *did.* Back at the academy in Daltenia."

"Wait a minute," Chall said, "are you trying to tell me you went to the academy, that an *empath* was going, and I never knew?"

"Um...yes?" Ned asked.

Chall frowned. "That's impossible. Seems to me I would remember you being in my classes."

Ned winced. "Right, well, thing is, I wasn't in any classes. Empaths bein' rare and all, the instructors decided to take up my...education, such as it was, separately from the rest."

"You mean they taught you alone?"

"That's right. I don't mind tellin' you it made it a pain in the ass to cheat on tests." He glanced between Chall and Priest, both of them watching him with frowns on their faces and grunted. "That was supposed to be a joke."

"Don't feel much like laughing just now, I'm afraid," Chall said. "Say that you are an empath and that somehow you *did* attend the university without my knowledge—I won't pretend I didn't get easily distracted, it was a failing which the instructors there made abundantly clear—"

"Hey, me too," Ned said, grinning.

"Either way," Chall went on, "none of that describes what you're doing in the poor district, and why you saved us."

Ned blinked, glancing between them. "Um...sorry, I guess? I reckon I was just under the impression that you fellas would prefer goin' on unstabbed."

Chall frowned, trying to find a way to approach that irrefutable logic, was still trying when Priest spoke. "While we appreciate your having come to our aid, that does not explain how you were able to do so in the first place. Specifically why you were *there*. Why you were following us."

Ned blinked. "Oh, well I can answer that easily enough. I wasn't."

Chall and Priest shared a look before turning back to the man. "You weren't?" Chall asked.

"Followin' you, that is," the carriage driver said. "I was there, of course. Would have been a pretty nifty trick to save you if'n I wasn't."

"What do you mean?" Chall said. "Of course you were following us. Or are we to believe that it's just coincidence that you happened to be in the poor district, happened to be at the *exact* tavern that that bastard Catham the Cu—"

"Not coincidence," Ned said. "After all, I was followin' someone, only it wasn't you."

"You were following Catham," Priest said, a tone of dawning realization in his voice which meant that he was several steps ahead of Chall.

"That's right," the carriage driver said, giving a nod.

"But...why?" Chall asked.

Ned winced. "Well, now that's goin' to take a bit of explainin'."

"Suppose you'd best get started then," Chall said. He glanced around. "Doesn't seem to me you've any cause to worry about being interrupted at any rate."

Ned gave him a humorless smile. "I s'pose that's true enough." He studied the two of them for a moment then finally gave a reluctant nod. "Very well. Follow me, the both of you—s'pose it's best if we were all sittin' down for this part."

The man turned without waiting for either of them to respond and started toward one of the cut-out "doorways" that Chall had noticed earlier. Chall glanced at Priest, and the man gave him a shrug before following, which left Chall to do the same.

Ned led them into a cavern that was considerably smaller than the last, the space dominated by a large dining table sitting at the room's center. The wooden table and the chairs surrounding it, like the rest of the caverns, were covered in dust, and Ned grunted. "Sorry, but I didn't have a chance to clean the place up. Still," he said, glancing around, his hands on his hips, "s'pose it'll serve. Have a seat." He extended his hands toward the table.

Priest eyed the carriage driver, and the chairs come to that, as if he didn't trust them in the least. Chall understood, for he was confused and feeling particularly suspicious himself, but his suspicions, at least, did not extend to the chairs. That was just as well considering that he'd spent the entire day and now night being rocked by revelation after revelation, not to mention a seemingly increasing likelihood of being murdered, and it was quickly becoming a case of sit down or fall down.

He moved to the table, slid one of the dust covered chairs out and, with a sigh of relief, chose to sit. There were still plenty of chances, he figured, that he would end up dead before the day was through, as there were a few hours left yet, but he was determined, if he did die, that he was going to do so sitting down.

Priest hesitated for another minute then finally walked over and sat beside him. Ned came last, moving toward the table, his eyes roaming the room and the walls, looking lost in memory. Finally, he walked to a chair and grabbed it to pull it out only to hesitate as his hand touched it.

He stared at the chair, and Chall saw what he thought was some great emotion—sadness, perhaps—glide like a dark cloud across the carriage driver's face. But it was gone in another moment, and Ned took a slow breath as if to steady himself before sliding the chair out and sitting, though from the way he'd sat he might have been sitting on a chair made of fire, so careful was he.

"Sorry," he said, glancing around himself, "it just...brings back a lot of memories. Being here."

"Well?" Priest said, sounding as impatient as Chall had ever known him. "You said you had an explanation?"

Ned nodded slowly. "Enough of the pleasantries, then. Well...might be..." He frowned, scratching at his chin. "Might be that I lied to the two of you before, about the Crimson Wolves, I mean."

"You mean you didn't create them?" Chall asked.

"No, no, I did," he said, "only...well, it wasn't *just* me. There was another, a friend of mine, Robert. Robert Palden."

Chall frowned. "I don't recognize that name."

"Nor would you," Ned said. "Fact is, we went to pretty great lengths back then to make sure nobody would recognize our names or our faces. Anyway, that ain't the point. Here's what you need to know—I wasn't lyin', before, when I told the prince he saved my village from the Fey, he and his men. That happened alright, durin' the war, and I wasn't puttin' him on when I told him I was grateful, neither. After all, if the prince and his men hadn't shown up, well, me and everybody else in the village'd be dead, eaten by those damned monstrosities. But while the bards love to write their songs about such battles, such rescues, they rarely spend much time on what follows." He shrugged. "Can't blame them, I suppose, for in my experience, after the celebration is done, after the rescuin' is done, well, the next bit ain't much worth singin' about. Diggin' graves and fillin' 'em, mostly. With dirt, sure, but with shed tears and broken dreams and bodies, too, those aplenty. Watchin' folks die, it's a hard thing—but I'll tell you, bad as it is, it ain't got nothin' on watchin' a whole village die."

"I...I don't understand," Chall said, his voice coming out in a little more than a whisper, for it seemed that the carriage driver's words had transported him back to that time, that place of grief and sorrow. Not by the magic of an empath, men and women who were said to be able to not only feel the emotions of others but to also manipulate them. Instead, this was a uniquely human type of magic, one comprised of regret and sorrow. "How does a village die? I mean, that is, the prince—you said he saved it."

"He saved the people," Ned said. "But the village...well. Imagine a village is a person, Challadius. That person might be being ravaged by a wolf and you might come to that individual's rescue, slaying or driving off the wolf only to find that the wounds the man had taken were fatal and that he would, in time, die. Such is what happened to my village. We had just taken too many wounds, that was all, lost too much blood. It wasn't just that nearly everyone had lost someone—although they had. It was that we had lost far more than that which remained to us. We had lost our loved ones, yes, and many of us lost our livelihoods as our shops and our fields, even our homes, were destroyed in the fighting. But we lost, also, our hope. And so, slowly at first but increasingly quick as the days went on, men and women of the village began to leave, not really knowing where they were going for the most part, I think, only wanting to get away. To flee from the ghosts that seemed to lurk around each corner, from the memories that would sneak up on you when you were least expecting it. You'd just be walking one minute, the next you'd find yourself in tears, or you'd hear the sound of a child laughing and think for sure it was a scream." He shrugged. "There were no more than a handful left when I decided it was my time to go."

"But...go *where?*" Chall asked.

"Anywhere at all," Ned said. "Anywhere I thought the ghosts wouldn't follow. Only, they did follow. I don't believe in haunted houses, Challadius, nor in haunted bed chambers or haunted fields. But I do believe in haunted people, oh yes, and how not? After all, I was one. In some ways, I still am. In some ways, I'm just another ghost."

"So...how did you end up here?" Chall asked. "In the capital, I mean."

Ned took a moment to answer, seeming to be lost in memories. Finally, he shrugged. "How does anybody end up anywhere? Truth is, I couldn't really say. You see, I showed up to the city a broken man, as I said, a ghost. Or if not a ghost, nearly one. There was only one person that saved me."

"Emille?" Chall guessed.

Ned gave a small, seemingly involuntary smile at the mention of his wife's name. "No," he said slowly, "not my Em. I didn't meet her until later. See, I was drinkin' in a tavern, nursin' a hangover and workin' on another, when I heard a serving girl's scream. I'm ashamed to say that weren't enough to even get me turned away from my ale. After all, the type of places I frequented in those days, well, there weren't anythin' all that unusual in the shout of a servin' girl as one bastard or another tries to get somethin' that ain't meant to be for sale."

"What does that have to do with the Crimson Wolves?" Priest pressed.

"I'm getting' there, fella," Ned said. "Just as quick as I'm able. It ain't easy, understand, rememberin' it all, travelin' back into it this way. Those memories, they're like traps, like dreams, and in those dreams, Priest, demons walk."

Priest let out a frustrated growl. "Just hurry up, damn you, and tell us what—"

"*Enough, Priest,*" Chall snapped, and the man recoiled as if he'd been slapped, his surprise at being shouted down by Chall clear on his face, and a surprise that Chall understood for he was equally surprised. "Enough," he said again, thinking as he did that it could not be a good sign of what they—of what the world—had come to that he was now forced to be the reasonable one. "Let's hear him out. If you want to lose your shit then, fine, but until he's finished just relax."

A look akin to betrayal passed across his companion's face, and Chall felt a momentary regret, yet he did not relent, continuing to scowl at him. Finally, Priest sighed, nodding. "You're right...I'm...I'm sorry."

Chall watched the man for a moment, deciding that whatever was going on with him would have to be addressed, and soon. For the meantime, though, they had other problems to worry about. He turned back to Ned. "What happened next?"

The carriage driver watched Priest for a moment then nodded slowly, turning back to Chall. "Well, as I said, I wasn't payin' all that much attention to the scream—fact is, I didn't pay much attention to anythin' in those days, except the ale in my hand and where the next one was comin' from. But then I heard somethin' else—not a scream, this, but a voice, tryin' for calm but shaky around the edges, tryin' for threatenin' but mostly just scared. A man's voice. Sayin' stop, sayin' to let her alone. Her, bein' the servin' girl, I s'posed. And while the woman's shout might not have drawn my attention for how common it was, this did. For whatever else might be said about the poor quarter, about the places where I lived my life then, if such an existence could even be called a life, they were not the places a man or woman went, if they were lookin' for heroes. So I turned to look."

He grunted what might have been a laugh. "Not sure what I was expectin' to see, but I can tell you that what I found wasn't it. You see, there was two men, big fellas, one of 'em pawin' at the servin' girl even as he and his companion loomed over a third man. This one barely standin' higher than five and a half feet, a hundred and thirty pounds soakin' wet with ink stains on his hands that marked him as a clerk. This, I knew immediately, was the fella who'd spoken, he of the shaky voice. His skin was pale, and his entire body was possessed of the same tremble his voice had betrayed, yet he stood there just the same, facin' the two men down, his expression a mixture of fear and determination. Lookin' at him, I realized three things at once. One, I saw that this stranger, whoever he was, knew about as much about fightin' as I knew about knittin'. Which, of course, is to say none at all. Second, the two he was squared off against, judgin' by their scars, had been in quite a few scraps and the little clerk, if he didn't back down—and maybe if he did—was about to get his ass kicked. But the last thing, the one that really drew my attention, that really *interested* me enough to pull me out of my drunken haze, was that the man knew all these things too and yet, he wasn't going to back down. He was going to stand there—at least for as long as he could stand—and get his ass kicked. Nothin' in it for him, no money or women, certainly no bards there to make a song about it, not that they would have done even if there had been. Yet, I could see in the man's eyes that he was going to go through with it."

"But...what did you see to make you think that?" Chall asked.

Ned considered that, scratching at his chin. "Well. He'd just had enough, that's all. You could see it in him, in his face, in his eyes. The poor bastard had just had enough. And I understood. You see, I left my village, came to the capital, thinkin' maybe things would be better here, safer. Thinkin' maybe I could find some peace among my own kind, safe from the Fey bastards who'd taken so much from me...and you know what I found? I found that we as a people didn't need no lessons from the Fey on how to go about doin' evil. In fact, I reckon we probably could show those bastards a thing or two. And that fella, well, it seemed to me that he'd come to about the same conclusion, that he was sick of it, sick of all the evil, all the badness. Me, I'd decided to drown that feelin' of helplessness it gave me in ale. Me, who knew a little somethin' about fightin'—and who'd learned a lot more in one barroom brawl after another. Meanwhile, this soft-faced, dewy-eyed clerk had decided to deal with the problem head-on. Foolish, maybe, but courageous too. Even I, in my drunken stupor, saw that. Just as I saw the way the clerk took the first punch on the side of his face, cried out and fell to the ground, only to rise again. And then I saw that understandin' begin to blossom in the eyes of the two men loomin' over him. Men who might as well have been giants as far as the clerk was concerned."

"Don't tell me they stopped," Chall said doubtfully.

"Stopped? Fire and salt no," Ned said, laughing. "No, I reckon they were all set to beat the ever-living shit out of this clerk, even if they were going to be slightly impressed about it. Only, as I said, I'd seen the man's courage, and it was enough for me to take notice. Enough, also, for me to find myself getting out of my stool, me surprised as anyone, and walk over to stand beside the bastard as he picked himself up off the ground. Now, I'll tell you, in the days that followed the attack on my village, I got in quite a few scraps. Some I won and some I lost, and the truth was the victories felt pretty much the same as the losses. I almost always ended 'em bloody, and almost always ended 'em regrettin' getting out of bed that day. This one, though, this one was different. You see, for the first time in a long time, maybe even for the first time in my entire life, I fought for something other than myself."

"For the serving girl," Chall said.

"For the man," Priest said quietly.

"No," Ned said. "No, not the girl—I figure even if I saved her from those bastards' pawin', so what? Just be another couple of bastards pawin' her tomorrow. And no, no it wasn't for the man, either. After all, he struck me mostly as a fool and fools have a tendency of gettin' their asses kicked in this life. No, I guess what it was that I fought for, more than anything, was the answer the clerk gave. An answer I'd been looking for ever since my village was attacked, had searched for it at the bottom of more mugs of ale than I care to mention or contemplate."

"What answer?" Priest asked, and to Chall he did not seem angry now. Instead, he seemed intrigued and, more than that, almost a little desperate. "What did he tell you?"

Ned shook his head slowly. "Oh, don't mistake me, he didn't *tell* me anythin', at least not with words. But he told me enough. But to understand the answer, you'd best know the question. And that—"

"Why is there so much evil in the world?" Priest blurted, sounding less like a child with his tutor and more like a victim with his torturer, spouting the answer out in hopes that the pain might stop, if even for a moment.

Ned gave him a small, half-grin, then nodded. "I see you know it. It's a common enough question, I s'pose, one asked by every man or woman when they see society's mask ripped away, when they see that their world, everything they know, is built upon foundations and those foundations are trembling, always in danger of coming down. And the answer the man gave me, not with words but by standing the way he did, his nose bloody, in pain, sure, but more than anything *defiant,* was this: it doesn't matter."

"What?" Priest demanded, sounding as if Ned had just cheated him at cards. "What do you mean it doesn't—"

"The world is what the world is," Ned said, "and they ain't no changin' it. What the clerk with his ink-stained hands made me realize was, that wasn't the point, not really. The point wasn't about changin' or fixin'. Instead, the point, the whole of it, was that given the world was what it was, what was a man going to *do* about it. Not because he thought it would help, but because it was simply what a man did. And the answer to *that* was, at least to my way of thinking, whatever he had to. A man can't fix the world, can't save it—it's too big. It's like a giant, drowning, and a man going to rescue it is only doomed to be pulled down by its struggles and drowned also. No, you can't save the world, can't take on the thousands of evils within it. But maybe you can take on one—or two, in the form of street toughs. And maybe you can't save the world, but maybe you can save a *person*—a serving girl, perhaps."

"But...but you said yourself that he was losing," Priest said. "That they were going to beat him."

"I did," Ned said, "and what difference does that make? A man's worth, I figure—I *decided* in that moment, or maybe had it decided for me—isn't in how many victories he's won, how many notches in his belt. Instead, it's in what he's stood for—what he's been willing to accept and what he hasn't. Normally, I would have been able to accept the serving girl's plight without so much as turning around. But just then, I found that...well. I couldn't."

"So what did you do?" Chall asked.

Ned shrugged. "As I said, I wasn't good for much in those days—unless you had a bunch of ale sittin' around in need of drinkin'. But there was one other thing I'd come to be somewhat of a hand at, and that was bar fights. So I did what I was good at—I took those two boys on, and I beat the shit out of 'em. And when it was done, I felt good. For the first time in a very, very long time I felt good and never mind the fact that I had a black eye comin' in and some bruises that'd last for weeks. I introduced myself to the fella—the clerk, I mean—and he gave his name as Robert Palden."

Chall hissed in a sharp breath of air. "That's where the two of you met."

"So it is," Ned agreed. "Anyway, Rob and I, well, both of us were doin' a fair amount of bleedin', but we ended up doin' a fair amount of talkin' too.. Spent the whole night at it, I guess, and for the first time since I could remember, I didn't do any drinkin'. Not that the grateful serving woman wouldn't have been obliged to bring us free drinks, for she tried it. Robert, he sipped, but I didn't. Didn't need to. The drink, you see, I'd just been usin' it to fill a hole in myself, a hole put there when the Fey came. Problem, o'course, is that while ale has its uses, it's damned shitty at patchin' holes, just keeps leak'n' out, needin' to be refilled. That night, though, it seemed to me that maybe that hole had closed up on its own, or had at least begun to anyway. We spent hours at it, talked until the mornin' came and then talked some more. And eventually, all that talkin' led to a plan and that plan to a purpose."

"You formed the Crimson Wolves," Chall said, unable to suppress the awe in his voice, for whatever else he was, the carriage driver was a damned fine storyteller, his words seeming to weave before them a moving tapestry telling the story of what he described.

The carriage driver winced. "Never did care for that name, Robert's idea, that. But yes, it all began then. Or, at least, the beginning began. A group of like-minded individuals who only wanted to do what the guards would—or could—not, to root out evil where we found it. It was just us at first, but there were more soon enough. Not many, you see, for we were careful, always careful, knowin' that our strength lay in our anonymity. The next one was an older man, one used to be a soldier in the army but who'd had his sword hand bitten off by a Feyling during the war. It was him who taught us to fight proper, me and the others. We found a place, too, or, well, several. Robert, see, just happened to be wealthy—not a clerk after all, but the son of a rich merchant who'd passed a few years gone and who'd been ink-stained from doing his own ledgers. So anyway, we went lookin' for places like this one, hidden places where we might not be found and, if there weren't any such places, well, we made 'em ourselves."

"The plague," Chall said in realization. "You made it up."

Ned gave him a small smile. "That's right."

"But what about the two priests who were here? You can't tell me you made them up too—I saw them once."

"No, they were actors, is all. Playin' a part they had no idea the point of but then with the amount of money Rob paid 'em, I don't suppose they much cared."

"And when they were finished with their job, you got rid of them," Priest said, frowning.

"That's right," Ned said. "Couldn't have 'em hangin' around, could we? Wouldn't do at all for priests of the Plague Church to be seen sittin' in some tavern drinkin', willin' to tell a story to anyone who'd listen, would it?"

Priest let out a growl at that, and before Chall—still stunned by the callous way which the carriage driver had spoken about killing two innocent men—could say anything, his companion rushed forward. His fist lashed out, lightning-quick, but instead of striking Ned in the face as it should have done, as Chall thought it *must,* the carriage driver moved to the side, narrowly avoiding the blow. He didn't stop there, though. Instead, he grabbed hold of

Priest's arm, pivoted, spinning so that his back was pressed against the man, Priest's arm draped over his shoulder. The next thing Chall knew, Priest was sailing through the air to strike the wall hard. The man fell to the ground, dust showering around him. "Sorry about that, fella," Ned said, sounding sincere as Priest picked himself up. "Another of the folks that joined us, she was a master of unarmed combat. Anyway, I don't know what's gotten into you, but we're all on the same side here and—"

"Same *side?*" Priest growled, stumbling to his feet, running an arm across his mouth where a trickle of blood leaked out.

"What's his deal?" Ned asked, glancing at Chall.

"His *deal?*" Chall said. "Oh, I don't know, I guess maybe he isn't a fan of killing innocent actors once they've played a role you want them to play."

"Kill them?" Ned said, shocked. "Fire and salt where did you get that idea?"

Priest, who'd started back toward the man, hesitated, and Chall himself blinked. "I...that is, that's what you said, that you got rid of them, that you couldn't have them hanging around."

"Yeah," Ned said, "we took care of them, as in, as part of the deal, they were forced to leave New Daltenia. I mean, gods be good, we didn't hurt them, except maybe the aches in their backs from havin' to heft the bags of coins Robert gave 'em before they left. The patients too."

"You mean...you didn't kill them," Chall said.

"Of course we didn't kill them," Ned said. "Have you been listening to anything I've been tellin' you? We formed our little...our group to do somethin' about all the evil in the world. Wouldn't make much sense to start by addin' to it, would it?"

Priest winced. "Ned, I'm...I'm sorry."

Ned waved a hand dismissively as if the man attacking him out of nowhere was of no great concern. "Don't worry about it, just a misunderstanding is all. Anyway, we went on that way for some time, stoppin' crime when we could, savin' folks what grief we could and doing everything we could to make it more difficult on the criminals of the city, those who would prey on the weak and the innocent."

"Including kill them?" Chall asked, glancing at Priest.

"You're damn right," Ned said instantly. "And if you expect me to feel guilty about that, you're to be disappointed. Durin' the wars, folks came to New Daltenia hopin' to be safe, thinkin' to find themselves a new life, and those bastards took advantage of them, robbin' them of what few possessions, what little coin they had left, and more often'n not leavin' 'em dead after it was all done. No, I don't feel bad for them. We were doin' good work, not savin' everybody, but savin' some. And each one saved made it worth it...at least for a while," he finished, his face getting a far away look.

"So...what changed?" Chall asked.

"Not what," Ned said, his voice grim now, "but who. Robert, you see. He changed over those years. You would think that it would make him feel better, seein' what good we did, those we helped, but it didn't. Instead, when we managed to excise some small bit of evil from the infection, Robert never noted what we took away, only what was left. Got to where he didn't think about those we managed to save—instead, he only thought about those we failed. Well, a man can't live like that, not forever, can't watch everythin' around him sour without, sooner or later, starting to sour himself." He shook his head. "We argued a lot in those days, Robert and me until, one day, when I'd thought he'd finally heard me, that I'd finally gotten through to him. Imagine my surprise, then, when I woke the next day to find out what he'd done."

"What?" Chall asked, finding himself leaning forward, his eyes wide in anticipation.

"There was a man we'd been following, a criminal, but not just any criminal—an important one. In point of fact, he was a nobleman, one whose connections throughout New Daltenia meant that he was in a unique position to further the criminal enterprise in the city like few others were. Only...not anymore. You see, while I'd been sleeping, and while I had *thought* that Robert was thinking over our conversation, he'd been busy instead. He went to the man—Lord Banham's—house, sealed the doors, and burned it down around him." He sighed, shaking his head sadly. "After that, well...things between us soured pretty quick, and that spelled the end of the Crimson Wolves."

"But why?" Chall asked. "No offense, Ned, but it seems to me that from what I've heard of the Crimson Wolves, brutality was sort of your mission statement, wasn't it?"

Ned grunted. "It's true, we didn't believe in mercy for those who had made their living off victimizing the innocent, and I won't apologize for it. Only, what Robert did, it went past that. You see, the good Lord Banham wasn't alone in his home that day—he rarely was. It was the reason we hadn't moved on him yet even though we knew how dangerous he was, how much trouble he'd caused. A family man, was Lord Banham, and we'd never yet managed to catch him out alone without them. But on that day, Robert decided he was done waiting."

Chall felt his breath catch in his throat. "You mean...you mean that the man's family was still inside?"

Ned nodded grimly. "That's right. After that...well. It's one thing, preying on predators. Always thought there was something noble about it, about what we done. But after that...well. Safe to say I lost the taste for it. Robert and I quarreled, and he left, along with some few who agreed with his way of thinkin'. That left me and the rest, not that there was anything left, really. We all dispersed, and I never heard about Robert or any of the other Crimson Wolves again. Not, at least, until a couple of weeks ago."

Chall frowned, glancing at Priest who shook his head. "A couple of weeks? The first we heard about the Crimson Wolves returning was today."

"The Crimson Wolves have not returned," Ned said sharply. "They could not have. But tell me, what makes you think so?"

Priest narrowed his eyes. "It is you who needs to explain himself, not us. Now, tell us wh—"

"Enough, Priest," Chall said, not angry this time only tired. "He's shared plenty—seems only fair that we'd do the same. Or do you want to attack him for no reason again?"

Priest colored at that, saying nothing, then Chall gave a gruff nod, turning back to Ned and recounting the events that had transpired since he had woken in bed with Maeve.

Ned listened, looking more and more disturbed by the moment. When Chall got to talking about the dead serving girl in the castle, he didn't look disturbed anymore, but angry. An anger that flashed in his eyes, and looking at it, Chall thought he saw that fury that had driven the man to forming the Crimson Wolves in the first place.

"I see," Ned growled when he'd finished. "Well, understand that was not the work of a Wolf, not a real one anyway. A Wolf wouldn't do such a thing."

"But that's not true, is it?" Priest asked, not challenging anymore but speaking in a soft, empathetic voice. "After all, a Wolf *did* do such a thing, according to the story you told us. And not just any Wolf, but the co-founder of the entire organization.

Ned frowned. "That was a long time ago. I haven't seen Robert in years—no one has. He wouldn't have come back, not after all that happened. And, if he had, I'd know."

"Would you?" Chall challenged.

The carriage driver sighed, scratching his chin. "This woman, the one you saw in His Majesty's chambers, what did she look like?"

Chall described her, trying to be specific as he could, and the carriage driver shook his head. "No, don't know anyone like that."

"Are you sure?" Chall asked. "I only ask because the woman *did* have a ring."

Ned sighed as if some suspicion he'd had had just been confirmed, and he wasn't all that happy about it. "Might be I've got an explanation for that."

"Oh?"

The carriage driver nodded. "Remember how I told you that I started thinking something might be wrong a couple of weeks ago? Well, that feelin' didn't come out of nowhere. You see, I was workin' a couple of weeks ago, and someone hired my carriage. Two someones, in fact, a young couple, bemoaning the fact that the priest who had married them had died, apparently in his sleep."

"So?" Chall asked.

"So," Ned said, "that priest just so happened to go by the name of Xavier. A pretty unusual name, but you see I knew a Xavier once, many years ago. He was one of the Wolves, if you'd believe it. And I also knew that he ended up, after the Crimson Wolves disbanded, joining the priesthood."

"But what difference does that make?" Chall asked. "I mean, people die, right?"

"Sure they do—it's one of those bad habits they can't seem to shake," Ned agreed. "And maybe that might have been all it was. Certainly I tried to convince myself of that fact. Only, try as I might,

I didn't quite manage it. You see, Xavier had been a friend of mine, a good man, and I thought that I needed to check into his death, just in case. And, if I'm being honest, that wasn't the only reason that I went. You see, I've spoken to Xavier quite a few times since the disbanding of the Crimson Wolves, enough to know that he always kept his ring hanging from a necklace he wore, a reminder, he told me, of his greatest shame and his greatest success. So I went to where they were keeping his body, along with his belongings, as they prepared for the funeral. I searched them all only to discover—"

"That the ring wasn't there," Priest finished.

"Exactly," he said. "I couldn't find any marks on Xavier's body, understand, but he'd been a healthy man, barely older than me, and I had a hard time imagining that he would die in his sleep like that. It didn't sit well with me, though I couldn't explain it at the time. Anyway, I'm thinking maybe now I can and that it might explain also where this killer of yours got her ring."

"But why?" Chall asked. "Why care about the ring at all, I mean?"

Ned shook his head. "I don't know. I mean, back then, we had plenty of people who tried to impersonate us, understand, men and women who were either sick of all the evil in the world the way we were or, more often than not, ones trying to use our reputation to benefit themselves. It was the reason we came up with the rings in the first place. Only those that possessed one could truly consider themselves—or truly *be* considered—a Wolf."

"All of this still doesn't explain why you were following Catham."

"No, but it will," Ned said. "You see, as I mentioned, I didn't feel good about Xavier dying that way—seemed unusual to me, and I told myself I'd at least look into it, find out what I could. I did so thinking that I would find that there was nothing, that all my suspicions about the reasons why the ring might be gone were just my fears, fears that my old life would come back to take what pleasure I'd found in the new one, fears for Emille. So I decided to look into his death a bit. Started by talking to those who came to see him, his flock, as it was. Those who sought him for guidance. I spoke to the young couple too and anyone else I could find that had dealt with him recently. I asked everybody that came to see him, trying to figure out where the ring went, trying to figure out if his death was innocent. The problem, though, was that Xavier had led a lonesome life. Finally, I found a fellow priest of his, one who he was as close to as anybody else, and I asked him. About the ring, I mean. And do you know what he said? He said that it had been taken, by Xavier's brother."

"And...that bothered you?"

"I'll say it did," Ned agreed with Chall. "The biggest reason being, you see, that I'd known Xavier for years. Why, we'd both stayed here, in this exact cavern, for quite some time. You stay in that close quarters with someone for any length of time—anyone—and you start to learn things about them. Things like Xavier hated snakes—had a real fear of them. Things like he had a scar on his back from where he'd been beaten nearly to death by the headmaster of the orphanage at which he'd been abandoned when he was just a kid. Things like the fact that Xavier didn't have a brother."

Chall frowned. "But...if he didn't have a brother, who was it that claimed the ring?"

"The same question I asked myself," Ned said. "So I started askin' around about this brother. Turned out, a few people had seen him, some of those good enough to give a bit of a description of him. Not much, but enough for me to be getting on with, just like I got an address for one of them on where the brother was staying. I went there one night, after work, and who did I see but your friend Catham. A man I'd never seen before. So I decided I might follow him for a bit, you know, see what he was all about. Imagine my surprise, then, when the supposed brother of a priest ended up being the second of a criminal organization. Surprise almost as great as, I imagine, that surprise Xavier felt, or at least would have felt if he'd been alive to feel anything anymore."

"So you mean...Catham has the ring?" Priest asked.

"Of course!" Chall said. "That explains why the bastard wanted us dead—it had nothing to do with that old shark woman. It was all—"

"Shark woman?" Ned asked.

Chall waved his hand dismissively. "It doesn't matter. But obviously that friend of yours," he said, glancing at Priest, "was worried that we would dig too deep, figure out what he was up to."

"But what *was* he up to?" Priest asked, sounding exacerbated. "Sure, we know that he stole the ring from the priest, and I suppose it only makes sense to assume that he was behind the man dying in the first place, but we don't know *why* he did it. I mean, it's just a ring, after all. What would be the point?"

"None," Chall said, then met the man's eyes. "Unless, of course, he was planning on resurrecting the Crimson Wolves. Him and that woman in the castle and whoever else might be with them. And based on the fact that they murdered a serving girl, I don't think their mission statement is going to be the same as it was twenty years ago."

Priest seemed to consider that then finally shook his head. "No, no I don't think—"

"Oh come *on,* Priest," Chall said. "It's obvious, isn't it? Why else would they want the ri—"

"No, you misunderstand me, Challadius. I do not mean to disagree about the idea that the Crimson Wolves have been reformed—that seems obvious enough, though to what purpose I cannot imagine. I only mean that, whatever that purpose and whoever is behind it, it cannot be Catham." He held up a hand, silencing Chall before he spoke. "I am not defending him— obviously, Catham is involved. I only mean that Catham is not a leader. Certainly he was not back then, and I am confident that that much, at least, has not changed. No, he has had opportunities in the past to take on leadership roles beyond what he currently enjoys, but he has always declined. I asked him about it once, and he said that when it came to such organizations, it never did to be at the top, just as it didn't do to find oneself at the bottom. After all, he told me, if men meant to chop a tree down, they most always started at the bottom, and when the storm comes, a building's top is most in danger of being struck by lightning, something like that."

Chall grunted. "Catham the Cautious indeed."

Priest nodded. "There is a reason why Catham is still alive when so many of our peers aren't."

"What about you?" Ned asked. "You cautious as well?"

Priest gave the man a humorless smile. "I am still around for a very different reason."

The carriage driver swallowed at that, and Chall thought it best, given the odd way in which Priest had been behaving, not to dwell on the fact that he had once been known as Valden the Vicious any longer than they had to. Instead, he chose to change the subject. "Anyway, there's no need to worry about the past. I'm more worried about the future. If this Catham wasn't the one who wanted to start the Crimson Wolves again, then who was? Do you think it was that woman, the one that was in the castle?"

The two men considered that for a moment, then finally Ned shook his head. "No, that doesn't make sense. If someone really is behind trying to resurrect the Crimson Wolves, for whatever purpose, then that same person wouldn't risk themselves by going on such a dangerous mission. No, I can't say for certain, but I do not think that the leader would risk him or herself so."

"Which means that there's a third," Chall said with a sigh.

Ned inclined his head in a nod. "And quite possibly considerably more than that. There's simply no way to know."

"On that," Priest said, his voice dark, "we'll have to disagree."

"Oh?" Ned asked.

"Yes," Priest said. "I can think of at least one person who would have that answer."

"You mean Catham," Chall said.

"I do."

"Sure," Ned agreed, "but just because he has the answers doesn't mean he'll be willin' to share."

"What about your gift?" Chall said. "I always heard that empaths could read minds."

Ned snorted. "Sure, and we can also fly." He looked at Chall's wide, shocked eyes and sighed. "There's a lot of lies that go around about empaths, but then there's a lot of lies go around about everythin', so I s'pose that ain't no surprise. Anyway, do you think if I could read folks's minds that I'd still be drivin' carriages for a livin'? Fire and salt, no. Why, Emille and I would live in some mansion, our feet always propped up, folks feedin' us grapes and pourin' us wine. No, we want answers from that fella, we're going to have to find another way of gettin' them."

"You let me worry about that," Priest said, and his grim tone of voice, along with his dark expression didn't leave much doubt in Chall's mind what he meant. It seemed to him that it was all too likely that Catham the Cautious would end up going by another name soon—Catham the Carved, maybe.

"Before we start planning out the best way to torture someone," Chall said, glancing sidelong at the man, "maybe we'd better consider if getting hold of him is something we're going to be able to do. After all, unless I'm mistaken the man's got somewhat of a reputation for being careful."

"Not careful enough," Priest growled. "Catham has made a mistake, has overextended himself, and any swordsman knows that doing so leaves you open for...retaliation. Come—we will go and find him. If we hurry, it should not be too difficult, for he could not have gotten far."

"You sure that's wise?" Ned asked, and Priest spun, glancing back at him. "I'm just sayin'," the carriage driver went on. "Seems to me that there's a whole tavern's worth of people out there lookin' to kill the both of you and that there's far better odds one of them will run into you before you run into this Catham fella. Better to wait, at least until mornin'. There's some old cots in the other room we could use. Though I can't promise they'll be comfortable, they ought to at least serve well enough to—"

"*No,*" Priest grated. "No, we cannot wait that long. There is not telling what atrocities Catham and the others might commit while we linger here. We must go. Now. Tell him, Chall."

Chall winced, glancing between the two men as they look at him. Finally, he sighed. "Ned's right, Priest," he said, hating the way the man's eyes widened in shocked betrayal. "Look, man, I want to settle this as much as you do, but we won't be a help to anyone if we get killed for charging in when we shouldn't. Besides, what, you think I don't want to get out of here, go back to the castle? For all I know, Maeve might be back by now. But if we leave now, like as not we'll stumble into one of those bastards from the tavern—or more than one—before we've walked a hundred feet. Better to wait, give them time to tire of the search. Besides, I'd just as soon travel the road in daytime if it's all the same to you."

Priest nodded, his jaw clenched. He turned to regard the carriage driver. "The cots in the other room?"

"That's right," Ned said.

Priest gave a second nod then, without another word, turned and walked out.

"Your friend," Ned said after Priest was gone, "he seems a bit...well a bit off. He alright?"

Chall stared at the doorway through which Priest had disappeared for a moment then finally shook his head. "No," he said softly. "No, I don't think he is. Come on—best we all get some rest."

CHAPTER TWELVE

"*Layna,*" he moaned in a trembling, barely audible voice, "*oh, how I've missed you.*"

Cutter watched his brother where he lay tossing and turning in his fevered sleep, a frown on his face. His brother had not fared well since their icy plunge in the water while fighting the lake monster. He had seemed fine at first, but he had only grown worse, more delirious as the day wore on. Now, he was under the grips of a fever, one that had only continued to worsen for several hours and never mind Cutter's efforts to collect herbs that might help it. Perhaps that was due to the fact that he knew nothing of the herbs himself and had to try to decipher Feledias's rambling, nonsensical answers to his questions to find what he needed. It was a task that had proven far more difficult than it might have, for even then, hours ago, Feledias had seemed only half-conscious, often making no sense, and if the herbs had helped his brother at all, Cutter could see no sign of it.

In fact, Feledias only seemed to have gotten progressively worse as the day wore on. Now he lay in troubled sleep, his skin almost painfully hot to the touch when Cutter checked on him, his breath pluming out in front of him in great frozen clouds of mist as he spoke to his dead wife.

Cutter had made a fire, meaning to keep his brother as warm as possible in the frigid darkness of the Black Wood, but it seemed a weak, pitiful thing, and even with his hands outstretched toward it, his fingers inches from the blaze, he could only barely feel its warmth. A fire that flickered and faded and threatened to die no matter how much he tried to help it, a brother that seemed to be doing much the same.

Cutter wondered then, as he stood silently regarding his brother, helpless to aid him any further, if his sins had finally come back to haunt him. Would that be his punishment, then, to watch as his brother slowly wasted away and died in front of him to the fever, an enemy that could not be slain and never mind with how much effort Cutter wielded his axe?

He had seen people die to the fever before. In this very wood, in fact, the last time he and some of the kingdom's soldiers had come, driving the Fey as deep into it as they had dared. It was as if the Black Wood was like a toxin, the very air they had breathed a poison, and some had simply been unable to bear it as well as others. He had watched, then, as they had given in one after the other, their minds going first, their sickness turning them into confused, frightened children before the fever finally claimed them. The deaths to the fevers had, in fact, been the biggest reason why he and what remained of his troop had eventually been forced to turn around.

"I'm...I'm sorry," his brother moaned within his troubled sleep. "*A whole village, Layna...their screams...gods help me, I can still hear their screams...can still smell them...burning.*"

Cutter tensed as he watched his brother. Feledias did his best while he was awake to hide his torment over the things he had done, likely thinking that it was a burden Cutter did not need. But in the darkness, in his dreams, a man could not hide—even from himself—those truths which in the day he might keep concealed. *Especially* from himself. And the truth of it, Cutter knew, was that no matter how Feledias tried to hide it, the knowledge of what he'd done, the *weight* of it, was crushing him. Cutter knew, understood, for he had felt that same weight, and it was only in watching Matt grow that he had felt some small bit of it taken away. Not much, but enough that he could labor on with his life...enough that he could breathe.

Cutter wished that there was some way that he could help his brother with that burden, but he knew that he could not. Such burdens could not be shared, only borne. Or not. There were plenty, he knew, who found that they could not stand up to that weight, the weight of burden which largely consisted of guilt and shame at a past lived and lived poorly and were crushed beneath it. There were others who simply chose to let it fall upon them, to stop fighting.

But even that burden of Feledias's, great though it must be, was not Cutter's largest concern, at least not now. Instead, that was the fever coursing through his brother's body like a poison, one that made him tremble with cold and never mind that his flesh felt so hot that it was nearly on fire.

And despite the small flame which Cutter had created with no small amount of difficulty—as if the very woods themselves hated the heat—it was cold. Very cold and, as night came on in full, it was only getting colder, the temperature seeming to drop by the second. As he stood there, watching his brother, watching him squirm in his troubled sleep and thinking that things could get no worse, Cutter saw a snowflake lazily fall before him.

No, he thought. *No, not now.* But then another came, and another, until soon it was no longer a peppering of snow but a true snow, falling thick and heavy, the little flame of the fire struggling to survive and slowly failing. And minutes after that, it was not a snow but a blizzard as the wind began to pick up, whistling through the trees and driving the flakes this way and that, so that it was difficult to even make out his brother through the curtain of shifting white.

He had hoped to allow Feledias to sleep, knowing well that often the best medicine for any ailment a man might suffer, physical or emotional, was sleep. But standing there, his breath pluming in great clouds in front of him, Cutter became convinced of something. This was no normal storm. If, that was, anything could be said to be normal within the confines of the Black Wood.

No, there was a malevolence, he thought, to the way the snowflakes struck him, like tiny shards of ice on his skin. Something was coming. Something that hated them, that wanted nothing but to destroy him and his brother. He knew that. He did not know how he knew it. Perhaps the voice inside him telling him so was an ancient voice, the primal voice of his ancestors from thousands of years before who did not consider themselves civilized, who understood, unlike so many of those living in the world today, that they knew little of the things that surrounded them and so came to rely on their feelings. On the wisdom of their souls.

Something was coming. He was sure of it. And he was sure of another thing, too.

There was little time.

He moved to Feledias, putting a hand on his brother's shoulder and giving him a shake. "It's time we were gone, Fel."

"*I want to take it back,*" his brother moaned, tears frozen on his closed eyelids. "*Please, I want to take it back.*"

Cutter gritted his teeth, his body beginning to tremble from the cold. He gave his brother another shake, this one a little harder than the first. "Fel, we have to go."

Feledias started, staring up at him with eyes that, for several seconds, were uncomprehending. "B-Bernard?" he rasped in a weak, croaking voice. "I-is that you?"

"It's me, Fel."

"*Have...you come...to kill me, then?*"

Cutter recoiled as if he'd been struck. "Fel? What? No, of course not."

His brother's eyes seemed to clear, and Feledias blinked. "Ah, Bernard," he said, "I do not mind telling you, brother, but I feel quite terrible. Perhaps we could have a chat some other time and—stones and starlight, have you dumped a bucket of ice on me? Why is it so cold?"

Cutter stared at his brother for several seconds and realized that Feledias seemed to not recall the question he'd asked him at all. Finally, he shook his head. "Not me, but someone has," he said, glancing around at the thickly-falling snow. "It's cold, Fel, very cold and getting colder. We need to find some shelter soon or..." He did not finish, but then he did not think that he needed to, for his brother was awake truly now, struggling to sit up. Feledias wrapped his arms around his chest tightly, staring out at the world as if he couldn't believe it.

"By the gods, what's happened? How did it g-g-get so c-cold?"

"I don't know," Cutter said, "and I don't want to." He offered his hand to Feledias who took it, groaning with pain and exhaustion as Cutter pulled him to his feet. "Can you walk?"

Feledias gritted his teeth, taking a step then giving a weak cry as the strength seemed to vanish out of his legs, and he would have fallen face-first had Cutter not caught him. "I-I don't think so," Feledias said, then he looked around again before meeting Cutter's gaze. "You need to go, brother," he said. "Now."

"Not without you."

Feledias snorted. "Now's not the time to try on a mantle of heroism, brother. Besides, it ill-suits you." He gave Cutter a small smile to take away the worst of the sting of his words. "What I mean is that I cannot walk, and if I cannot walk, I cannot run. I am just too weak. The storm...it seems intent on claiming us, and I, at least, do not seem in any position to argue. You, though...you can still make it away."

"Not without you," Cutter repeated.

"Listen, damn you," Feledias shouted, or at least tried to, *"I cannot go any farther.* And, brother...part of me, maybe the greatest part...it does not even want to. I...the memories, Bernard..." His brother paused, and when he spoke again it was in a shaky, uncertain voice. "They are a foe I cannot fight. They torment me. Always, and I deserve to be tormented."

"Listen, Fel," Cutter said, "that's just the fever talking. You're not in your right mind and—"

"No, *you* listen, Bernard," Feledias said, meeting his gaze. "I am not a good man. The truth of the matter is that the world will be better off without me. Brighton, all those people, they died because of me, because of my order, and Bernard—they died badly. I do not...I do not want to remember it, anymore. And even so, it makes no difference because I cannot *walk,* do you understand? I do not have the strength."

"No," Cutter agreed, "maybe not. But I do. If you cannot walk, Fel, then I will carry you."

Feledias let out a weak, outraged squawk as Cutter stepped forward and unceremoniously lifted him, tossing him over one shoulder like a sack of potatoes. His brother struggled against him for a moment, saying words—curses mostly, Cutter thought—that he could not make out over the sound of limbs cracking with the sudden frost.

Cutter ignored him, lifting his axe from where he'd set it with his other hand, and he started forward, hewing away the bracken and undergrowth in his path. Behind him, more branches cracked in the frost, and he became increasingly certain that they were indeed being chased. Not by a creature, perhaps, but by some force, a force which came at them in a great wall, almost like a giant wave crushing everything in its path. Glancing back, he could almost *see* it, or at least the edges of it. The ground and trees looked normal enough, for the moment at least, but beyond them the twisted, snapping trees and branches were instantly laden with a heavy frost as the cold reached them. It was coming.

Not particularly fast, but it was coming nonetheless. Cutter growled, turning and increasing his efforts as he hewed this way and that with his great axe, chopping away anything that stood between them and their escape as he forced his way forward.

He was not sure, later, how long he was about it, for how long he forced his way through those woods. It might have been minutes or hours or days. All he knew was the swinging of the axe, again and again, the ache in his arms each time and, most of all, the cold. A cold that seemed to spread within him like some sickness or plague, threatening to steal the strength from his limbs, a cold that spread even into his mind, seeming to try to convince him to stop, to rest. To give up.

But he did not. The Crimson Prince, after all, was known for many things but giving up too easily could not be counted among those. And so he did the only thing he ever did, the only thing, it sometimes seemed, that he had ever done—he fought. He fought against a growing sense of despair as he continued to search and not find anything that they might use as a shelter. He fought against the ache in his arm and his shoulder where he still carried his brother, against the cold spreading through him, striving to steal what strength remained.

He fought against it all, putting one foot in front of the other, taking a step, then another, and another still, glancing back from time to time to watch the wave growing slowly closer. Not moving quickly but moving just the same, moving, *shifting*, coming on with a sort of inexorable, inarguable procession, one that could not be stopped.

Feledias had long since stopped struggling, that much he knew, had either fallen asleep once more or passed out from exhaustion, and so Cutter toiled on alone beneath the great pregnant moon of the Black Wood, hounded by that encroaching frost in much the same way that his past had hounded him all these years.

Yet for all his efforts, the undergrowth in front of him grew thicker and thicker, requiring more swipes of his axe to clear, and each stolen glance behind him showed that the frost was drawing closer, spreading across the ground in a great wall of ice, the sound of tree branches cracking like the sound of its footsteps as it approached.

He abandoned any attempt to clear the bushes then. Instead, he simply plowed into them, doing his best to keep Feledias above the bushes while thorns scratched and cut at his flesh like thousands of little knives wielded by malevolent faeries.

Still the frost came on, unhampered by anything so trivial as the trees and bushes which crowded the forest floor, and Cutter was just beginning to think that he would not escape that now, finally, the sins of his past had caught up to him. That was when he topped a rise, began running down the other side of the hill and saw, off to his right, what looked like a cave. People commonly thought of caves as great places to shelter, and they were right, so far as it went. The problem, of course, was that animals also considered them fine places and so a person seeking to make use of one would most likely have competition, competition that wouldn't hesitate to make its case for ownership with tooth and claw. That was in a normal wood. In the Black Wood, there was no telling what horrors might lurk within those shadowed confines.

But as Cutter half-ran, half-staggered down the hillside, he decided that it really didn't matter what danger the cave represented, only that it was some place he might use to protect them from the encroaching freeze. True, there might be another better, safer place farther on, but then again there might not. Besides, his legs were already aching terribly, sharp pains stabbing through his thighs, another sharp pain in his side where his breath rasped painfully from his lungs. And so the choice, he decided, wasn't really any choice at all.

He lumbered toward the cave as quickly as he could. It was almost directly to his right now and so he was forced to turn and head in that direction, meaning that he was no longer heading away from the frost which was gaining on them. He looked back and forth between the cave entrance and that moving line of white, trying to gauge the distance and deciding that it would be close, too close to call.

So he did not try. Instead, he only pushed on, summoning every ounce of the strength remaining to him, forcing his weary legs forward again and again. He reached the cave entrance and stumbled through it. There was a large boulder right inside, and he quickly lay his unconscious brother down before turning to it. He grabbed hold of it and, grunting and straining with the effort, his veins writhing like snakes beneath his neck and arms, he heaved. At first, the giant rock did not move, and he felt sure that it would not. But finally, just when he thought it was too late, it did, groaning with its own weight as Cutter rolled it toward the cave entrance. It did a fair job of blocking it. He had no idea how much it might help, but neither did he take time to consider it. Instead, he moved back to Feledias and lifted his brother up, groaning himself with the effort as his weary arms burned.

He turned back to the cave entrance just in time to see a rime of frost spreading across the entrance, across the boulder blocking it. He backed up into the darkness, unaware of what lay behind him but confident that, should that frost touch them, they would freeze to death. One step, then another as the frost seemed to stretch out with conscious enmity, like some great hand reaching toward them. Cutter's back fetched against something, and he was forced to stand and watch as the frost reached farther still.

Ten feet away from them, then seven, then five and then, as if whatever malevolent power had fueled it had finally run out...it stopped. Cutter stared at it, his breath coming out in great panting clouds in front of him, waiting to see if it would move once more. When it remained still, and he was confident—or at least as confident as he might be—that it did not mean to start up again, Cutter gently laid his brother down on the cave floor.

It appeared, then, that they would not die, at least not for the moment, and if that was the case, there was only one thing to do— get about the business of living. Which meant warmth, fire, for while the greatest of that magical frost may not have touched them, it might yet claim them if he tarried. Already his teeth were chattering, his fingers numb from the cold, and he knew that, now that he was no longer running and working up heat from the exertion, it would only get worse. So he removed his pack from his back, searching for his flint and tinder, a job made more difficult by the fact that the cave, with the boulder mostly occluding its entrance, was pitch black. That and of course the fact that his numb fingers could hardly feel anything at all.

Finally, though, he managed it. He pulled it out, eager at the prospect of the warmth the fire would bring, more eager than he could ever remember being.

That was when he heard a growl in the darkness behind him.

CHAPTER THIRTEEN

While they waited, Maeve examined the room she and Emille had been led to.

A large, circular wooden table sat at the room's center with chairs scattered around it. Stacks of paper decorated the table's surface, and along one wall sat a large easel with several parchments on it. What drew her eye, though, was a diagram hung from the wall. A diagram that depicted a naked man. Dashes indicated several parts throughout the body, showing each of the tendons and arteries as well as labeling muscles and organs.

Maeve was still staring at that diagram when the door opened, and she turned to see two men step into the room. The first was large and muscular, wearing trousers and a sleeveless vest which contrived to show off the not inconsiderable size of his biceps, so large that it looked to Maeve as if the bastard had been stung by something. He was six-and-a-half feet tall if he was an inch, and scowled at her with a face that might have been hewn from stone as he stepped into the room, taking up position on one side of the door.

The second man was as different from the first as he could have been. He was short, a few inches shorter even than Maeve, and where the other man was built like a bear, this one reminded Maeve of some large, prairie cat. He was thin but not in an emaciated way—instead, he possessed whip-cord muscle that shifted beneath his skin as he moved, further making her think of some great cat. This second man did not walk into the room so much as stalk, and from the way he moved alone Maeve was confident that the man was an expert in the use of the thin sword currently sheathed at his back, and in fact she suspected that he was the more dangerous of the two.

The second man took up position on the opposite side of the door from the big man. The two said nothing, only stood at their positions and regarded Maeve and Emille, the big man with a scowl, the other with an expressionless face.

Maeve shared a look with Emille and did not think she had imagined the way the woman's skin had grown a shade paler. Only, it was not the two men that she stared at as one might have expected, but instead at the doorway. Maeve followed her gaze and was rewarded a moment later by a third figure stepping into the room. This one was far different than the other two and as soon as Maeve saw it she had to bite back a curse, for it was a face she recognized.

The woman appeared to be in her sixties, with long gray hair pulled tightly back in a severe bun and a presence that somehow made her manage to look like by far the deadliest of the three and never mind that she lacked the first man's muscles and the second's sword. She stepped into the room as if she owned it, and glanced at Emille before turning to regard Maeve with eyes as sharp as the point of a dagger. "Ah, it seems that I owe Brunhilda an apology. She told me that Emille had brought a guest, one who went by the name of Lady Maeve. I, however, was quite certain that she was mistaken. I told her, in fact, that the woman to whom she referred could not be Lady Maeve. After all, Lady Maeve gave up this life a long time ago, chose to leave us all behind to become the Crimson Prince's consort."

"Not consort," Maeve said, frowning and noting a fourth person, also a woman, easing into the room behind the older woman, this one young with her head bowed down low, her hands clasped in front of her, a servant eager to attend her lady's wishes.

The other woman grinned. "Very well, pet then. Regardless, yours is a face I did not expect to see again. Not alive, anyway."

"And what a pleasure it is to see you again, Mistress Agnes."

The big man let out a growl at that and started forward. The older woman did not even glance in his direction, only raised her hand, and he froze as if under the grips of some mighty spell. "That will be quite enough, Gideon," she said.

The big man frowned but moved back to his position. Maeve's heart was racing, but she knew that she could not betray her fright, for to do so in such a place as this was as good as begging for death, so instead she raised an eyebrow. "Speaking of pets, yours seem eager enough."

The woman gave another humorless smile, her lips a thin, dagger-cut in her face. "Gideon is...protective, and I suppose he well should be. After all, what trait is more important than protectiveness in a bodyguard?"

"That they're house-trained?" Maeve asked.

The big man said nothing to that, but Agnes let out a soft laugh. "Clever. But then you always were clever, Maeve. Clever enough to leave the Guild on your own two feet instead of carried out on your back like everyone else who takes it in mind that they no longer want to be a part of it. And just how did you manage that anyway?"

Maeve gave the woman a humorless smile. "Just lucky, I guess."

"Lucky," the woman said slowly, as if tasting the word. "Well, I suppose that would explain how you have managed to find your way here after so long when all the ways are far different than those you once knew. For surely—" she paused, glancing at Emille, not smiling now—"no one would think to bring you here without permission, a transgression which, if I am not very much mistaken, carries a most...*severe* punishment."

"Mistress Agnes," Maeve began, "it is not Emille's fault. I forced her to—" She cut off at a growl from the big man and the old woman turned on her, her eyes sharp enough to cut.

"It is not 'Mistress Agnes' any longer, *Lady* Maeve. Instead, it is *Head*mistress Agnes."

Maeve felt a momentary bout of panic at that. She had known Agnes for many years, for they had been peers when they both worked for the Guild—but more than peers, they had been rivals. The best two assassins of their generation, it had been believed, and so they had set themselves against each other, making of everything a contest. As for the leaders of the Guild at the time, they had not tried to discourage the behavior—in fact, if anything, they had encouraged it, supposing, Maeve guessed, that the competition would only bring out the best in them. And, perhaps they had even been right, but what the competition had also brought out in them was an intense hatred, a jealousy, an envy for each other that had meant that twice, the woman had tried to kill Maeve and if she was being honest with herself, Maeve had been little better.

She had been bitter in those days before she had met the prince and he had given her a purpose for existing beyond causing others some small bit of the misery she felt. She had been full of anger and hate, resentful of the world which she had thought had taken her husband and her child from her. And so she had returned the woman's scorn, had shared it, and now that woman, the woman with whom she had been in competition for years, the woman who she had strove against and made, at every opportunity, to look like a fool, was now the leader of the Assassin's Guild.

Maeve glanced at the two men by the door. How long, she wondered, before the woman ordered the two men forward to kill her? She could, Maeve knew, and there would be no consequences, not for the leader of the Guild.

"Well?" the headmistress asked, eyeing Maeve with a humorless smile. "Aren't you going to congratulate me on my promotion, Maeve?"

Her mouth was dry, but Maeve nodded. "Of course. Congratulations, Ag—forgive me, *Headmistress* Agnes."

The woman watched her, that dagger-cut smile still slashed across her face, and Maeve did her best not to fidget beneath Agnes's pleased gaze. Maeve realized, standing there, that it had been a mistake to come. If she'd had any idea that Agnes had risen to such heights since her absence from the Guild then surely she would not have. Normally, she would have asked about such a thing, done her due diligence as she had been taught by this same Guild so many years ago. Her younger self would have spent days, perhaps even week studying, learning before she'd made any move—certainly she had done so with each mark she had taken for the Guild before she had met Cutter and the others. It was a time-consuming part of the job, sure, but also an important one. After all, those hours spent talking to this person or the other, watching a building to see who came and went and a thousand other things, had saved her life and that more than once.

The truth was that those hours were probably to be credited with her success as an assassin—any assassin who lived to reach her age, she thought, might be considered a success—as much as, if not more than, her skill with her knives. After all, anybody could stick a knife in somebody, particularly if that somebody didn't see it coming. The real trick to being an assassin wasn't killing someone else. The *real* trick, the point of those hours spent listening to rumor and gossip, sifting the truth from it the way a man might sift through ash in the hopes of finding something retrievable from a fire, was not carrying a few knives sheathed in your own back.

An assassin was trained to be dangerous, yes, but more than that they were trained to avoid danger, to survive it. Certainly not to blunder into it blindly like some fool cow shouldering its companion aside to ensure that it would be the first to reach the butcher's block. Or like an old woman far past her prime allowing her emotions to get the best of her and send her stumbling to her doom like a drunkard shambling in front of a runaway carriage. The drunkard might survive such a foolish decision, but it was unlikely and even if he did survive it, he did not deserve to.

She was like that drunkard, that cow, allowing her emotions, her fear for Chall, fear of losing the love she had only so recently discovered—or perhaps accepted was closer to the truth, to make her make a foolish, rash decision. She had come here unprepared, and when disaster struck, it was always the unprepared who suffered most.

"How long has it been, Maeve?" the woman asked finally, watching her with a hungry look in her eyes. "How long since you and I last spoke?"

"I'm...not sure," Maeve said, then gave the woman her best attempt at an apologetic smile. "My memory, you see, I'm afraid it isn't as good as it used to be."

"Oh, come now, Maeve," Agnes said, "I'm sure you're just being modest. Why, you were considered by many to be the best the Guild had to offer years ago, and I'm sure that hasn't changed." She smiled sharply. "After all, the prince himself was impressed with your...skill, is that not so? I mean, that was after all why he brought you along, why you spent the years during the war feasting in great halls with nobles and diplomats, wearing jewels that cost more than most people make in a year and dresses sewn by the kingdom's greatest tailors. Indeed, it is your talent, your inherent *betterness* that made the prince see fit to allow you to attend ball after ball while myself and the other poor souls of the Guild, who could never hope to be your equals, toiled away to survive. A task, of course, made all the more difficult as the *greatest assassin in the world, Maeve the Marvelous,* could choose any contract she wanted and we others were forced to exist off her *leavings* like hogs at the trough, devouring the slop and scrap of their masters table with pathetic eagerness because they know that not to do so will mean only that they will starve."

"Listen, Agnes, I didn't—"

"Oh, please, *Maeve the Marvelous,*" the woman said, holding her hand up, "do not think to explain yourself to me, for I am far below you and not worthy of an explanation. Besides, I would not dream of asking for one lest I give offense and you show me, personally, those skills for which you are famous. Skills that, according to the stories, make you more of a goddess than a woman. Why," she said, leaning forward, "I do not doubt that, if you grew offended, you could butcher each and every one of us right here. Don't you think so, Gideon?"

The big man said nothing, but he let his opinion be heard by the way his upper lip pulled back from his teeth in a silent snarl.

"Sorry, Lady," Agnes said to Maeve, "not much of a talker is Gideon, I'm afraid. Certainly, he would be out of place in those fine dining halls, surrounded by those pampered and powdered nobles with which you were once accustomed to spending time. Still, he does have other qualities to recommend him, though none that I am sure need concern one such as yourself."

Toying with her, making a game of it. Maeve didn't like it, but then the alternative, which was more than likely the ordering of those two assassins, Gideon and his smaller, unnamed companion, forward to kill her was, she thought, considerably less desirable. And so, as long as Agnes was willing to talk, she was happy to listen. Maybe some words might hurt, but in Maeve's experience, they hurt a damn sight less than a dagger. Once, she might have listened to the challenge in the woman's words and chosen to attack head-on, but then she was not the woman she had been in those days. She was in some ways, more than that woman, but in many ways less. And just as it would not do for a once-great fencer, long into his retirement to step foot into a circle with the current champion, neither would it do for her to antagonize the new leader of the Assassin's Guild.

"Is that why you have come back, I wonder?" the woman pressed. "To take up your position within the Guild once more? Or is it, perhaps, that you wish to challenge me for the position of Guild Headmistress?"

Maeve was shaking her head before the other woman was finished. "Agnes, I swear it's nothing li—"

"*Headmistress,*" the man, Gideon growled.

Maeve winced, starting to speak but the woman beat her to it. "Relax, Gideon," she said, flashing a smile that did not touch her eyes. "After all, this is Maeve the Marvelous—what need does one such as she have to show others the respect of using their titles? She who is so far above us? Is that it then, Lady Maeve?" the woman asked, raising an eyebrow. "Have you come to take my place? To wrest control of the Guild from me? Has Emille here brought a lion into my home?"

"Headmistress, please," Emille said quickly, "I can assure you, Maeve means you no harm and—"

"*Silence,*" the other woman hissed in a furious tone, her eyes suddenly wild with rage. The two men flanking the door started forward, only stopping when Agnes jerked a hand up. "You, I will deal with later, daughter," Agnes said, all the while her smoldering gaze watching Maeve.

Emille opened her mouth, clearly meaning to say more, but the woman stabbed a finger at her. "If she says another word without my permission, Arel, you have permission to cut her tongue from her mouth."

The small man gave a small smile at that, nodding his head.

"Look, A—Headmistress," Maeve said, "there's really no need for this. I haven't come here looking for trouble. In fact, quite the opposite. I've come to—"

"*Shut your mouth,*" the woman snarled, and Maeve saw in her features, twisted with rage, one thing which made her skin grow cold. Madness. The truth was that for the last many years she had thought little of the woman, Agnes, her former rival. Had all but forgotten her, in fact. But it seemed that whatever the years might have done for her, they had done nothing to diminish the hatred the woman felt for her—had, in fact, if anything only seemed to grow it.

Maeve shut her mouth.

The woman watched her, trembling with her rage, and Maeve tensed, preparing to defend herself and Emille should the woman order her two bodyguards forward. Not that she thought it would be likely to do much good. She was not as dangerous as she once was, a blade left to rust and dull in its scabbard, if she might still be considered a blade at all. But even if she had been the woman she once was, she was not sure it would have made a difference. The two men were no doubt some of the best the Guild had to offer—it was why they would have been given the privilege of such a posting—and she and Emille were weaponless. Maeve did not like their chances if it came to a fight, not at all.

"Now," the woman said, "let me tell *you* why you're here. You have come back, after all this time away from the Guild, after being the only one ever to leave it—at least while still standing—because you have realized your mistake. Finally, you have come to understand all that you gave up, the power that you gave up. And so you have come back with the intention of wresting it from me."

"Agnes, that simply isn't—"

"*Enough,*" the woman snapped. "Gideon, Arel, take *Instructor Emille* out of here, but see that she is not harmed, not yet. I will speak to *Lady Maeve* alone."

"Are you sure, Headmistress?" Arel asked, glancing at Maeve with an expression that seemed to show that he would be more than happy to kill her, if killing was wanted.

"I'm sure," the woman said, then turned to the other woman who'd followed her in. "You as well, Eloise."

"Ma'am?" the woman said, looking surprised.

"You heard me," Agnes said, her voice sharp. "I suspect I will be able to survive five minutes without your assistance. But do not fret should I require you to pull on my shoes or lace my gown I will be sure to give a shout."

The woman nodded meekly, her head bobbing quickly before turning and moving toward the door, still cradling her stack of parchments and her quill as if they were her favored children. The small man, whom she'd called Arel, gave a small smile, bowing his head to Emille. "After you, sister."

Emille glanced at Maeve, who gave her the slightest nod. The woman frowned but, in the end, turned and walked out of the door. The small man went next, followed by the big man, Gideon, who took the opportunity to shoot Maeve one more parting scowl before walking through the doorway and closing the door behind him.

Maeve did not like the way that door sounded when it closed, so final, and she turned to regard Agnes, expecting that the woman might threaten her—or perhaps attack her—eager to resume their decades-paused contest and prove that she was the better.

Maeve was surprised, then, to find the woman not looking at her at all but instead studying the closed door with a troubled, almost fearful expression on her face. After a moment, she seemed to start as if waking from a light doze and she turned to regard Maeve.

"Listen, Headmistress," Maeve said, "I swear, I did not mean to—"

"Let it be 'Agnes,' please," the woman interrupted in a voice that was not unkind. "And I hope it will suffice should I call you Maeve?"

"O...of course," Maeve said, more than a little confused by the woman's abrupt change of demeanor.

"That is good then," Agnes said, sounding suddenly not angry at all but instead very tired. "Sorry," she said, wincing, "you know, about before. The threats and all of that. It is just a game, that's all, one that I am expected to play and so I must."

Maeve blinked. "You...you mean...that is...that you don't..."

"Hate you?" Agnes asked. Maeve nodded, and the woman gave a small smile. "No, Maeve, I don't hate you. I did, you know. For a while. For a long while. Hated you because you were given what I thought were all the best contracts. Hated you because the instructors of our time used to always hold you up as an example.

213

'If you were more like Maeve,' they'd say, or, 'Thank the gods we have Maeve, if the rest of you lot are so worthless as this.' Those sorts of things and many others, taunts, ones I now understand, and perhaps even understood at the time, that were contrived to make us better. To create in us a hatred for each other which would fuel us to be smarter, faster. And, I must admit that it worked. Only...that hatred remained for a long time after. Hatred that they always seemed to dote on you, hatred mostly, if I'm being honest with myself, that you were better than I was."

"Agnes, I don't—"

The woman waved a hand in dismissal. "Relax, Maeve. I bear you no ill will for that—we both tried as well as we could. You were just better, that's all." She shrugged. "Someone had to be, didn't they?"

Maeve stared at the woman before her feeling as if she was seeing her for the very first time. The calm, reasonable person speaking with her now was a far cry from that angry, bitter woman she had once known, the one with which she had competed about everything.

"Now then," Agnes went on, moving to the table and waving a hand at a seat before taking one for herself, "why don't you tell me the real reason you've come."

Maeve hesitated, glancing around, feeling very much like she was preparing to walk into a trap. True, Agnes *seemed* sincere, but then assassins were trained in many things and not all of it combat—the woman knew how to act, as all members of the Guild did, better than any costumed and face-painted actress from a mummer's show. The woman turned to her, raising an eyebrow, and Maeve considered it for another moment before finally moving toward the table.

She did so for two reasons. The first being that, if the woman had meant to kill her she could have done so easily enough without any trickery necessary. After all, her two bodyguards looked more than capable and, in the big man's case at least, more than willing to do the job themselves. Secondly, what choice did she have? She could either risk giving offense to the leader of the Assassin's Guild or she could play along and pursue the reason she'd come here to begin with.

She sat, but she did not allow herself to sink into the chair and get comfortable. She turned to the woman. "Well, as to that, I think you probably know why I'm here."

The woman frowned. "Say that I don't."

Maeve sighed. That was how she was going to play it then. However much the woman claimed that she didn't hold the past against Maeve, it seemed that she hadn't completely let it go after all. Or perhaps she just enjoyed her petty cruelties—certainly she had in the past. "Very well. I've come because an assassin tried to kill me and Challadius this morning—and very nearly succeeded."

The woman's frown deepened. "An assassin?"

"That's right."

"And you think that this assassin is one of ours?"

"Was," Maeve said, and it was her time to frown. "Anyway, I *know* he was one of yours. I've been gone for a long time, but not so long that I don't recognize the Guild marks when I see them. So I've come to get the contract on Challadius and I removed."

Maeve was watching the woman carefully as she spoke, for even the world's best actors might give away some small bit of their thoughts from time to time, and indeed her efforts were not in vain. But what she saw in the woman's eyes, only for a moment before she covered it once more, was not what she had expected. Not satisfaction or anger at a job done poorly—instead, it was surprise.

Agnes rose, pacing away for a moment before turning back and, had Maeve not known better, she would have said that the woman looked scared. "There must be some mistake."

"That *mistake* very nearly killed Chall and I this morning before we even so much as rose from bed," Maeve snapped, "so if you—"

"Wait a minute," Agnes said, her eyes going wide. "Did you say that you and Challadius were abed when the assassin came?"

Maeve felt her face heat. "That's right, but what difference does that make?"

"None, I suppose," Agnes said, a small smile coming to her face. "Only, I fear that I owe a few people some coin. I suppose I'm lucky that in our business most people don't live all that long, or I'd likely be broke."

Maeve frowned. "I don't understand."

"Oh, come now, Maeve," the woman said, "we are far from blushing young brides, are we not? The only place farther than where we now stand is the grave we will one day crawl into. Those of us who were closest to you, your peers, we were aware of when you met the prince and Challadius and the other, the priest. Just as we were aware of how you grew to love the mage."

Maeve snorted. "That's impossible—why, all I ever did was complain about the bastard and…" She trailed off, her face heating further. Then, "Why…why didn't you say something?"

"Me?" Agnes asked, laughing in seemingly genuine mirth. "Me, your greatest rival point out your affection for a known rake, possibly the world's best-known philanderer? No, I think not, Maeve. First, I must admit that some part of me—a large part—at that time did not want you to find happiness and, even if I *had* pointed it out to you, you would have only assumed it was some kind of trap I was attempting to lure you into. Which, had I pointed it out, of course I would have made sure that it was."

"And…and you claim that everyone knew?"

The woman shrugged, smiling. "I would say that we all suspected, yes. Though we had our doubts—or, at least, *I* had my doubts—that you would ever do anything about it. You were a great assassin, Maeve—our best, I can admit that now—but that does not mean you were skilled in matters of the heart." She gave her a tight grin. "Unless, of course, that meant carving into that heart until its owner died a quick death."

"I…see," Maeve said, feeling particularly foolish. To think that so many people had been able to see more of her than she had herself. But then, that was another of the world's truths—this one not learned from the Guild but from a lifetime of living and breathing on its surface—that a woman or a man never saw themselves as clearly as others. And how could they? After all, even when they did catch a glimpse of themselves, it was only in part, for their eyes were a part of them as much as anything else. Unless, she supposed, they gazed into a mirror or a lake surface, but even then what looked back at them was backwards, an imperfect reflection colored by their own expectations, their own thoughts.

"I am glad that you found each other, Maeve," Agnes said, and Maeve jerked her gaze up to see the woman watching her. She had thought, at first, that she was being mocked, but the woman appeared genuine enough.

"If you don't mind my saying so, Agnes…" Maeve said, "you…have changed."

The woman gave her a small, almost sad smile. "Time changes us all, Maeve. For some, perhaps even for most, it makes of us bitter, cruel, hateful things. But in some few instances, it might change us for the better."

"And you would have me believe that is what happened to you?"

The woman considered that then finally shrugged. "No. You can believe what you want to believe, Maeve. I will not try to persuade you one way or the other."

Maeve grunted. This woman had made her life torture for years, and now somehow *Maeve* was the one who felt guilty. "Anyway, about this contract: if you truly are changed, will you remove it?"

Agnes sighed. "I am afraid I cannot. For I know of no such contract."

Maeve snorted. "Come now, Agnes. I might be old, but I'm not so addled that I don't know when an assassin is making an attempt on my life. Anyway, he bore the mark of the Guild, and unless things have changed dramatically since I was here, I seem to recall the Guild not liking the idea of people under their employ choosing to freelance. As I recollect, the punishment was most…final."

"You misunderstand me, Maeve," Agnes said. "I believe that you saw, as you have claimed, the mark on the man, and you are correct in supposing that the Guild frowns upon its members taking other jobs. But what I mean is that *I* know of no such contract."

Maeve narrowed her eyes, watching the woman. "But…but you're the Headmistress. You're the leader of the Guild. All contracts pass through you."

"Or at least they should," Agnes agreed, frowning.

"I…don't understand."

"Neither do I, at least not fully," Agnes said, "and that, I'm afraid, is the problem. You see, Maeve, when we were young and just starting out in this life—" she paused, grunting a bitter laugh—"if life it can be called, well we were focused on our own purposes. Fulfilling contracts, competing with each other, climbing the ladder of the Guild. And I, like most, like even you, I suspect, contrived to sabotage my peers so that they might lose favor with the guild masters. The guild masters themselves approved of it, of course, believing that the contest would make us all stronger. The problem is that when I aged and began to take up a position of power within the Guild, so too did the others, those who I had spent the better part of twenty years sabotaging, and who, in turn, had spent that time sabotaging and targeting me. You remember the Tribunal?"

Of course Maeve remembered the Tribunal, the three scariest men and women in all of New Daltenia as far as she was concerned. Assassins, one and all, or at least former assassins, the best of what the Guild had to offer, those who had risen to power among their peers, who had garnered reputations as being the most dangerous, the most cunning, the most *deadly* assassins of all. They were also the ruling body, such as it was, of the Guild, with the Headmistress or Headmaster of the Guild—currently Agnes—sitting at their front. The Headmistress served as a sort of king or queen within the Guild, but unlike the king of New Daltenia, the leader of the Guild's power was not paramount, but might instead be checked by the Tribunal, assuming a majority vote. "I remember," she said. "The ruling body of the Guild, aside from...well. You, of course."

"Vipers, more like," Agnes hissed. "Snakes lying in wait in the grass, poison dripping from their fangs. And who do they lie in wait for, Maeve? Who but me?"

Maeve frowned. "You mean that you think they are conspiring against you?"

"I do not *think*, Maeve," the woman said, looking at her as if she were a fool. "I *know*. There have been two attempts on my life already in the last year. Not so unusual a thing, I suppose, for no sooner does a person reach the top than there's someone eager to push her down so that they might watch her fall from so great a height. What *is* unusual, though, is that these attempts both have come at times when no one knew where I was. No one, at least, except the members of the Tribunal."

"Ah," Maeve said. "That is the reason for the bodyguards then?"

Agnes raised an eyebrow. "That was my intention but, as it turns out, hiring them was a foolish mistake."

"Why?"

The woman gave her a sharp, humorless smile. "The problem with swords for hire, Maeve—or in Gideon's case, *fists* for hire—is that they care very little who hires them, or who *pays* them. They *do* care, however, about how *much* they are paid. They remain loyal to their charges only so long as those charges continue to have the best offer."

"You're saying that they've been...hired by someone else?"

The woman glanced back at the door as if expecting someone—her bodyguards, perhaps—to come charging through it with blood on their minds, then she turned back to Maeve. "Bought and paid for, yes. Gideon belongs to that old crone Bethesa."

Maeve's eyes went wide at that, for the woman to which Agnes referred had been old—ancient, really—even twenty years ago. "She's still alive?"

"Of course she is," Agnes said, frowning, "evil doesn't die, Maeve, haven't you ever heard as much? And that woman is as evil as they come, no matter how she enjoys her play-acting. It's all just a show she puts on, that's all. As for Arel, the swordsman, well he works for that old wretch, the Weasel."

"The Weasel," Maeve repeated.

The woman nodded. "My name for him, and apt enough, I think. You would know him, of course, as Tribune Piralta. Not quite as old and not quite as evil as Bethesa, perhaps, but not far from it either."

"And you're sure? That your bodyguards work for them, I mean?"

"Of course I'm sure," the woman snapped. "I wouldn't claim it if I didn't know it was true. You think I haven't done my research? I do not come to such conclusions lightly, Maeve, particularly when my own life might well be forfeit if I am wrong."

"I see..." Maeve said, "but if you know that they're traitors, then why do you continue to keep them in your employ? Why not simply fire them?"

"Under what pretense?" the woman asked. "And what would be the point? After all, they would only immediately set about finding other eyes and ears to watch me, ones I might not discover.

No, better that they remain, better that I know to whom their eyes and ears belong. That way, I can at least control what they see, what they hear."

Maeve watched the woman carefully. She hadn't spoken with Agnes in a long time, but she had known her well once. After all, they had been bitter rivals, and one of the lessons the Guild had taught her was that an assassin should know her enemy—or her mark—better than she would know her best friend or her sister. Maeve had taken that lesson to heart and so she knew the woman before her well, despite the passing of the years. Well enough, anyway, to see that there was something else troubling her. "What is it, Agnes? What is it really?"

The woman looked at her, hesitating. Then, finally, she sighed. "I am afraid, Maeve. Once, I would have never said as much, certainly not to you, but I am older now, and what pride the years have left me is a pathetic, shriveled thing. The main reason that I do not rid myself of the two men is that I fear what the Tribunes might do should I try. In truth, I'm not even sure that I *could* dismiss this from my service. For all I know, the men are under strict orders to kill me if I try. Perhaps it does not make sense given how miserable and untenable my life has become, but I am not yet ready to lose it."

"Miserable?" Maeve asked, surprised.

The woman gave her a soured smile. "Yes, perhaps it is strange, considering that you know me from years ago, to hear me say as much. Certainly I was ambitious then, and the me of the past would not understand how I could be anything but satisfied—even overjoyed—with my current position. After all, it is the position for which I conspired for years. I am like a thief who has long coveted a jewel only to find, when he finally acquires it, that what he has taken for a precious gem was nothing more than costume jewelry. Worse yet, that it had been coated in poison so that whatever fool thought to take the prize for themselves might be made to regret that decision."

"Poisoned?" Maeve asked.

"More than you might imagine, Maeve," the woman said. "A poison that is slow acting, but that is no less fatal for that."

"It seems to me that that is often the case, when we get what we thought we always wanted," Maeve said, thinking about how her life had been since she had become the kingdom's most famous—or infamous, depending on who you asked—assassin. Certainly, it had not made things easier. Then she found herself thinking of Chall, and a small smile came to her face. "At least...most of the time."

"You think of him, don't you?" Agnes asked. "Your mage." She shook her head slowly. "I am happy for you, Maeve, but I must admit to some small bit of envy as well." She held up her hand as if to stop Maeve from saying anything. "I have no designs on Challadius the Charmer, understand. Only I am jealous that you have found someone else, someone with which you might share the burden of life with."

The burden of life. Maeve wasn't sure what the woman had been through, but it was clear that it had not been easy to leave her viewing her existence in such a way. She thought that it was too bad Priest was not with her, for the man had a way of helping people, granting them peace from such thoughts. He had certainly helped her countless times over the years. But then she considered the way he'd been acting of late and decided it was probably best he had not come. "It is...*he* is...more than I deserve. It is why I came, to make sure that he is safe. Listen, Agnes, about the contract—"

"Yes, yes, to business," the woman said. "Well, as I said, Maeve, I am afraid that I have no idea of any such contract on you or your man, Challadius. But then, that is no great surprise. They hide things from me, you see, working behind my back. Always working. When I turn to investigate, they appear innocent enough—they are skilled at that—but there are too many of them, and so I spend all of my time only turning this way and that while those out of my sight work against me, undermining my authority."

"But to what end?" Maeve asked.

The woman gave her a small smile. "To the only end that matters for those in the Guild, of course, Maeve. Power. The Tribunes seek the power I possess—or at least, what power they *imagine* I possess. Those who work for them seek the seats of the Tribunes themselves, and on and on it goes all the way down to the least of the scullery maids. Such is the Guild, such is what it makes us. As for the contract, I do not know why they would keep it from me, only that they have. And I doubt very much if that is all they have kept from me."

"So…there's nothing you can do?"

"I did not say that," the woman said slowly. "There are, perhaps, some options, some courses I might take. Only…these courses, they are fraught with peril, Maeve, and to travel along them I would need some…incentive."

Maeve fought back an inward sigh. Here it was, then. Never mind all of her condemnation of the Guild and what it stood for it seemed that Agnes had not changed so much from that woman she had once been as she pretended. "A price," Maeve said. "Well, I guess there always is one."

The woman inclined her head in a nod. "Of course—it's how the world goes 'round, isn't it?"

"What is it, then?" Maeve asked. "How much?"

The woman cocked her head, watching her. "How much? You think that I want your money?"

Maeve frowned. "Well, it seems that—"

Agnes laughed without humor. "I have all the coin I need, Maeve. And should I get more, what would I spend it on? What need does a prisoner have of coin?"

"Are you sure you're not being…a bit dramatic?" Maeve asked.

The woman only smiled, saying nothing to that. "No, Maeve, it is not your coin that I want."

"Then…listen, Agnes, if it is a contract that you want…"

The woman shook her head. "No, Maeve. I do not wish for you to kill anyone—I know plenty of killers, after all. The truth is that I know little else. Still, it would be interesting, to see you in action once more, to see how much of your skills you have retained."

"I've retained enough," Maeve said sharply. "I would say your guildmember, Felara, would agree, if she were alive to do so."

Agnes smiled. "I heard of that. It is true that Felara was talented, but she was also impatient, an unfortunate combination that was bound to get her killed sooner or later, though I will admit I had not expected that death to come at your hands. Still, you need not posture for me, Maeve, for I mean you no harm. Indeed, your appearance has given me an idea, has given me something else, too, something that I have lacked for a very long time: hope."

"I'm...not sure what you mean, Agnes. If it isn't money or a contract you want then what..."

"I want *out,* Maeve," the woman blurted. "I want to *escape.* I want to pass this poisoned jewel to another, *any* other, and run as far from the Guild as I can."

Maeve stared in shock at the woman, who was suddenly panting from her outburst. She had not expected that, not from Agnes, and she decided that the woman had changed, after all. The woman she had known had been all hard surfaces and sharp edges, without any softness to her, or, if there had been any, then a man or woman would have cut themselves to ribbons trying to reach it. One of the deadliest women—deadliest *people*—Maeve had ever met and that with no small amount of competition. But she did not seem so now. Instead, she seemed scared, desperate. "But...if you no longer want to lead the Guild, why do you not simply...give up your position?"

The woman gave a cackling laugh at that. "Give up my position. Oh, if only it were that simple. You see, Maeve, being the Headmistress of the Assassin's Guild is like a woman climbing to the top of a great mountain who suddenly finds that she can climb no longer and that there is only one way left to her. Down. And only one path to take her downward, if he so chooses—and that is to fall. No, I would not be allowed to simply quit. There is only one way a person leaves the position that I'm in—and that's dead."

Maeve winced. "Well, if that's true, Agnes, then you have my pity, but I'm not sure what else I can do for you."

"*Damn your pity,*" the woman snapped, then winced. "Forgive me, only...I do not ask for your pity, Maeve. I ask for your help, just as you have come to ask for mine, though you did not know at the time that it was me who you would ask."

"My help?" Maeve asked.

"Of course," the woman said. "After all, who better to consult about leaving the Guild than the only person I have ever known to do it successfully? At least, that is, alive."

Maeve blinked, the pieces finally clicking into place. "I see. But, Agnes, surely you understand that those were special circumstances. It wasn't as if—"

"Oh yes, I am quite aware of those special circumstances," she interrupted. "Circumstances, of course, by the name of Prince

A Warrior's Penance

Bernard. After all, even the Guild had no interest in getting on the Crimson Prince's bad side."

"Right," Maeve said, "but that doesn't mean that *I* can help you, Agnes."

"Of course you can," the woman said. "And in turn, *I* will make sure to figure out the specifics of the contract on you and your man, will make sure that it disappears." She leaned forward then, quickly, her eyes dancing with a desperate sort of madness, "Come on, Maeve. It will be better for both of us."

"But...how?" Maeve asked.

"It's obvious, isn't it?" Agnes asked. "You need only speak to the prince—the two of you are close. I'm sure that if you but asked him—"

"It's impossible, Agnes."

The woman cut off her exciting blurting and frowned. "For a woman who has come seeking assistance, Maeve, you sure do not seem overly prepared to give it."

Maeve winced, shaking her head. "It's not that, Agnes. You see, Cu—that is, Prince Bernard is not in New Daltenia any longer. He was escorted out of the city. I am surprised that you have not heard of it."

"I heard," the woman said frowning, "but then a lifetime spent in the Assassin's Guild has taught me not to trust anything I do not see with my own eyes and only half of that which I do. Now, are you trying to tell me that Prince Bernard and the rest of you returned to New Daltenia, somehow avoided being murdered by Prince Feledias—who, by all accounts, has thought of little else for the last fifteen years—and then managed to appoint Prince Bernard's son as king only for that same son to exile the prince because of crimes committed before said king was even born?" The woman raised an eyebrow at her. "Come, Maeve. Even a child could not credit such a tale."

"And yet, it's true," Maeve said, remembering Matt's possession by the Feyling all too clearly. "You have my word on that."

"So you mean to say that the prince's newly-discovered son, who he rescued from death in that backwater village of Brighton, sent him to the Black Wood as thanks?" She snorted. "He would have been better off simply sticking a dagger in his back. It would have been painful, perhaps cliché, but far preferable than placing oneself in the hands of those creatures of the wood."

Maeve blinked. "I'm...didn't know you—"

"Didn't know that I had heard of Brighton?" the woman asked. "Oh yes, Maeve. I have heard rumor of it."

"I thought you didn't trust rumor."

Agnes shrugged a thin shoulder. "Trust or lack of it is no reason for a person to remain uninformed. In my business, in what once was *our* business, you know as well as I that a lack of knowledge will kill you quicker than any executioner's axe."

"But...but how did you hear of it?" Maeve asked.

Agnes waved a dismissive hand. "How does not matter, Maeve, only that I did and that, by your reaction, I can see that this rumor, at least, was a true one. So tell me, Maeve," she went on, leaning forward, "what would possibly possess Prince Bernard's son, after his father had gone through all that trouble for him, to send him to his death?"

Possession is right, Maeve thought, but did not say as much. The woman before her was far different than the Agnes she had known a long time ago, but she was still not just a member of the Assassin's Guild but its leader. "I'm afraid we all have our secrets, Agnes. Anyway, it makes no difference. What does is that you can see that the prince isn't here—I cannot ask him for his help in this, even if I wished to."

The woman sighed, seeming to deflate as she sat back in her chair, slumping. "Well then, Maeve, it seems that we are, both of us, bound to be disappointed. I suppose there will be one last contest between us after all—seeing who dies first, you to your assassins or me to mine."

Which one of us dies first. The words stuck in Maeve's mind and, for several seconds, she couldn't figure out why. Then, suddenly, realization struck. "That's it, Agnes," she said. "You have to die."

The woman raised an eyebrow. "That Maeve sounds less like a plan and more like something to do when a plan fails."

"No, no, Agnes," Maeve said, "I don't mean to kill you. In fact," she went on, her mouth spreading in a grin, "I mean to help you."

"Really?" Agnes asked, sounding suspicious, true, but Maeve could see the spark of hope in her eyes.

"Really," Maeve agreed. "You did say you wanted to get out of the Guild, to leave New Daltenia and start a life somewhere else, isn't that right?"

"That's right," the woman said slowly.

Maeve nodded. "And if I agree to do that for you then you'll cancel the contract on me and Challadius?"

"Of course," she said, "but I will not risk myself to do that simply on your word, Maeve. I will want to know what your plan is."

"Sure," Maeve said, "it's simple, really, Agnes. We just have to kill you."

The woman frowned. "I told you, Maeve, you would be wise to—"

"No, no," Maeve said hurriedly, "not *truly* kill you. We need only to make people *believe* you've been killed."

"You mean lie," the woman said.

Maeve shrugged. "Yes."

Agnes scratched at her chin, seeming to consider it. Finally, she shook her head. "It is not without merit, Maeve, but it will fail. Those who seek to replace me might be ambitious fools, but they are not idiots. If I were to die out of their sight, they would not believe it. They would search for me and, sooner or later, in the searching, they would find me. As you well know, no one can hide from the combined might of the Guild, not forever, at least."

"Then we had best make sure they are convinced you're dead," Maeve said.

The woman raised an eyebrow. "The only way they will be satisfied of that is to be standing over my corpse, Maeve, and actually *being* dead defeats the whole purpose."

"Oh, they'll be satisfied alright," Maeve said, grinning. "Just leave that part to me."

The woman stared at her, a confused expression on her face for several seconds then her eyes slowly widened, and Maeve watched as realization dawned. "You mean to make use of the mage, Challadius the Charmer."

Maeve smiled. "I do."

Agnes nodded slowly. "I suppose there are some benefits to bedding an illusionist."

Plenty, Maeve thought, aware of her face heating—the man might be overweight, but he was surprisingly energetic for all that. "Yes, well, either way."

"And you believe he will be willing to help?"

"I think he might be convinced."

"Sounds like a lot of convincing all around," Agnes said. "I've heard that the man's a good illusionist, one of the best who has ever lived, but he would have to be a master indeed to fool the Guild. After all, they will want to be *sure,* and such people as this leave nothing to chance."

"They'll be sure," Maeve agreed with more certainty than she felt. After all, she'd heard Chall bitch enough about creating illusions over the years to know that they were much more difficult to fashion—and maintain—than most people thought, far more than just a simple snap of the fingers. But then, what choice did they have?

Agnes watched her for several seconds, no doubt searching for some sign of deceit or trickery—after all, an assassin who trusted easily was also one who did not live long. Finally, the woman gave a single nod. "Very well," she said. "I can think of no better way. How long will it take to start, do you think?"

"Not long," Maeve said. "I just have to get back to the castle and speak with Chall—he'll know the best way to get it done. Then I'll come back and we can set about it." Maeve started toward the door, paused as the woman spoke.

"No."

Maeve tensed, turning, resisting the urge to reach for her knives at the abruptness of the woman's tone. It wouldn't make sense for the woman to attack her or order her killed now, not when she had a chance to get what she wanted. It would not be in her best interest—but then Maeve had lived long enough to know that people could often be counted on to do things against their best interest and they rarely made sense.

"No?" she asked, turning to regard the woman who had risen from her chair.

The woman shook her head. "It would not do for you to simply walk out the door. No, it would cause too many questions. Why, for example, did Lady Maeve, the once most celebrated assassin in all the world, come to the Guild in the first place? Then, from there, why was she allowed to leave without any...punishment? After all, those people for whom my bodyguards work will not accept that you came here for no reason, and that once having come, we simply made up. They would doubt it, would doubt you and your presence, and so in the days to come, the days when we might enact this plan of yours, they will look back on this moment, do you see? They will look back and believe that there was a purpose to your visit after all, and a good reason why you left unharmed."

Maeve winced. Agnes was right, of course. Maeve should have seen the angle of it, but she was too excited at the prospect of ending the contract on her and Chall—or perhaps it was simply that she had been out of the assassin's life too long, had lost her edge. "True," she admitted, "but do you have some idea about what to do about it?"

Agnes gave her a sharp smile, one that did little to offer Maeve any comfort. "Oh, I think I do."

Maeve raised an eyebrow. "An idea, one hopes, that doesn't involve me being whipped or stabbed."

"You know, Maeve, you always were a spoil sport. But don't worry, I don't mean you any harm. After all, I wouldn't dream of hurting another member of the Guild."

Maeve raised an eyebrow. "I don't mean to quibble, Agnes, but I left the Guild twenty years ago."

"So you did," Agnes agreed, "but now, returned to New Daltenia, you have decided that you wish to rejoin the fold once more. After all, with your prince gone and with your advancing years, what else is left to you but to try to relive the glory days of your past?"

Maeve winced. "You still don't bother to pull your punches, do you? Anyway, I don't recall those days being all that glorious, if I'm being honest."

"Forgive me, Maeve, but I have more important things to worry about than your feelings. And so do you, unless I'm mistaken, and you've decided you are no longer concerned with the contract on you and Challadius."

"You know I haven't," Maeve said. She considered for a moment, then sighed. "Fine," Maeve said, "fine, you're right. But how are we going to fool them into thinking that I rejoined the Guild?"

The other woman flashed a vulture-like grin. "Oh, but Maeve don't you see? We're not going to fool them at all."

"I don't understand," Maeve said, though the truth was she had a suspicion that she understood all too well what the woman meant.

"Don't you?" Agnes asked, raising an eyebrow. "Our plan is difficult enough, Maeve, without adding to it. What's the easiest way to make the members of the Tribunal believe that you have rejoined the Guild? Well, that's simple enough, isn't it? You *do* rejoin. Not pretend, but in truth."

"But...how?" Maeve asked, resigning herself to the fact that Agnes was right. "I mean, is there a procedure for it?"

"No," Agnes said, "in fact there is not. After all, every other soul who has left the Guild hasn't exactly been in a position to attempt to rejoin it...largely owing to the fact, no doubt, that they were dead."

Maeve winced. "Right...so what do we do?"

The woman's eyes roamed up and down Maeve. "Tell me, Maeve, how are you with those knives you're carrying? Still got any talent?"

"I suppose I still have something left," Maeve said warily.

"Good," the woman said. "Because it seems to me that if you want to return to the Guild—"

"Which I don't."

"Then you'll need to prove that you still belong among our number."

Which I don't. Maeve sighed. "And I suppose there's no written exam for that?"

"I regret that there isn't," Agnes said, though by the grin on her face Maeve thought that if the woman did feel any regret she was doing a damned fine job of hiding it.

Maeve sighed. "What did you have in mind, then?"

Agnes smiled, an expression that Maeve did not care for, not in the least. "Well, Felara was not the only assassin in the Guild seeking to make a name for herself as its best member. There are plenty of others, any of whom would be more than a little eager to take on Maeve the Marvelous herself—even a washed-up, admittedly withered version of her."

"Again with the flattery," Maeve said dryly.

"Such a one," the woman went on as if she hadn't spoken, "would be thrilled at the prospect of making his or her name by besting you."

"Look, Agnes, I'm sure you'd enjoy watching me get skewered by someone half my age, but me being dead isn't going to fix either of our problems."

"You're right, of course," Agnes said, tapping her chin thoughtfully. "Tell me, Maeve, just how good of a friend is Emille to you? Obviously she must be at least pretty close, for she risked everything by bringing you here without permission."

Maeve frowned, thinking she was beginning to understand where this was going and not caring for it. "Emille has helped me several times, far more than I deserve and with little recompense for it."

"I see," Agnes said. "It seems to me, then, that she has made a habit of helping you and might well be convinced to do so one more time."

"You mean for her to challenge me," Maeve said.

"I do."

"And for her to lose on purpose."

The woman bared her teeth in what might have been a grin. "Hopefully she will not have to try too hard for that. After all, it will have to be a public affair, won't it? With all, or at least most of the Guild present. And not only will it need be public, it will also need to be *believable*."

Maeve considered it then shook her head. "I cannot ask it of her. It...it would not be fair."

"Perhaps not," Agnes agreed. "Then, I suppose, you have a choice to make, Maeve. Would you like to be fair, or would you like to have the contract on you and Challadius canceled? I do not think that you can have both."

"I hope you don't take offense, Agnes," Maeve said, "when I tell you that I hate you a little bit."

"Well, I should hope so," the woman said. "After all, you're going to kill me, aren't you?"

Maeve sighed. "When are we going to do it?"

Agnes's mouth slowly shifted into a vulpine grin. "How does now suit?"

CHAPTER FOURTEEN

Chall woke to a hand on his shoulder, made some sleep noises—not words, not really, or at least, if they were, they were incomprehensible even to himself—and opened bleary eyes to see a form standing over him. One he recognized, when he blinked and rubbed the sleep away from his eyes, as Priest, the man wearing what was becoming a depressingly familiar and depressingly dour expression. "Chall," he said. "It's time."

Chall grunted, rising. "Where's Ned?"

Priest frowned, glancing toward the carved-out hollow which led to the main cavern. "Only just returned. He went out into the city."

"Why?" Chall asked, surprised.

"I do not know," Priest said, his frown deepening.

Chall watched the man for several seconds then shook his head. "You don't trust him, do you?"

"No."

"Then you're a fool," Chall said matter-of-factly.

Priest recoiled as if he'd been struck. "What?"

"You heard me," Chall said as he rose from the small, dusty cot on which he'd lain. "I mean fire and salt, Priest, what does the man have to do to get you to trust him? How many times has he saved our lives now? Two? Three? What's the cut off?"

"Perhaps you're right," Priest said slowly, "but he has secrets."

Chall snorted. "All men have secrets, Priest, you and I included. That doesn't mean anything except that he, like the rest of us, is human. Anyway, I don't think your mistrust is about Ned at all, not really. I don't know what's going on with you, but I'll tell you what I think, Priest—I don't think you're in a position to want to trust anybody or any*thing* isn't that right?"

The man looked angry at that, and Chall wondered if perhaps he had stepped too far, if perhaps he was going to see the man's hand-to-hand fighting skills personally. Priest finally opened his mouth as if to say something, but never got the chance as a voice called from the doorway.

"Mornin', mornin' glories."

They both turned to see Ned standing there, his smile doing little to hide the deep circles under his eyes or his haggard, exhausted appearance. "Good morning," Chall said.

"Sleep good?" Ned asked.

"Slept, anyway," Chall said, rubbing at a crick in his neck. "How about you?"

"Didn't have the time," the carriage driver said, "had something I had to be about."

"Oh?" Chall asked. "You mean you haven't slept at all?"

The man waved a dismissive hand, even the simple gesture betraying his exhaustion. "Don't you worry about me none. Plenty enough time to sleep when...well. Anyway. I suppose we'd best be going. It's daylight out."

Chall shook his head. "Even with it being daylight, I must confess I don't love the idea of traipsing around the poor district."

"Guess we'd best get you back to the castle then," Ned agreed.

"No."

They both turned to regard Priest who'd spoken. "What's that?" Chall asked.

"I said no," Priest repeated. "We cannot go back to the castle, not now. We still have yet to discover enough about the Crimson Wolves. We need to speak to Catham—he seems to know more than he let on; why else would he try to have us killed when Nadia did not order it?"

"You're telling me you want to walk around the poor district— a district full of people who want to see us dead—searching for one man in the hopes of finding him before one of the no doubt many he's got out there looking for us finds us?"

"It's the only way to get the answers we need," Priest said.

"Maybe not the only way," Ned offered.

They turned to look at him, and the carriage driver shrugged. "Well, seems to me that it's little better than suicide, you two goin' lookin' for Catham. After all, he knows the both of you. He or one of his men would mark you before you got within a hundred feet. Me, though, well he don't know me from anybody, does he?"

"So what?" Priest said. "Just because he doesn't know you doesn't mean anything. You'd still have to find him, to follow him without him knowing until you had an opportunity to capture him."

"Sure," Ned agreed. "But then, I've found him and followed him before. After all, it was the reason I was on hand to rescue the two of you, wasn't it?"

"He's got a point," Chall said, his mouth suddenly dry as he recalled the dozens of people that had been ready—eager, really—to kill them. "We ought to just let Ned look into it."

"No," Priest said.

Chall frowned. "What do you mean, 'no?'"

"What I *mean*," Priest said, frowning at the carriage driver, "is that I don't trust him."

Chall blinked. "You still don't trust him. The man who saved our lives last night."

"He is, by his own admission, a member of the Crimson Wolves," Priest said, watching Ned with narrowed eyes. "The same Crimson Wolves who were behind the murdering of an innocent castle servant, in case you've forgotten, not to mention infiltrating Matt's—that is, His Majesty's—quarters."

"Not the same."

They both turned to look at Ned. "What's that?" Chall asked.

"Not the same," the carriage driver repeated, a frown on his face. "Whoever is behind the Wolves' return, if indeed they *are* returned, I already told you, it's got nothin' to do with me. Why, that's the whole reason I'm lookin' into it in the first place. Fact is, nobody wants to know who's behind all this more than I do."

"If you're to be believed," Priest said, "but I *don't* believe you. After all, up until last night you were content to allow us to think you were a carriage driver, nothing more."

"That's because I *am* a carriage driver," Ned said, sighing. "Damn, fella the Wolves ain't existed for years now."

"And what of your wife, Emille?" Priest challenged. "Does she know of this? Have you told her the truth?"

The carriage driver had endured Priest's jabs up to that point with good humor and patience, but at mention of his wife, his mouth drew down into a deep frown, his eyes narrowing. "I'd watch myself awful careful right now, I was you," he said. "I don't reckon I'd be proud of hittin' a priest, it came to it, but I don't reckon that'd stop me neither. Won't be the first thing I've done I ain't proud of."

"You would regret the attempt," Priest hissed, his hands knotting into fists at his sides.

The carriage driver met the man's gaze and they looked moments from coming to blows. Chall stepped forward. "Damnit enough!" he snapped, coming between them. "Like we ain't got enough folks already volunteerin' for the job of killing us, now we mean to do it to each other? There some sort of reward ain't nobody told me about, is that it?"

He was watching Priest, saw the man frowning, then sighed, glancing over his shoulder at the carriage driver. "You mind givin' us a second, Ned?"

"Sure," Ned said, watching Priest for another moment before turning and walking away.

"That's damned ridiculous," Chall said after the man was gone.

"I know," Priest said. "Look, Chall, I think we should—"

"I mean *you*," Chall said, turning on him.

Priest blinked as if he couldn't believe what he was hearing. "I'm sorry, what?"

"Fire and salt, Priest, what's wrong with you? Don't like bein' saved, is that it? Well, congratulations, because after the way you've acted, I'm fairly sure we won't have to worry about Ned makin' that mistake again anytime soon."

Priest frowned. "But...he lied to us, Chall. He was a Crimson Wolf—you heard him say as much yourself."

"You're right," Chall said, "I did hear it. So what?"

"So...what?"

"You heard me," Chall said. "And maybe you're forgetting, Priest, but if the man would have decided he wanted to keep that secret a bit longer all he would have had to do was nothing, just sit there and watch us get bled out by those bastards in the tavern and, from the way they were lookin', I don't think it would have taken all that long, do you?"

"No, probably not, but—"

"No 'buts,' Priest," Chall said. "That man saved our lives—risked his own in the doing of it, in case you forgot, not to mention losing Catham, the man who he was following in the first place. He saved our lives and all you've done since was your level best to make him regret it. All because, what, he was part of some vigilante group twenty years ago? Who cares?"

"You don't understand, Chall," Priest said. "You did not know the Crimson Wolves, the fear they struck into the people of the city."

"Criminals, mostly, from what I hear," Chall said. "And I got to imagine scared criminals are just about the best kind."

"They didn't just scare them though, Chall," Priest said, sounding desperate to be understood now. "The Wolves, maybe they started out wanting to fight for something good—perhaps he was telling the truth about that. I don't know. But what I do know is they were brutal, toward the end. The things they did..." He shook his head. "They were worse even than those crimes perpetrated by the criminals."

"Yeah, well, you'd know, wouldn't you?"

Priest recoiled as if he'd been slapped, his face paling. "What are you saying?"

"I think you know damn well what I'm saying," Chall said, unaware that he had raised his voice until the last. He winced. "My point, Priest," he went on, focusing on sounding calmer—it wasn't easy—"is that we all have pasts. Stones and starlight, I was a pick pocket, not to mention an irredeemable philanderer, and I only gave that second one up because when a man puts on so much weight that standing is a chore, climbing out of windows to avoid angry husbands is simply out of the question."

"You were a pick pocket?" Priest asked.

"Sure I was," Chall said, "though it was a long time ago."

"I...I didn't know that about you," the man said quietly.

"Of course you didn't," Chall said. "It isn't exactly somethin' I go around telling folks when we first meet. Anyway, like I said, Priest, we all got pasts, and I've yet to meet the man or woman that doesn't have somethin' in that past they aren't proud of, something they wouldn't change if they could." He met the man's eyes. "So Ned's got a past—he aint' the only one. Is he?"

Priest frowned consideringly. "What do you want to do then, Chall?"

"I want to trust him," Chall said. "What choice do we have? Anyway, the man seems to know what he's about, and he's right—unless he's suddenly developed a case of amnesia, that friend of yours, Catham, will see us coming from a mile away. He's known you for what, twenty years? And as for me, well..." He paused, glancing meaningfully down at his bulk. "I'm not exactly easy to miss, am I?"

Priest scratched at his chin, not speaking for several seconds, clearly thinking it over. Chall let him, knowing that the man would have to see reason. In the end, though, when Priest spoke, Chall saw that he was wrong. "No," the man said. "I can find Catham myself—we don't know Ned, not really, and we have no idea of what his motivations might be. I can't trust him."

Before Chall knew it, he was moving forward, grabbing the man by the front of his shirt—which was insane. After all, they both knew that Priest could beat him to death, likely with one—or both—hands tied behind his back. Chall's gifts in a fight had always lain in different areas than direct confrontation. Areas like turning and running as fast as he could at the first sign of danger and letting someone else sort it out.

Priest grunted, clearly as surprised as Chall was himself, a surprise that only increased when Chall gave the man a shake and heard his own voice, coming out rough and raw and furious. *"Then you'd better learn to trust him,"* Chall roared. "Because I have had *enough* of your bullshit."

Part of Chall tensed then, expecting the man to retaliate, expecting that, in another moment, perhaps two, he'd be lying face down on the ground, conscious of some fresh aches and pains that hadn't been there before, or perhaps not conscious at all. Priest did not attack him though. Instead, the man only stood there, staring at him as if seeing him for the very first time.

"Chall," Priest said, "I don't...I don't understand why you're angry, I—"

"*Don't you?*" Chall demanded, giving the man another shake, his hands, his voice, his *mind* seeming to operate independently of himself. He was aware that his breathing was ragged, his chest heaving with shallow breaths, his hands shaking where they held the front of the man's shirt. "Don't you?" he said again, quieter this time, his voice trembling with fury as much as his hands. "I don't know what's been going on with you, P—" He started to call the man Priest, but then realized that didn't feel right, not anymore, and that made him angry all over again. "I don't know what's wrong with you, *Valden*," he went on. "It seems you've lost your faith somewhere—in people or the gods, maybe in yourself. I've given you time, thought maybe it would get better, but it hasn't, thought maybe you'd talk to me about it, preferably maybe Maeve...shit, preferably just about anyone else, when you were ready. You didn't, though, so you tell me now—what is the damned problem?"

Priest winced. "Chall, you don't understand, the Crimson Wolves—"

"No, *you* don't understand, Priest," Chall snapped. "I don't give two shits about the Crimson Wolves. What I *do* give a shit about is that we're alive when we ought to be dead on account of *that* man over there!" He stabbed a finger in Ned's direction. "And that not for the first time. What I care about is your way of thanking him for saving our lives—what, three times now?—is to treat him like some sort of criminal. What I care about is making it back to the castle safe, makin' sure the lad is alright. I care about making sure that *Maeve* is okay. And also, I care about figuring out what's wrong with this damned city and fixing it."

"And if we can't?" Priest said, avoiding his gaze, his voice little more than a whisper. "Fix it, I mean?"

"Then I, at least, will die trying," he said.

"To save the world?" Priest asked, a small, fragile smile on his face.

"I don't give a shit about the world," Chall said. "I'll do what I can because it's the only way to make sure that the people I care about are safe. Or at least as safe as I can make them."

Priest nodded slowly. "Certainly we might help to make Matt safer, and should we do so quickly, we might yet aid Prince Bernard. Very well, Chall. You're right, and I'm sorry...I will get you back to Maeve."

"I didn't just mean them, you damned fool," Chall said. "You're my friend too, Priest. A better friend than I ever deserved, and that's a fact. I care about makin' sure you're okay just as much as the rest. And as to that, will you now tell me what's bothering you?"

The man winced. "I...I have...I suppose you would say that I've lost—"

"Your faith?" Chall supplied.

"Yes but more than that...my identity," Priest said, a look of desperation on his face, looking lost and uncertain. "Chall, without my faith, I...I don't know who I am anymore."

"Well it's good for you that I do then," Chall said. "So how about you let me tell you? You're a good man, Priest—" The man started to say something, clearly an objection, and Chall held up his hand to forestall him. "A good man," he repeated, "no matter what you once were. You're a man who has made a difference, who can *still* make a difference, a man who many—myself among them—have come to rely on for his wisdom. You, Valden, are my friend, and that is no small thing, not for me, at least, for I do not have many."

The man gave him a fragile smile. "A friend...I thought...I thought I got on your nerves."

"You do," Chall said immediately. "So what? But what you are most of all, Priest, is a man of faith, a man who I could always count on to remind me of the coming morning no matter how dark the night got."

"I...I do not know if I can be that man any longer, Challadius. It seems to me that the night only grows darker and that the coming morning is only an illusion, a lie we tell ourselves to make the night more bearable. Once...once I believed that things would work out, in the end, that they *had* to work out, that there was some grand design which was being followed. One which we might not understand but one which was there nevertheless."

"And now?"

"Now...I do not know. Cutter has been sent away and a conspiracy threatens all New Daltenia. I am no longer sure if there is a grand design, Challadius, and *if* there is, then I am no longer sure that its designers were benevolent."

"You'll find your faith again, Priest," Challadius said. "I believe that. Just...give it time, alright? The night is dark, that's true, but that doesn't mean it will never end. We will find out what's going on with the Crimson Wolves, Priest. We'll save the city, then save Prince Bernard."

"But...how can you believe that?" Priest asked.

Challadius considered that then shrugged. "It seems to me that a man has to believe something, Priest. Knowing that, there doesn't seem much point in believing it's all going to shit. Things might seem bad, sure, but they're not so bad as all that. There's still time to fix them. Then, one day, you can find your faith again."

"And in the meantime?"

Chall gave him a cynical smile. "I'll tell you the same thing I'd tell a high-priced prostitute forced to suffer the awkward pawings of a wealthy patron."

Priest raised an eyebrow at that, saying nothing, and Chall shrugged. "Fake it."

Priest stared at him for several seconds, blinking and then, after a moment, he began to laugh. A low, quiet laugh, but the first genuine sign of mirth Chall had seen from the man in days, so he thought he'd take it and gladly.

"Very well, Challadius," Priest said. "You are right, of course. You lead...and I will follow."

Chall came aware that he was still holding the man's shirt, and he cleared his throat, letting it go. When he'd first grabbed him, he hadn't been thinking much—mostly he'd just been angry—but what little thinking he *had* done had been around expecting to end up beaten and bloody for his trouble. He'd given very little thought to the man actually listening to him. *You lead and I will follow.* Which was what Chall had wanted, of course, or at least, he thought it was. He only hoped, then, that he did not lead them both off a cliff. He wondered if this was what Prince Bernard felt all the time, this sort of responsibility for him and the others, knowing that they had put themselves into his hands. If it was, then Chall decided that maybe there was more to being a prince than servants eager to do your bidding and fancy clothes after all. Maybe even too much.

"Come on," he said, his mouth suddenly painfully dry, "I guess we'd best get going."

He started toward where the carriage driver sat, his back propped against the doorway and obviously doing his best to look anywhere but at them. The man turned to regard them as they approached. "Nice chat?"

"Wasn't bad," Chall said.

Ned nodded. "Ready to go, then?"

"Ye—"

"I wanted to tell you," Priest said before Chall could speak. "Ned...I'm sorry."

Chall wasn't sure what the carriage driver had been expecting, but from the look of surprise on his face—a surprise Chall shared—it hadn't been that. The man blinked. "No problem."

"No, it is a problem," Priest said. "You have done nothing but shown me and my companions kindness, a kindness which put you and your wife in danger, and as thanks I have behaved terribly. I am sorry, truly, and I thank you for all that you have done."

The carriage driver fidgeted, clearly less comfortable with genuine thanks than he had been in facing down a room full of would-be murderers. "It's nothing."

"No," Priest said, "whatever it is, Ned, it is not nothing, and I promise that I will not forget it. Now, you mentioned getting us back to the castle...I wonder if you would share your thoughts on the best way of getting that accomplished?"

Chall grunted. "Preferably thoughts that don't end with us getting beaten or stabbed to death in the street. Got to be honest, I don't much love the idea of trying to walk back to the castle just now, not with a fair portion of the poor district wanting to see us dead."

Ned stared at Priest for another moment, then turned to look at Chall. "Well, it might be that I have a solution for that."

"Oh?" Chall asked.

The man smiled, nodding. "Well, I am a carriage driver, ain't I?"

"That's where you went earlier, when you left," Priest said.

Ned inclined his head. "That's right. Believe me, I'm not anymore interested in getting killed than the two of you. Anyway, I figured even if I didn't go back to the castle with you, lady Maeve would likely make me regret letting her beau get killed, and if even half the stories about her are true I think she's got more than the necessary skills to make that regret last just as long—or as short—as she'd like."

Chall tried to offer the man a smile, but the thought of Maeve—and, more specifically, of where she'd been meaning to go the last time he'd seen her—made the simple gesture impossible.

Priest must have seen something of his worry on his face, for in another moment the man was putting a reassuring hand on his shoulder. "She'll be alright, Chall."

"Right then," Ned said, "you all ready to leave, or would you like to sit around here a while longer, see if we can't get a layer of dust to match our surroundings. There's still some ale left in those barrels," he went on, motioning toward the corner where several dusty barrels were stacked. "We could take some drinks, see who gets sick first, maybe make a game of it."

Chall grunted. "I think maybe I'll choose a quick death instead."

Ned grinned. "Thought you might."

And with that, the carriage driver walked toward where the ladder waited and, without another word, started up. Chall glanced at Priest who was watching him. "It'll be okay, Chall," he said, his reassuring smile, if not exactly the same as the one Chall remembered, a welcome improvement over the last few days.

"You really believe that?"

The man said nothing, only continued to smile for a moment before starting after the carriage driver. *Fool,* Chall thought, *of course he doesn't believe it. You told him to fake it after all, didn't you?* He didn't much love the idea of going back into the poor district, carriage or not. It felt to him an awful lot like tiptoeing through a field of lions and hoping that maybe they wouldn't wake up, that maybe, if they did, they wouldn't decide to give him a good chewing. But then that was the thing about maybes. A man could live his life off of them…until he couldn't.

Still, he thought that if Priest could pretend to have faith, then he could pretend at courage. He walked toward the ladder, then began climbing up behind the others. This time, light filtered through the covering overhead, so that the trip upward was nowhere near as scary as it had been coming down. And he was grateful for that—after all, the scary shit lay somewhere ahead and, if experience served, he did not think it lay so very far.

Above, the ruins of the Plague Church were as they had left them, and although Chall now knew that the plague had only been a lie, its victims only actors, a sickly warmth seemed to spread in him the moment he stepped off the ladder. "That plague of yours…" he said, suddenly feeling out of breath—and was he only imagining the unusual beating of his heart in his chest?—"you're sure it's all pretend?"

The carriage driver glanced at him then flashed a smile. "Well. Pretty sure anyway—come on, the carriage is over here."

Chall found himself stopping then, glancing around at the ruins. Just a story maybe, but as far as he could tell, if there was ever a place where a man might catch the plague this seemed like it. And just why did his damned chest feel so damned tight? That was the real question.

"Chall?"

He glanced up to see that Priest had turned back and was staring at him. "He was just messing with you. You know that, don't you?"

Chall cleared his throat which suddenly felt thick with mucous. "Are…that is. Are you sure?"

Priest considered that, grinning. "Well…pretty sure," he said, then he turned and sauntered off after the carriage driver. Like a real son of a bitch.

Chall watched the man go, not thinking of the plague, at least in that moment, but thinking instead about how he'd like to push him down—assuming of course he could avoid the inevitable ass beating that would follow. "Beginning to think I liked you better when you were miserable," he muttered, walking after him.

He did not have to go far before he saw that they were both stopped in the street, Priest glancing around as if expecting to discover an army of murderers which had been lying in wait. Ned, meanwhile, watched him as he walked up to them. "Get lost?" the carriage driver asked.

Chall frowned. "Something like that."

The man nodded. "Very well then, milord. If you have found your walk sufficient," the carriage driver said, sketching an extravagant bow. "Then might I just inform you, your carriage awaits," he pronounced as he indicated the carriage and team of horses in the street with a grand, sweeping gesture."

CHAPTER FIFTEEN

He was hot—burning up, really—fire racing through his body, his muscles, even his veins. Yet even while he was burning up, he was freezing. An icy cold seemed to spread through him, and it was not a question to him, as he tossed and turned in delirium, if he would die. Instead, it was only a question of what would kill him. The fire or the ice, the fever or the cold.

He was plagued with troubled fever dreams, ones that were confusing, not dreams in truth but only flashes of images and sounds, smells and feelings, all of which were conjured by his fevered mind. They did not make sense, those images, those sounds, but they left him feeling scared and uncertain, very small and unimportant. Neglected by the world or, if not neglected, then, worse—hated.

It was as if he was cast about on a roaring sea, the waves shifting, rising and plummeting in the grip of some mad storm, and he could do nothing to save himself, could only fall gasping into the waters of sickness one moment just to be tossed aside the next.

He thought as he was cast about, that he would die. That he *must* die. And as his torment dragged on and on, he did not think—he hoped. He did not know how long it lasted, that agony, that listless, lonesome suffering. He knew only that, one moment, he was being wracked by fever and chills, and the next, someone was there. He knew this, recognized it just as he recognized that same someone gently lifting his head and slowly pouring something into his mouth. It was hot, but this heat, unlike that fevered sickness spreading through his body, was a good heat, but more than that, it tasted good. The liquid, whatever it was, tasted of cooked meat and some sort of herbs—sage, perhaps.

The soup hit his empty stomach and awakened there a great hunger, one that he had felt for so long that he had forgotten it was there at all. Then he was drinking quicker, reaching up trembling hands in an effort to tilt the bowl and pour its contents into his mouth.

"*Slowly,*" a voice said, "otherwise, you will not be able to keep it down."

Feledias frowned—or at least he would have, had he still not been using his mouth to slurp ravenously at the bowl's contents. He knew that voice, had heard it often enough to recognize it. "B-Bernard?" he asked, slowly opening his eyes and looking up at his brother who was cradling his head, feeding him like someone might feed a child.

"I'm here," Bernard said.

Feledias meant to ask another question—several, perhaps—but he decided that, for the moment at least, it was enough to know that the figure was his brother, that he was here. He continued to eat the stew until the bowl was empty, yet still his stomach roiled hungrily.

"Just a moment," his brother said. "I'll get some more—but not much. Too much and you'll get sick."

"Sicker, you mean," Feledias rasped as his brother lay him carefully down.

No longer distracted by the stew—his hunger, if not resolved then at least sated to some small degree—Feledias became aware of a warm, pleasant heat beside him. He glanced over at a small fire flickering beside him. A pathetic blaze, really, but he didn't think he'd ever seen anything so fine. He rolled onto his side, reaching out his trembling hands to it, aware that he was acting like an invalid and not caring. The sickness, after all, had done its work on him, and if he was acting like an invalid it was because he was not that far from one. Not so very far at all.

He felt weak, weaker than he could ever remember feeling, and while he suspected he would be ashamed of the way his brother had cared for him, later—the same way that a mother might have cared for her child, cradling his head just so—at the moment, he could be only grateful. The cave where he lay felt comfortable, homely, the fire nice and warm, and with his brother watching over him, the most feared man in the Known Lands, possibly the entire world, he felt safe.

He felt comforted. At least, that was, until he turned and let out a sound that was a mixture of a shriek and a gasp as he noted some giant creature. He didn't get a good look—mostly just a flash of wet fur, splattered with crimson, of teeth and claws and a monstrous body—before he turned and leapt to his feet, fleeing the opposite direction.

At least, he meant to. The sickness had left him weak, and his intended flight instead manifested itself with a twitch of his hands and feet and a terrified whimper.

"Easy," his brother said, his deep voice resonating in the cave. "It cannot harm you—not anymore."

Feledias's heart began to slow where it was threatening to rip out of his chest, and he glanced behind him. Bernard was moving back toward him now, and in the light of the small campfire Feledias noticed something that he had not seen before—his brother was covered in blood. The one reassuring thing of note—if anything *could* be reassuring at such a time—was that the blood at least looked dried, old.

And it did not take even Feledias's fever-numbed mind very long to realize where the blood must have come from. He turned to regard the creature again, avoiding the urge to flinch away as he noted that he had not overestimated its size. The creature took up one whole side of the cave, its bulk—thankfully dead, unmoving bulk—reaching almost to the ceiling where it lay. In some ways, it appeared almost like a bear, though far bigger, and lacking the elongated snout of a bear or most animals. Instead, its face was flat, revealing a massive mouth which had slipped open in death to reveal rows of needle-like teeth, some of which, he saw, were stained with blood.

"What...what *is* it?" Feledias asked, his stomach revolting in disgust as he stared at the grisly form.

"I don't know what it was," his brother said. "As for what it *is*, well, that I can answer easy enough. Dinner."

Feledias's gorge threatened to rise at that, and he swallowed bile. "Gods help me if I'm ever so desperate as to eat something like that. I'm pretty sure it'd kill you as quickly as the bastard's claws and teeth."

"Hasn't so far."

Feledias frowned, not understanding what his brother meant, maybe not *wanting* to understand, but despite his mind's efforts, realization dawned a moment later. "You mean..." he asked, staring wide-eyed at the bowl of soup his brother had brought to him.

Bernard gave his massive shoulders a shrug. "There wasn't any roast pheasant or boiled chicken, I'm afraid."

Feledias didn't counter with an immediate rejoinder—mostly because he was too busy trying to keep from emptying what little he'd eaten out of his stomach. "Is it really too much to hope," he rasped, finally, "to find a rabbit or a wild turkey, perhaps, on which to break our fast?"

"Normally?" his brother asked. "Probably not. But in the Black Wood...I'm afraid so. Anyway, our supplies have been out for days, as you're well-aware."

"And starving men can't be picky, is that what you're saying?"

Bernard only gave another shrug, as always demonstrating the fact that he didn't care to squander words when a good shrug or frown would do. "So how...how long have we been here?"

Bernard's eyebrows drew down in thought as he sat down beside Feledias. "I'm not sure, not exactly," he said. "Not easy to tell, what with daytime looking exactly like night but...well. I'd guess a day, maybe two."

Feledias raised an eyebrow. "You didn't go outside?"

Cutter shook his head. "Very little." He let his gaze travel to the corpse of the giant creature. "I thought it best not to leave you alone for long, not in your current state. After all, not all the world's monsters announce themselves with a roar."

Monsters. The word stuck in Feledias's mind. "No, brother," he said, his mouth suddenly dry, "you're right...often, they do not. Often the monster does not announce himself at all." He was talking low, in little more than a whisper, but he found that he could raise his voice no further. "Often...he comes in the darkness, like a thief." He was looking at the campfire, but not seeing it, not really. Instead, he was seeing another fire, this one far greater, not one fire at all in truth but many of them, blazes several times taller than a man. And the warmth he felt on his skin from the flame reminded him of the heat he'd felt on that day, the day that Brighton burned. Not a warmth, not then, but a heat so great that some part of him thought, in that moment, that he would burn. And another part, a small part but one that had been present, even then, had believed that he deserved to. "A thief," he went on, "one of which the owner of the house is unaware, at least until his home begins to burn down around him."

"Fel," Bernard said, his voice soft, "I'm sorry. I did not mean..."

"To remind me of my crimes?"

His brother said nothing, and Feledias sighed wearily, shaking his head. "It is not your fault, Bernard. It is mine and mine alone. The truth is, everything reminds me of it, and of course it should. Those people...what I did..." He shook his head. "If I'm haunted, brother, it's because I deserve to be. I know what people smell like when they burn, Bernard. Who but a monster might say as much? I know the sound their flesh makes when it pops from the heat, the sound of their screams when they—"

"*Enough, brother,*" Bernard growled. "Leave it."

Hot tears were running down Feledias's face, but he did not bother wiping them away. "Very well, Bernard," he said. "If it troubles you, I will not speak of it."

"Damnit, Fel, don't you get it?" Bernard demanded, rounding on him. "It is not myself I think of—it's you."

That hurt, hurt in a way, to a degree, that Feledias would not have expected. But it was a good hurt, and the teary-smile he flashed his brother was a sincere one. "Thank you for your concern, brother, but I'm afraid it changes nothing, nor should it. I am damned, it is true, but you are not at fault—I am." He drifted back into memory then. He was only barely aware that he was still speaking as he relived those moments, a tableau of destruction and death and desperation as the villagers of Brighton tried—and failed—to escape their gruesome fate, either at the burning flames of the fire or at the sharpened steel of his troops. "They follow me, brother, in the day and in the night, too, waking or sleeping. A line of ghosts, all speaking with one voice, all condemning me, and they are right to do it. They are right, and yet knowing that does not ease my pain. It only makes it worse. They never stop, the ghosts. They are always there, when I turn to look behind me, always whispering their words of condemnation, their hatred."

Cutter nodded slowly. "I know."

Feledias met his eyes, and in that gaze he could see the same kind of pain he felt, the same kind of shame and regret and self-loathing. "Yes," he said quietly, "yes, I think you do. Perhaps even better than I know it myself. But...I do not think I can live like this, Bernard. It...it's too much."

"I know."

Feledias heaved a heavy sigh. "Please, Bernard, give me some good news, lie to me if you have to, I don't care. Just...anything to make it not hurt so much."

Bernard watched him for several seconds, then nodded. "It will get better, Feledias. A little better each day until it's...until it's bearable."

"Really?"

His brother raised an eyebrow. "Yes," he said, "really."

Feledias nodded, choosing not to hear the lie. After all, he had asked for it. "Thanks, Bernard. So...what now?"

"Now, we wait for you to get your strength back."

"And then?"

His brother did not answer that, but then he did not need to. Once Feledias felt better, they would continue, that was all.

After all, their death lay somewhere up ahead; it would be a shame to make it wait. Feledias sighed. "Anyway...can I have some more monster stew?"

His brother grinned. "Of course."

CHAPTER SIXTEEN

"Are you sure this is a good idea, Maeve?" Emille whispered.

They were following Agnes and her three-person entourage down a long hallway, and Maeve could not help but notice the way the Headmistress's bodyguards had spread out to either side of her and Emille. The bigger of which, Gideon, was scowling in Maeve's direction—as he had been doing for the last ten minutes—as if she were a bug he'd very much like to crush. Maeve glanced over at Emille, seeing some of her own worry mirrored in the other woman's expression. "It'll be fine," she said with far more confidence than she felt.

The truth was that she was worried. After all, it was her fault they were here, not Emille's and whatever happened, she would be the one responsible for it. And it seemed all too likely that something *would* happen. Agnes might have acted nice enough when they'd been working out the plan, but as they walked down the hallway, the two bodyguards flanking them, Maeve couldn't help but think that it would be an easy enough thing for the woman to change her mind. And if that happened, if Agnes decided that Maeve suited her better dead, she wouldn't have to wait long to see it done.

Maeve and Emille had spent the previous night at the Guild—ostensibly as Agnes's prisoners. At least Maeve *hoped* ostensibly. There had been two small cots for them to make use of, but there might as well not have been. As Maeve had grown older she'd found it harder and harder to sleep, as if she'd just lost the knack for it, and if there was a more difficult place to go to sleep than a cell in an assassin's guild then she'd never heard of it. And the dark circles under Emille's eyes were proof, if any had been needed, that her companion had also found sleep elusive. Instead, they had sat worrying over the plan, talking it out again and again in their nervousness until Maeve imagined they had both taken both sides of the conversation at least half a dozen times. Then they had waited—Maeve, at least, doing so terribly impatiently.

She had been frustrated with each minute, each hour that slipped away as she waited for morning to come, for Agnes to return and say that everything was ready. However, now that the time had finally arrived, she almost wished that she was back in the cell, waiting. At least there she didn't have to worry about the bodyguards' scowls or those suspicious looks of the people they passed as she and Emille were led through the winding hallways of the Assassin's Guild. She was worried about dying, it was true, but not just that—what was worse was that if she died, no one would ever know it. After all, they were underground, beneath a healer's academy in hidden rooms even the instructors and students of which had no idea existed at all. No, if Agnes decided Maeve needed to die she was confident it would be an easy enough task for them to dispose of her body without anyone knowing.

But it was too late now—she was committed. She would just have to trust that Agnes was being sincere and meant her no harm. A woman who had always hated her, an *assassin* who had risen to the highest rank within a guild of killers. Sincere. And meaning no harm.

Maeve hoped Chall would be okay alone. Despite the man's incessant complains about people, he needed someone to look after him.

"Ah," Agnes said, pulling her from her thoughts, "here we are."

Maeve looked up to see that the Agnes had stopped in front of a wide set of double doors. She was currently glancing back at Maeve with a toothy smile. The sort of smile, Maeve thought, that a cat might flash, were it able, while watching its prey struggle to get away, knowing all the while that there was no chance of that.

Maeve didn't much like the idea of going through that door, but then, as she already knew, it was too late. Likely, it had been too late the moment she had stepped across the threshold and entered the Guild. Despite the woman's assurances, Maeve thought it was likely—perhaps even probable—that the door at which she stood led to some dark, out-of-the-way room, one particularly well-suited for murder.

Maeve winced, glancing at Emille. "I'm sorry for involving you in this," she said.

The woman shook her head. "It is not your fault, Maeve. No one can make me do something I do not want to, after all, and I went along with it."

Maeve nodded at that, turning back to Agnes.

"Ready?" the woman asked, arching an eyebrow, clearly relishing the moment, savoring it the way a wine lover might savor a newly-discovered vintage.

Maeve sighed. "Ready."

Agnes inclined her head, her smile still well in place, then turned and opened the door, stepping inside. The Headmistress's bodyguards turned toward Maeve and Emille, making it all too clear they expected her to go through the door. She didn't want to, but then that was why she had come, why she was here in the first place. So Maeve took a moment, as she had so many times in the years before meeting the prince and the others, to clear away her emotions. She took the fear she felt at being here, the regret at not listening to Chall, and she bundled them up, tucking them away in some far corner of her mind.

It was a trick she had done often in the past, thousands of times, but she felt rusty now, the fear and the shame slipping through her fingers as she reached for them like piles of clothes dropped from careless hands.

She gritted her teeth, trying again, aware of Emille and Agnes's bodyguards watching her. In the space of one deep breath, she gathered up those emotions that would not serve her here, gathering up also the tattered remnants that tried to remain behind. She kept at it until she had it all or at least as much as she thought she could carry, and then she tucked them away out of sight...and out of mind.

This time, it worked, and she felt a mixture of relief and satisfaction at that. Old, yes, far slower than she used to be, a dull blade to be sure, but then even dull blades could cut if you put in enough effort.

"Maeve?" Emille asked. "Is...is everything alright?"

Maeve turned to the woman, not having to fake the confident smile that spread across her face. Not the smile of Maeve the Marvelous, maybe, but not that of a frightened old woman walking to what she was sure was her death either. Somewhere in between the two, and she counted that a marked improvement. "Perfect," she said, and meant it. Then she turned back to the guards and walked toward the door. Before she entered, she paused long enough to tip a wink to the big man, Gideon, and got the satisfaction of seeing his seemingly perpetual anger give way to confusion before she stepped through the door.

But no sooner had she done so than she felt the smile give a threatening twitch. Not going away completely, not yet, but close.

"So many?"

Maeve glanced at Emille, who was staring around the room in awe—not that she could blame her. After all, the room in which they found themselves was far from some abandoned storehouse where a certain inconvenient old assassin might be forcibly retired. Instead, they stood at the edge of a very large circular room. And around the edges of that circle were hundreds of chairs. Not all of them were taken up, which she supposed was a good thing, but there were far more men and women filling the chairs than Maeve ever would have expected. At the opposite end of the circle, seated on a raised dais behind a long oak podium were two women and a man, ones who needed no introduction. The Tribunal, the three that, along with Headmistress, ruled the Guild, making them some of the most dangerous men and women in the city, if not the entirety of the Known Lands.

When Maeve had first walked through the door, the room had been alive with the low, droning buzz of dozens of conversations as those seated around the circular audience chamber talked. But by the time she walked to where Agnes and her assistant waited, the conversations had cut off and a thick, smothering silence had settled over the room.

The smile on Maeve's face faltered again, and for a moment she thought it would abandon her altogether. In the end, it stayed, but it was a close thing, and the drawer in her mind, the one into which she had tucked her fears and anxieties slipped open slightly.

Agnes glanced around the room at all those gathered, making them wait, reminding them that she was in charge. Then, finally, she turned to regard Maeve, speaking in a barely-audible whisper. "Not a bad turn out, all told."

"Yes, Headmistress," Maeve said tightly, sticking to the woman's title and bowing her head in obeisance, showing her respect just as they had planned. Not a woman come back to get the contract on her removed but instead an assassin who had abandoned the Guild and was now returning full of regret and shame, hoping to be allowed to rejoin it. She had spoken in a low voice, but she was shocked to hear it reverberating around the circular space so that everyone in attendance could not have helped but hear.

"Headmistress," a sharp voice said, and they all turned to regard the podium where one of the three Tribunes sat, a woman with dark hair pulled back into a severe ponytail who had a large aquiline nose and a frown on her face—one that, from the looks of it, Maeve imagined rarely left her expression. "I wonder if you might not tell us why we are all gathered here. After all, you have called an emergency meeting, and I am sure I am not the only one who is curious as to what that emergency actually *is*."

Maeve was surprised by the tone the woman used, one of ill-concealed challenge, just as she was surprised by how young she was. When Maeve had been part of the Guild, the Tribunes, as well as the Headmistress, had all been very old. Ancient, really, gray-haired men and women—when they had hair at all—not dangerous in and of themselves but instead because of the connections they'd made over their long lives, because of favors others owed them. This woman, though, seemed all too ready to do the work herself, and young enough to still do it well. In fact, she had to be at least ten years younger than Maeve, possibly as many as fifteen.

Agnes turned to the woman, raising her nose. "Ah, Tribune Silrika, it is with great pleasure that I see that you were able to attend. And perhaps that attendance will be of benefit to you—

after all, you cannot solve every problem by poking holes in it, can you?" The woman frowned at that, and Maeve figured that if they were keeping score, Agnes was one ahead. "Besides," the Headmistress went on, "perhaps you might even learn something."

"*Learn* something?" the woman sneered.

"Just so," Agnes said, smiling widely and inclining her head. "Such as that sometimes a measured response is what's called for. A measured, *considered* response, and it is to that end that I called an emergency meeting. An action which, I believe," she went on, her voice suddenly turning sharp, menacing, "is well within *my* power as Headmistress of the Guild. Or do you disagree?"

It was an open challenge, barely veiled if veiled at all, and the Tribune's face colored an angry, splotchy shade of crimson, her entire body seeming to tense as if she'd just been struck by lightning. For a moment, Maeve was convinced that the woman would rise and rush across the room to attack, so much anger was revealed in her posture, her expression.

In the end, though, she settled, like a raging forest fire slowly dying out until only the embers of the blaze—or in this case, the woman's anger—remained.

Maeve found herself breathing a quiet sigh of relief, but based on the fact that Agnes did not seem in the least moved by the woman's anger, Maeve thought that such challenges were common things.

"Of course, you are, as always, correct, Headmistress," another voice said, this one a man's wheedling tone, and Maeve's attention was drawn to the other side of the podium and the old man sitting there. He appeared to be in his late fifties, and considering that he was the only man on the platform he had to be the man Agnes had told her of, Tribune Piralta. And based on his over-flattering tone as well as his obsequious manner, and the way his head was bowed low enough that his nose was in danger of scraping the podium surface, Maeve thought that Agnes's nickname for the man, "the Weasel," held up. "It is your prerogative," the man went on, "to call such a meeting whenever you deem it appropriate. We all await your pleasure."

"Thank you, Tribune Piralta," Agnes said, her tone sounding bored, "my boots needed a good cleaning."

It was the man's turn to color then, and there was a flash of emotion across his face. It only lasted for a moment, but it was enough for Maeve to recognize it for what it was—anger. Whatever love, whatever fawning the man showed for Agnes, Maeve was willing to bet that it was no more than a show.

"Yes, yes," a third voice said, and Maeve directed her attention to the center of the podium where the woman Agnes had referred to as "the old crone" sat. A woman Maeve recognized, if only vaguely, from her time at the Guild. "Now that we've got the niceties out of the way, Headmistress," she said in a country accent someone would have expected to hear in some out of the way village but not the Known Land's capital. "I wonder," the woman went on, "if it wouldn't be possible to get on with the purpose of this meeting? No disrespect, of course, only it is a bit of a task, haulin' my old bones all the way here. I'd hate to think I did it for no reason."

"Of course, Tribune Bethesa," Agnes said, "I would not think to call so many of our...*illustrious* members away from their duties without good reason."

Maeve glanced over at Agnes and saw that while the woman had looked annoyed by Tribune Piralta's flattery and amused by Tribune Silrika's challenge, now she appeared to be neither. Instead, she appeared cautious, watching the old woman as if afraid to miss anything.

Agnes continued to watch her for another moment before finally continuing. "As to the reason that I have called you all here, I trust that once you have heard it, it will prove worth your time. You see, I have been approached by someone who wishes to join the Guild."

"And for that you have called an emergency meeting?" Silrika sneered—Maeve got the impression that the woman did a lot of sneering.

"That's *Headmistress,*" Agnes corrected, a sharpness to her tone that caused the woman sitting at the podium to tense.

"Of course," the woman said dryly, "forgive me, Headmistress."

"Forgiven," Agnes said, giving a smile that never touched her eyes. "As to your question, yes, I have called an emergency meeting. Normally, it is true that such a thing would not be handled by me—after all, we have systems in place to take care of that sort of thing. However, this time, this potential *recruit* is…shall we say, unusual."

The three tribunes, along with what Maeve would have guessed was every single person in the room, turned to look at her. Maeve could feel their regard on her, could see them sizing her up, trying to determine if she were a potential opponent and, if so, trying to determine how dangerous of one she might be. And based on their largely dismissive glances, they were not all that impressed. Not that Maeve could blame them—after all, whatever she had once been, *whoever* she had once been, now she was just an old woman and of no threat to anyone. Or so she appeared, and in this case, appearances were only slightly deceiving.

"She doesn't look like anything to me," Silrika said. "Except perhaps someone's grandmother." There were some titters of laughter from among the watching crowd at that, but Maeve was unbothered. After all, it was far gentler than the things she told herself.

"Forgive me, Headmistress," Tribune Piralta put in, "but while I would never think to question your judgement, I must admit that I do not see what might make this woman so special. She seems quite…" He eyed Maeve, his nose high in the air, his incessant flattery, it seemed, reserved for people he deemed more important than an old woman. "Quite…ordinary," he finished. "Quite…old."

Maeve did feel her back go up a little at that. Maybe she was old, but she was no older than the bastard himself, a few years younger, if she had to guess. She opened her mouth, preparing to say something particularly foolish, but before she could say anything that she would inevitably be made to regret, laughter filled the air. Though it was really more of a cackle as the third and oldest of the Tribunes wiped a leathery hand across eyes that had grown teary from her mirth.

"Old, is she?" she asked. "Why she looks like little more than a child compared to you, Piralta," she said, to which the man only sniffed, turning away. "And as for me, well, it's been so long since I was that young I expect I can't even remember it well anymore. Still," she went on, turning back to Agnes, "the two fools do have a point, Headmistress. Seems awful strange to bring such a woman here, to gather us all together. She ain't old, I'll say that—if anyone in the world knows old, it's me—but then she ain't exactly no spring chicken either, is she?" she asked, glancing at Maeve.

Maeve realized the woman didn't recognize her and supposed that was no great surprise. After all, she was far removed from the celebrated beauty she once had been. Still, she returned the woman's stare and noted that although the tribune acted friendly enough, simple enough, there was a calculating coldness in her gaze. She realized, in that moment, that without doubt, this was the most dangerous of the three Tribunes, quite possibly the most dangerous person in the room, save Agnes, and even on that score Maeve was not sure.

"I suppose I've well and truly sprung, Tribune," Maeve said with a bow before turning to the younger woman, "though I would not suffer many to call me chicken."

Tribune Silrika colored an angry crimson at that, but Tribune Bethesa only let out another cackle. "Well and truly sprung, sure and why not? You know what, it might be that you're alright."

"Thank you, Tribune," Maeve said, inclining her head, "I certainly like to think so."

"Still," the old woman went on, turning back to Agnes, "that doesn't go toward explainin' why you've called us all here, Headmistress. I imagine if you don't tell us soon, Silrika here's liable to throw a fit."

Agnes smiled. "Of course. You see, the reason I saw fit to bring a new recruit before the Tribunal—not to mention so many of our number—is because she is, in fact, not a new recruit at all. Indeed, it could be argued—and I doubt it would need be argued very much—that she is the most famous, or infamous of all our members."

The younger two Tribunes looked genuinely confused at this, but the oldest woman, in a display that showed that while her body might have lost some of its fervor, her mind was still quick enough, let out a low gasp, her eyes widening. "It can't be," she said. "Do you mean to tell me, Headmistress, that before us stands the Crimson Courtesan?"

Maeve frowned. She never had liked that name, mostly because it was as inaccurate as it was stupid. For one, she had *never* been a courtesan and secondly—and, as far as successfully assassinating someone went, far more importantly—she, like every assassin ever, had made it a point of not getting any of the blood which she inevitably drew in her work on her clothes. After all, an assassin who walked around coated in her victim's blood wasn't likely to make it very far. Besides, it was no easy thing to wash out blood. A careless assassin could easily spend a fortune replacing her wardrobe. Her frown deepened. She wasn't sure what it said about her that she hated the idea of being thought careless more than being thought a whore, and she wasn't sure she wanted to know.

There were whispers around the room at that, mostly those of confusion, and Maeve understood. Many of those gathered hadn't been around during her tenure—one necessity of running a successful assassin's guild, she supposed, was a heavy focus on recruiting. After all, in such a profession there were always spots opening up.

"You have surmised correctly, Tribune Bethesa," Agnes said, clearly enjoying the old woman's surprise. "Before you stands Death's Mistress." Maeve winced. She had forgotten that moniker and that with great effort, but Agnes was not done. "The Dame of Death." She winced deeper at that—the bards really were fools with far too much time on their hands. "The woman," Agnes went on, "known throughout all New Daltenia as the Red Beauty."

Emille glanced at Maeve, raising her eyebrow, and Maeve considered it for a moment then shrugged. She had always kind of liked that last one.

She glanced around the room and still saw uncertainty painted on most of the gathered faces, watched as they whispered between each other in obvious confusion, trying to figure out who she was. Agnes allowed it to go on for a moment then rolled her eyes. Even assassins, it seemed, were not immune to the feelings the old often felt for the young and their ignorance. The Headmistress's hand shot up, asking for silence—demanding it, really, Maeve supposed—and the room instantly went quiet.

"It seems, instructors," Agnes said, glancing to one side of the gathered people where men and women who were clearly older than most of those in the room stood side by side, "that we must focus our lessons more on recent Guild history. This woman," she went on, talking louder, her gaze slowly traveling around the room, "the one seeking admittance into the Assassin's Guild, is none other than Maeve the Marvelous."

Those gathered might not have recognized her other monikers, but they recognized that one quickly enough. Once more, the crowd broke into conversation, though not nearly so quietly as they had the other times. This time, they spoke loudly, the drone of their voices full of shock and wonder and more than a little disbelief. Maeve couldn't argue with that disbelief, never mind that it pained her. After all, she wasn't sure what she looked like standing there—only hoped it wasn't a victim waiting to be victimized—but she knew that whatever she looked like, it was certainly *not* the world's greatest assassin.

"Maeve the Marvelous," Tribune Bethesa said, her voice a mixture of wonder and disbelief, and what sounded to Maeve like caution. The woman eyed her carefully, slowly, the way someone might eye a dog that, while it looked friendly enough, also possessed a reputation for biting. "I remember when you left the Guild," the old woman said. "Caused quite a stir, as I recollect and no surprise that, as the conventional way of leavin' the Guild is a bit more...straightforward. As surprisin' as I reckon that was, though, for me and for a lot of folks back then, I'd say it's even more surprisin' to see you standin' here now. Is what the Headmistress says true? Do you mean to seek entrance back into the Guild?"

Maeve glanced at the Headmistress who gave her a small smile, extending her hand as if to say that she had done what she could, and now it was up to Maeve.

Maeve inclined her head in a nod, then stepped forward clearing her throat. "The Headmistress speaks truly," she said, "I...I have come seeking to re-enter the Guild."

"I see," the old woman said, nodding slowly, scratching at her chin thoughtfully. "To that end, Lady Maeve, I have but one question—why?"

Maeve blinked. It was a simple enough question, one she should have anticipated in the time she'd spent waiting for Agnes to gather the other assassins and organize this meeting. The problem, though, was that she had not. In fact, she had been far too busy focusing on what she would do should the woman betray her—mostly coming up with die horribly—to consider what she would do if she did not. Now, though, the Tribune, along with the other two of her number as well as hundreds of trained assassins, were watching her carefully, waiting for her answer. Which meant that it had best be a good one. Something a little better than, I've come seeking admittance so that I can kill your Headmistress, only not really, to rejoin, only not really, so that I can cancel a contract on myself and the man I love—and yes, really on that part, thanks.

Do better than that, old woman, she thought, *assuming that you want to walk out of here instead of have your corpse carried out.* "I...I know that I have been gone for a while," she said, trying to buy herself a little time to think.

"I would agree that twenty years counts as a while," Tribune Bethesa said, a small smile on her face. "But all of us present are aware of your extended absence, Lady Maeve. I imagine they are far more curious—as am I—about the manner and, in particular, the *reason* for your return."

"As for the manner, that I can answer easily enough—I came in the front door. The same way most folks come in, I'd guess."

There was some scattered laughter at that, and Maeve winced inwardly, cursing her sharp tongue. It was a habit of hers, when she was nervous or anxious or...well, when she just felt like being an asshole, and one that had rarely done her any good. She expected the woman to grow angry, perhaps to condemn her, but instead Tribune Bethesa only flashed a toothy grin one that, Maeve noted, did not touch her eyes. "I see," the old woman said, watching her with a knowing gaze, as if she was well-aware that Maeve was scrambling. "And the reason?"

Maeve's mind was a whirl as she scrambled for reasons for her unexpected—most of all by her—return. But as many of those reasons that she saw in her mind, they swirled too fast for her to grasp. So instead she stood there with her mouth half-open, well aware that she looked like a complete idiot, and soon might end up looking like a completely dead one.

"What's more," the Tribune pressed, "I would also be curious as to how you hav,e found yourself here, after so many years. After all, the avenues by which one may come to the Guild are not the same as they once were. It is disturbing to think that any...civilian might so easily find her way here."

Maeve winced, trying to find some way to explain her presence, at least a way that didn't implicate Emille any more than was necessary.

"She found her way here because I showed her the way."

Maeve and the rest of the attendants turned to regard Emille as the woman stepped up to stand beside her.

"Instructor Emille," the old crone said, eyeing her. "Am I to understand that you brought Lady Maeve here, and as one can only assume as it was never discussed, without permission?"

Emille inclined her head. "I did, Tribune Bethesa. I thought...I thought it would be wise."

"Nobody cares what you *think*," Tribune Silrika snapped. "You overstepped yourself by bringing her here without the Tribunal's acceptance."

"Yes," Tribune Piralta intoned thoughtfully, "you did indeed take liberties, Instructor Emille. And such liberties must indeed be punished."

Emille paled slightly at that, as well she should, for the Guild was not known for doling out easy punishments. She opened her mouth, hesitating. Maeve started to speak, to try to come to the woman's rescue—not that she was in much of a position to do so, of course. After all, a woman falling from a cliff face was hardly in a position to save another from doing the same.

But Agnes stepped forward instead which was just as well as Maeve still had no idea of what she might say. "She did not require the permission of the three of you," the woman said, eyeing them, "because she had mine."

"You mean that you were behind this, Headmistress?" the old woman, Bethesa, asked, her eyes narrowing slightly.

"I was indeed," Agnes said. "You all were no doubt as aware as I that Prince Bernard had arrived back in town to crown our new king. And I am also sure that, like me, you all heard the rumor that he was accompanied by his companions of old, including Maeve the Marvelous."

"I had heard such a rumor, it's true," Bethesa said slowly.

"Of course," Agnes agreed. "And having heard it myself, I thought it prudent to send Instructor Emille on an...investigation of sorts. The purpose of which was to determine if Lady Maeve was indeed returned to New Daltenia."

"And...if she found that such was the case?" Bethesa asked.

Agnes glanced back at Maeve, an expression on her face to show that she had better appreciate this, before turning back to regard the Tribune. "If Emille discovered that Death's Mistress had indeed returned to New Daltenia then she was to bring her here."

"And to what purpose?" the Tribune asked.

"Isn't it obvious?" Agnes asked in a voice that seemed to indicate that anyone who did not see the point of bringing Maeve back was a fool. Which, unfortunately, made Maeve a fool because the possible reason for bringing her back to the Guild was not obvious to her, not at all. Unless maybe the floors were in need of a good scrubbing.

"Forgive me, Headmistress," the old woman said, "but I am an old woman and not as clever as I used to be. Perhaps you had best pretend that it isn't."

Agnes sighed. "Very well. You should all be aware that with Felara's death we are short a combat instructor. And knowing this, I thought who better to fill that role than Maeve the Marvelous. Assuming, of course, that she had any interest in returning to the Guild. Imagine my surprise, then, when Emille came to me with the news that not only had Maeve seemed to consider the idea, she was in fact eager to return. Isn't that right, Lady Maeve?" she asked, glancing at her and raising an eyebrow.

"O-of course," Maeve stammered, then took a moment to take a slow breath, gathering herself. "I was excited to return," she finished, well-aware of Tribune Silrika staring at her with open hostility.

"Impossible," the Tribune spat. "It is not enough that you are the only person to have ever left the Guild, choosing to abandon them after they had done so much for you. Now, you wish to return, but not *only* to return, to return to a position of authority?"

Maeve opened her mouth to speak, but Agnes beat her to it. "Just because a thing has not been done before does not mean that it *cannot* be done, Tribune Silrika. I am surprised you do not know that."

She said the last with an obvious contempt, and the woman bared her teeth for a moment in equally obvious anger.

"Indeed," Tribune Bethesa said, her voice sounding bored. "Since we are speaking of Instructor Felara, she had, as I understood it, garnered a reputation for having never been beaten in single combat. But now that has changed. As the Headmistress said, just because it has not been done does not mean that it cannot be done. In fact, if the rumors are true, it is none other than Lady Maeve who defeated Felara."

"She cheated," Silrika hissed, "she must have. There is no way Felara would be beaten by a-a—"

"Careful, Tribune Silrika," Bethesa said, her tone somehow conveying both a warning and, to Maeve, at least, amusement. "You overstep yourself."

"Over*step?*" the other Tribune demanded, the furious expression on her face making it clear that she heard the other woman's enjoyment as much as Maeve.

"That's right," the old woman responded. "If the Headmistress has seen fit to bring Lady Maeve before us then we, as her subordinates, are in no position to argue. Besides which, I would caution you to not so easily lose your temper. After all," she went on, flashing a grin, "Felara was known for having a short fuse as well—and now she is dead."

The other woman turned a furious red at that, and if looks could kill Maeve imagined that the old woman, Bethesa, would have died where she sat, along with dozens of others, collateral damage caught in the woman's furious scowl. "So she is," Silrika said, "and I can assure you that I will discover the true manner of her death."

"Yes, and good luck to you," the older woman said in a voice that was at once bored and dismissive. "Still," she went on, turning to regard Maeve, taking her time, "Tribune Silrika does bring up a good point, I'm afraid."

"And what point is that?" Agnes asked warily.

"Forgive me, Headmistress, but it is now my turn to say it is obvious," the old woman said. "And by that I mean that if you intend for Lady Maeve to instruct our students on the arts of combat, well, I think that well and good. Only, there's one problem."

"What problem?" Maeve asked, thinking she knew all too well.

The Tribune favored her with a small smile. "Forgive me, Lady Maeve, for I mean no offense, but it seems to me that you have been gone a very long time, left the city during the war, as I recall.

We have not seen you in what, twenty years? Why, there are some among us here who were not even born when you left. It seems—"

"She means you're soft," Silrika snapped.

Maeve turned to regard the woman. "Forgive me, Tribune, but war does not make a person soft. In fact, all the soft ones who go are dead. Like Felara."

The woman let out a furious growl, starting to rise and the older woman, Bethesa, raised her hand. They were, ostensibly, the same rank, but that didn't stop the woman from freezing and slowly sitting down again, glaring at Maeve all the while.

"Be that as it may," the older woman went on, "it still seems to me that there must be some sort of means by which we can demonstrate that you, Lady Maeve, are indeed capable of training the students."

"Yes, well, as to that," Agnes said, "I have already had an idea."

"Of course," Tribune Piralta interjected, "for in your wisdom, Headmistress, it is apparent that you would have thought of all eventualities and addressed them so that—"

"Enough, Piralta," Agnes snapped. "You're a man, not a dog. Have some damned respect for yourself."

The man turned a furious, angry red at that, and Maeve winced. She knew that Agnes's anxiety level was high—certainly her own was—but she knew also that the woman had just made a mistake, could see it as the man's mouth worked, his jaw clenching and unclenching. However much of a danger the man had been to Agnes before, she had just ensured that he would be a far greater one going forward. "Forgive me, Headmistress," he said. "I will...consider your words carefully."

"And what then did you have in mind, Headmistress?" the old woman asked.

"Why, a trial by combat, of course," Agnes said.

There were murmurs of excitement from the crowd at that. *And why not?* Maeve thought. *After all, they're not the ones risking getting murdered.*

"I see," Tribune Bethesa said, as if she had expected as much. "And who, I wonder, did you have in mind to serve as the opponent for our Lady Maeve?"

"Who else?" Agnes asked. "It seems only fair, given the effort she put in to find her and speak with her that Instructor Emille be given the honor of doing a bout of mock combat with Lady Maeve to determine if, indeed, she still retains those skills which made her famous."

"If indeed she *does* retain her skills," the old woman said, her eyes seeming to shine as if she understood clearly what they were trying to pull, "then I am not sure that would be an honor. Or at the least it would be a painful one. While I am well aware of Instructor Emille's abilities, the name of Maeve the Marvelous is famous the world over."

"At any rate," Agnes went on, "Instructor Emille has already graciously agreed to participate in a little...demonstration for us. One that will either prove—or disprove—that Lady Maeve is indeed qualified to teach the students the art of combat."

"A demonstration," Bethesa said thoughtfully. "And you two are agreed to this?"

"I am, Tribune," Maeve said.

"As am I, Tribune," Emille said.

The old woman nodded slowly then glanced back at Tribune Piralta.

The man still wore a sullen expression from when Agnes had berated him, but he inclined his head. "I have no issue with it," he said.

Bethesa then turned to regard the woman, Silrika, who frowned for several seconds before finally, slowly smiling, somehow making the expression not less menacing than her frown but more so. "I agree with it," she said, and the old woman began to turn back, but Silrika wasn't finished. "Except, that is," she went on, her smile widening as she regarded Maeve and Agnes, "for one thing."

There was something about the way the woman said it that Maeve did not like, and alarm bells began to ring in her mind. Then, suddenly, realization struck.

Agnes, though, had apparently not realized what the woman intended. "Oh?" she asked in a voice brimming with anger at the woman balking her. "And what's that?"

"I do indeed agree, Headmistress," Silrika went on, watching Maeve with a small smile on her face, "that Lady Maeve might prove her talents in a mock demonstration. And while I, like everyone here, respect Instructor Emille and know well her worth, it seems to me that a woman of Lady Maeve's *legendary* talents might be better served fighting someone a little more...experienced."

"I see," Agnes said, speaking through gritted teeth. "And just who did you have in mind?"

The woman pretended to consider, though Maeve was certain she already knew exactly who she meant to recommend, had known from the moment she'd objected. "Hmm, well now that is a question, isn't it?" Silrika mused. "Were Felara here, I would recommend her for the task but...well..." She met Maeve's eyes, and something very much like insane anger flashed in her gaze. "Felara is not here, is she? She is dead, the exact *manner* of that death still uncertain."

"Yes, yes," Bethesa said, "we are all well aware of Instructor Felara's fate, Tribune Silrika. Now, is there a point to all of this?"

"The point," the woman went on, "is that I would be honored to serve in this demonstration along with Lady Maeve...personally."

The room went deathly silent at that, so that Agnes's snort sounded terribly loud. "You mean you intend to fight her yourself? That's ludicrous, Silrika. You might be the youngest Tribune, but you are still far past your fighting prime. Why, as a member of the Tribunal you no longer even take out contracts. No," she said, shaking her head, "it will be Emille—it only makes more sense. Now—"

"Forgive me, Headmistress," Tribune Bethesa said, "but there might be some merit to what she says."

"You can't be serious," Agnes said, but while she tried to sound angry, perhaps even amused by the ridiculousness of it, Maeve at least thought she could detect a hint of unease in the woman's tone. Tribune Bethesa gave a small smile, as if in apology, but Maeve thought she could see something in her eyes that seemed to indicate that she knew her speaking up was conflicting with their carefully laid plan, and was glad of that fact.

"I'm afraid I am, Headmistress," the old woman said. "After all, while you are correct that Silrika has not actively taken contracts for several years, neither has Maeve, and however old Silrika is, I hope I do not offend Lady Maeve by pointing out that she is, without question, her senior. In fact, it would seem unfair to me to place Lady Maeve in contest with such a talented assassin as Emille, one who, as it happens, is in the peak of her youth. For none knows better than I the ravages that time visits upon the flesh."

"No," Agnes said, sounding almost desperate now, "no, the very idea is ridiculous. We cannot risk one of our own Tribunes in such a contest. After all, as a member of the Guild's ruling council, Silrika is an important part of—"

"Oh, I wouldn't worry so much about it, Headmistress," another voice said, and Maeve was surprised to find that this time it was Tribune Piralta who had spoken. The man gave her a sharp smile, as if to say that this was payback for the way Agnes had treated him. "After all, such a demonstration would no doubt be of inestimable value to all the students here to watch, yes, I dare say even the instructors. And of course, I am quite sure that two women of such skill as Lady Maeve and Tribune Silrika can ensure that, however it turns out, neither of them suffers any lasting harm."

"Forgive me, Tribune, but perhaps—" Emille began, but cut off as the old woman held up her hand.

"Not now, Instructor Emille," Bethesa said, her eyes never leaving Agnes's. "You have done well to bring Lady Maeve to us, but your part in this is done."

"Are you attempting to dictate to me how things will play out, *Tribune Bethesa?*" Agnes hissed.

"Of course not, Headmistress," the old woman said, "I wouldn't dream of it. Though, with such a matter as this, I would think that, according to Guild law, it would have to be taken to a vote, one in which you, as well as the Tribunal participated." She paused, smiling, "Luckily, thanks to you, we have all of the Tribunal present even now, so that a vote might be taken. All in favor?" she asked, not even bothering to look back as she raised her own hand, followed in another moment by the hands of Silrika and Piralta.

"*Fine,*" Agnes hissed, turning to Maeve. "If you get the chance," she said quietly in a voice nearly too low even for Maeve to hear, "kill the bitch. There's plenty who would thank you for it."

The woman's words weren't really what bothered Maeve. Instead, it was the fact that, by the look on her face, she didn't seem all that confident that Maeve would get such a chance. Agnes said nothing else though, only turned and walked to the sidelines, her bodyguards and assistant following behind her without a word, though Maeve didn't miss the way the smaller of the two bodyguards watched her with a small, amused smile that she didn't care for.

That left her and Emille standing there, the woman not having walked off yet. "So," Maeve said quietly as she turned to her. "Just how good is she?"

Emille winced. "Look, Maeve, perhaps there is another way. If you were to say you didn't want in the Guild after all, maybe—"

"How good, Emille?"

The woman sighed softly. "Silrika has the highest contract completion count in the Guild, at least out of those who have claimed those contracts openly. She used to train with Felara and there were many—myself included—who believed that she was Felara's better."

"I see," Maeve said, her mouth suddenly terribly dry, as if she'd gargled with road dust. Contract count, after all, actually meant *kill* count. "Well, at least it's just a practice bout, right?" she tried a smile, but it died a quick death. "I mean we're not *actually* out to hurt each other. It's just a friendly competition."

"Right," Emille said, doing her best to give Maeve a reassuring smile and coming up about the same as she had herself.

"What is it, Emille?" Maeve asked. "What are you not saying?"

The woman winced. "It's just...well, Maeve, I won't lie to you—Silrika is known for her brutality. It was her calling card of sorts, when she was taking contracts, and if anything retiring to become a Tribune seems to have made it worse. Anyway, does she seem particularly friendly to you?"

Maeve frowned, turning in looking in the direction of Silrika as she climbed down from the podium on which she had sat, the woman's gaze watching her with a degree of eagerness that was in stark contrast to Maeve's own. "No," Maeve said as the woman bared her teeth in an expression that could not even loosely be called a grin but was instead a sort of feral challenge. "No, she doesn't."

"Alright, Instructor Emille," the old woman, Bethesa intoned, "if you would clear out of the way, we can get started."

Emille glanced at Maeve, a helpless expression on her face. "Lady Maeve, I'm sorry, if I'd known this was going to—"

"It's okay, Emille," Maeve said, offering her a smile. "I'm the reason we're here, not you. Whatever happens, it's not your fault. Best you get out of here."

The woman nodded, yet she hesitated, clearly wanting to say or do something. "It'll be alright," Maeve said softly. "Go on now."

The woman looked at her for another moment then finally turned and left. Which was just as well. Maeve had done her best to reassure her, but she never had been very good at lying. That was Chall's arena. Lies and manipulation, diplomacy and negotiation—which to her, were just fancier lies—were not her strong suit. Oh, she'd had some talent in getting men to do what she wanted, but that had really come from her fearsome reputation and her looks, neither of which she had any longer. The reputation had diminished in the years of her absence and the looks had diminished far faster.

No, her real talents lay in different areas—specifically in the direct, often bloody approach, letting her blades do the talking for her. Problem was, it had been quite some time since her blades had done much talking, though to be fair they'd been forced to get back in the hang of it lately since Chall had interjected himself into the safe—if pathetic—life she'd built for herself.

Not that she blamed Chall for that interruption, not any more than she blamed Prince Bernard who had led her to battle after battle. No, she did not blame either of them for her being here, in this place, where her knives would be called for once more. Instead, she blamed herself for allowing those knives to become dull.

Figuratively, of course. She might no longer be the woman she once was, but she was also not a complete fool, and even she knew it was better to have your knife sharpened, lest you need it, than to need it and find it unequal to the task.

The Tribune stalked forward, stopping a dozen feet in front of her. Maeve turned so that her right side, her dominant side, faced the woman. "What type of contest, then?" she asked. "Blunted weapons or…?"

"Oh, I'm sure that won't be necessary," Silrika said quickly. "After all, we are both well-trained. I am sure that we might forego using those novice's tools and use our own weapons instead."

"You can't be serious," Emille shouted. "Someone could die!"

"I'm sorry, Instructor Emille," Tribune Bethesa said, "but Silrika is right. After all, we're not the Guild of Puppy Dogs and Rainbows, are we?" she asked.

No, you are not, Maeve thought, as there was some scattered laughter around the room, *more's the pity.*

Emille looked to Agnes as if for help, and Maeve followed her gaze, but the moment she saw the other woman's face she decided that there would be no help from that quarter. Agnes was furious, that she could see, but more than that, she appeared nervous, and Maeve thought she understood that. After all, the woman had been outmaneuvered in front of a large portion of the Guild by the old Tribune. A Headmistress might be outmaneuvered in such a way once or twice, but if people were able to get by with such things often, they would begin to think they could get by with bigger things too. No, she could not afford to be made to appear a fool, at least not if she wanted to keep on breathing.

The woman looked angry, her jaw clenched, but she said nothing, and Maeve knew that she would not. Agnes had done what she could for them, for Maeve. Now she was on her own.

"The bout will continue until one party yields or is unable to carry on," Tribune Bethesa intoned in a formal-sounding voice. "A bout to determine whether Lady Maeve is worthy to return to our illustrious ranks. Do either of you have any questions?"

"None," Silrika said immediately, drawing two knives, one in either hand, from the inside of her tunic.

"I'm good," Maeve answered. *At least for the moment.*

"Do you have any of your own weapons?" her opponent asked, grinning. "If not, I'm sure someone around here has some that you might borrow."

"I think I'm alright," Maeve said, reaching into her own tunic and withdrawing two blades, holding one in each hand.

"For now," the woman said, coming uncomfortably close to echoing Maeve's own thoughts from seconds ago.

"Are both contestants prepared?" Bethesa asked, an eagerness for bloodshed in her voice that the woman's affected, down-to-earth tone didn't quite manage to conceal.

Silrika nodded and Maeve nodded as well. "Very well," the Tribune said, "then...begin!"

The other woman bucked, as if she meant to rush forward, and Maeve tensed. Silrika subsided though, flashing her teeth in a wide grin as she began to circle. *"Maeve the Marvelous,"* the woman said, widening her eyes in mock-admiration. "I've heard stories of you since I first joined the Guild. Stories of your skill...your beauty." She made a point of eyeing Maeve up and down. "It seems that some of those, at least, were exaggerated."

"Stories often are," Maeve said. The woman was trying to rile her, to make fun of her looks, but she would have to try far harder than that. After all, it wasn't as if Maeve had just woken up one morning and found that her beauty had been stolen. Instead, she had watched, helpless, as it was taken bit by bit over the years, and she had had no choice but to grow used to those seemingly daily thefts. "Still," she went on, flashing the woman a smile, making a point of looking her up and down as well, taking in her squat form, her too-wide shoulders and plain face, "I suppose it's better to have had and lost than to have never had at all, wouldn't you agree?"

Her opponent gritted her teeth at that, turning an ugly shade of crimson, and that was good. Anger could be a weapon, it was true, but it had a way of cutting the one wielding it as much as anyone else. Anger, after all, made people reckless, and if reckless people could be said to be good at anything, they were fair hands at dying.

"I have not risen where I am because of a pretty face," the woman snapped.

"That much is obvious," Maeve agreed, and the woman gritted her teeth tighter still, hard enough that Maeve fancied she could hear her jaw muscles straining. She let her smile go wider. It was all a game of course, for any warrior worth her salt knew that in a duel such as this, the fight began long before blood was drawn. It began often before the two opponents even met on the field of battle. A battle not of muscle and tendon, of speed and strength, at least not then, but one of will and mind. And far more often than not, the loser of *that* battle was the same one who ended up losing the real thing.

Not always though. After all, while words, while thoughts might indeed hurt, in Maeve's experience a knife hurt a considerable bit more. As if eager to test that idea out, the Tribune suddenly rushed forward, her left hand leading, and Maeve didn't have time to think anymore, didn't have time to do anything at all but back up, twisting away from the woman's flashing blades.

A lot of people looked at knives like smaller swords, thinking that a fight with one or the other would be very similar, but this could not have been further from the truth. Swordfights—at least duels of the kind fought in castle courtyards—were largely made up of precise parries, precise steps. Knife fights, on the other hand, despite their smaller size, were almost always wilder, more brutal. You did not parry a knife with a knife—you were either cut or you were not.

So Maeve did not engage the woman's vicious onslaught. Instead, she focused on staying out of her reach, hoping the woman would tire herself out. The problem, of course, was that the woman didn't *look* as if she was getting tired. And then that wasn't the only thing to concern Maeve. After all, even if she lost, she thought it possible that she would be inducted into the Guild. Assuming that she showed some skill in fighting and didn't spend the entire fight retreating as she was doing now.

The real issue was that the woman was fast—very fast. She was fast, and she was angry, the knives she wielded flashing this way and that, twin metallic blurs. And while Silrika might not have appeared to be getting tired, Maeve certainly was. Tired enough, in fact, that she was too slow to back up and cried out as the woman's blade sliced across her forearm.

A shallow cut, one that was far from life-threatening, and yet looking at it, at the crimson line across her arm, Maeve felt a sort of panic.

The Tribune grinned cruelly as she paced around Maeve. "Felara was a friend," she whispered in a voice too low to be heard by the others in the room. "I don't know how you bested her, but know this, *Lady* Maeve—you will die here."

There had been times in Maeve's life when she had thought she wanted to die; certainly, there had been times when she thought she deserved it. Despite that, though, she found, listening to the woman's words, that she was angry. Not just angry—furious. Perhaps she had earned her death a thousand times over, but she would not die today, not now. If she did, she knew that the contract on Chall would continue and that the mage would be dead within the week, likely within the day.

But anger, she knew, would not serve her, not here. After all, while anger might have been one of Cutter's strengths, it was not hers. So she did her best to ignore the pain in her arm, that stinging, incessant pain, and took a slow deep breath as the woman watched her, that cruel grin on her face. The woman was fast, it was true, but she was also confident. Confident, as perhaps she should be, that she would easily best the old woman standing before her.

There had been a time when Maeve would have beaten her, if not easily, at least solidly. The woman was fast, but there had been a time when Maeve had been faster, stronger, too. Of course, that had been twenty years ago. The woman did not fear her, and she was right not to fear her, for Maeve was exactly what she looked like—an old woman. An old woman far past her prime, who didn't have much fight left in her.

But then she found herself thinking of Chall, of the assassin that had been lurking outside their window, meaning to kill them while they slept. As she backpedaled away from the woman's ferocious attack, she thought of those moments before the assassin had shown up, when she'd lain awake watching Chall sleeping beside her. She thought also of Matt, the boy so eager to do good and so scared he would fail, of Priest. The man kept himself to himself, but there was no doubt he was having some kind of crisis, that he needed help. And then there was Prince Bernard to think about also. Prince Bernard who had traveled to the Black Wood. She might have written anyone else off by now, considered them beyond saving, but then Prince Bernard wasn't just anyone, and she had long since lost count of the times he'd faced certain death—her reluctantly along for the ride—and come out the other side. Bloody and battered, sure, with some fresh scars to keep him company but breathing. No, he might still be alive, and if he *was*, then he needed her help. That much she knew for any mortal entering the Black Wood was in great peril.

The prince needed her. Chall, Priest, and Matt needed her. But if she was killed she would be of no use to anybody. True, she was past her prime, and true she didn't have much fight in her. But as she continued to back in a circle, the woman slashing at her again and again, Maeve decided that there was a big difference between not much and none at all.

But she could not allow herself to give into her anger, as tempting as that might have been. Assassins concentrated on retaining their calm, their composure. While others might get scared or angry, they kept their focus. It was a skill the best of assassins mastered, and one that had always come naturally to Maeve the Marvelous, for after what she had lost at the hands of the Skaalden everything else had meant little to her.

And so she called on that woman now. Perhaps Maeve the Marvelous did not remain, but at least the *memory* of her did, and the memory was enough. Maeve felt that cold, calculating calm suffuse her, spreading through her and, as it did, it took away her fear and her anger, took away also the pain in her arm.

There was nothing but her and the woman in front of her: her mark. And so Maeve did what she had been trained to do—she studied her. She knew already that the woman was quick to anger, that it was that anger that she had learned to harness to make herself dangerous, that was currently granting her the ferocious energy that drove her forward, that powered her arm as she slashed at Maeve again and again with her knives.

Maeve studied the woman, the way she moved as she came on again. Not stalking forward methodically but barreling forward, putting her momentum behind each swing. This meant that her strikes were stronger—more deadly than they might have been—but it also meant that she over-committed with each one, leaving her weight unevenly distributed.

Maeve continued to watch her, analyzing her movements, growing used to her pattern of attack, the way she tended to follow up a left-handed jab with a right-handed hook. A hook which she telegraphed with a slight dip of her right shoulder as she prepared to launch the strike.

The woman hissed, pausing in her assault for a moment to slowly circle Maeve. "There is no way you beat Felara, not fairly. You are weak."

"Maybe I didn't beat her fairly," Maeve said, giving the woman a small smile, not because she found anything humorous, only because she knew the reaction it would cause—was, in fact, counting on it. "But I *did* beat her. I'd say you could ask her, but then..." She allowed the grin to widen.

Her words caused an instant reaction in the woman, as Maeve had known they would, fueling the flames of her anger. Silrika's face twisted in furious rage, and she charged forward—also as Maeve had known she would. She came on fast, leading with a wickedly-quick jab of her left knife. Maeve did not retreat from the blow this time, but instead stepped to the side of it, a thing she was only confident in doing because she had expected the jab, had known what shape the attack would take. She waited until she saw the slight dip in the woman's shoulder, the one that indicated that the right-hook was coming.

Then Maeve stepped forward, ducking before the strike even started. If she was wrong, of course, then she was in some serious trouble. If, say, the woman was performing an uppercut or a downward strike instead, then Maeve had just positioned herself perfectly to accept a knife in the back or, as it happened, in the stomach. But she was not wrong, and the woman did indeed attack her with a right hook of her knife, stepping forward aggressively, putting her full weight into the movement. Which added considerable force to the fist that Maeve planted in her stomach.

Silrika let out a gasping wheeze as the breath exploded from her lungs, folding over Maeve's strike. Maeve, though, wasn't finished. She let go of the knife she held in her right fist, letting it fall to the ground before delivering a ridge-handed strike to her opponent's throat. Not hard enough to do permanent damage but enough to cause some serious pain, to incapacitate her for at time. Silrika stumbled backward, wavering, wheezing for breath as she brought her hands to her throat, her pain making her blind to everything else around her. Everything...including Maeve's foot, positioned behind her. The woman let out a grunting hiss of surprise before she tumbled over onto her back.

Silrika had dropped one of her knives, but her right hand was still clasped around the handle of the other. At least, that was, until Maeve stepped forward, giving it a kick and sending the weapon skidding across the ground. Groaning in pain, the woman started to rise only in time to freeze as Maeve knelt, placing her knife at the Tribune's throat.

"Someone should have told you," Maeve said, loud enough for her words to carry around the large chamber. "Assassination has very little to do with strength."

The woman stared at the blade, her body tensing, her eyes dancing with insane fury and, for a moment, Maeve thought that she meant to attack, even though doing so would mean that the blade, poised at her throat, would do its bloody work. In the end, though, she remained still, save for her upper lip that lifted in a snarl. "I could have had you," the woman hissed.

"Yes," Maeve said, "you could have—but you didn't."

"Go on then," she spat. "Finish it."

Maeve considered doing just that. After all, the woman wasn't her biggest fan—that much was clear. And what Maeve and Agnes were about was already dangerous. The woman being alive, remaining a Tribune, could only be bad for her. But she found that she could not do it. She was not that woman anymore, the woman who had been able to kill someone, to snuff out a life with no more thought or consideration than one might give to snuffing out a candle flame. That woman, one who had just recently lost her husband and her child, had had nothing to live for, nothing that meant anything to her. Now, Maeve had found a family again, people that she loved and who, in turn, loved her.

Maeve flashed the Tribune a smile, giving her a wink. "Maybe next time," she said. Then she rose, leaving the woman lying with an undeniable mixture of relief and confusion on her face, as she glanced around the room. Everyone gathered watched her for several seconds, clearly stunned by this turn of events. Then, as one, they all burst into applause.

Maeve stood there, in the midst of that applause, that adulation, feeling very strange indeed. It was as if she stood victorious, in some tourney circle instead of the midst of a guild of assassins. She stood there awkwardly for several seconds until Silrika growled in fury, rising to her feet, her face a deep, angry crimson, her hands clenched into fists at her sides. She looked around the room with a scowl sharp enough to draw blood, then, instead of moving back toward the Tribune podium, she turned and stormed off, toward the door Agnes had led Maeve through earlier.

In another moment, the woman was gone, the door slamming shut behind her. Maeve became aware of movement out of the corner of her eye and glanced over to see Emille hurrying up to her. "*Maeve,*" the woman said, a grin spreading across her mouth, "that was...that was amazing. Are you okay?"

"I'm fine," Maeve said, offering the woman a smile she didn't feel. "Thanks."

Emille nodded, glancing around the room as the clapping and cheering slowly began to die down. "Looks like you've got some new fans."

"Some new enemies too, I expect," Maeve said, glancing back at the door through which Silrika had disappeared.

Emille followed her gaze and winced, nodding. "Still...it could be worse. I've got to be honest, Maeve, for a minute there, I thought..." She trailed off, not finishing, a guilty look on her face.

Maeve gave the woman a smile, nodding herself. "So did I," she said honestly.

"That was a mistake," a voice said quietly.

They both turned to see that Agnes had walked up. To Maeve's surprise, the woman did not look happy or relived but instead, if anything, she seemed even angrier than when Tribune Bethesa had outmaneuvered her.

"If it was then it wasn't the worst one I might have made," Maeve said dryly, "and I'm glad to see you're happy to see me still breathing, Agnes."

"Sure, but for how long?" the woman snapped, keeping her voice down so that it would not carry. "Silrika will not thank you for letting her live, Maeve. You have embarrassed her, wounded her pride, and there is nothing more important to such a woman like her than her pride."

Maeve raised an eyebrow. "You seem awfully confident of that."

Agnes's eyes narrowed. "Do you think that she would have shown you such mercy if your roles were reversed?"

"The thought never crossed my mind," Maeve said honestly.

The Guild's Headmistress gave a frustrated toss of her head. "Better if you had killed her," she said out of the corner of her mouth as she looked around the room. "Better for you and better for me as well. What person, Maeve, finding her foot poised over a poisonous spider, chooses not to stomp on it?"

"Maybe a person who knows that the spider beneath her boot is far from the only spider she needs to worry about," Maeve said archly.

Agnes rubbed at her temples. "She will not count it as a favor. You have embarrassed her, have made her look weak, and that, to Silrika, is a fate far worse than death."

"Maybe she won't thank me for it," Maeve said, "but that's alright—fact is, Agnes, I didn't do it for her. Anyway," she went on, glancing around as she noted the cheers finally beginning to subside, "it might be that you'll want to leave off scolding me now and attend to all these people—sorry *assassins*."

Agnes gave her one more parting scowl—in case, Maeve supposed, her disapproval hadn't already been made clear—then turned to the room at large as the last of the cheers died away. "Now then," Agnes began, her gaze traveling to the two remaining members of the Tribunal and despite her scolding, there was no denying a tone of gloating in her voice as she regarded Tribune Bethesa. "I hope that this...*exhibition* has satisfactorily put to rest any...*doubts* the members of the Tribunal might have entertained regarding Lady Maeve's usefulness to the Guild?"

It was, on the surface at least, a question, but Maeve could hear the challenge in it, just as she could see, from the sour expression on Tribune Bethesa's face, that the old woman recognized it for what it was as well.

"Still," Agnes went on when the remaining tribunes didn't immediately respond, "I suppose we might vote on it." She pretended at mock concern then. "Though, we must find someone to track down Tribune Silrika. She left rather...abruptly, I'm afraid."

"That won't be necessary," the old woman, Bethesa, croaked, seemingly having to force the words out of her mouth.

"Oh?" Agnes asked, all mock-innocence.

The Tribune gave her a tight, fragile smile. "Of course not," she said. "After all, the match has served its purpose, proving well that your reputation, Lady Maeve," she went on, turning to regard Maeve, "is well-deserved."

"Thank you, Tribune," Maeve said, playing her part and giving a deep bow, more than a little satisfied to still be standing to disappoint the woman. "It was my honor to fight one so...worthy."

"Quite," the old woman said, her smile fading. "Now that this piece of business is concluded, is there anything else, Headmistress?"

"Hasn't this been enough for you, Tribune?" Agnes said, smiling deeply, and Maeve winced, not loving the way Agnes was using her victory as a weapon. True, she didn't intend to remain in the Guild—at least not any longer than necessary to get the contract on her and Chall canceled and figure out if there were any others. That and to fulfill her promise with Agnes. But then it didn't take all that long for someone to stick a knife in your back. While many of those gathered around the room were smiling or staring in wide-eyed shock—it wasn't everyday that you watched a woman that might be your grandma beat one of the Guild's most dangerous assassins—there were those among their number who looked none too pleased.

The old Tribune scowled, turning to regard Maeve again. "It was well-fought," she said with obvious reluctance. "Welcome back to the Guild, Instructor Maeve." And then, with anger dancing in her eyes. "Though, I might warn you—things have changed since last you were here. It is my belief that, this time, you might find it far more...difficult to leave."

"Yes, yes," Agnes said, waving her hand dismissively at the woman's words. Bethesa clearly wanted to utter some angry retort, but she did not, subsiding into a sullen silence and why not? After all, Agnes was winning—for the moment at least. "Thank you so much for your *exhaustive* input, Tribune Bethesa. Now then, you may all return to your duties—I will personally see to the reacquaintance of Lady Maeve with the Guild and what will be expected of her." She turned to regard the room at large, her gaze sweeping across the gathered students. "In time, one of you might well find yourself in a class with her as your instructor. If so..." She paused, smiling a dagger-sharp smile as she turned her gaze on the old Tribune." You would do well, I think, to remember what transpired here today."

The words were clearly meant for the old woman, so clearly, in fact, that no one in the room moved, save the woman, Bethesa, who trembled slightly with fury. Finally, it seemed that Agnes's proddings had disturbed the mask of casual disregard which the woman had worn, giving Maeve a glimpse of the furious, hateful, twisted thing lurking beneath.

The two continued to stare at each other until, a few seconds later, Agnes appeared to realize that no one was moving, and she turned to glance around at the auditorium as a whole. *"Well?"* she demanded. That was enough to get them moving, and in another moment the air was filled with the sounds of shuffling feet and hushed conversations as the students and instructors left, discussing what they had seen. Unless things had changed dramatically since last she was in the Guild, Maeve expected that many of them were already plotting how to use her return to their advantage and, failing that, how to dispose of her as quickly and quietly as possible.

"Come."

Maeve turned to see that while she'd been looking around the room, noting those faces—far too many—who watched her with angry or sullen expressions as they filtered out, Agnes had come up on her from behind. *Careful, Maeve,* she thought. After all, Agnes might pretend to be her friend right now, but she did not doubt that would change the moment she appeared to lose her usefulness.

"Where are we going?" she asked carefully. After all, just because she could think of no reason why Agnes might have lied and did all of this as some elaborate way of setting her up, didn't mean it wasn't true.

The woman gave her a small smile, as if she knew well what she was thinking. "To my office—unless you want to hang around here a bit longer. See if maybe Silrika or perhaps one of her friends returns to finish the job."

"No, no I think I'm ready to leave," Maeve said.

"I thought you might be," the woman said. "Come—this way."

"And what of me, Headmistress?"

They turned to regard Emille, standing there with an uncertain look on her face. "You may return to...whatever it is you were doing, Instructor Emille," Agnes said. "Your work here is done."

Emille glanced at Maeve in question, and Maeve gave her a slight nod of her head. Despite the fact that everything had gone according to plan, she didn't *feel* safe—at least not any safer, she imagined than the frog who let the scorpion climb on his back to cross the river—but whatever happened, she thought it wise to distance herself from Emille as much as possible. After all, it would not do for those meaning to make her pay for embarrassing Tribune Silrika to include Emille in their anger.

She saw the woman still hesitating, and Maeve glanced at Agnes as the woman's bodyguards and assistant seemed to appear as if by magic behind her. "May I have a second to speak with Emille?" she asked. "I'll be along in just a moment."

"Of course," Agnes said, "but do not take long—you know what Quelaash used to say about slow assassins." And with that, she turned and walked away to stand a short distance off, speaking with her assistant.

"Who is Quelaash?" Emille asked.

"An old instructor, one that Agnes and I shared," Maeve said grimly as she stared after the Headmistress. She turned to Emille. "He used to say that slow assassins made dead assassins."

The woman winced. "Maeve, I'm still not sure this was a good idea."

"Me neither," Maeve admitted, "but it's too late now. Listen, Emille, I know that I've asked far more from you than I deserve, but I have one more favor to ask."

"Name it," Emille said, and Maeve at once felt honored and also ashamed by the woman's willingness to help her.

"If...if things go wrong," Maeve said. "I need you to find Challadius and Priest and tell them what happened, that I failed."

Emille nodded, her face slightly pale. "Is...is that all?"

"One more thing," Maeve said, clearing her throat. "If...if something *does* happen...tell Chall that I love him. Would...would you do that for me?"

"Of course, Maeve," Emille said, "but I'm sure you'll be alright." She tried to sound certain, but Maeve could hear the doubt in her voice. Not that it was all that hard—after all, it was a doubt she shared.

"And Emille," Maeve said, "if I can offer you one small bit of unsolicited advice…find that husband of yours, and you ask him to his face what he's been doing lately."

Emille winced. "I…I don't know if I want to know."

"Maybe not," Maeve agreed, "but trust me, Emille, take it from someone who has spent the last twenty years of her life wondering if a certain illusionist with a penchant for being an asshole loved her…it's always better to know."

"Even if what you learn is bad?" Emille asked, giving her a fragile smile.

Maeve put a hand on the woman's shoulder, offering her a return smile. "Especially then. Now, I'd best go. Good luck, Emille."

"And you too, Maeve," she said.

The woman started to turn away then paused, glancing back. "Go on," Maeve said, offering her a smile. "I'll be okay." *Until I'm not.*

Emille gave another nod, then turned and walked away. Maeve had only known the woman for a short time, and so she was surprised at the feeling of loss and discomfort she felt as she watched her leave. Still, she took a moment to wish Emille all the best with her husband, for she deserved happiness. From what she had seen, Maeve was sure the man would never have stepped out on Emille. She'd been wrong before, of course, but she sincerely hoped that this time was not one of them.

Still, whatever happened, Emille would have to deal with it by herself. Maeve had more than enough problems of her own to keep her busy. She turned back to one of those problems now, giving a nod to Agnes. "I'm ready."

"About time," Agnes said. "Come—my office is this way."

CHAPTER SEVENTEEN

Half an hour later, Maeve sat in Agnes's large study. If the assassins of the Guild themselves were subtle, the Headmistress's office most assuredly was not. The study was decorated with ornately carved bookshelves, and along the walls were several paintings that looked so real Maeve was possessed of the crazy idea that she could step directly into them. Not that she would want to, for many of those paintings depicted some scene of violence or tragedy. What appeared to be a violent uprising, complete with a torch-bearing mob in this one, and then a brutal execution in the next. A third depicted a bed in which a man lay, a man who might have been sleeping save a fresh pool of spreading beneath him, staining the coverlet and sheets crimson.

Maeve suspected that the contents of the painting were meant to throw off visitors to the study, to make them uncomfortable, and she at least could vouch for their effectiveness.

Across the massive oak desk from her sat Agnes, the woman shaking her head, a malicious grin on her face. "My, but did you see that old bitch Bethesa's face?" she cooed. "That isn't an embarrassment she's likely to forget anytime soon."

"Nor I," Maeve said, glancing down at her arm where the cut she'd taken from Silrika was freshly bandaged by Agnes's personal healer before the Headmistress had sent her away, along with her bodyguards and assistant.

Agnes nodded. "Yes...you did surprisingly well, Maeve," she said. "I must be honest, I did not expect for Silrika to challenge you, though perhaps I should have. When she did...I would be lying if I didn't say that I thought she would best you. She is a brutal fighter, Silrika, even by Guild standards, and you are...well." She cut off, shrugging.

"Old?" Maeve asked.

Agnes smiled as if to say that was exactly what she meant. "Anyway, as I said, it was well done."

"With little help from you, I might add," Maeve said.

The other woman shrugged, clearly not apologetic in the least. "You came out alright. And I can't say I minded watching Silrika be embarrassed so...thoroughly. Anyway, it wasn't as if I could be seen to show you favor. We don't want anyone thinking that we're friends—"

"No problem there," Maeve interjected.

"Yes, quite," the woman said, giving her a small smile. "Anyway, I dared not help you anymore than I did and risk the plan."

"And if I would have died?" Maeve demanded.

The woman didn't even have the good grace to look apologetic as she shrugged again. "You didn't. Anyway, I didn't want you to die, if that's what you're getting at. After all, do you have any idea how inconvenient it would be for me to have to find someone else to execute this plan with?"

"I hate the thought that my death would *inconvenience* you," Maeve said.

"Oh, I wouldn't worry about it overly much—after all, you didn't die. Did you?"

Maeve rolled her eyes. "No, I did not. Still, I don't like where we left things."

"Oh?" Agnes said. "For to me it seemed most...satisfactory," she finished, grinning at the memory, and Maeve knew she was thinking of Bethesa.

"While I am thrilled that you got the opportunity to embarrass your rival," Maeve said dryly, "I don't think things went as well as you seem to think."

"And why is that?"

"For one, you offended Tribune Piralta far more than you needed to. And from what little I've seen of the man, he does not appear to be the type to forgive and forget easily. What's more, I get the distinct impression that he's going to hate me all the more because of that."

Agnes waved a dismissive hand. "The Weasel is the least of my concerns, and he should be the least of yours. The man is a pathetic worm, a flatterer. Truth to tell, he is barely even a man. He is no real danger."

"Maybe he isn't much of a man," Maeve said, "but then a person doesn't need to be a man to stick a knife in someone's back. And speaking of danger, what of Silrika?"

Agnes avoided her gaze then, busying herself with adjusting one of the stacks of papers on her desk. "What about her?" she asked in a decidedly affected off-handed manner.

"What do you mean, *what about her?*" Maeve asked. "She seemed dangerous enough for the both of them, if you ask me."

"Yes, well," Agnes said, "I suppose it's true that Tribune Silrika has a bit of an anger problem. Still, you came out alright."

"Did I?" Maeve demanded. "I don't know Silrika well—we only just very nearly killed each other—but she seems to me the type that holds a grudge. And unless I miss my guess, there were quite a few among those other students and instructors who weren't all that pleased to see her beaten."

"Yes, well, it may seem surprising, but Silrika does enjoy a fair number of friendships...though how that is possible considering her nature, I am sure I do not know."

"And let me guess, it's those friendships that explain why such a hot-headed individual has somehow found herself on the Tribunal?"

Agnes inclined her head. "Just so. While Silrika might be belligerent and often openly hostile, the amount of people who follow her lead cannot easily be discounted. She pursued her spot on the Tribunal the same way she does everything else— aggressively—and despite my reservations I really had no choice but to see her appointed."

"And the other Tribunes were okay with it?"

Agnes stared at her as if she were a fool. "Tribune Piralta expressed very little opinion on the matter save pleasure at the appointment—but then how the man acts and how he actually feels are often quite different."

"And Bethesa?"

Agnes frowned. "Yes, she was quite amenable to the idea, and I suspect I know why."

"Do you think the two of them are in collusion?" Maeve asked. The thought was a troubling one, for while the two women seemed dangerous enough, if they were working together they would be far more of a threat.

But Agnes shook her head. "No, no, it isn't that."

"How do you know, though?"

"I *know*," Agnes said testily, "because when Silrika's name was first put forward to replace the previous Tribune, I did my research. There is no connection—however tenuous—between Silrika and Bethesa. If there had been, I would have found it. You see, Maeve," she went on, frowning, "I am not so foolish as you appear to think."

Maeve winced. "Sorry. Anyway, speaking of Bethesa—"

Agnes nodded. "She is the true danger. I can only hope that the show we put on was enough to convince her, for if she suspects any sort of alliance between the two of us she will not stop until she uncovers it. Do not let her outwardly friendly manner fool you, Maeve—that woman is a viper, and her teeth have only grown sharper with age."

Maeve, who had caught a glimpse of those fangs when the woman's frustration had caused her mask to slip, did not need convincing of that. "So what now?" she asked.

Agnes raised an eyebrow at her. "I was preparing to ask you the same question."

Maeve nodded, sitting forward. "Well, I suppose it's about time we kill you then." The woman frowned, and Maeve offered her a smile. "Or, well, only pretend to kill you, of course."

Agnes frowned. "You need not look so happy about it."

"Why Agnes," Maeve said, "the very idea of anything happening to you sends shivers of dread through me. I only pretend it doesn't matter, you see, for the good of the plan—much as you pretended not to care when I was attacked by a homicidal Tribune."

"Right," the other woman said, clearing her throat. "Anyway…am I to assume you have a plan?"

"So I do," Maeve said. "Or, at least the beginnings of one." She leaned forward then and they spent the next several hours hunched over, talking in quiet whispers.

CHAPTER EIGHTEEN

"Alright, lads. We're here."

Chall opened his eyes, blinking to see that Ned had peeked his head back through the screen separating the carriage's driver's seat from the back.

He was surprised—and more than a little mortified—to realize that he'd fallen asleep on their trip through the city. True, he had not slept well the night before, and true, when he was stressed he tended to sleep more than normal, but neither of those things would matter much if he was caught unawares by someone working for that bastard Catham. It was a foolish mistake, unforgiveable really, and he might as easily have been waking up in the land of the dead.

"Here?" he asked blearily.

The carriage driver gave a small smile. "Sleeping hard, were you? I'll take that a compliment on my smooth driving. Anyway, we're at the castle."

Chall nodded, glancing at the back of the wagon. The screen was closed—the better to hide from the murderers seeking to kill them—and anything might have lain beyond. "Priests first," he told his companion.

Priest smiled. "Of course."

The man moved to the back of the carriage, then climbed out. When he remained unstabbed, Chall followed him, exiting the carriage to see that Ned had pulled them up in front of the castle gates. The guards stationed there were watching them with the slightly bored, slightly suspicious expressions that, to Chall's mind, all guards seemed to be assigned along with their uniforms and weapons.

He and Priest walked to the front of the wagon. "Thanks," he told the driver and meant it. "For the ride."

Ned smiled. "It's what I do."

Chall hesitated, wanting to say something more but unsure of what that something might be. "You'll...that is, are you going home to see your wife now?"

Ned winced. "Not yet; much as I want to, there's something I need to be about first. Some questions that need answering."

Chall nodded. It didn't take much to realize that the man meant to go find Catham again, to resume his investigation into the sudden reappearance of the Crimson Wolves and what it might mean. "Be careful, alright?" Chall said. "I've only met your wife a few times, but I've seen enough to know I wouldn't want to be the one that had to explain to her what happened to you."

Ned grinned. "I'll be fine."

Priest cleared his throat, and they turned to him. The man fidgeted, clearly uncomfortable. "Ned...I...that is, I want to say again, how sorry I am. And to thank you...for all your help. Without you, we would have died. There's...there's no way we could ever repay you."

The carriage driver laughed. "No worries. Anyway, if you want to give it a go, repaying me that is, well then, when this is all said and done, maybe you can buy me an ale, how'd that be?"

Priest gave the man a small smile, inclining his head. "You've got it."

Chall snorted. "Shit, if we come out the other end of this thing alive, I reckon I'll be buyin' more than one ale."

Ned grinned. "Well. Best I be goin' now. Things to do and all that."

"Alright then," Chall said. "Just...be careful."

"Yes, Mom," Ned said. He gave a wide wave then clucked at the horses and in another moment the carriage was moving down the street.

Despite the fact that he wanted nothing more than to rush into the castle and find Maeve—she was surely back by now, and no doubt terrified wondering where he'd gone—Chall found himself standing there, watching the carriage driver depart.

He continued to stand there, worrying, until he felt a hand on his shoulder, and he turned to see that it was Priest, the man giving him a small smile. "He'll be okay, Chall."

"How do you know?" Chall asked.

The man gave a soft laugh, turning and glancing at the departing carriage as it disappeared down the street. "Because a wise friend of mine once told me that a man has to believe in something, and left with a choice to believe in the good or believe in the bad, I choose the good."

Chall snorted. "Sounds like a pompous asshole to me."

Priest winked. "Yes, well, there are worse things. Now, I suspect you are eager to go back to the castle and find Maeve. I'm sure she's back and waiting for us by now."

"The thought had crossed my mind," Chall admitted. He had known, over the last several days, that he'd loved sharing a bed with Maeve, both when they were awake and when they were not. But spending the previous night in the abandoned hideout had made him appreciate even more fully just how *much* he enjoyed it. "Come on," he said. "We can find Maeve and the king and tell them what's happened. With any luck, they'll have some idea about how we should proceed."

Priest nodded. "You lead. I'll follow."

Then may the gods help us both, Chall thought, but he only nodded, moving toward the gate and waving at the guards as he did.

"Ah, Sir Challadius, Sir Valden," one of the guards said as he and Priest approached, then he paused, glancing up and down at their dust-covered forms—Ned's safehouse might have been safe, but it most certainly hadn't been clean. "Is...everything okay, sirs?"

Chall nodded, thinking that if all the dust made the man uncomfortable, he couldn't imagine what he would think if he knew just how close they'd come to being covered in blood instead. "Everything's fine, thank you." A thought occurred to him to ask if anything had happened while they were gone—anything like another assassination attempt. But then, he didn't know how secret Matt wanted that little bit of information, so he chose to take a different tack. "How's...that is, how have things been here?"

The guard looked surprised by the question. "Quiet, sir."

"Sure, of course," Chall said. "Anyway, guess I'd best be going."

The guard bowed. "Of course, sir." He motioned to one of the others who moved at his command, and in another moment, the gates were swinging open.

As they walked down the path Priest let out a soft grunt.

"What is it?" Chall asked, turning to glance at him.

"I'm...only a little surprised, to be honest," Priest said. "That they recognized us, you know, looking as we do. I had not expected to be let in so easily."

"I wouldn't be too proud if I were you," Chall said dryly, "they let in assassins, too, in case you've forgotten. Now, come on—let's get a move on."

"Where to?" Priest asked. "To your quarters to find Maeve, I assume?"

Chall wanted to say yes to that, wanted it just as badly as he'd ever wanted anything. Certainly it was the type of thing the old him would have done. Old as in the version of him from yesterday. But then, that version had spent a night lying on a dusty old cot—one he suspected was a prototype of some unique but particularly creative torture device—thinking that if most of the decisions a man made led him to near-death experiences, he was probably making the wrong decisions.

Besides, it wasn't just about him, *couldn't* just be about him. There was Matt to think of, and Priest as well. The man had clearly been making an effort to be in a better mood, but he was also clearly still struggling with his own demons. And then, of course, there was Prince Bernard and, indeed, the entire kingdom. They might not know exactly what the man, Catham was up to, but whatever it was, it couldn't be good, that much was clear. They still didn't know who the man worked for—cautious bastard like that, there was no way he allowed himself to be the head of the snake, not when it was the bit most likely to get chopped when the chopping started. No, the man had a boss, and they could only hope that Ned found out more.

Still, they knew more than they had—and they were still alive—so overall he counted the last twenty-four-hour period a win. Or at least, would, just as soon as he was able to track Maeve down and give her a dramatically inappropriate kiss. But there was one thing to do first.

"No," he said, giving up trying to hide his disappointment as a lost cause, "first, we need to go see Matt—that is, the king. We need to tell him all that we've found out. Besides, likely as not, we'll find Maeve right there with him."

He caught sight of a serving woman busily wiping the dust from a statue, one of a man that, with his jawline and terrifying visage, could only be one of Cutter's ancestors. "Excuse me, ma'am," Chall said.

The woman turned, and Chall found his gaze going to her fingers, found himself breathing a low sigh of relief when he saw that she wore no ring bearing a wolf crest.

The woman bowed deeply. "Yes, milord, how may I help you?"

"I was wondering," Chall said, "if you could tell me where the king is? His quarters, perhaps?"

"Forgive me, Sir Challadius, but no, the king and Commander Malex, they both went to the dungeons."

Much more of this, and Matt may as well get them to move a bed in there for him, he thought. Still, he was surprised, for he had thought Matt had agreed to get some rest when last they'd spoken. "The dungeons," he repeated, "you're sure?"

"Yes, milord, quite sure," she said, then gave her head a shake, her face paling. "Terrible thing, that."

Chall frowned. "What thing?" he said, noting well that the woman had not mentioned Maeve, feeling his heart hammering in his chest as if it were some creature meaning to rip its way clear. "What's happened?"

"P-please, milord," the woman said, recoiling at the vehemence in his tone, "I-I'm sure it isn't my place to say."

"And Lady Maeve?" Chall demanded. "What of her?"

The woman looked confused at that. "What of her, milord?"

Chall wanted to scream, but he fought the urge back...barely. "What I mean," he said, "is have you any knowledge of her whereabouts? Is she with the king? Or...or perhaps is she in ou— that is, in her quarters?"

"Forgive me, milord," she said, "but I had not heard that Lady Maeve had returned to the castle. If you would like, I'd be happy to find her for you and—"

"No, no," Chall said, "that won't be necessary. Thank you. For your help."

"Of course, Sir Challadius," the woman said, but Chall was already turning, hurrying through the castle hallways, Priest beside him.

It didn't take them long to reach the dungeons—a few minutes, no more—yet Chall was sweating by the time they got there, his heart beating an uneven staccato rhythm in his chest. He stepped inside and was surprised to find that where there were normally two guards standing watch at the entrance leading down to the prisoners' cells, there were currently four. One of whom, he recognized. "Guardsman...Benedict, isn't it?"

The man bowed to him and Priest. "That's right, Sir Challadius," the man said, but Chall was barely listening to his words. Instead, he was taking in the man's expression, the way he looked pale, uncertain, perhaps even scared. And however bad he looked, the youngest of the four guardsmen was sheet-white, terrified and, more than that, as if he might throw up at any moment—which judging by his smell, would be a repeat performance instead of an original. "You've been summoned by the king, then?"

"That's right," Chall said, not bothering to correct the man. "Is he through here?" he asked, pointing at the stairs leading down into the dungeon proper.

"Yes, sir," he said, "just a moment, and we'll unlock the door for you."

Chall frowned. "You locked the king in?"

"By his own order, sir," the guardsman said, nodding, his expression grim. "He thought it wise not to...well, not to take any chances, I suppose."

"Right," Chall said. "Well...suppose we'd best be going then."

The guard nodded. "Of course, sir," he said, and Chall waited impatiently, doing his best to keep from tapping his foot while he waited for the man to unlock the door. After only a few lifetimes, the guardsman finished unlocking the door, stepping out of the way.

Chall hurried past, Priest beside him.

"Oh, forgive me sirs, but one more thing."

Chall wanted to scream, but instead he turned to regard the man, smiling as pleasantly as he could. "Yes, Guardsman Benedict?"

"Might be you'll want this," the man said, withdrawing a leather thong from around his neck. From the end of the band hung what looked like a small bag. Chall took it, bemused, to realize that there was a powerful, flowery fragrance emanating from it.

"Go on then," Benedict growled to one of the other guardsmen who seemed to reluctantly withdraw a similar necklace, proffering it to Priest.

"Healer Malden came by a little while ago, brought some along."

Malden. Chall recognized that name as belonging to the crotchety old healer who had worked on Guardsman Nigel when he'd been poisoned, as well as on Prince Bernard himself after the assassins had attacked him in one of the castle's storerooms. "Brought them along for what, though?" he asked.

"Why...the smell, of course, sir," the guardsman said.

"The smell," Chall repeated.

The young guardsman nodded vigorously, taking a deep whiff of his own bag. "I know it seems...s-strange, sir, but they really do h-h-he—" He cut off, making a gagging noise as he clamped a hand over his mouth and rushed out the door.

"Right," Chall said, turning back to Guardsman Benedict. "Well...thanks. You know. For the bags."

"Don't mention it, sir," the man said.

Chall glanced at Priest, saw his own confusion and worry mirrored on the other man's face, then swung the dungeon door open and stepped inside. The smell struck him first, and he staggered, immediately having to force back his gag reflex. It was the smell of blood, thick, pervasive, but not just that—the smell of excrement and urine, too, and one other thing...fear. Chall found himself grasping for the perfumed bag, clawing at it with desperation before bringing it to his nose and taking a long, grateful smell, telling himself he would have to remember Guardsman Benedict on the next holiday that came around. If the man wasn't a saint, then he was the closest to it Chall had met in a while—which, he supposed, wasn't all that impressive when you stopped to consider that most of the people he had met lately had tried to kill him.

The dungeon corridors were lit by torches hung at intervals along the earthen walls, their flames flickering at a slight breeze, the origin of which he could not imagine. The sporadic orange light they provided illuminated the cells lining the hallway, as well as their occupants—at least, what could be seen of them. Most of the prisoners were curled into balls at the backs of their cells, their faces buried in the corner.

Chall frowned at that. He'd been in the dungeons before. In fact, it wasn't very long ago that he had been a prisoner instead of a visitor, along with Cutter and Feledias. And while he'd been distracted at the time—mostly contemplating his imminent doom—he had noticed something about the dungeons. Well, the truth was, he'd noticed a few things. The stench was one, though to be fair he realized now as he clutched desperately at the perfumed bag, that what he had taken for a stench was only a mildly off-putting smell and was nothing compared to what he now faced. The main thing he'd noticed, though, was that it was never quiet. The prisoners put up a terrible, incessant racket. Some screamed and shouted with anger, some with disbelief and denial about their current state, and some with desperation. It had been loud, surprisingly so. Now, though, the dungeons were nearly completely silent, save for the snap and pop of the fire in the torches and what sounded like muted conversation from somewhere up ahead.

Chall frowned, peering into the cells as they walked, wondering at the source of the silence, of the terror which clearly gripped the prisoners. He had hated those screams and shouts when he'd spent time in the dungeons, had thought them like the screams of the damned in some tortured afterlife. But as bad as they had been, he found that the unnatural silence was even worse. He passed one cell in which the prisoner, apparently braver or more terrified than his fellows, risked a glance over his shoulder from where he was huddled against his cell wall.

A furtive, quick glance, like a woodchuck or a gopher, poking its head out of its burrow to check to see if was safe. The man turned away in another instant, drawing in on himself, scrunching into a tight ball, but Chall had managed to catch a glimpse of his parchment-white face, covered in grime save for lines where it looked like tears had traced their way down his cheeks.

Chall didn't love the idea of confronting whatever it was that was bad enough to make a hardened criminal cry—and not only cry, for he could see a foul puddle spreading beneath the man, one that at least gave some answer to where the smell of urine was coming from. Chall took another deep breath of the perfumed bag, glancing at Priest before moving farther into the dungeon.

The sound of conversation grew louder as they walked, and soon they took a turn in the dungeon corridor and were brought face to face with two guardsmen, both of whom wielded bared blades. Chall let out a squeak of surprise and fear, stumbling away and only just managing to avoid impaling himself on one of the swords.

His foot struck a bar of one of the cells, and he would have fallen had Priest not caught him.

"What the *shit*," Chall hissed.

"*State your business*," one of the guards demanded in a stern voice, the point of his blade not wavering.

"Shitting myself just now," Chall muttered as he used the wall to regain his balance.

"Your business," the guard repeated. "Now."

Chall glanced at Priest then back to the guardsman, surprised by the man's hostile demeanor. "We've come to see the king—preferably unimpaled, if it's all the same to you."

"I have been made aware of no such visit," the guard said, the sword unmoving. "Now, what's your na—"

"*Chall?*" a voice called. "*Priest? Is that you?*"

Chall looked past the guardsman—and the sword hovering far too close for his liking—to see Matt approaching. He was walking beside Commander Malex. The king's face was pale, and he looked as if he might be sick at any moment. Even Commander Malex, Chall noted, looked disturbed, which was unnerving considering all the terrible things the man had seen over the years.

"It's us, Majesty," Chall called back.

"Well, let them through, guardsman," Matt said.

"As you say, Majesty," the guardsman in question replied, making a face that seemed to indicate to Chall that the man would have more happily complied with a request to cut them down where they stood. Still, he did move, stepping aside along with his companion.

Chall walked past, watching the guardsmen warily until he stood in front of Matt and Commander Malex. Then he looked past them, farther down the hallway, hoping that he would see Maeve walking up.

He did see two figures approaching, but as they drew closer into the light of the torches he saw that neither of them was Maeve. Instead, they were two more guardsmen. These did not have their swords drawn, but they looked ready to do it, their hands grasping the handles of their blades.

"Majesty," Chall said, "forgive me, but what news of Lady Maeve?"

Matt looked confused at that. "Maeve?" he asked, glancing between the two of them. "I...haven't seen her. I just assumed that she met up with the two of you."

Chall's mouth suddenly went terribly dry at that, and a cold chill ran across his back.

"Chall?" Matt asked. "Are you okay?"

"F-fine," he managed in a voice barely loud enough to hear himself.

Priest's hand was on his shoulder again. "It's okay, Chall," the man said quietly. "It doesn't mean anything. I'm sure Maeve is fine."

Chall was close now. He could feel it, a sort of *slipping.* Similar to what a man might feel if he were standing above some great precipice and his feet began to slide across treacherous ice. He was close to the edge, so very close. And should he fall, he thought that he might never stop. But if she was gone, he did not care. There was nothing left for him without her. He had thought that he had lived his life these many years, but he had been wrong. He had not lived, not truly, had only existed. But now, having felt what it was to be alive in truth, he could not go back to that pseudo-existence any longer, no more than a baby bird, once it has discovered how to fly, could go back to living a mundane existence within its nest once more.

Chall pulled his thoughts away from that, pulled his *mind* away from the edge with desperation. She was okay. She had to be. And so he was okay. *He* had to be, for he would not do anyone any good by losing himself now. "So what's happened here then?" he said, his voice a rasping, emotional croak.

Matt frowned. "Chall, listen, we can go look for her, all of us right now, and—"

"*No,*" Chall blurted, then shook his head, taking a deep, shuddering breath. "No, Majesty, that's quite alright. I'm..." He paused, clearing his throat. "I'm sure that Maeve is fine. Now, what's happened here? Is everything alright?"

Matt glanced uncertainly at Priest, and Chall was aware of the man giving him a small, almost imperceptible nod. Matt cleared his throat, nodding. "Right. Well...no, Chall, to answer your question, I'm afraid things are very, very far from okay."

"So...what is it then?" Chall asked. "What's happened?"

The king paled, swallowing hard and looking sickly. "Perhaps...that is...perhaps it would be better if we showed you." He nodded to Malex.

The commander inclined his head in a bow. "Majesty." He turned to them then. "This way, gentlemen, though I will warn you, what you are about to see...it is quite...disturbing."

"Oh, I wouldn't worry overly much, Commander," Chall said. "In truth, the last several days have been little else."

Malex nodded. "Very well—this way."

And with a particularly grim expression, the man turned and started back down the hallway, Matt following with obvious hesitation. Chall glanced at Priest again. He did not want to follow them. Yet, he knew that while there were times in a man's life when he might be able to afford being a coward with little punishment for it, this was not one of those times. And so he walked after the two men. If reluctantly.

They continued down the corridor for only a minute or two before Malex stopped, turning back to Chall and Priest, his expression even grimmer than it had been. "It is here," Malex said, gesturing to a cell that Chall couldn't see from where he stood.

"Wait a minute," Chall said, thinking. He and the others had spent some time in the dungeons recently with Matt while the king had desperately sought to gain information from the prisoners that Guardsman Nigel had helped them discover. These were traitors who'd been working in the castle, who they'd hoped had information that might allow Matt to end the conspiracy and save his father and uncle from their doomed venture into the Black Wood. In that time, Chall, along with Matt and the others, had come to the dungeons several times, enough that he knew well where each prisoner was kept. "This...this is Rolph's cell, isn't it? That bastard from Two Rivers who was your bodyguard?"

"It was," Matt agreed, and there was something about the way he said "was" that made Chall think it wasn't that the man had been taken to another cell while his previous one was cleaned. "Go ahead, if you like," he said to Chall and Priest, gesturing. "I...I think I've already seen enough."

Chall nodded grimly, taking a slow deep breath in an effort to prepare himself. An effort which, when he stepped forward, gazing into the cell, proved useless. At first, he wasn't even sure what he was looking at, had no more than a vague image of crimson, as if red paint had been splashed everywhere and among the puddles he could see pieces of something strewn about the cells, pieces that might have been a butcher's leavings after harvesting a cow or a hog.

For a brief, blessed moment, Chall's mind could not make sense of what he was seeing. Instead, he only had a powerful sense of wrongness. Then, slowly, his thoughts, which had scattered before the sight confronting him like a pile of dry leaves before a massive wind, began to reassert themselves.

Saliva filled his mouth and bile suddenly rose in his throat and Chall began—despite his efforts—to understand. The paint was not paint at all but blood, and the torn pieces of flesh he saw scattered throughout the cell did not belong to cows, but instead to a human. He opened his mouth to speak, but all that came out was a dry croak. He had seen much in his time, far more than most people and certainly more than he'd ever wanted, but standing there, gazing at the devastation that had been wrought in the cell, Chall decided that nothing could prepare a man for this.

He understood, in that moment, why the guardsmen in the hallway had acted so hostile, why, too, Guardsman Benedict and the other three had seemed so reserved and troubled. The sight here was enough to shake a man, sure, enough to turn him upside down and rattle the shit out of him until all his contents—or at least his sanity—came falling out.

The mess was not confined to the cell floor either—though it did a fine job of filling up that space. It was also splashed along the bars of the cell, along the back wall, and indeed, some had spilled out into the hallway. Chall had seen many dead men—sometimes he thought he'd seen more dead ones than ones still breathing—but he found himself shocked at the thought that one man could hold so much blood inside of him. So much that it was a wonder there was room for anything else. He stood there, stunned—might well have stood there for an hour or a day, or the rest of his life, had Priest not spoken.

"It...is it Rolph?" the man asked. His voice sounded hollow, as if it came from some great distance, across the vast, tumultuous waters of Chall's consciousness.

"We...think so." Malex's voice.

"What do you mean, 'think'?" Priest asked.

"It's not so easy, I'm afraid, to identify the body. We...we're still working on it to be sure."

That Chall could understand. It didn't seem right that the mess in front of him could have ever been Rolph, didn't seem right that it could have ever been a person at all. He thought that unless those poor bastards given the task of identifying Rolph were the world's best puzzle solvers—and even if they were—they had their work cut out for them.

"Have you not found his...his face?" Chall asked, bringing the perfumed bag to his face, pushing it against his nose. It helped his nose at least, but as the guard at the dungeon entrance had warned him, it did nothing for his eyes. Neither did it begin to approach the torture his soul was currently undergoing.

"Parts of it," Malex said, clearing his throat, "but unfortunately, it hasn't yet been enough to identify him."

Parts of it. That was it. That was what did it. He stumbled farther into the dungeon, preparing to retch just about anywhere, so long as he did He caught sight of a bucket that seemed to have already been used for the task and stumbled toward it, barely reaching it before the entire inside of his stomach seemed to decide, all at once, that it wanted to be on the outside and gave a damned good attempt at it.

"Chall, are you—" Priest began, cutting off as Chall raised one hand away from where he'd been grasping the top of the bucket, not bothering to turn. When the worst had passed, and his stomach only felt like someone had grabbed hold and was clenching their fist, Chall ran an arm across his mouth. "Better off than...him, anyway," he managed, waving his hand in what he thought was the vague direction of the cell.

"But...how is this possible?" Priest asked, "I thought you increased the guard on the dungeons after arresting your advisors?"

"I did," Matt answered.

"So..." Priest said.

Chall slowly rose, aware of his stomach roiling threateningly. He started to walk back toward them then paused, thinking that maybe his stomach was going to rebel again. When it settled—at least as much as he thought it meant to—he moved forward again. "So what happened?" he asked, finishing Priest's unasked question. "How could anyone manage to get in here? And not *just* get in here but—" he glanced at the cell and immediately regretted it, turning away even as he waved a hand at it, "also manage to do...*that*. It would have taken time. Effort. And I got to think that poor bastard Rolph—assuming that's who it is in there—would have voiced a complaint or two." *Fire and salt, for all we know it might well be more than one person,* Chall thought, *certainly there's enough blood for two.*

"We...we're still looking into it," Malex said, glancing at Matt. "It appears that two guardsmen by the names of Falder and Callum might be responsible."

"Oh?" Priest asked.

Malex nodded. "According to Guardsmen Benedict and Alder—those stationed outside—they asked to switch shifts with them."

"And what have this Falder and Callum said in their defense?"

"Nothing," Matt said. "Because we can't find them."

Chall blinked. "They're gone?"

"That's right," Matt said. "No one we've spoken with has seen them since yesterday."

Chall grunted. "Seems pretty guilty, disappearing into thin air after there's been a murder on your watch."

"We thought as much as well," Malex said, nodding.

"First Belle, now Rolph…" Chall said. "Do me a favor, Majesty, if you ever decide to put me in the dungeon again, maybe just go ahead and have me executed, huh? Save me the walk anyway."

It wasn't a great joke—that much was evidenced by the fact that no one so much as giggled—but then with what waited inside the cell Chall thought that even the best joke would have fallen on deaf ears just then.

"Do we know why anyone would want him dead?" Priest asked.

Matt frowned. "That much, we do know. Falstid Aberath, the Chief Interrogator, came to visit me last night."

"What did he say?"

"Nothing," Matt said, shaking his head in frustration. "I was asleep. He came back this morning, and told me that Rolph had said he wanted to talk, that he had information for me regarding the conspiracy in the castle. But when we got here…"

"He was already dead," Chall finished.

Matt nodded. "Yes," he said, running a hand through his hair, clearly frustrated.

"So…if the head questioner came with you, where is he now?" Chall asked.

Malex answered. "Questioner Falstid is currently interrogating the other prisoners and the guards, trying to discover if any of them saw anything but so far no one has seen anything or…"

"Or if they have, they're not talking," Matt finished.

"Can you blame them, Majesty?" Chall asked, glancing back at the room and wincing as his stomach immediately rebelled. "This poor bastard here wasn't just killed, was he? Someone wanted to make an example of it, likely to teach anyone else a lesson about what would happen to them if they meant to spill what they knew. And it's a lesson, at least judging by the look of the prisoners when we came through, that I'm thinking they learned well enough."

"How long until we know for sure if it was him?" Chall said, keeping his gaze firmly averted from the mess in the cell.

"I don't know that we ever will," Matt said.

"Who's working on it?" Priest asked.

"Healer Malden," Malex said, "and one of his assistants. They were here earlier, but they have since gone to take a break."

"At my insistence," Matt pointed out. "We thought that they would have the best chance of being able to piece something together, you know, them being healers. They would have stayed, but..." He shook his head. "Even they need breaks with something like this."

"Only two?" Chall asked. "Wouldn't it be faster if, I don't know, you had others, working in shifts maybe, or..." He trailed off, thinking that he was sounding far too much like a man trying to volunteer, which was just about as far away from what he wanted to do as possible.

Malex and Matt shared a look. "We thought...with all that's been going on in the castle and the city, lately, that it might be better if we kept this under wraps...at least as much as we can."

Malex nodded. "Since the slaying of the serving woman in His Majesty's quarters, we have had several of the castle staff quit, but even this is not the real problem—maids can be replaced, new guards trained. The real problem is with the city itself."

"The people of New Daltenia have already suffered enough, been through enough," Matt said. "What they need is hope, the ability to believe that things are going to get better. I would spare them this, if I could."

Chall nodded slowly, thinking that while Matt was, in many ways, his father's son, he was also his own man. It was not that Cutter was not kind or considerate, for he often was in surprising and disarming ways. The difference, though, was that the prince's mind worked in a very simple, straightforward way. It was what made him so effective on the battlefield, Chall thought, what made him the world's greatest warrior. It was also, though, what would have made him a poor king. "That is...wise of you, Majesty," Chall said.

Matt gave him a weak smile. "Thank you."

"But what of the guardsmen?" Priest asked.

"We have spoken to them," Malex said. "They have been told not to talk of what they've seen."

"I don't much care for the odds of them listening, though," Chall said.

"No," Matt said grimly, "neither do I. But what else can we do? Anyway enough of this—what can be done is being done. Tell me, where have the two of you been?"

Chall and Priest shared a look. "Majesty?" Chall asked.

Matt gave him a small, humorless smile. "I sent for you both when I got Falstid's message this morning. I thought to bring you along. I was surprised to find that neither of you were in your rooms and that, according to the guard I sent to retrieve you, neither of your beds had been slept in. When I came here and saw Rolph...I was worried."

Chall stared at the young man, looking close to tears, and found that he was touched. Maybe Chall wasn't a good man—he didn't think there'd be many people prepared to argue with him about that—but he found that he was proud to at least *know* a good man. Oh, he'd known *great* men all his life, such as Cutter and his brother Feledias, or the famous professors at the Academy of Magic back in Daltenia before the Skaalden had come. But he had known very few good ones. There was Priest, of course, but there was no denying that the man had his own problems just now.

"I tasked several men with searching for you," Matt went on, "for I thought that surely you would not have gone anywhere, not without at least mentioning it to me."

Chall winced, glancing at Priest and seeing an expression of guilt on the other man's face to match that he felt himself. "Yeah," he said, "well, sorry about—"

"It was my fault, Majesty," Priest said. "I meant to leave without telling anyone. Challadius only came along as a friend."

"Came along where?" Matt asked.

Priest and Chall shared a look at that. "About that, Majesty..." Priest said. "We need to talk."

Matt looked between the two of them then nodded slowly. "I see. Well, once we're done here—"

"Forgive me, Majesty," Malex said, "but I can keep watch on things here."

Matt frowned, and if the man felt relieved by the idea of escaping such a grotesque task he hid it well, actually appearing, if not disappointed, guilty. "Are you sure?"

"Yes, Majesty," the commander said. "I'll let you know as soon as we learn something."

Matt nodded. "Very well, thank you, Malex." "Of course, Majesty," the other man said, clearly surprised to be thanked for doing his job.

"Now then," Matt said, turning back to Chall and Priest. "What is it you wished to talk about?"

"I think...maybe it would be better if we didn't talk about it here, Majesty," Chall said, glancing around the dungeon at the prisoners in the nearby cells. They were all turned away, surely thinking—rightly so far as Chall was concerned—that in the case of witnessing a murder as horrendous as this one...well, it was preferable to be blind than dead. But while they might have been willfully blind, Chall was also confident that their ears worked well enough, and with everything that was happening in the castle and the city, the last thing they needed was to destroy what little faith the citizens of New Daltenia still had left in their leaders by letting information about the Crimson Wolves leak into the populace.

"Right, of course," Matt said, glancing back at the cell and turning noticeably paler. "I...I think I could use some fresh air anyway."

Chall wasn't about to disagree with that, so the three of them turned and headed for the exit to the dungeons. Soon—but nowhere near soon enough as far as Chall was concerned—they left the dungeon corridors, which smelled of blood and worse, behind them and stepped out into the castle courtyard. They might have gone back to the castle, had their discussion in the prince's quarters, but it didn't take long for Chall to realize he wasn't the only one among them who didn't much fancy being inside just then. Besides, it wasn't as if the king's quarters were secure—the woman with the Crimson Wolf ring had proven that much.

They walked around the courtyard and into the carefully maintained gardens, moving to stand in front of a burbling fountain which, Chall hoped, would serve to make their words more difficult to hear by anyone that might be listening in.

"Now then," Matt said, looking between the two men, "are you going to finally tell me what all this is about?"

Chall and Priest glanced at each other, and Chall nodded to him. "Go ahead—priests first."

Priest gave him a sour smile, obviously knowing well enough that the privilege was a dubious one at best. Still, he went on to describe to Matt everything that had happened since they'd left the castle, recounting their meeting with Nadia, a murderous crime boss, and then Catham—her murderous second. After that, Priest told the king about their meeting with quite a few murderous murderers in the tavern...or would-be murderers, he supposed, though he suspected most of them had some practice at it already.

Matt listened intently, asking questions here and there, never frivolous, always clarifying a particular point or driving to the heart of the matter with surprising speed. Listening to him, Chall found himself once again reminded of the young king's father, Prince Bernard. The prince liked to think the only thing he was good at was swinging that axe of his—and while the man certainly *was* good at that, anybody who might have argued it had likely died to that same axe—the man also had a way of cutting to the heart of things in speech as well as war. A way of paring away the fat that Matt, based on his questions, seemed to share.

Finally, the story was done, and Matt said nothing for several seconds, taking his time, thinking it through. Eventually, he sighed, shaking his head and clearly frustrated. "Fool," he muttered.

"What's that, Majesty?" Chall asked.

"I said I'm a fool," Matt said, giving a humorless laugh. "After we got rid of Emma, I thought things would get better. And when they didn't, I told myself that once we got rid of the advisors, once we questioned them and spoke to Nigel about what he knew about the castle guardsmen, things would get better, but they aren't. If anything, they're getting worse."

"I think you're wrong, Majesty," Chall said. "That is, things *are* getting better. You've made a difference."

Matt sighed. "What difference, Chall?" he asked, meeting his gaze, and Chall was surprised to see that the king's eyes were brimming with unshed tears. "Rolph might have been a prisoner, but he was killed under *my* protection. But then, at least he committed a crime. Unlike the serving girl whose only crime was cleaning my quarters. And *that's* before you even think about the assassin that came for you and Maeve or these Crimson Wolves." The tears began to overflow then, and he shook his head angrily, wiping an arm across his face. "I told myself that we could get it all sorted out, that *I* could make a difference and that, when things were better, I could save my father and uncle. But things aren't getting better, they're getting worse, and my father...my father is as good as dead."

Chall and Priest shared a troubled look, and Chall waited for the other man to take over, to do as he had done so often in the past and seem to find the perfect words to say, words that would give Matt comfort, give him hope. Priest opened his mouth, as if he meant to do exactly that, but in the end, he only closed it again, as if those words, words which had once come so easily, were nowhere to be found now.

Chall felt a powerful anger at the man, in that moment. Anger that he would not fix it, that he would not offer the boy comfort. It wasn't fair, of course, for Priest clearly had his own troubles on his mind. Anyway, he wasn't just angry at Priest. He was also angry at Maeve. If Maeve had been here, she too would have known something she might say, something that would give Matt some comfort. She *wasn't* here, though, because she had gone to the Assassin's Guild, *despite* Chall begging her not to. The truth, though, was that he was not mad at her for not being there to say something to comfort Matt—he was simply mad at her for not being there. And the real, *truthful* truth was that he wasn't mad at all—he was only scared. Scared much like Matt was.

"Forgive me, Majesty," Chall said, "I'm, not usually good at these sorts of things, but I just found myself thinking of something your father once told me, something that always gives me comfort."

Matt looked up, his teary eyes dancing with what might have been hope—or simply tears, Chall never had been good at judging a person's thoughts from their expressions.

"What's that?" Matt asked.

"It was after a particularly brutal battle," Chall said, thinking back, "during the war. Your father was a very different man then than who he is now but, even then, he was possessed of wisdom. Even if it was a particularly...*hard* kind. You see, we'd come upon a village that the Fey had attacked. Too late to save it, for all the people were dead, but the Fey were still there, and so it was not too late to avenge them. And avenge them we did," he said, aware that his voice was a low rasp as his memory brought him back to that moment.

"We were outnumbered," he went on, "but that didn't stop us, not when we saw what those things had done to the villagers, saw how some of them had been..." He paused as his already mistreated stomach lurched. "Chewed on," he managed. "Outnumbered or not, we avenged the villagers, killing every single one of the creatures, and losing quite a few of our own in the process. Anyway, this was…after."

"It was dark when the thing was done, you see, and everyone was exhausted, both in body and mind and soul. We left the ruins of the village, far enough that we could not see the devastation, far enough that the smell of death was not quite so…thick. We would have gone farther but we were all simply too tired. At least, those of us who survived…there were plenty that did not. Anyway, I do not need to tell you that it was a solemn group of us—about fifty in all—that set up camp. In time we had fires going—far more than were necessary in truth, for it was in the middle of the summer, and it was hot."

"Then…why the fires?" Matt asked.

Chall glanced at Priest, and saw an expression on the other man's face that said he knew well enough, and why not? He'd been there, of course. But then even if he hadn't been, he would have understood the way any man accustomed to bloodshed would have. Chall hesitated, trying to think of how to explain it, to share with Matt that knowledge one normally only earned after he had killed and watched his friends die in countless battles. "It…you see, lad, the world, well, it can be a pretty cold place. Dark, too. The sort of cold, the sort of dark that seeps into a man's heart, into his soul, so that even in the middle of summer he might find himself shivering from it. So that even in the middle of the day, with the sun shining on his face, he might see only shadow. The fires, then, work to ward off that cold, those shadows."

Matt nodded slowly, as if he understood, but Chall knew it was just to humor him. The boy did not understand—how could he? Chall's greatest hope for him was that he never did, for it was an understanding that came at a steep price, and it was one without benefit. It did a man, forced to stumble through the darkness, no good to learn the shape and sizes of those things which prowled it around him, tracking his progress.

"Anyway," Chall went on, "I was sitting by the fire but not really feeling it, trying to rid myself of the ghosts of the memories of what I'd seen—they were always stubborn, those ghosts. It was about that time your father walked up." He met Matt's eyes. "He hadn't yet wiped the blood from his clothes, and I'll tell you this much—if there's a sight to strike fear into a man's heart it's the Crimson Prince himself, covered in the blood that was his namesake, appearing out of the darkness like some apparition or, perhaps, some creature sent from the land of the damned to fetch his prize. His axe was still in his hand—in those days, he was rarely without it, and it, like its owner, was covered in blood and worse. He was like...death, just looking for someone to happen to." He glanced at Priest. "You remember how he was in those days, how...imposing."

Priest inclined his head. "I remember."

"At first, he said nothing," Chall said. "He only stood by the fire, not even seeming to notice it, certainly not gazing into it as if somewhere within those flames lay salvation, the way that many of the men—myself included—did. He stood that way for a few minutes, which made me nervous. After all, your father was a dangerous man, deadly, and sometimes, when the battle lust was on them, men acted strangely, sometimes mistaking their friends for their foes. But your father did not attack me...instead, he did something *really* strange."

"Stranger than attacking you?" Matt asked, frowning.

"Yes, Your Majesty," Chall said, "yes, I'd say so. You see, your father turned away from where he'd been gazing out at the other men and women soldiers all sitting at their own campfires and looked at me. And he told me to laugh. Growled it at me, not a request at all but a command."

"I...don't understand," Matt said.

"Neither did I," Chall admitted. "And while normally, I'd agree with anything your father said—particularly when he was toting that axe of his—just then, I was just about as far from laughter as any man can be and still be breathing."

"So what did you do?" Matt asked.

"I apologized," Chall said, remembering. "And I did it quickly. Forgive me, Prince, I said, but I just don't feel much like laughing at the moment."

"'What you feel's got nothin' to do with it,' he told me. He said that a man's job was to do what was necessary and never mind what he felt like doing. And he said that, just then, what was needed was for me to laugh.'"

Matt blinked, on his face the confusion Chall had felt at that moment. "So...did you?"

"I tried," Chall said. "But as I told you, I didn't have any laughter in me just then. What came out was more like a rasping wheeze than a laugh—blame it on spending several hours before that fighting and screaming in terror."

"So what did he do?" Priest asked, his voice eager, and they both turned to stare at him. The man fidgeted, looking embarrassed. "Forgive me, but I do not remember this."

"Nor would you," Chall said. "As I recall, you were off avoiding work as usual."

Priest raised an eyebrow. "Scouting."

"His word for it," Chall said in a confidential tone to Matt who grinned. He sighed. "Anyway, what the prince—your father—did, was he put that axe of his down and then he did the last thing I ever would have expected." They were both leaning in now, like children eager to hear the end of a mummer's tale. "He told me a joke."

Priest frowned. "A joke?"

"A joke," Matt said.

"That's right," Chall said. "And truth to tell, not a very good one. Or, maybe it was, but he just mangled it...like most things. You see, the prince had—*has*—many talents, but the jesters of the world need not fear him stealing their jobs, that much I can tell you with confidence."

"What...what did you say?" Matt asked.

"I didn't say anything, so much," Chall said. "Instead, I only stared at him, wonderin' if he'd finally snapped, if the pressure of being him, of doing the things we did had finally gotten to him. And then...he did something that was equally as strange as the joke itself—he waggled his eyebrows at me. Waggled them like an old lech walking into a brothel with a stolen coin burning a hole in his pocket, and gave me a wide, toothy grin. It was the waggle and the grin that did it—next thing I knew, a laugh burst out of me, one I hadn't even known had been there. Then another, and another, and soon I was laughing so hard I was crying."

He shook his head in memory. "I was still laughing when your father spoke again. 'Men died today, Chall,' he said. 'Perhaps we will die tomorrow or the day after. In the end, scared or smiling, death takes us all. That being the case, a man ought to smile as long as he's got the strength to do it. He ought to smile if he can, and if he can't, then at least he ought to keep going. As long as he's got the strength to do it."

"And even as he spoke, I began to notice something. That laugh—the one that had erupted from me in surprise at the waggling eyebrows and toothy grin—had been like a spell. Or, more accurately, I suppose, like the magical words that might break one. For the gloomy, grief-stricken company of soldiers had changed. Oh, they were still sad, sure, still grieving, but they were no longer sitting in silence and staring at the flames. Instead, they were talking, laughing quietly. And one even shouted at me from a nearby fire. *'Go on then, Charmer, tell us the joke.'*"

Chall shrugged. "As I said, it wasn't a good joke, but I rose to do just that, remembering the prince's words, that a man did what was necessary. I started forward then turned back to ask the prince if he was coming—only to see that he was gone. Vanished into the darkness of the night."

"But where did he go?" Matt asked.

Chall sighed slowly. "I don't know, lad," he said. "But I think that, on that night, in many ways, your father grieved for all of us, grieved so that we wouldn't have to. A cold man, sure, a hard one, but a wise one too." They were silent for a time, the two men considering his words, Chall reliving the memory. Odd, maybe, but it was one of his best memories and never mind how it began. Prince Bernard had seen to that.

Suddenly, he was possessed with a desperate, almost overpowering urge to rescue Bernard. To go charging off into the Black Wood—alone, if necessary—to see it done. The man might not know it, might think himself a monster and that only, but Chall thought that the truth was the world would be a far darker place without him in it. At least, *his* world would be. Still, he knew that to charge after the man was a fool's errand, one that could only end in his death. After all, if there was a single person in the world who might survive an excursion into the Black Wood, Chall was most certainly not him—and the prince most certainly was. "My point, Majesty," he said, pushing the urge away, "is that what your father said was true. What we ought to do is to smile and keep going, but if we can't smile then we need to keep going anyway. There's nothing else to be done."

Matt nodded slowly, and Chall didn't think he imagined the way the king seemed more at ease than he had before. "Very well, Chall," he said, "I will keep going. But then what is the next step? Should we look into these Crimson Wolves, or…?"

"No, I think Ned will do that well enough," Chall said, glancing at Priest. "I think what we ought to do is figure out who might have snuck into the dungeons and killed Rolph. But more importantly, *why* they did it in the first place."

Matt nodded grimly, his head down, and Chall put his hand on the young man's shoulder, waited until his gaze slowly rose. "And then, Matt, then we'll go to the Black Wood, together, and we *will* find your dad."

A childlike hope flashed in the king's eyes then. "You mean it?"

"You're damn right I mean it," Chall said. "I'll burn that whole damned cursed forest down if I have to, and I'll do it all smiling."

"Thanks, Chall," Matt said. "And you're right."

"Of course I am," he said, still smiling.

"So…would the two of you accompany me back to the dungeons?" Matt asked.

"Of course, Majesty," Priest said, inclining his head in a bow even as he stared at Chall with a surprised, impressed expression.

"Happy to, Majesty," Chall said, "only, I need to visit the privy first. Then I'll be right along."

"Everything alright, Chall?" Priest said, watching him closely.

"Sure it is," Chall said, grinning wider still. "Why wouldn't it be? Now go on—unless that is you mean to stick around, hold my hand."

"I'm afraid I'll have to pass," Priest said dryly, then he and the king turned and started back toward the dungeons.

Chall watched them go, keeping his smile in place as well as he could for as long as he could. It trembled on his face, that smile, then, like an ancient dam finally succumbing to the strain of the water pushing against it, it broke altogether. Only, this dam was not holding back water but instead fear and grief. He knew that should either of the two men hazard a glance behind them, all his words of comfort would mean naught, for they would see his true feelings, his true worries on his face. But neither turned and in another few minutes they were disappearing through the door leading into the dungeons.

Chall took a slow deep breath wondering if this was how Priest had felt when he'd lied to the people who trusted him and loved him most. And that lie had not just been about the smile on his face, of course. It had also been that he would be right behind them. For he would not. Maeve was not back yet, and he meant to go find her. Even if it killed him.

Which, considering that finding her meant traveling to the Assassin's Guild, it almost certainly would.

He took another long, slow breath in an effort to rid himself of the fear he felt at the thought—it didn't help. Then he turned, meaning to start toward the gate. His eyes caught on something—or, more accurately, some*one*—standing less than a dozen feet away. The breath froze in his lungs, and a tremor went through his body, as if he'd been struck by lightning as he stared at the figure.

She stood there, a small, almost shy smile on her face. He was reminded of the first time he'd seen her. Beautiful now as she was then, somehow confident and vulnerable all at once, imposing and delicate, a contradiction only she could manage and that without trying. "*Maeve?*" he breathed, realizing, in that moment, just how sure he had been that she was dead. "Is...is it really you?"

"If it isn't, someone's got a lot of explaining to do," she said, the smile widening for a moment before it fell apart, and she didn't look happy anymore, what she looked like was scared, or maybe ashamed. "Listen, Chall," she said, "you were right. I shouldn't have—"

He didn't give her time to finish. Instead, he charged forward—as much as a man whose protruding gut had long since blocked enough of his sight that he had to take it on faith that he still had knees could, that is. She let out a sound of surprise and then he was on her, wrapping his arms around her and pulling her into a tight embrace. "Fire and salt, Mae, I thought something had happened to you. I thought—" He shook his head, unable to say the words even now, as if her returning to him alive was some sort of miracle the acknowledgment of which might spoil it.

"I'm okay, Chall," she said, sounding taken aback and amused all at once. But when he did not laugh along, only held on tighter, she pressed her head into his shoulder. "I'm okay," she said again, softer this time.

He nodded, clearing his throat and finally stepping back. "It's good to see you, Mae."

"It's good to be seen," she said.

He breathed a heavy sigh of relief, aware for the first time just how much he had missed her. He'd known that he missed her, of course, but he hadn't realized how *much*, how truly great the burden of his worry had become until he was no longer being crushed beneath it. "Maeve," he said, as his mind began to catch up, "you just missed Priest and Matt. Stones and starlight, but they'll be happy to see you. Come on—they're just in the dungeons. There's a story there, and I'll admit it might put a damper on the mood, but then Rolph wasn't really a good guy anyway and—"

"Chall."

He'd started away, but there was something in her voice, a strange tone, that made him turn back to regard her, noting as he did that she had not moved. "Yeah?"

"I can't go there."

He winced. "Right, well, okay so it is bad. But Guardsman Benedict, he gave me this." He paused, brandishing the perfumed bag that still hung around his neck. "I know it looks a little ridiculous, like something some noble fop would have, but it helps. Doesn't block the smell completely, understand—I don't think anything could. But it helps. Anyway, if you don't want to look, you don't have to. We'll just catch up with Matt and Priest—Malex is there too. They can tell you all about i—"

"No, Chall," she said, interrupting him, her tone sounding apologetic and impatient all at once. "What I mean is I can't go into the dungeon at all, can't talk with Priest and Matt yet."

Chall frowned. "But...why?"

"Because they would try to talk me out of doing what I'm going to do. Anyway, they have enough to worry about already without me adding to it."

Chall snorted. "You have no idea."

She tilted her head. "What does that mean? Wait, you know what? You can tell me when we're on the move."

"The move to where, Mae?" he asked.

She suddenly looked uncomfortable, avoiding his gaze. "That, right, well...you see...Chall I need your help."

He couldn't help but swell up with a little bit of pride at that. Maybe men like the prince were used to women needing their help, but he wasn't. Besides, Maeve the Marvelous wasn't the sort that needed anybody's help very often. "What is it then?" he asked. "Something on a high shelf you need me to get you, is that it? Or is there some ruffian who's besmirched your honor, and now it's in need of defending? Because if that's the case, I'll defend the shit out of it."

Maeve stared at him, blinking. "First of, Chall, you're literally an inch taller than me, and unless there were cookies on the top shelf I'd give myself far better odds of retrieving whatever it was before you. Secondly, I misplaced my honor years ago and have never looked back. And assuming I *did* still have it, I can't imagine how you intend on defending it against this...ruffian. Unless you mean to challenge him to a drinking contest, that is."

"The only contest I know of where a man can lose and win anyway," Chall grumbled. "And so what, then? If it isn't your honor, what is it?"

Maeve fidgeted uncomfortably. "See, that is, well...it's just a little thing."

"Of course, anything for you, Maeve," Chall said. "So...what is it, then?"

Maeve cleared her throat and when she spoke she blurted out the words almost too quick to follow. Almost, but, unfortunately for Chall, not quite. "Last night, I rejoined the Assassin's Guild—which is now led by a woman who was once my biggest rival. I was forced to fight in a duel with one of the three members of the Tribunal—the Guild's ruling council—and am afraid that I made a few enemies in the process, quite possibly more than a few. Now, to get the contract off our heads, all I have to do is fake Agnes's—that's the Guild's Headmistress and my rival, well, ex-rival's—death. In return she has promised to get the contract on us removed."

Maeve finished and took a long, deep breath, necessary, no doubt, after the amount of words that had just spilled out of her mouth. Chall, meanwhile, found that he could barely draw a breath at all. "So no big deal then," he said, hearing a definite squeak in his voice but unable to stop it. "You just have to fake the death of the leader of a guild of assassins that, if they figure out what you're really up to, will no doubt be eager to kill you."

"Don't forget to mention that I'm still not sure the Headmistress herself doesn't want to kill me," Maeve said. "But you did get one thing wrong."

"Thank the gods, what's—"

"*I* don't have to fake her death..." Maeve gave him a small smile. "We do."

"We do," Chall repeated.

"Well," she said, "you did say anything."

"Sure," Chall stammered, "when I thought the whole traipsing into an assassin's guild where people were offered a fortune to kill us bit of the week was over."

"Why assume a fortune?" Maeve asked. "I hate to ruin it for you, Chall, but I don't think we're all that difficult of marks."

"Difficult?" Chall said. "Fire and salt of course not—I got my head stuck in my shirt a week or so ago and almost killed myself by running into the wardrobe in our room, that isn't—"

"You said one of the servants made that dent," Maeve said.

"Well, I lied. Turns out, it was all my forehead." He took a deep breath. "Still, Maeve, are you sure you've thought this through? I mean...this is sounding like a 'last' mission to me. Last on account of it'll be the last one we do and *that* on account of we'll be dea—"

"I get it," Maeve interrupted. "And if you don't want to help, Chall, I completely understand."

He sighed, shaking his head. "Of course I'm going to help, but when we're about to be killed, expect a few 'I told you so's. Anyway, you came to me, your man, because you wanted my help and trusted me to do a better job than the others. That means a lot, Maeve."

He noticed her giving an uncomfortable look, avoiding his eyes again, and he sighed. "That's not why you asked me for help."

"Not...exactly," she said. "You see, if we're going to make this work, make people think Agnes is dead, that is—"

"Fire and salt, with a name like that can you blame her for wanting to—"

"Then who better to help," Maeve interrupted, "than an illusionist."

He frowned. "An extremely capable, extremely handsome, extremely *deadly* illusionist."

"Of course."

He watched her for a moment, but her expression remained fixed, and he sighed. "An illusionist. Now, do you want to tell me the plan? Preferably one that doesn't make me an extremely *dead* illusionist."

"Yes, but I'll tell you on the way—we have to move fast. We've got a window to get this done, but it won't last long."

"Can't wait," Chall grumbled, but more for the sake of consistency than anything else. The truth was that he was so glad Maeve was alive that he would have followed her to far worse places than a guild of assassins...not that any such places came to mind, but there it was.

Maeve flashed him a smile then started away down the street, and he fell into step beside her.

They didn't talk as they walked toward the gate where the guards stationed there waited. "Leaving so soon, Lady Maeve?" one of the guards asked.

"I'm afraid so," she said, glancing at Chall. "We've got business in town."

The guard nodded at that, and in another moment the gate was swinging open. Soon they were walking down the street, and when he judged that they were a good enough distance from the guardsmen, Chall turned to look at Maeve. "Now then, are you going to tell me what this is all about?"

Then she did, and for the next several streets as she led them through the city, he listened as she relayed the events that had transpired once she left the castle. When she was finished, Chall decided that the old saying was true...ignorance really was bliss. The problem, of course, was that ignorance also made a poor shield against a crossbow bolt like the one the assassin had tried to use on him only two days ago.

"Fire and salt, Maeve," he said, finding that he was annoyed with her, "you're lucky you aren't dead. I told you; you shouldn't have gone."

"I know, Chall," she said, "and as I said, I really am sorry. Only...I could think of no better way to keep us safe, to keep *you* safe. I know assassins, Chall, I know the Guild, and they would not stop, not until the contract was finished or the contract was terminated."

Chall immediately found himself feeling guilty for his annoyance. After all, Maeve could take care of herself—far better than nearly any person he'd ever met, a list which certainly included him. "I just hate the thought of you going in there alone like that."

"I wasn't alone," Maeve said softly. "Emille was with me."

He frowned. "A fact which would have made no difference at all if this old rival of yours had decided she wanted you dead. I mean, stones and starlight, weren't you scared?"

She paused, grabbing his hands gently in hers and meeting his eyes. "I was terrified," she said sincerely. "But as scared as I got, Chall, I did it for us, and no matter what happened, I took comfort in knowing that you were here, safe in the castle."

He raised an eyebrow at that, and she sighed. "Well, as safe as anyone can be in such times."

It was his time to shift uncomfortably. "Right, right...anyway, what's the plan? How are we going to—"

"Hold on a minute," Maeve said, frowning. "Why are you acting strangely all of a sudden?"

"I'm not," Chall blurted, far too quickly. "That is, I mean if I *am*, probably it's because talk of assassins puts me a bit on edge—you know like it would do any rational person."

Maeve watched him for a moment, her eyes narrowed suspiciously. Then, finally, she shook her head. "No, that's not it. Or at least, not only it. There's something else. Something you're hiding—so what is it?"

Chall thought about lying to her, but he decided that there really wasn't much point. It wasn't a question of whether or not she would figure out the truth—it was only a question of how pissed-off she would be when she did. He sighed. "Thing is...I might not have spent *exactly* the whole time you were gone in the castle."

"Oh?" she asked.

He cleared his throat, and then despite his cowardly urge to try to keep it all to himself, he told her everything that had happened with Priest and the carriage driver and the man, Catham.

When he finished, Maeve sighed. "I am glad, at least, to hear that Ned hasn't been cheating on Emille..I did not think him capable of it. It is good to know that some things, at least, some people are as good as they seem."

"Cheating? What do you mean?"

"Never mind that," Maeve said. "You've got some of your own explaining to do. Such as about how you were giving *me* so much grief about risking my life, considering what you've been doing."

"Trust me," Chall said, "if I'd had my way I would have spent the entire time you were gone locked in a room—preferably one without any windows an assassin might shoot at me through. But...I couldn't leave Priest alone, Maeve. Something's going on with him...I'm not sure what but..."

She nodded. "I've noticed. But we can only hope that Priest can take care of himself for a while. We have our own troubles to deal with. As soon as this is all settled we'll talk to him." "Assuming it ever *is* all settled," Chall said, "or that, when it is, we'll still be around."

"Right," she said dryly. "Assuming that."

They did not speak for some time as they traveled deeper into the city, as quiet as two prisoners heading to their execution. Which, as far as Chall could see, wasn't all that far from the truth.

CHAPTER NINETEEN

Cutter's arm ached from swinging the axe, cutting away the undergrowth before him. But he swung the axe again anyway, tearing away a fresh swath of brambles and thorns. His legs burned from walking mile after mile, feeling as if he'd spent his entire life walking and that only. But he took another step anyway, telling himself that he was one step closer now to his destination. His back and shoulders also hurt from the burden he carried. But he went on carrying it. The only options now were to move forward or to lie down and die, and he was not ready to die. Not yet. He would do what his son had sent him to do or else he would give himself in the effort. There was nothing else.

The burden on his back shifted, and Cutter grunted as a bony elbow dug into his shoulder. "Fire and salt but this is embarrassing," Feledias said. "My only hope is that no one back in the Known Lands hears of it."

"I don't think that'll...be a problem," Cutter rasped as he took another swing of the axe, another step. "Do you?"

Feledias sighed from his position riding on Cutter's back. "I suppose not. Still...it's ridiculous. I'm not a little child, am I? One to go riding piggy back."

"Maybe not," Cutter said, wincing as he raised the axe yet again, "but then the alternative would have been to leave you behind."

"Don't tempt me," Feledias said.

They both knew what that would have meant. Feledias was weak, barely able to stand on his own, let alone walk. And like a wounded animal stumbling into a wolf's den, it didn't take much effort to guess at what would have happened to him. For in the Black Wood, a man could not afford to be weak.

Cutter paused, running his free arm across his forehead, sopping away some of the sweat as he looked around at the dark, shadowed woods around him. He felt as if he had been at it for hours, days. He had no real sense of what time it was, for in the Black Wood, it was always dark, and the shadows always lingered.

They were deep in the wood now, deeper than he had ever been. Deeper than any *man* had ever been—any living man, at least. They were closer to the wood's center, to the heart of Fey power. Cutter did not doubt that closeness, for he could feel it. He could feel that alien strangeness in the air against his skin, could taste it in the breath in his lungs. He almost thought, at times, that he could hear it in the rumbling thunder that was like the beating of some great heart, far in the distance, the sound of which lay just beyond his hearing. Or perhaps it was not beyond his hearing at all, only his understanding. For the Black Wood was not of men, and it was not for them. It was as inimical to them as water to fire, and the metaphor was a good one, for here there was no light, no warmth. Only the dark. Only the cold.

"How much...farther, do you think?" his brother asked.

"Farther," Cutter answered, swinging his axe once more, cutting away another knotted tangle of vines.

Feledias sighed, saying nothing, and that was alright with Cutter. His brother needed to save his strength—they both did. He did not know how much farther they would have to travel, how much farther they *could* travel, but he had the feeling that whatever came, they would need every ounce of strength they could muster or save.

They pressed on, both of them weary, Feledias even too tired to utter anymore complaints, which said a lot for his true level of exhaustion. Cutter did his best to ignore his own weariness, suffering it the same way he suffered his brother's constant complaining. He focused on taking one step after the other, swinging the axe one swing after the other—it was the only way to get it done. The only way, in his experience, to get anything done.

He kept at it until, finally, his next step didn't lead to more of the tangled snarl of bushes he had been navigating. Instead, he found that they stood in a large clearing.

"Well, now that's a blessing," Feledias panted from his spot on Cutter's back, the first words he'd spoken beyond muttered curses in some time.

"Yes," Cutter agreed quietly, taking a moment to get his breath. "But for who?"

He didn't like that clearing. It looked easy, but he had traveled long enough beneath the shadowed boughs of the Black Wood to know that nothing was ever easy. In fact, he would have felt more comforted had they stepped into the clearing and come upon some snarling monster.

Still, there was nothing to be done for it. His path lay before him, as it always had. All he could do, the same as any man, was to walk it.

And so he did.

He moved forward, his gaze traveling left and right to the shadowed bushes on either side of the clearing as he did.

"Did I ever tell you, Bernard, about the first time I saw Layna?"

"I was there," Cutter said, and the truth was that he needed no reminding of it, for he remembered that moment well. After all, it had not only been Feledias that had seen her, just as it had not only been Feledias who had, in that moment, come under the grip of some powerful emotion. For Feledias, it might have been love or something similar, some sort of pure, clean emotion, one that spoke to the best parts of human nature. For Cutter, it had been a very different thing, a carnal sort of lust. His own feeling had not been clean or pure, but like some lurking, creeping thing rousing awake inside him, turning to study her as she stepped away from the stall of some street vendor.

There had been a crowd in the street, New Daltenia's citizens gathered to watch their princes and attendant retinue travel through the city. The woman, though, seemed completely unaware of it, moving into the street and in front of the horse of the lead guardsman, one of the many that made up their escort. The woman gave a cry, and the guardsman cursed, giving his horse's reins a hard jerk. The beast reared, narrowly avoiding crushing the woman who fell to the ground, the parcel she had been carrying—which later turned out to be bread she'd bought, as she often did, for the orphans in the poor district—spilled onto the street.

The guard captain berated her angrily, ordering her to move, but Feledias hopped down from his horse, rushing forward and helping her to her feet. Cutter had watched them from his place atop his own horse, watched Feledias offer comfort to the woman, watched the woman grace him with a smile. He had been jealous, then, that much he remembered. Jealous and, even in that moment, plotting how he might make her his. It wasn't that he had decided he didn't care about his brother's feelings; no, the truth had been worse. The truth had been that he had not even considered them in the first place.

"I think I loved her," Feledias said softly, his voice thick with the memory. "Even in that moment."

"Yes," Cutter said, feeling the shame of the man he had once been.

"And she loved me too, I think. Not then, no," Feledias laughed self-consciously. "But later. In time."

"She did," Cutter said, thinking that he knew well what was coming next, the recrimination, the question of "why" and him with no answer to give. No answer except for while it was the role of some things to be pure and clean, it was the role of others to defile, to sully.

But Feledias surprised him by saying something else instead. "If someone like that, someone so...good, loved me...then I wasn't all bad, was I?"

"No, you weren't."

"At least then," Feledias said, his voice sounding grim. "But—"

"Wait," Cutter said, slowing to a stop and glancing around them.

"What? What is it?" his brother asked, his voice sounding tense. "Did...did you see something?"

"No."

"Hear something?"

"No," Cutter repeated as his gaze slowly traveled around the bushes surrounding the clearing.

"So what then?" Feledias asked. "Look, if it's the smell, I'll have you know that you've spent the last several nights in a forest just like me and you don't smell one whit better. Worse, likely, as I've done a lot of lying around in the meantime, while you—"

"Something's coming," Cutter said, turning slowly in a circle.

"How would you know?" Feledias asked. "If you can't hear it or see it then—"

"I just know," Cutter said. He might not have recognized the truly good, truly pure when it approached, but he knew evil well enough. How could he not? After all, he had lived with it, *in* it, for nearly his entire life. "I must set you down."

He suited action to words, easing his brother onto the ground. Then he gripped his axe in two hands and waited for what would come. It felt heavy, the axe, heavier than he could ever remember it feeling, but he did not let that bother him. He knew from experience that it would feel light enough when it was called to its purpose. At least, he hoped as much.

Seconds passed, the silence uninterrupted, and he had just begun to think he'd only imagined that feeling of foreboding—a perfectly reasonable thing to do in the Black Wood—when he heard a sound. It was quiet, almost imperceptible, but even as he listened harder, he heard it again.

Then again.

It was a sort of rasping hiss, as if something were being dragged across the dry leaves littering the ground. And it was coming from behind them.

Cutter turned slowly, Feledias craning his neck as well, to stare into the undergrowth. That was when the same kind of sound came from the direction he'd been facing only a moment ago. Then another sound, and another still until the clearing was filled with that dry, rasping hiss. It was unnerving, that conglomeration of sound, somehow making Cutter think of hundreds, thousands of snakes slithering their way across the forest floor toward them.

Only, when he began to catch faint glimpses of the figures moving toward them through the tangled undergrowth, Cutter saw that they were not snakes. Neither were those things which approached some wild Fey creatures out of nightmare, as he had expected, creatures that no man had ever seen or would likely ever see again. For as the figures began to emerge from the undergrowth surrounding the clearing, dozens, hundreds of them, Cutter saw that they were, in fact, the last thing he had expected. Men.

Men and women both, but even that was not the strangest thing about them. They wore the uniforms of soldiers of the Known Lands, uniforms that, without fail, bore rips and tears, gouges and holes, the fabric marred with dried blood stains. Their arms hung lank at their sides, and they did not even use them to push away the thorns and vines of the undergrowth, instead walking through them in a shambling shuffle, oblivious to the nicks and scratches they endured as they did. In their hands, many carried swords or maces, though some few held tree limbs. The weapons looked old and ill-treated. Even as he watched, the figures allowed the weapons, hanging from their limp hands, to drag across the ground as they moved into the clearing.

"What is this?" Feledias asked in a low, scared voice.

"I don't know," Cutter said, continuing to watch as the soldiers—for soldiers they were, there was no denying that much—continued to appear out of the bushes, stepping into the clearing only to stop along its edge. By the time it was done, hundreds of them surrounded Cutter and his brother, all of them standing perfectly still, not even seeming to so much as breathe, like marionettes waiting for their master to take up their strings.

"What do you want?" Cutter asked.

The creatures—for despite the fact that they looked like men and women, still Cutter found himself thinking of them as creatures—said nothing, did not so much as flutter an eyelash in response. Instead, they only stood there silently, regarding him and Feledias with lifeless gazes.

"Stay here," Cutter said to his brother, then he lifted his axe and started forward.

"I would not do that were I you, Destroyer."

Cutter turned to look in the direction from which the high-pitched, almost squeaking voice had come, to see the men and women who'd stood there so still suddenly begin to move, stepping to either side to open an avenue in between them.

And through that avenue, a man walked, one that, with his massive size, towered over those others around him as he lumbered through the empty space, dragging a mace the size of a small tree behind him. The figure was even taller than Cutter himself, and there was a deep gash going across his face. A large flap of skin hung off and one of the figure's eye sockets had been turned into a ruin, but if it bothered him he didn't show it.

But it was not the man's features that sent a shock of surprise through Cutter. Instead, it was those features which remained intact. Features which, coupled with the man's size, were familiar to Cutter. And the man was one who he recognized.

It would have been impossible not to, for he had fought with the man, and against him, for over a year during the Fey War. With him against the creatures of the Black Wood and against him in many practice bouts, for the man had been one of the few who had been a true challenge to Cutter's own skills. He had also been completely loyal and possessed of a bawdy sense of humor and a lust for life to match his great size. Not that either of those things showed in his dead-eyed, lifeless stare. "Ferrik?" Cutter asked, his voice little more than a whisper.

But Ferrik, if indeed it was the giant warrior, said nothing, only stood there regarding him with a blank, lifeless expression. So still was the man that Cutter would have thought him no more than a corpse someone had propped on its feet had he not just witnessed him taking a stroll.

Cutter looked into the figure's eyes, trying to see some trace of life, some trace of the man he'd once known, but he saw nothing, only an empty void. Whatever the creature was, it was Ferrik no longer. It was as if what had made him *him* had been hollowed out, scoured away, leaving only a shell which moved only because it knew nothing else. Staring at him, Cutter noticed something else that was strange. There were ripples underneath the man's bald head, as if something—or, to be precise, several somethings—was beneath the skin. And whatever they were, they were long and thin, like large worms or baby snakes, and like worms, they seemed to wriggle even as Cutter watched.

Then, a moment later, something crawled up onto Ferrik's massive shoulders, a gray-skinned creature that was toadlike in appearance, though its face looked eerily human, wrinkled like an old man's. The figure itself was small, the size of a two or three-year-old child, and its head was proportionately too large for its body. Its eyes glowed a pale blue, and its mouth spread into a too-wide grin displaying too-large teeth.

Staring at it, Cutter realized something even more disturbing than the appearance of the small figure huddled on the big man's shoulders. What he had at first taken as snakes or worms beneath the skin of the man's head were neither of those things. The creature's hands were on the big man's head, and those long, thin shapes Cutter had seen were its fingers, stretching *into* the man's head.

"*Oh gods, Bernard,*" Feledias gasped from his spot on the ground, sounding very close to being sick, "*i-it's inside his head.*"

"Yes," Cutter said, staring at the creature with its head still cocked, still smiling, studying them. "What have you done to Ferrik and these others, creature?" he called. "Release them from whatever spell you have them under or I warn you, I will make you suffer before the end."

The creature continued to smile, not moving to respond, but Ferrik's mouth opened, seemed to *yawn* open, and then he began to speak. His mouth did not move, though, and he did not speak in the deep, rumbling voice that Cutter remembered the giant man having. Instead, he spoke in a lisping, hissing, high-pitched tone that grated against Cutter's ears, his mind.

"*He will not answer you, Destroyer, for he cannot. He has no voice, not anymore, no life, either, save that which I give him, like these others gathered here.*"

Though the little creature perched on Ferrik's shoulders did not speak itself, Cutter realized that it was the one communicating with him, and he could not help the disgusted frown that came to his face. "What are you, creature? And what have you done with them?"

"*What am I, Destroyer? Well, my kind, here, in the Wood, are known as Sveldersleys. It does not translate well to your crude tongue, but the closest you might come is to call me the lifebreather.*"

Cutter glanced around at the figures standing unmoving in the clearing then back to the creature. "It does not look like life to me."

"*There are many forms of life, Destroyer,*" the creature said, "*just as there are many forms of death. Now, drop your axe and follow me.*"

"No."

The creature's grin seemed to widen further still, so that it appeared to take up nearly its entire face, nothing but two glowing blue eyes and bared teeth. *"You would fight these, your own people? For they are yours, Destroyer. Those who came into the Wood long ago. You came with them, I think, you and some others, your brother among them, but while the two of you left, not all who came did. Some remained to become part of the Wood, part of me."*

Cutter felt his jaw muscles clenching, his hands gripping his axe haft so tight they ached. It was not enough that these men and women had given their lives, now their bodies were paraded around by this *thing*, made a mockery of. "They are not my people, not anymore," he growled, "and I can promise you that when I finish with them, you're next. You tell me that there are different degrees of death and perhaps you are right, but I will make sure you experience it for yourself."

"And I wonder, Destroyer, what will happen to that brother of yours, while you fight? For even should you somehow manage to defeat me—and you would not, even these husks can see that it takes all your strength to remain on your feet, axe in hand—still that will not save your brother. For you cannot fight me and protect him all at once, not from so many."

Cutter gritted his teeth. He opened his mouth to retort, only to realize that he had no retort he might give. The creature was right, after all. He would not be able to watch over Feledias while fighting. His brother was still terribly weak from the fever, could not even stand. It would be a simple enough thing for one of those creatures to slip by Cutter while he was engaged with the others, to come upon his brother and kill him before he could do anything about it.

"What do you want?" Cutter demanded.

"What an odd question," the voice said, *"for I want what all the living want. I want more."*

"More," Cutter repeated.

"That's right. I want more. To have more. To think more. To be more. And now, that more, Destroyer, is you and your brother. Do you understand?"

Cutter frowned, glancing again at the figures around them. "That's not going to happen."

The creature laughed, and that was the worst sound of all, a piercing, grating laugh that felt like spikes being driven into Cutter's mind. *"Oh, do you think, Destroyer, that I would make you like these, my pets? No, you need not worry of that, for that is not your fate."*

Cutter stared at the creature for several seconds, thinking. "Where would you take us?"

"Does it matter?" the creature asked. *"Come with me, Destroyer, deeper into the Wood. Come or your kin will die. It is that simple."*

Cutter glanced at Feledias. His brother looked back, a pale, sickly expression on his face, but he gave a shrug. "Deeper into the wood...it's where we were going anyway, wasn't it?"

Cutter grunted, turning back to the figure. "Very well. Lead the way."

The creature stirred, cocking its head the other way, an incredibly long tongue flashing out to lick its lips before going back into its face, baring its teeth in a macabre grin once more. *"So eager. So strong. Now it is time. I will have my pets carry your brothe—"*

"No," Cutter interrupted. "He is my brother. I will carry him."

Feledias let out an audible sigh of relief at that, and the figure watched him for a moment. *"Very well, Destroyer. This way."*

The figures parted, revealing a path. Cutter moved to Feledias, lifted him up onto his back once more, then stared at that path, a path that led between hundreds of men and women who he had once fought with, long ago. Men and women who were now no more than shells, their bodies, which should have long decayed, somehow kept together, either by the magic of the Wood or of the creature possessing them.

"I don't like this, brother," Feledias said.

"What's to like?" Cutter asked. And then, since there was no other option, he started forward.

CHAPTER TWENTY

Maeve sat at the counter of the Tipsy Tankard, doing her best to look unobtrusive. She held an ale in one hand, taking a sip from time to time. She also focused on nodding every once in a while, murmuring replies to the person seated beside her who did a good job of keeping up a steady stream of whispered chatter, never mind that none of the sounds were actual *words.*

An unintentional mistake, she wondered, or simply Chall's way of taking shortcuts so that his mind could be elsewhere? Sitting there, listening to the murmured conversations of dozens of people, watching the barkeep move back and forth, busying himself with barkeep things, she realized that she had always given Chall far less credit than he deserved. She had thought being an illusionist was just something he was, just a facet of his character that gave him an advantage, not so different than a tall man being able to reach things on a shelf that a short man could not. She had thought his illusions interesting, but taking little effort, a thing you could either do or not do.

Now, sitting in the middle of one of his illusions, certainly the biggest she had ever seen the mage make, she realized how wrong she had been, how much went into it that she hadn't realized. The barkeep, for example, who kept right on doing barkeep things. Only if someone looked very, very closely, and that for some time, would they notice that he repeated himself over and over again, operating on a roughly fifteen-minute circuit.

Only if they listened very closely would they notice that those dozens of conversations going on all around the tavern weren't real conversations at all, the words being strung together in quiet voices no more than random nouns, adjectives, and conjunctions. It was a very odd sensation, one which made Maeve feel as if she had just stepped into a world gone mad. Which was ridiculous, of course—she'd stepped into that world a long time ago, had been born into it, in truth.

She resisted the urge yet again to turn and look at the doors. Agnes and her retinue would arrive soon or they would not, and her looking would do nothing to change that.

Still, it felt that she had been here for hours already, and she had long since lost count of the times she had watched the barkeep—who didn't actually exist—clean the counter with an equally non-existent rag, wipe down non-existent glasses with that same non-existent rag, then tend to several non-existent customers only to start the whole thing all over again. It wasn't impatience that she felt, though; it was fear. Fear that something had happened, that Agnes had been forced to change the plan at the last minute, fear that they had been discovered somehow. She was also afraid that they *would* show up, and that Chall wouldn't be able to maintain the illusion for long enough, that it would all fall apart. But mostly, she was scared that she would fail. That she wouldn't be good enough, that the battle with Silrika had been a fluke and nothing more and that she was about to be proven to be just an old woman after all, one who had bitten off far more than she could chew.

She was on the verge of calling the whole thing off, of trying to find some other way to get the thing done, when she heard the wooden creak of the door opening. Her entire body tensed, but she did not turn, at least not at first. She waited, listening as Agnes and her two bodyguards moved to the table against the wall, one intentionally left empty so that they might choose it. Assassins, Maeve knew, had a tendency not to trust people—the product of murdering those same people for a living—and she'd yet to meet one that didn't want to be able to put their back against a wall when they sat so that they could see anything coming at them.

Sure enough, she was gratified to hear the sound of footsteps moving in that direction as the bodyguards took advantage of the open table in the otherwise bustling common room. Maeve tensed, fearing that now would come the mistake. One of them, the bodyguards or Agnes herself would bump into a tavern patron only to pass right through them—which would no doubt leave them with some questions.

She waited anxiously for a shout of alarm or challenge, but she heard nothing and in another few seconds the bodyguards, along with the woman they guarded, were seated at the table in the corner. Which put them in line of her view, as intended. It was the reason, after all, why she had picked out this spot at the bar in the first place. People, assassins in particular, were liable to pick up on someone following them or marking their progress. They were far less likely to be suspicious, though, when they stepped into someone's field of view instead. Or so she had reasoned with herself.

Still, she made sure not to look too much, to pay attention to her pretend companion and their pretend conversation, all the while keeping her head low so that her hood would disguise her features from view. Chall had included her in the illusion, of course, and according to him she would appear like an old, gray-haired woman—far closer to the truth than she'd like—with stooped shoulders and a long beak of a nose that had caused the bastard no small amount of laughter. A woman hobbled by age and one that was no threat to anyone. She only hoped that last was an illusion and not what it felt like, which was the truest truth that ever truthed.

She winced. That sounded like something Chall would say. He was getting into her head, that was a fact. Still...she supposed there were worse things. A small smile came to her face at the thought, a smile that shattered like a glass thrown to the ground as soon as she heard a call from the other side of the tavern.

"*You, serving wench, are you blind?*"

Maeve tensed. *Fool,* she thought. She'd sat here wasting time, trying to convince herself that she wouldn't fail; meanwhile she was doing exactly that. She rose, trying to hurry but appear to be taking her time all at once, as she moved around the room, stopping here and there as if to talk. As she did, she kept checking on the two bodyguards. Gideon, the big man, was intent on the serving woman who was currently at a separate table, a frown on his face, clearly not enjoying being ignored. The second bodyguard, the swordsman, looked around the room slowly, studying everyone, watching for potential threats. He didn't appear to be paying Maeve any particular attention, so she moved on, circling wide as if heading for the stairs which were adjacent the table at which Agnes and the other two sat.

She was nearing them when Gideon shouted again, angrier this time. *"I know you hear me, wench! Answer at once."*

The woman did not answer, though, mostly because the man was wrong—she did not hear him. And *that* mostly because she wasn't, strictly speaking, a woman at all. Or at least not a real one. And while illusions were amazing, they were also, as it happened, terrible conversationalists. The man rose, and Maeve increased her pace, well aware that should he reach the woman and try to put a hand on her, the illusion would be revealed for what it was, and she would miss her chance.

The man was approaching the serving woman, his expression a storm cloud, and Maeve knew that she would not make it in time. So she did the only thing she could do. "Excuse me?" she said, doing her best at an old woman's voice as Chall had told her he would not be able to alter the sound of her actual voice. "Can you spare a coin for an old woman?" she asked as she approached the man at a hobble.

She winced, thinking that there was no way anyone could be fooled, but judging by the man's look of disgust she did a good job—depressingly good, in fact—of sounding exactly like an old woman.

"Get you and your nose away, you old hag, before you end up getting hurt."

That was cleverer than she would have given the man credit for, that was sure, but Maeve ignored it, continuing to shamble forward, holding her hands up to show she meant no harm—which, of course, she did.

"You should have listened," the man growled, starting forward, confident and why not? She was just an old woman, after all. Only, she wasn't *just* an old woman. She also happened to be an old woman carrying a short, stout iron rod. Certainly, it wasn't the smith's finest work, but she thought it would serve its purpose well enough. A theory she put to the test as soon as the big man came within range. He grabbed for her, but Maeve stepped to the side, no doubt considerably faster than he would have credited the old woman she appeared to be—and mostly was—with. Then she brought the length of steel hard into the man's temple. Not hard enough to kill, at least she hoped not, but hard enough to render him decidedly unconscious.

The big man's eyes rolled up in his head, and he fell backward, crashing into a table. Even as he did, one of the figures in the common room walked by. It was well done, nearly perfect, the woman's movement coinciding with the big man crashing into the table and sending it, and him, to the ground. You wouldn't have noticed anything amiss unless you were looking for it—which, of course, Maeve was. She noted the figure—Emille wearing a hooded cloak—move past, just as she noticed the trail of liquid spilling out of the bottom of the cloak onto the ground. Then, after that, a small bit of burning wick, and a moment later a fire roared to life, chasing its way hungrily across the floor of the tavern as if eager to devour the building and all those within it. And unlike those men and women who ran this way and that, screaming as if in agony and never mind that the blaze never seemed to *actually* touch them, the fire was all too real.

Should Maeve be too slow or too careless, it would not pass through her the way it did the illusions. Already she could feel the heat of it against her skin as the blaze, fueled by the flammable liquid they had procured from an alchemist's shop and which Emille had spread throughout the tavern, spread like wildfire.

Maeve could not worry about that, though, not yet. Instead, she spun back to the table where Agnes looked genuinely terrified—unsurprising as she had only been privy to part of the plan. The Headmistress of the Assassin's Guild had shared her schedule for the next two days with Emille and Maeve, but they had not deigned to share their plans with her, assuming that it would be easier for the woman to fake surprise if she was actually *surprised.* Which, as it turned out, was nothing but the truth.

But the woman also wasn't Maeve's worry, not then. Instead, it was the swordsman, Agnes's second bodyguard, who'd risen to his feet, his sword appearing in his hand so fast it looked like magic.

That wasn't good. The plan had been to take the two men by surprise and never give the bastard a chance to draw the sword at all. It had certainly *not* been to get stabbed or burned to death. But then plans, as Prince Bernard had told her before, had a way of becoming useless the second the bloodletting started.

And that was the reason why she had taken Chall's own ideas into account—make a plan, he'd said, but then plan for that plan to fail. That way, you can never be surprised.

Which was why Emille, after having to improvise and start the fire when the big man fell, had circled back around the room and now stood behind the swordsman. She was standing leaned over a table in conversation with several people—who weren't actually people at all. When the swordsman started toward Maeve, a look on his face that said he had murder on his mind, Emille spun, striking him in the back of the head with the second stout length of steel they'd commissioned the smith to make.

The swordsman had the same reaction as his big companion—really the only reaction Maeve suspected a man *would* have: he promptly collapsed to the floor, unconscious.

Maeve, aware that time was of the essence, was jogging toward the woman when Agnes let out a shout and suddenly dove forward, producing a knife from her jerkin.

Maeve interposed herself between the two women, grabbing the Headmistress's wrist, and Agnes snarled and spat, thin but surprisingly strong as she fought in Maeve's grip. *"I don't know who you are,"* the woman snapped, *"but I'll be damned if—"*

"Agnes, it's me!" Maeve shouted, and the woman's eyes went wide.

"Maeve?" she said, her eyes narrowing as she tried to stare past the illusion that Chall had created. "Fire and salt, I'd heard that man of yours was good with illusions, but this..." She reached out, brushing her fingers tentatively against the illusory face Chall had overlayed on Maeve's real one then jerked her hand away with a hiss. "Remarkable," the woman mused, then glanced around the room at the tavern's patrons, still busily running in circles and shouting incoherent, frightened noises, many of which were running through the flames, oblivious to their touch. "And all of these...also an illusion?"

"Yes," Emille said, withdrawing her hood to reveal her features, and Agnes grunted.

"Instructor Emille, you are in on it as well?" She glanced at Maeve. "And the fire—fake I imagine?"

"All too real," Maeve said.

"Ah, to destroy any evidence—nicely done."

"Or to burn us all to death if we're fool enough to keep standing here chatting," Maeve said. "Besides, we're not done. In case you haven't noticed, you haven't died yet."

Agnes raised an eyebrow. "I would certainly like to think that I would notice such a thing."

Keep it up, Maeve thought. *Pretending at assassination and actually doing it aren't, as it turns out, all that different.* "I'll get this one," she nodded to the bodyguard. "You two get the other."

Emille nodded, starting toward Gideon, but Agnes frowned. "What do you mean *get* him?"

"I mean drag him out into the street, out of the fire, obviously," Maeve said.

Agnes glanced at the unconscious man at her feet, her upper lip peeling back in a silent snarl. "Neither of them cares anything for my welfare, only pawns working for the Tribunes, pawns that would kill me in an instant, if given the chance. Better to let them burn."

"Maybe," Maeve hissed, aware that the fire was growing by the moment, "but then who would be alive to witness your murder?"

The woman grunted, nodding slowly. "You're right," she said. "It seems you have really thought this all through—except for one thing, Maeve."

"And what's that?" Maeve asked impatiently.

The woman gave her a sly smile then, before Maeve could react, she knelt and buried her knife in the unconscious man's throat. The man spasmed as blood fountained out before growing still in a moment, and Agnes rose, grinning a humorless grin at Maeve. "We only need one witness."

Maeve stared in shock at the stark reminder that, no matter how their purposes had happened to align, the woman, Agnes, was a monster and likely the world would be better off if she killed her in truth. Agnes must have seen some of her thoughts on her face for she frowned, watching Maeve the way a reptile might.

Maeve thought she probably should kill her, that she would be doing the world a favor, but she was not a cold-blooded assassin anymore, one who placed no value on human life. Besides, what would she tell Chall? What would she tell herself? Finally, she let out an angry growl. "Come on, damnit," she said, "and put that blasted blade away."

Maeve turned away, tensed, giving it even odds that the woman would attack her. She didn't, though, only sheathed the knife and then the three of them were cursing and grunting as they dragged Agnes's remaining bodyguard toward the tavern's exit. They were nearly there when the door swung open and a man wearing a guardsman's uniform hurried inside.

Agnes hissed, dropping her side of the unconscious man to draw a knife, and Maeve growled in pain as the extra weight felt as if it might pull her arm out of socket.

"Relax, Agnes," she said quickly before there was some sort of fatal misunderstanding, "that's Chall."

"Challadius the Charmer?" Agnes said in shock as she stared at the broad-shouldered, handsome man in a guardsman's uniform approaching them through the fire like some hero out of a storybook one come to rescue the princess—not that he was likely to find any princesses here. "I see why you're interested in him," she finished as he walked up.

"You ought to see me with my shirt off," Chall said, flashing her a winning smile. Maeve rolled her eyes as the illusory version of Chall glanced down at the unconscious bodyguard then up at Maeve. "Where's the other?"

Maeve frowned at Agnes. "He didn't make it."

"Ah," the man said, swallowing hard, as if just becoming aware that he was in a burning tavern with not one but three assassins. "Right. Here, let me help."

He bent to the task then, and with his help, the four of them dragged the bodyguard to the exit then out into the street. They were all panting by the time the man was what they deemed a safe distance from the tavern which was quickly becoming a raging inferno.

"You sure about this, Mae?" Chall asked doubtfully. "Maybe we can just do it in the street and—"

"You know we can't," Maeve said grimly. "It has to be in the fire."

Chall nodded. "Okay, but hurry."

"I don't plan to take anymore time than I need to, I can promise you that," Maeve said, then she turned to Agnes. "Come on, let's get it done then."

"Get what done?"

"Why, I've got to kill you, of course."

They started toward the burning building, and Maeve glanced back at Chall. "Make sure the bastard sees."

"You got it," Chall said.

They moved toward the building and were still a dozen feet away when Maeve began to feel the heat from the flames, an uncomfortable feeling against her skin. Still, she knew they couldn't tarry. It would only be a matter of time before a crowd began gathered in the street, drawn by the blaze, and no doubt some of them would be very curious to know why two people were walking *into* the burning building instead of away from it.

"I'm beginning to lose some respect for this plan," Agnes muttered.

"You're the one that wanted to die," Maeve said.

"Yes, but not *actually*," Agnes said. "A minor point, perhaps, but an important one."

"Let's just get it done and fast," Maeve said, "otherwise you won't have to pretend to be dead—you will be."

They stepped into the burning flames, Maeve drawing a dagger as she did, then they waited. Maeve felt as if her skin was blistering as she stood there, but she knew she had to wait for the signal from Emille. A moment later, just when she was sure she could take no more, that signal came, a scream as if of shock by someone stumbling upon the blaze—but it wasn't that. It was Maeve's cue.

She made sure that they were positioned in the doorway so that anyone looking in from the street could see them, then she thrust forward, making sure to over-exaggerate the move, to telegraph it so that Chall would have time to form the necessary illusions.

She grabbed Agnes's shoulder in her left hand even as her right buried the blade she carried in the woman's stomach, or at least, appeared to. In truth, she pulled the woman in and with a dramatic roar—one that she had never actually done in real life—she bent Agnes forcefully toward her as she thrust the blade into the space in between the woman's arm and side. Illusory blood erupted from the wound, a bit more than was realistic, but she supposed Chall was taking liberties for the benefit of the bodyguard and those citizens which had begun to gather. Twice more Maeve stabbed the empty air, then there was a loud *cracking* from overhead, and she did not have to fake the scream of surprise as the roof collapsed around them in a shower of wood and flame.

Only, it didn't, not really, and she swallowed hard, shocked to still be alive despite the fact that she had been the one who'd planned this out and promised herself to show Chall some proper thanks when all of this was done. But there was still one small part to finish yet, and it wasn't one she was looking forward to.

Aware that Chall wouldn't be able to use the smoke and the illusion to block the view from the street forever, Maeve grabbed Agnes and pulled her farther into the inn, away from the open doorway.

"I'm impressed, Maeve," Agnes panted from the heat, "but it all seems convoluted if we end up burning to death. So what now?"

"There's a back door, behind the bar," Maeve said, running an arm across her sweat-drenched forehead. "It's the reason we chose this place to begin with."

"You mean that bar?" Agnes asked, and Maeve followed her gaze to see that the bar counter—and the rest of it for that matter—were on fire.

"That'd be the one," Maeve said. Then she took Agnes's hand. "Come on." It was only twenty feet to the door at the back, but it felt as if it took an eternity to reach it, and when they finally did, Maeve grabbed the handle only to cry out from the heat. Gritting her teeth, she grabbed it again, hissing with pain and effort as she forced the door—that suddenly didn't want to budge—open.

Then she and the woman stumbled, coughing and hacking, into the street, black smoke billowing out with them. Maeve slammed the door shut then bent over with her hands on her knees, wheezing for breath.

"Maeve! Are you alright?"

She looked up to see Chall moving toward her, not some storybook knight like the guardsman he'd appeared as now, but her Chall, and she couldn't help but grin, a grin that only spread as he pulled her into a tight embrace. "I'm alright, Chall."

"Stones and starlight, that was terrifying."

"Did he see?" Maeve asked.

Chall snorted. "Yeah, him and about twenty some odd other people—you really missed your calling, Mae. You would have made a fine actor."

"Who says I don't act?" she asked, raising an eyebrow, and he frowned at that.

"What now?"

They both turned to look at Agnes, the woman standing there looking lost. Maeve nodded to a burlap bag sitting against the opposite alley wall. "Now you leave, Agnes, and go wherever you want to go. There are fresh clothes in that bag and some money—not much, but I expect you've got that part taken care of yourself. Take them and find yourself a new life. You're free."

"Will they not be curious when they don't find my body among the rubble?" she asked, glancing at the burning building.

"But they will find it," Maeve said, "or at least one that looks like it enough that, with the fire, they will not be able to tell the difference."

The woman gave a nod. If Maeve had been expecting the woman to break into tears or gratuitous thanks, she was to be disappointed. Instead, Agnes only gave her a single nod, snatched up the bag, and disappeared down the alley.

"Suppose we'll ever see her again?" Chall asked.

"Fire and salt I hope not," Maeve said. "Now, come on."

"Where to?" he asked.

"First, I mean to get my hand seen to," she said, "and then back to our quarters."

Chall grunted. "Could use some rest myself."

"Rest?" she said, glancing at him as they moved toward the alley's exit. "Who said anything about rest? I mean to celebrate, Chall, and you are going to celebrate with me."

He somehow managed to look nervous and excited at the same time—which was exactly how she liked him—and he cleared his throat. "Yes, ma'am."

CHAPTER TWENTY-ONE

They walked for hours, Cutter carrying his brother, surrounded by dozens of what had once been men and women but now were no more than puppets, husks. It was an eerie, silent journey. The creature riding on Ferrik's back did not speak. Instead, it only rode hunched on the big man as he moved in front of them, the creature glancing back to check on them from time to time, always with that too-wide grin displaying its too-large teeth, its blue eyes shining.

They walked a path that Cutter could have sworn had not existed before, winding easily through the trees and underbrush on either side. Eventually, Ferrik—or the body that had once *been* Ferrik—came to a stop at the edge of a large clearing, though Cutter could see little of it past the man's massive frame and the other dead men and women gathered around him.

Ferrik opened his mouth and, once more, that strange, hissing, squeaking voice came from him. "*Rejoice Destroyer and brethren of the Destroyer, for now you have come to a place no mortal has ever seen and, likely, will never see again. You have come to the very heart of the Fey. You have come to the Glade.*"

Even despite the creature's strange alien tone, there was no denying the reverence with which it spoke. Feledias, though, didn't seem impressed, grunting from his spot on Cutter's back. "Do you suppose they have sweet cakes?"

"Only one way to find out," Cutter said, as the creature atop Ferrik favored him with an even wider grin before turning and moving forward into the clearing.

Cutter followed. He did not know where he expected the creature to lead them. Some cave it had taken as its den, perhaps, but whatever he had expected, it was not what he found waiting for him as he stepped into the clearing. Or, in more particular, *who*.

Thousands of fey creatures of all shape and size, those which appeared wistful and those which appeared deadly, were gathered around the clearing in a great throng, all of them watching as if they had known the exact hour, the exact moment of Cutter's arrival.

An avenue was open in their midst, in front of Cutter and Feledias, an avenue at the end of which stood a familiar figure, green eyes studying them.

Ferrik and the creature riding atop him bowed low, extending a hand as if in invitation.

"What is this, Bernard?" Feledias asked, his fear making his voice weak, thready.

"I do not know," Cutter said. What he did know, though, was at the end of that lane stood Shadelaresh, known as the Green Man. The one he had come to speak with. And so, he started down the open lane. Perhaps he should have been afraid. Perhaps a part of him even was. Mostly, though, he just felt relief. The journey was nearly done now, and that was good, for his strength, legendary or not, was very nearly spent. He was tired, physically and mentally, wrung out.

He hoped that it would end as he had meant for it to, as Matt wished for it to, in peace. But even if it did not, he thought he might be okay with that, just so long as it did end.

The creatures on either side of the lane studied them as they passed, some hissing or growling or speaking in echoing whispers, threatening. Cutter recognized some few of them, but most he had never seen before; most he thought no man had. Here a creature with a head similar to a human's, only there were no features, just skin stretched tight across it, its mouth in its throat, a single eye on the palm of a pure-white hand which it held to its forehead. On his left, Cutter saw a creature, if it could be called a creature, who

A Warrior's Penance

seemed to be made entirely out of water, water that shifted and moved restlessly even as it stood there.

He continued on and was surprised in another moment to see a familiar face, one formed and shaped from branches and vines, leaves and twigs, the visage of the one who had called himself the Gray Man. The figure was largely expressionless, but Cutter thought he detected a hint of disappointment in it to see him there. Still, he paid it little mind, just as he paid those other creatures little mind.

If they attacked, then they attacked, and he would kill as many of them as he was able. He would fight until he was able to fight no longer. But they did not attack, and so he pushed on, coming to stand a short distance away from the Green Man.

The figure regarded him silently for several moments, his emerald, glowing eyes seeming to shine brighter and brighter, to produce a sort of heat, as if they were boring holes into Cutter.

Then the figure of the Green Man silently yawned open his mouth and spoke.

Welcome, Destroyer, he said in a voice that sounded like the rustle of leaves in the wind, the creaking of a tree's branches. *Welcome, Betrayer. It is good that you have come, for we have waited for you.*

"I am here," Cutter said. "And I have come to speak of peace."

Peace, the figure said. *These are strange times indeed, for the Destroyer to come and speak to me of peace with the Breaker of Pacts in his hand.*

Cutter said nothing, only waited, and the figure shifted.

Very well then, Destroyer, the Green Man said. *You have come seeking peace and so peace you shall have. The only peace that any of your kind ever truly receives. You will die. And so, you will find your peace.*

Cutter had hoped for a better response but hoping and expecting were two different things. He hefted his axe and prepared to do what he had done for seemingly his entire life—to fight. After all, it was all he knew.

He was going to die, and he thought that was alright. His only regret was that in dying, he would fail.

"I am sorry, Matt," he whispered as the throng of creatures in the clearing started forward. "But what do I know of peace?"

Nothing, that was the truth. He knew of one thing and one thing only—killing. And so, as the creatures of the Black Wood surged toward him, running and loping and slithering forward, he prepared to do exactly that.

THE END *Of* SAGA OF THE KNOWN LANDS

BOOK FOUR

And now, dear reader, we have reached the end of *A Warrior's Penance.*

It is my hope that you have enjoyed journeying with Cutter and his companions once more. The next book in the Saga of the Known Lands will be out soon.

While you wait, why not give one of my other series a shot?

Want another story of an anti-hero in a grimdark setting where a jaded sellsword is forced into a fight he doesn't want between forces he doesn't understand?
Get started on the bestselling seven book series, The Seven Virtues.

Interested in a story where the gods choose their champions in a war with the darkness that will determine the fate of the world itself?
Dive into The Nightfall Wars, a complete six book, epic fantasy series.

Or how about something a little lighter? Do you like laughs with your sword slinging and magical mayhem? All the world's heroes are dead and so it is up to the antiheroes to save the day. An overweight swordsman, a mage who thinks magic is for sissies, an assassin who gets sick at the sight of the blood, and a man who can speak to animals...maybe.
The world needed heroes—it got them instead.
Start your journey with The Antiheroes!

If you enjoyed A Warrior's Penance, I'd really appreciate it if you'd take a moment to leave an honest review. They make a huge difference, and there are few things better than hearing from readers.

If you want to reach out, you can email me at Jacobpeppersauthor@gmail.com or visit my website at JacobPeppersAuthor.com.
You can also give me a shout on Facebook or on Twitter. I'm looking forward to hearing from you!

Turn the page for a limited time free offer!

Sign up for my new releases mailing list and for a limited time get a free copy of *The Silent Blade*, the prequel book to the bestselling epic fantasy series *The Seven Virtues*.

Go to JacobPeppersAuthor.com to get your copy now!

Note from the Author

And now, my friend, we have reached the end of A Warrior's Penance. It would appear that Cutter and Feledias have reached the end of their journey, might well have reached their own ends, too, for they are in the heart of the Black Wood now, in the center of Fey power.

Still, there is reason to hope. With Emille's help, Maeve has successfully re-entered the Assassin's Guild, and Chall and Priest have found an unexpected—and unexpectedly powerful—ally in the form of Ned, the carriage driver.

Meanwhile, Matt grows into his role as king, showing a cleverness and compassion that is sorely needed in the Known Lands. Perhaps it will even be enough…

As always, I would like to take a moment to thank all of those many people who have made this book far better than it might otherwise have been.

Thank you to my wife, Andrea, whose support has made not only this book better but my life, too.

Thank you to my kids, Gabriel, Norah, and Declan. Your mother and I are outnumbered now, but I'm confident that I speak for the both of us when I say I wouldn't trade it for anything.

Thank you to my friends and family—I say this in lieu of payment for the hours you've spent listening to me talk about this plot point or that character.

Thank you to my beta readers. You all are simply awesome. I really don't know another way to say it. This book—every book I write—is far better for your input, and I remain incredibly humbled that you sacrifice your time and energy to help.

Lastly, thank you, dear reader. Thanks for coming on this journey with me. It would be lonely to travel these paths alone, perhaps even a little scary. Your being here…it means everything, and I cannot thank you enough.

I do not know what the future of Cutter and his companions holds—I do not know what truths the shadows hide. But if you stick around, I promise that we'll figure out together.

Until next time,
Happy Reading,
Jacob Peppers

About the Author

Jacob Peppers lives in Georgia with his wife, and his children, Gabriel, Norah, and Declan, as well as their three dogs. He is an avid reader and writer and when he's not exploring the worlds of others, he's creating his own. His short fiction has been published in various markets, and his short story, "The Lies of Autumn," was a finalist for the 2013 Eric Hoffer Award for Short Prose. He is the author of the bestselling epic fantasy series *The Seven Virtues* and *The Nightfall Wars*.